S0-BYN-015

Literary Lives

Founding Editor: **Richard Dutton**, Professor of English, Lancaster University

This series offers stimulating accounts of the literary careers of the most admired and influential English-language authors. Volumes follow the outline of the writers' working lives, not in the spirit of traditional biography, but aiming to trace the professional, publishing and social contexts which shaped their writing.

Published titles include:

Clinton Machann
MATTHEW ARNOLD

Jan Fergus
JANE AUSTEN

John Beer
WILLIAM BLAKE

Tom Winnifrith and Edward Chitham
CHARLOTTE AND EMILY BRONTË

Sarah Wood
ROBERT BROWNING

Janice Farrar Thaddeus
FRANCES BURNEY

Caroline Franklin
BYRON

Sarah Gamble
ANGELA CARTER

Nancy A. Walker
KATE CHOPIN

Roger Sales
JOHN CLARE

William Christie
SAMUEL TAYLOR COLERIDGE

Graham Law and Andrew Maunder
WILKIE COLLINS

Cedric Watts
JOSEPH CONRAD

Grahame Smith
CHARLES DICKENS

Linda Wagner-Martin
EMILY DICKINSON

George Parfitt
JOHN DONNE

Paul Hammond
JOHN DRYDEN

Kerry McSweeney
GEORGE ELIOT

Tony Sharpe
T. S. ELIOT

David Rampton
WILLIAM FAULKNER

Harold Pagliaro
HENRY FIELDING

Andrew Hook
F. SCOTT FITZGERALD

Mary Lago
E. M. FORSTER

Shirley Foster
ELIZABETH GASKELL

Neil Sinyard
GRAHAM GREENE

James Gibson
THOMAS HARDY

Linda Wagner-Martin
ERNEST HEMINGWAY

Cristina Malcolmson
GEORGE HERBERT

Gerald Roberts
GERARD MANLEY HOPKINS

Neil Roberts
TED HUGHES

Kenneth Graham
HENRY JAMES

W. David Kaye
BEN JONSON

R. S. White JOHN KEATS	*Michael O'Neill* PERCY BYSSHE SHELLEY
Phillip Mallett RUDYARD KIPLING	*Gary Waller* EDMUND SPENSER
John Worthen D. H. LAWRENCE	*Tony Sharpe* WALLACE STEVENS
Angela Smith KATHERINE MANSFIELD	*William Gray* ROBERT LOUIS STEVENSON
Lisa Hopkins CHRISTOPHER MARLOWE	*Lisa Hopkins* BRAM STOKER
Cedric C. Brown JOHN MILTON	*Joseph McMinn* JONATHAN SWIFT
Linda Wagner-Martin TONI MORRISON	*Leonée Ormond* ALFRED TENNYSON
Priscilla Martin and Anne Rowe IRIS MURDOCH	*Peter Shillingsburg* WILLIAM MAKEPEACE THACKERAY
David Rampton VLADIMIR NABOKOV	*William Christie* DYLAN THOMAS
Peter Davison GEORGE ORWELL	*David Wykes* EVELYN WAUGH
Linda Wagner-Martin SYLVIA PLATH	*Jon Bak* TENNESSEE WILLIAMS
Felicity Rosslyn ALEXANDER POPE	*Caroline Franklin* MARY WOLLSTONECRAFT
Ira B. Nadel EZRA POUND	*John Mepham* VIRGINIA WOOLF
Richard Dutton WILLIAM SHAKESPEARE	*John Williams* WILLIAM WORDSWORTH
John Williams MARY SHELLEY	*Alasdair D. F. Macrae* W. B. YEATS

Literary Lives
Series Standing Order ISBN 978–0–333–71486–7 hardcover
Series Standing Order ISBN 978–0–333–80334–9 paperback
(*outside North America only*)

You can receive future titles in this series as they are published by placing a standing order. Please contact your bookseller or, in case of difficulty, write to us at the address below with your name and address, the title of the series and one of the ISBNs quoted above.

Customer Services Department, Macmillan Distribution Ltd, Houndmills, Basingstoke, Hampshire RG21 6XS, England

Toni Morrison

A Literary Life

Linda Wagner-Martin

First published 2015 by
PALGRAVE MACMILLAN

Palgrave Macmillan in the UK is an imprint of Macmillan Publishers Limited, registered in England, company number 785998, of Houndmills, Basingstoke, Hampshire RG21 6XS.

Palgrave Macmillan in the US is a division of St Martin's Press LLC, 175 Fifth Avenue, New York, NY 10010.

Palgrave is a global academic imprint of the above companies and has companies and representatives throughout the world.

Palgrave® and Macmillan® are registered trademarks in the United States, the United Kingdom, Europe and other countries.

ISBN 978–1–137–44669–5

This book is printed on paper suitable for recycling and made from fully managed and sustained forest sources. Logging, pulping and manufacturing processes are expected to conform to the environmental regulations of the country of origin.

A catalogue record for this book is available from the British Library.

A catalog record for this book is available from the Library of Congress.

Typeset by MPS Limited, Chennai, India.

For William and Evan Duff and
Jessica Kate Wagner

Contents

Preface

More than 20 years ago, when Toni Morrison was awarded the Nobel Prize in Literature in 1993, the world of literary devotees turned to a new page in accolades presented to American (and African American) writers. It was not exactly the start of this wise woman's successful career, because that had officially occurred in 1977 with the publication of her third novel, *Song of Solomon*. This startling presentation came after decades of the Swedish Academy's slighting the most prolific achievements of United States writers: rather, the awarding of the Nobel Prize to Toni Morrison marked the merging of African American literary achievement with the more conventional, and perhaps more anticipated, attention to mainstream American fiction.

During the twentieth century, no other country had produced such aesthetic bounty. Within the United States, aesthetic accomplishment outdid itself year after year – nurtured particularly by the democratic freedoms to write whatever an artist chose. In America, the freedom to create paralleled the freedom to say. Toni Morrison, having been a senior editor for more than 20 years at Random House, understood how much freedom she had been given: she poured her considerable ability into her novels, aiming high and individually with each book. From *The Bluest Eye* in 1970 through *Sula* in 1973, *Song of Solomon* in 1977, *Tar Baby* in 1981, *Beloved* in 1987, and *Jazz* in 1992 – the latter coupled with her blockbuster book of literary criticism, *Playing in the Dark: Whiteness and the Literary Imagination* – whatever Morrison published was truly unanticipated. It was deserving of not only attention but praise. It was a statement of such significance that newspapers and magazines (and all kinds of Internet sources) carried multiple reviews. Morrison's work prompted waves of commentary, both print and electronic, despite the supposedly "dying" market for fiction and literary critique. When Toni Morrison chose to pick up her pencil, even before the Nobel Prize was given to her, the readers of the world paid attention.

One reason Morrison was so important to the world of writing was that she spoke for a populace that had had only sporadic representation: African American culture, like its typically African American life, could count on one hand the writers who spoke truly for this body of richly expressed narrative. As Morrison envisioned African American culture, she harvested as well much about the African culture that underlaid it. And Morrison claimed not only the African American palm; she claimed the African American *woman* writer's palm. She did not flinch at what she saw as her significant task: she approached telling the stories of black women's lives, no matter when in history those lives occurred, with indefatigable energy, accuracy, and passion. She also understood from the start that no woman's life existed in a vacuum, so she became adept at creating the lives of African American *men* (and it is for that reason that this study begins with her third novel, *Song of Solomon*, 1977, rather than her first, *The Bluest Eye*, 1970).

In a literary world where publishers demanded uplifting writing, where best-seller lists judged literary excellence by sales of books in the millions, Toni Morrison seldom reached records at all close to those commercial markers. Rather, she wrote what she saw as truth. She expressed the lives of African American characters with a deft grace that guided the reader's imagination to truths that might never previously have been acknowledged: she created and recreated all parts of inextinguishable lives so that readers understood the joys, and the pains, of those figures. She did not write autobiographically, except with the human impulse that took her into the souls and the experiences of her characters: *humanity expressed as seldom before* was her chosen topic.

After the admitted disruption of her winning the Nobel Prize for Literature, Morrison continued her steady path of accomplishment. In 1998 she published *Paradise*, the third of the books she considered her trilogy – *Beloved, Jazz, Paradise* – working for the first time on issues more spiritual than historical. In 2003 her treatise on men's lives as sources of community power appeared in a novel titled *Love*. In 2008 she continued her testament about forgiveness and love in *A Mercy*, and in 2012 she brought a number of aesthetic and philosophical issues together into one of the shortest – but perhaps, most powerful – of her novels, *Home*. Within this latter book, many of the tormented historical prisms of what was cast in *Beloved* as issues of slavery reappeared as issues of different kinds of trauma, some associated with warfare – again proving Morrison's skill with the creation of male characters as well as female.

Wherever and whenever Morrison turns to fiction, readers wait with intense suspense. Can she maintain her admittedly difficult route into the minds and souls of her readership? Can she continue to work the magic that arises with such calm from each of her printed pages? This book itself is one small testimony to her ability to evoke such magic, and such truth, as she writes and polishes – over and over – her unique, and much loved, novels.

Acknowledgments and Conventions

It has been a pleasure once more to work with the editors and staff of Palgrave Macmillan, a partnership which began in the late 1990s with my book on Sylvia Plath (and a second, revised edition of that study in 2002). In 2007 came *Ernest Hemingway, A Literary Life*; and in 2013, *Emily Dickinson, A Literary Life*. I have long appreciated the support and attention of Benjamin Doyle, Sophie Ainscough, and Tomas Rene (as well as the editors who came before them). Thanks also to Caroline Richards for her copyediting and Linda Auld for her managing of the production process.

For this book, I have assumed that three in-print collections of Toni Morrison's interviews and nonfiction will be available to readers: (1) Danille Taylor-Guthrie's collection of interviews with Morrison, published in 1994 as *Conversations with Toni Morrison* by the University Press of Mississippi; (2) Carolyn C. Denard's collection of Morrison's interviews, published by the same press in 2008 as *Toni Morrison: Conversations*; and (3) Professor Denard's collection of Morrison's essays, titled *Toni Morrison: What Moves at the Margin, Selected Nonfiction*, also published by the University Press of Mississippi in 2008. I have used the abbreviations *Con I* to cite the Taylor-Guthrie collection, and *Con II* to refer to the Denard collection of interviews. I refer to Denard's collection of Morrison's essays as *Nonfiction*. The essay by Toni Morrison in Brian Lanker's edited collection, *I Dream a World: Portraits of Black Women Who Changed America*, is referred to as *Lanker*.

Although I have included many of the excellent essays and books on Morrison's oeuvre in the Secondary Bibliography, there are still other works that – space permitting – might well have appeared. For their omission, my apologies. I also thank the many students at both Michigan State University and the University of North Carolina-Chapel Hill who brought energy and insight into the reading of Morrison's fiction.

Introduction: Morrison's Early Years

She was born Chloe Wofford in February 1931, to the wintry Lorain, Ohio, weather – and to her family, which included the Willises, her maternal grandparents and great-grandmother, as well as her parents and older sister Lois. In the steelworkers' neighborhood of mixed-race, lower-class people hard work was valued. Few people understood that lives elsewhere could be marked by a family's accumulation of wealth, not by their day-to-day earnings. But for these Lorain residents (some from Poland and central Europe; others from Mexico, Italy, and Greece; others – like the Woffords – from the American South), work or the promise of work comprised a primary element of the American dream. What such an ethic and such a household meant to the bright Chloe Ardelia Wofford was an atmosphere of reading and learning, of being useful. Morrison remembers that when she began school at five, she was one of the few children who could already read. In sixth grade, she was chosen to read to "the partially sighted" (Con II, 132). One of her middle-school teachers sent home a note to her mother which said, "You and your husband would be remiss in your duties if you do not see to it that this child goes to college" (Als 68).

In high school, Chloe was selected to work in the school library, and some accounts say she did secretarial work for the head librarian. She studied hard and was a non-stop reader, but she was also active in debate, the drama club, and on the yearbook staff (Li 11). Her tendency to be modest about her successes shows in an essay decades later, when she recalled, "I remember myself as surrounded by extraordinary adults who were smarter than me. I was better

1

educated, but I always thought that they had true wisdom and I had merely book learning. It was only when I began to write that I was able to marry those two things: wisdom and education" (Lanker 36). She was already a writer: many of her essays were read aloud to her classes. Chloe Wofford was not only one of the few African American children in the Lorain, Ohio, public schools – she was also one of the smartest within the school population.

In retrospect, Morrison called Ohio "neither plantation nor ghetto" (Con I, 158). She insisted, as had Eudora Welty, that knowing *place* was crucial for a writer. "It is a feeling, it is a perception about the past, a matrix out of which one either does come or perceives one's beginnings. ... It has very little to do with geography. ... [In fact] you get closer to the truth when you sometimes ignore the facts of the 'place'" (in Cooper-Clark 192). About growing up in Lorain, Morrison was matter-of-fact: "We all shared the small space, one high school, three junior high schools, these totally dedicated teachers, poverty, and that kind of life" (Con II, 132). During the decades that followed, her descriptions of being poor are never self-pitying. Later in the interview, Morrison noted: "Being one of 'them' [the poor, the disadvantaged] for the first twenty years of my life, I'm very, very conscious of all – not upward mobility, but gestures of separation in terms of class" (Con II, 133). Years later, speaking at an international library congress in New York, Morrison admitted to then facing the life that was starting to unroll before her if she had not gone to college: "Had I lived the life that the state planned for me from the beginning, I would have lived and died in somebody else's kitchen, or somebody else's land, and never written a word. That knowledge is bone deep, and it informs everything I do" (Sanna 22).

Family unity provided a reliable and safe matrix. Morrison remembers the strength of her mother, grandmother, and great-grandmother, and speaks frequently about their behavior. The Willis family – her mother's – came from Alabama, her grandmother leaving home with seven children and 18 dollars, taking the train north; secretly, her husband joined them from Birmingham, where he worked as a violinist. In Morrison's words, "Since it was possible for my mother, my grandmother and her mother to do what they did, which to me is really scary, really scary – snatching children and roaming around in the night; running away from the South and living in Detroit, can't read or write; in a big city trying to stay alive and keep those children when you can't even read the road signs – now, these are hard things to do" (Con I, 131). Her great-grandmother was a midwife, who stood six feet tall and whose skin was darker in color than that of the rest of the family. It is this group of women Morrison reveres. She describes them as "women who would run *toward* the situation rather than putting someone up in front of them, or retreating" (Con I, 54). Her mother was something of a social activist; Morrison recalls:

> My mother, when she would find out that they were not letting Black people sit in certain sections of the local theater, would go and sit in the white folks' section, go see *Superman* just so she could come out and say, "I sat there, so everybody else can too." It's a tradition ... It's an old technique that black people use – you know, the first one in the pool, the first one in the school. (Con I, 134)

For much of Morrison's childhood, the Great Depression made money scarce. Although her father was ingenious about finding work, sometimes there was none to be had – then the Woffords (including the two sons born after Lois and Chloe) lived on welfare. Not to be pitied, Chloe's mother once wrote an angry letter to President Roosevelt, complaining about the quality of the food given to the poor (Matus 6). Eventually, George Wofford was working two union jobs, a situation that meant he could have lost both of them. When questioned, he explained that he needed every dollar for Lois's college education (with Chloe to start school immediately after her older sister), and the union officials gave him permission (Li 12).

At 12, Morrison herself went out to clean. Writing about that experience years after the fact, she described the day's experience: "The best news was the two dollars and fifty cents. Each Friday she would give me ... enough money to see sixteen movies or buy fifty Baby Ruth candy bars. And all I had to do for it was clean her house for a few hours after school." Morrison really didn't know how to clean with the woman's new and fancy supplies – but she was unquestionably proud that she could give half her munificent earnings to her mother. As the weeks passed, her employer began offering Morrison used clothing as part of her pay – in time she learned how to refuse those items so that she still had her earnings. It was tiresome to see her position, and her money, whittled away and so, eventually, she complained to her father. He advised her: "Listen. You don't live there. You live here. At home, with your people. Just go to work; get your money and come on home." Morrison translated this into several rules about work: "Whatever the work, do it well, not for the boss but for yourself." "Your real life is with us, your family." "You are not the work you do; you are the person you are" (Nonfiction 16–17).

As this anecdote shows, Morrison early learned the importance of work, of doing things the right way and to the best of her ability. This attitude was a part of the Willis–Wofford family tradition. When the economic depression eased and George Wofford was employed as a welder, he explained to Chloe that he sometimes signed the seam he had just completed. When she pointed out that no one would ever see that signature, he told her that it was important to *him* to claim that ownership (Con II, 14).

Whereas many of Morrison's reminiscences focus on her mother and grandmother, the presence of her stalwart father is never diminished. He was the family's best teller of ghost stories. In Morrison's recollections, she grew up being what she called "a radio child. You got in the habit of gathering information that way, and imagining the rest. You made it up" (Con I, 90). All her life, Morrison was a listener:

> In Lorain, Ohio, when I was a child, I went to school with and heard the stories of Mexicans, Italians, and Greeks, and I listened. I remember their language, and a lot of it is marvelous. But when I think of things my mother and father or aunts used to say, it seems the most absolutely striking thing in the world .... It's always seemed to me that black people's grace has been with what they do with language. (Con I, 45)

Within the Wofford home, everyone told stories. Critic Karla Holloway describes Morrison's comments about her families' narratives:

> The spoken library was ... children's stories my family told, spirituals, the ghost stories, the blues, and folk tales and myths, and the everyday ... instruction and advice, of my own people .... I wanted to write out of the matrix of memory, of recollection,

and to approximate the sensual and visceral response I had to the world I live in … to recreate the civilization of Black people … the manners, judgments, values, morals. (Holloway, "Narrative Time" 104–5)

In the Wofford–Willis home, parents and grandparents also privileged dreams, and Chloe was an avid dreamer. Her grandmother thought her dreams were lucky, and frequently asked her about them: then she consulted the dream book, which charted dreams by a three-digit code that could be used for playing the numbers. Morrison explains:

> You dream about a rabbit, or death, or weddings, and their color made a difference – if you dreamed about dying in a white dress or a red dress – and weddings always meant death and death always meant weddings. I was very interested because she used to hit a lot on my dreams for about a year or two … Then I stopped hitting for her, so she stopped asking me. It was lovely to have magic that could turn into the pleasure of pleasing one's grandmother and was also profitable. My dream life is still so real to me that I can hardly distinguish it from the other. (Con I, 100)

More generally, Morrison remembers that "I grew up in a house in which people talked about their dreams with the same authority that they talked about what 'really' happened. They had visitations and did not find that fact shocking and they had some sweet, intimate connections in things that were not empirically verifiable" (Con I, 226).

The Wofford household was also filled with music. Her grandfather played the violin by ear; her mother played the piano for silent movie houses (Con I, 283). Her mother also sang – sometimes for hours on end – moving from classical songs to jazz to spirituals to blues. (She sang regularly in the choir at the Greater St. Matthew A. M. E. Church' Con II, 210.) Chloe's family wanted her to take piano lessons but doing so confused her and made her feel "deficient" (and much less talented than her other family members) (Bigsby 262–4). So pervasive was her mother's singing that Morrison later compared the presence of song to meditation: "The singing and dancing that I remembered was not limited to entertainment; it was a kind of meditation. I know that it's true in my own family because I came from people who sang all the time. It was a kind of talking to oneself musically." Morrison thought that her mother's constant singing, and the choices of the songs she chose, was "a kind of probing into something and then working it out, in addition to whatever release it provided. It had a great deal to do, actually, with my feeling that writing for me is an enormous act of discovery ... It's a way of sustained problematizing for me, writing novels." (Con II, 136–37).

It was Morrison's mother, Ramah, who had graduated from high school, whereas her father had had to work so hard during his Virginia childhood that his formal education ended before twelfth grade. There was little question that Chloe would not only graduate high school, but that she would – like her uncle – attend college, and would become, with Lois, the first person in her immediate family to do so. To help her, Ramah took on a series of what Morrison called "humiliating jobs" – largely custodial – for extra money which she sent to her daughter at Howard University in Washington, DC.

Morrison attended Howard from 1949 to 1953, majoring in English literature and minoring in classics. She joined a sorority and, in the words of Amiri Baraka, who was two years younger than she, was "one of the most beautiful women I'd ever seen" (Con II, 211). During several of those summers, she went south with the Howard Unity Players dramatic troupe; after her graduation, she went to Cornell University in Ithaca, New York, to get an MA degree in English. During her college years, everything that gave her comfort about Lorain, Ohio, disappeared: both the city of Washington and points south were visibly segregated. Morrison was suddenly all too aware that she was an African American woman, and on some occasions, that the most important fact about her was her skin color. As she insisted to Bigsby, during the years when she had lived in Lorain, "there was a lack of racial tension – being black was no worse than being Irish or Jewish." She continued, "I never believed I was inferior .... I thought I was interesting because my parents thought we were all interesting" (Bigsby 262, 265). But facing the punitive strictures of racial difference taught Morrison quickly.

Tranquil as she usually is when discussing race in Lorain, by the time Morrison becomes more candid, her personal bitterness surfaces. In a later interview, talking about the poverty of African American children in the United States, she admits that she understands that life – "I have seen it and I know about it and I know when it doesn't work and I know in some instances why. When you haven't got the resources to get through it – it's not an easy life – it is NOT an easy life" – and such knowledge gave her much of the story of Pecola in her first novel, *The Bluest Eye* (Con II, 43). She describes the pain of coping with the racially divisive signs in DC; she also admits that on tours of the South, she sometimes did angry things:

> I can remember I hated New Orleans because they used to have these beautifully made wooden signs saying "coloreds only" that you could move, depending on who was getting on the bus. If there was a neighborhood where there were lots of white people, and a black person came on, you could take the sign and move it back or forward. I remember stealing one of those, at great pains and with a great deal of plotting with the other actors in the troupe, to take it home ... once you have seen separate fountains and separate toilets in Washington, and I hadn't seen it before I got there, the South was an extension of that. (Bigsby 271)

After her two years of graduate study at Cornell, and her graduation with a Master's degree, Morrison returned to the South for a teaching position at Texas Southern University in Houston, Texas. In this all-black school, she began to come into political consciousness. (Despite courses at Howard from noted African American poet Sterling Brown and Alain Locke, the creator of the rubric "the New Negro" and the "Harlem Renaissance," much of Morrison's college education was not marked by racial politics. That her lengthy MA thesis at Cornell focused on the way both William Faulkner and Virginia Woolf drew their "outsider" characters, such alienated figures as Septimus Smith in the latter's *Mrs Dalloway* or Quentin Compson in Faulkner's *Absalom, Absalom!*, again showed a consciousness based more on aesthetics than on race.) By 1957, Morrison had returned to Howard University to teach, and she stayed in that teaching position until 1964, through her marriage to Jamaican architect Harold Morrison, the birth of two sons, and her eventual divorce from Morrison.

During the early 1960s, however, it was hard to stay distant from African American politics. Among Morrison's students at Howard were Houston Baker, Jr., Andrew Young, Claude Brown, and Stokely Carmichael, one of the founders of SNCC, The Student Nonviolent Coordinating Committee. Because her children were babies, she could not be politically prominent but she sometimes sat in on a writing group, along with the painter Charles Sebree and the playwright Owen Dodson (writing the story that would lead to her first novel). During later decades, when Morrison was asked about her absence from politics during the 1960s and the 1970s, she would admit, "I am really awful at organization. I do not show up and I have no good administrative skills and I really don't take orders well ... I think I knew there was something an art form could do in that milieu that journalism and television could not. It could identify, it could interpret, it could clarify, it could pose all the right questions" (Bigsby 271).

By 1964, Morrison had returned home to live with her parents in Lorain. There she had help caring for the two little boys, one just a baby, and getting her divorce. The next year she applied for a job as a textbook editor in Syracuse, New York, and took that position with a subsidiary of Random House. She recalled "having a baby sitter during the day and coming home after 7:30 at night." Soon she and her boys were moving into the New York environs: Random House had offered her a position as an editor in New York. Although her mother worried because they had no immediate family in the city, Morrison found friends and supporters. And most of those friends and supporters were women.

Morrison's first novel, *The Bluest Eye*, 1970

For a woman well trained in the study of literature, particularly in the mainstream texts of England, Italy, Germany, Russia, France, and – to a lesser extent – the United States, nothing in her classic preparation would have prepared Chloe Wofford Morrison to write a novel. Insistent as she was even early in this somewhat secretive endeavor, Morrison knew she wanted to write books that *African American* readers would want to know and study. The models for such books, however, were few. About the relevant writings by Richard Wright, Ralph Ellison, James Baldwin and a few other African American male writers, Morrison complained that they seemed to be writing sociology, explaining black lives to white readers, white *male* readers. As she later told Jean Strouse, "Those books and political slogans about power were addressed to white men trying to explain or prove something to them. The fight was between men, for king of the hill" (Strouse 55).

Morrison wanted no part of such efforts. Her aim was to write about the reality of African American family lives, focusing where possible upon the mothers and daughters of those families. It was the lives of *women* that most fascinated Morrison. As she worked on *The Bluest Eye*, she saw that fiction as "something separate from the harangue and the confusion" that existed elsewhere in African American writing (Lanker 36).

The novel that became known as The *Bluest Eye* grew from Morrison's recollection of a beautiful black girl who was her friend in Lorain, Ohio. This girl had given up any belief in God because, as she told Chloe, she had prayed to Him for two years asking for blue eyes – and nothing had happened. Morrison remembers being shocked that this beautiful girl would have such a warped sense of what beauty was. (She had also joined the Catholic Church when she was 12, so perhaps her sense of what God might be asked to do was already well developed; Bigsby 269.)

As she wrote and rewrote the book during the evenings after her sons were in bed (and early in the mornings before they were awake), Morrison drew from what she as a youngster had experienced living in Ohio. She recalled, "I was very, very conscious of that mood and atmosphere of my hometown in the first book, *The Bluest Eye*. I used literal descriptions of neighborhoods … but the description of the house where we lived, the description of the streets, the lake [Lake Erie], and all of that is very much the way I remember Lorain" (Con I, 171). She also realized that no simple narrative would do justice to the complex story of physical beauty and its power in contemporary culture. In a later draft of the book, she added the characters of the MacTeer girls as her primary storytellers, and the MacTeer family, based visibly on her own parents, to the text. Then the story became a racial prolegomenon: the MacTeer family was stalwart and completely moral. The Breedlove family had drifted away from social conventions and had grown envious of all the trappings of *white* culture.

The Bluest Eye speaks to the lives of very young women, so crippled in their desires that they all appear to be victims. Pecola Breedlove, the most damaged of all, is never going to recover and even though readers appreciate the conscience of the MacTeer sisters, Frieda and the younger Claudia, their grief over the fact that their communities of women have failed Pecola and her mother, Pauline Breedlove, creates a grim resonance around the story. Deprecation and abuse, regardless of the race of the oppressor, is a story no one wants to pass on. *The Bluest Eye* is a cautionary tale, and its presentation of real evil exists in the lack of parenting that both the Breedloves – Cholly as well as Pauline – experienced when they themselves were children. Torn from families that could have cared for them, placed in the deep poverty typical of the Southern migrant, the Breedloves are homeless when the story begins; they cannot care for their two children any better than their parents cared for them. The novel works in a downward and increasingly negative spiral.

Except for its bleak tone, *The Bluest Eye* might have fulfilled Morrison's early aim in her fiction. As she explained to Paul Gilroy, "I write what I think is of interest to black people ... This is about me and you. I have to deliver something real" (Gilroy 177). Adding more description to that concept, Morrison noted, "I always wanted to read Black books in which I was enlightened, I as a Black person ... There are not many books like that. ... there are a lot of critics who believe that our books are there to tell them what our lives are all about" (Con II, 15).

Morrison explained her relative lack of self-consciousness about writing her first novel:

> I just didn't think anybody was ever going to do what I was doing. They couldn't judge me. Nobody was going to judge me, because they didn't know what I knew, and they weren't going to do it. No African American writer has ever done what I did, which was to write without the *white gaze*. This wasn't about them ... I really felt original. I really did. I hate to admit that because it sounds so self-regarding. ... There was nobody else who was going to make the center of the novel "the most helpless creature in the world: a little black girl who doesn't know anything, and who believes all that racist stuff, so *vulnerable*, so *nuts*." This was brand new space. (Con II, 252–3)

She had repeated to Jean Strouse, "When I wrote my first novel ... I wanted to capture that same specificity about the nature and feeling of the culture I grew up in" (Strouse 53–4).

Because Pecola is raped by her father, among Morrison's 1970s readership – regardless of their skin color – *The Bluest Eye* was considered a sensational and sensationalized novel. Sabine Sielke, one of the foremost rape theorists of the feminist period, noted, largely on the basis of this novel, that Morrison was a pioneer in writing about "the incest trope": "Sexual violation looms large throughout Morrison's work, beginning with *The Bluest Eye*" (Sielke 152). Surrounded as Morrison's novel was by such mainstream (white) feminist novels as Joan Didion's *Play It as It Lays* (1970), Sue Kaufman's *The Diary of a Mad Housewife* (1967), Sylvia Plath's *The Bell Jar* (available in England in 1963 but in the States only after 1970), Margaret Atwood's *Surfacing* (1972) and Erica Jong's *Fear of Flying* (1973), the fact that Morrison's first novel sold comparatively few copies meant that the marketing of African American fiction was to take a different route. Sad as Pecola's life is, mainstream readers did not want to read about the sorrows of poverty, especially poverty intensified in raced conditions. The comedy that infused much of this early feminist writing – particularly Jong's fiction – was absent in *The Bluest Eye*, though Morrison gave Mrs. MacTeer some scenes, and some language, that came close to humor.

Morrison also made Cholly Breedlove a complex figure. Deprived as he had himself been by his loss of parents, and by his being forced by the "whitemen" to rape Darlene, Cholly seemed unclear about both his act – of raping his daughter – and his motivation for that act. Years later, in Morrison's "Afterword" to the reprinting of the novel, she suggested that part of her dissatisfaction with *The Bluest Eye* lay in the fact that Cholly's brutal act against his helpless child should have been seen as a reflection of his own powerlessness, as he was forced to perform sexually in the glare of the white men's flashlights: "connecting Cholly's 'rape' by the whitemen to his own of his daughter" ("Afterword" 215). Donald B. Gibson was one of the earliest observers to see Cholly's complexity; he went against the usual negative readings of this character by connecting Cholly's rape of Pecola with his earlier love for Pauline. He pointed out, "It would be on the whole easier to judge Cholly if we knew less about him and if we could isolate the kitchen floor episode from the social context in which it occurs and from Cholly's past. But we cannot; we are neither invited to nor allowed ..." (Gibson 170).

In a subsequent interview, Morrison tries to recapture the difficulties of her writing *The Bluest Eye* during the late 1960s. She posits her role as both an *African American* writer and a *woman* writer: the significant stream of African American writing in the 1960s was by men who wrote, and much of that writing stemmed from Ralph Ellison's *Invisible Man*, which had – since its publication in 1952 – become a central text in the teaching of all contemporary fiction. Whereas Richard Wright's *Native Son*, published more than a decade earlier than *Invisible Man*, had often been included in syllabi, by the 1960s – when the mood of race relations was changing into promise rather than despair – the Ellison novel, with Invisible Man's psychological search for self as its primary theme, had replaced the sometimes shocking horror of the acts of Bigger Thomas, *Native Son*'s protagonist. In the retrospective view of Carsten Junker, African American writing was changing visibly:

> critics had to recognize the growing participation of Black women in the field ... to their increasingly effective assertion of gender issues in Black men's writing, and racial biases in white women's writing. Essay writers like June Jordan, Audre Lorde, Toni Morrison, Barbara Smith, and Alice Walker explicitly demanded and reflected the repudiation of worldviews organized according to race or gender as sole axes of differentiation. (Junker 91)

Morrison always thought that writing by women would be read differently – and attacked differently – than writing by men; and she had been long enough in the publishing world to understand that African American writing would naturally constitute a category separate from mainstream writing.

These are Morrison's words about the problems of creating her Pecola:

> Because when I began to write, it [sexual violence] was unmentionable. It is so dangerous, it is so awful, so wicked that I think in connection with vulnerable black women, it was never talked about. I wanted to write books that ran the whole gamut of women's sexuality in literature. They were either mothers, mammies, or whores. They were not people who were supposed to enjoy sex, either. That was forbidden in literature – to enjoy your body, be

in your body, defend your body. But at the same time I wanted to say, "*You can still be prey.*" (Con II, 104–5; italics mine)

Years later, Morrison revisits the incestuous rape, saying, "Before we even knew who we were, someone we trusted our lives to could, might, would make use of our littleness, our ignorance, our need, and sully us to the bone, disturbing the balance of our lives as theirs had clearly been disturbed" ("Foreword" to *Love* x).

In the later "Afterword" to her first novel, Morrison also mourns the lack of attention given to *The Bluest Eye*, saying that it was "dismissed, trivialized, misread" ("Afterword" 216). That *The Bluest Eye* in 1970 was consistently overlooked was no surprise. Morrison had published it with a house – Holt – other than the one she worked for, Random House. Neither publisher had a specific category for African American writing and, even in the case of Ellison's *Invisible Man*, the important fact that the author was African American was rarely mentioned. Even when readers knew that African American literature existed, few critics were providing ways to discuss that body of work – and those who were focusing on African American works concentrated, sometimes exclusively, on writing by black men. Although not the case with the Ellison novel, much African American writing was marked by the duality that existed in culture – black endeavors (and heroes) set against the inimical circumstances that existed because the white culture was all-powerful.

It was clear that Morrison's *The Bluest Eye* could not be read within that dynamic. First of all, in this novel, white culture seems not to exist at all. The differences between the MacTeer family and the Breedlove are charted among an all-African-American cast. The risk Morrison took was that readers would stop trying to decide where moral right existed and chalk off the Breedloves' cruel behavior to their children as an acceptable condition, given that the characters were black and poor. For the middle-class white reader, the Breedloves (and the MacTeers as well) were definitely "Other."

Making the literary world create an entirely new category for *The Bluest Eye* meant that few readers would be aware of the novel at all – and yet, given her immersion in publishing, Morrison knew she needed to stake such a claim. Whether intentional or accidental, *The Bluest Eye* fulfilled the aim Morrison later expressed to critic Nellie McKay, that,

Black people have a story, and that story has to be heard. There was an articulate literature before there was print. What you hear is what you remember. That oral quality is deliberate. It is not unique to my writing, but it is a deliberate sound that I try to catch. The way black people talk is not so much the use of non-standard grammar as it is the manipulation of metaphor. The fact is that the stories look as though they come from people who are not even authors ... They are just told – meanderingly – as though they are going in several directions at the same time. (Con I, 152)

Intricately structured as *The Bluest Eye* was, it would fall to some of Morrison's later writing to create the movement she described here as "meanderingly." But in scene after scene, the reader was struck with the authenticity of her created African American language.

Morrison's language throughout *The Bluest Eye* was convincing, but the narrative itself was so modern – even postmodern – that readers found the reading process difficult. The book bombarded readers with characters and events hard to sort through. Chief among those difficulties was the fact that Morrison had incorporated layers of separate stories, often without explanation or signal. Added to the Breedlove and MacTeer lines and interchanges were unexpected stories involving Maureen Peel, Geraldine, Mr. Henry, the three prostitutes, Soaphead Church, and – toward the conclusion – Pecola's unnamed imaginary friend. In her attempt to show the irreparable damage that Cholly's rape had done to his daughter, Morrison draws from characteristics William Faulkner had created decades earlier for the figure of Benjy Compson in *The Sound and the Fury*. Neither Benjy nor Pecola has any effective language. Both live in a surreal enclosure of inhuman behavior as others – even their family members – mistreat them. Benjy, eventually, knows his own sexual violation. Morrison's emphasis – which is illustrated quite differently from Faulkner's – is that Pecola Breedlove could have lived a normal life, were it not for the abuses of her family and her culture. Morrison's novel is one of sorrow and blame; Faulkner's book is more generally read as one of unrelieved pity.

Morrison knew that African American writing would not exist, except marginally, until critics helped to create opinions about that body of work. She wrote in her Lanker essay, "You can't evolve good criticism until you have good books ... it was hard to get the balanced attention of critics and reviewers because they wanted to talk about anything but political implications. Then they started talking about the political implications and they never talked about the artistic strategies. They didn't give you two legs to walk on, always one" (Lanker 36).

The appearance of *The Bluest Eye* did make review markets aware of Morrison's existence – and in the early 1970s, her own reviews of black writing created a kind of shadowy presence for her. Her appearances in the *New York Times* (both the *Book Review* and the *Magazine*) were meant to counter what she later called the critics' "attempt to reduce the area about which I wrote, to ghettoize me, and I was very forceful about turning that around. Now I insist on being identified as a black woman writer because these are the sensibilities of which I write" (Con I, 125).

Morrison's second novel, *Sula*, a feminist conundrum

Morrison had several regrets about publishing *The Bluest Eye* in 1970. The first was that her publishers used a name she thought seemed wrong: she had assumed that she would publish the novel as Chloe Wofford, or perhaps as Chloe Wofford Morrison. She wanted her father's name, her family name, to appear on the book jacket. But because her submission process had been informal (contacting the young editor she knew, giving him the manuscript but not typing it up with title page or copyright information), she did not know how her professional name had been changed. Once she had chosen "Anthony" as her baptism name, some of her friends began calling her "Toni." Once she married, as was the custom at mid-century she changed the name Wofford to Morrison. There was no malice in her name's appearing as "Toni Morrison," then; it was the way people in New York had come to know her – and it was a designation that would become permanent (Bigsby 272).

Her more pervasive regret about *The Bluest Eye* was that she had chosen a narrative strategy that was difficult for readers to process. While the arrangement of sections in *The Bluest Eye* was in keeping with such modernist innovation as Faulkner's and Dos Passos's, it was not easily accessible to general readers. For all the writing that Morrison was to do after 1970, she never again used so many different levels of metaphor and scene, such fragmented chronology. Yet for all its technical difficulty, *The Bluest Eye* told a comparatively simple story.

By the time of Morrison's *Sula* in 1973, it had become clear that creating nothing less than an African American *world* was the author's aim. Within *The Bluest Eye* she had drawn three prostitutes – Maginot Line, China, and Poland (the novel was, after all, set during World War II) – as well as the prudish and self-satisfied middle-class character Geraldine. She had shown mean children growing into their own mean self-righteousness from prideful families. She had imagined the Trinidadian fanatic Soaphead Church who, like Mr. Henry, the MacTeer boarder, was a God-obsessed pedophile. And she had already described the kind of exclusionary women's community that would – four novels later in *Beloved* – damn Sethe Suggs to an isolation worse than the judgments of hell. Again working against stereotypes, Morrison's drawing of a women's community was much more negative than were the communities she herself had experienced.

As she would throughout her writing career, Morrison chose to pit herself and her abilities against the expected concepts of *who* black women were, and *what* such women were capable of doing. Facing the unjust stereotype that all African American women are mammies or nymphomaniacs, Morrison chose a unique pattern for the character of Sula. Almost masculine in both her strength and her disdain for social propriety, Sula went defiantly away from her family's matriarchal culture, so powerful within the small Ohio town of Medallion. Sula went to college; she also slept with whomever she chose – but she did not marry; and when she came back to Medallion after a decade, she then slept with her best friend's husband, and so ended the years-long Sula–Nel friendship. Sula also incarcerated her vindictive grandmother in a home for the aging, although there was no financial necessity for this act. (Readers who knew Zora Neale Hurston's *Their Eyes Were Watching God*, a novel about Janie's long-standing friendship with Phoeby, understood how different the tone of *Sula* was.)

Like most beginning writers, Morrison drew from personal knowledge. As she said about *The Bluest Eye*, "I used the geography of my childhood, the imagined characters based on bits and pieces of people" (Con I, 96). With Medallion, she created a new town from her mother's descriptions of their moving from the South to Pittsburgh – so Morrison the author was leaving Lorain, Ohio, but she was not going far from the town's tangible markings. As she said about *Sula*, "I was obsessed with the idea, and totally enchanted by it. ... I always thought *Sula* was the best idea I ever had, but the writing was on its own" (Con I, 98). In those three years between the publication of Morrison's first novel and her second, she had been forced to delve into her own definitions of African American women: in 1971 the *New York Times Magazine* asked her to write about the feminist movement. Accurately, in "What the Black Woman Thinks About Women's Lib," Morrison defined that social condition as a white (and middle- to upper-class) woman's effort.

In her essay Morrison points to the elite economic concerns of the movement, which contrast with the concerns of African American women: "not getting into the labor force but in being upgraded in it, not in getting into medical school but in getting adult education, not in how to exercise freedom from the 'head of the house' but in how to *be* head of the household" (Nonfiction 21–2).

Much of the lengthy essay describes the strength of African American women. They, of necessity, stand on their own two feet. In fact, Morrison says, black women are people who have "nothing to fall back on: not maleness, not whiteness, not ladyhood, not anything" (Nonfiction 24). Later, she recalled to an interviewer,

Feminists were saying that we had to become friends, *begin* to call ourselves sisters. I remember thinking, what do they mean we have to *begin*. I reflected on those women in my family, my mother and her friends, who liked each other's company and in their church called each other sister. I knew what the relationship among those women was, how they cared for one another, liked one another. I can hear them now, all that wonderful laughter about their husbands and sons. (Bigsby 273)

Morrison was also reviewing for the *New York Times Book Review,* and there she often critiqued authors' views of African American life. She was working in her editorial capacity at Random House to help construct what she called a kind of "Whole Earth Catalogue" about contemporary African American life – and its relevant history. *The Black Book* was published in 1974, following *Sula* by less than a year.

It could easily be said that in the early 1970s Morrison had undertaken the study of African American existence. She had been well educated but that education had little to do with her knowledge that she was African American. Now she was empowering herself as writer to educate readers about the myriad situations that developed in black people's lives, and she was not averse to using issues from her own single-parent life to illustrate those issues. As she wrote years later in a Foreword to the novel *Sula*, divorced from her sons' father and living in Queens,

> commuting to Manhattan to an office job, leaving my children to childminders and the public school in the fall and winter, to my parents in the summer, and ... so strapped for money that the condition moved from debilitating stress to hilarity. Every rent payment was an event; every shopping trip a triumph of caution over the reckless purchase of a staple. The best news was that this was the condition of every other single/separated female parent I know. The things we traded! Time, food, money, clothes, laughter, memory – and daring. Daring especially, because in the late sixties, with so many dead, detained, or silenced, there could be no turning back simply because there was no "back" back there. Cut adrift, so to speak, we found it possible to think up things, try things, explore. Use what was known and tried and investigate what was not. Write a play, form a theater company, design clothes, write fiction unencumbered by other people's expectations. Nobody was minding us, so we minded ourselves.

Remembering the late 1960s, Morrison added, "We were being encouraged to think of ourselves as our own salvation, to be our own best friends" ("Foreword" xv).

Besides Morrison's personal situation, she was interested in writing about women's intimate friendship that was not lesbian. (One of the early ways of casting suspicion on "women's lib" was the charge that same-sex friendships were sexually based.) In Morrison's terms, friendships between women were often "discredited" (Con II, 79). At best, such a narrative as the friendship between Nel and Sula would be seen as boring.

She was also interested in describing Sula as different from Nel, and thereby expanding the notion of what an African American woman of a certain age was like. Sula, for her author, was an "outlaw" woman, a figure who created her own roles of behavior. For Nel to think that Sula's sleeping with her husband was the most cruel betrayal jarred against Sula's thinking that she simply wanted the pleasure of that man's body. (As Morrison said in her New York Public Library interview, December, 2013, "Sula slept with him – she did not KILL him.") In the "Foreword" to *Sula*, Morrison had pointed out that "Female freedom always means sexual freedom – even when – especially when – it is seen through the prism of economic freedom" ("Foreword" xiii).

Dominant in the matrix of women characters in Medallion stands the figure of the war-damaged Shadrach, who returned home after losing his best friend to the horrors of combat. That man was beheaded as he ran beside Shadrach – but his body kept moving and Shadrach – years later – still saw the grotesque sight. In his friend's honor, Shadrach created for Medallion what he called National Suicide Day: annually the town revered its wartime losses. In this new emphasis on a cherishing ceremony, Morrison was beginning to introduce a broader life sensibility: the dignity of a global response to war's (and life's) horrors was etched here.

According to critic La Vinia Jennings, by 1973 and 1974 Morrison had absorbed a quantity of information about African culture. She had been the sponsoring editor of both *Giant Talk*, an anthology of Third World writing (edited by Quincy Troupe and Rainer Schulte), and the work of Chinweizu, the important African historian, *The West and the Rest of Us: White Predators, Black Slavers, and the African Elite*. As Linden Peach described the latter, "white power gives rise to and maintains racism ... while white power in turn serves white power." Complete with outright suggestions for ways the white races can avoid brainwashing "by European propaganda" and avoid "self-hatred," the thesis, coming as it did in the early 1970s, was one avenue for exploration of real strengths within African American unrest in the United States (Peach, *Toni* 7; Mbalia 106). She had helped to publish Ivan Van Sertima's radically significant *They Came Before Columbus: The African Presence in Ancient America* (Li 22).

Morrison had pored over Camara Laye's novel *The Radiance of the King*, as well as works by such other African writers as Ayi Kwei Armah, Wole Soyinka, and Chinua Achebe. She also was absorbing this non-American philosophy through her position as editor at

Random House for Leon Forrest, Toni Cade Bambara, Angela Davis, Gayl Jones, Lucille Clifton, James Alan McPherson, Muhammad Ali, Ishmael Reed, and – though posthumously – Henry Dumas.[1] She had worked long and hard on all stages of *The Black Book*, which was a compendium of African and African American history and culture, particularly popular culture, although Random House was not sure the project was viable (Li 28).

One of the principal differences that study of Africa and its philosophies brought into the Western mind was an acceptance of the fourth power, that of evil. The African mind focuses on "causes and effects of evil, not its origin, since the concept of evil does not exist." Of particular relevance to Morrison's absorption with women characters and their lives is the African belief that "African witches [almost always considered to be female], the principal agents of moral evil, unconsciously and inadvertently visit dis-ease, death, and material misfortune" (Jennings 7). "Sula" itself is an African name. Throughout this novel, Morrison creates situations best explained by African beliefs – Eva's burning her son Plum, for example, in her role as mother of the family; Sula's cutting off her finger's end, to protect Nel from the mean boys; the deaths in the Bottom of Medallion residents who investigated the tunnel in the hope of finding ways that they could be hired to work on that project. Again, Jennings devotes nearly a chapter to describing the ways *kindoki*, African witchcraft, is "almost exclusively unilinear in its patrilineal and matrilineal descents." Sula receives Eva's line, as her mysterious facial mark may suggest (Jennings 54).

Another difference between Western and African belief systems is the timelessness of considerations of time. In African thought, past, present, and future merge (and such distinctions grow meaningless). As Missy Kubitschek emphasized, African time is neither linear nor progressive. So long as the memory of a person lives, so does that person. Tangentially, the self and other people are not truly separable, and the "dead" as ancestors remain important influences. (Morrison repeatedly uses the phrases "the ancestors" and references to the *ancient properties*.) Most elements of life and ritual, no matter how commonplace, are considered sacred (Kubitschek 22–3; see also Higgins; Zauditu-Selassie).

Replete with a new symbology, African thought privileges the circle with a cross through it (the mark Morrison will later give to

Sethe's mother as her slave brand; the round shape of Medallion with the river bisecting it) – the circle suggesting the repetition of patterns, always including sorrow. Morrison's increasingly visible use of folktales – as in the flying motif of *Song of Solomon* and the metaphoric use of "tar baby" in the novel of that name – draws as well from African legend. The similarity between Native American beliefs and African – underscored in both *Song of Solomon* and *A Mercy*, and interesting to Morrison because of her great-grandmother's Native American blood – stems from, in Jennings' assessment, "their reverence for land. In African consciousness there is a great reciprocity or unity between land or space and time. One is the coefficient of the other. Often one word serves for both" (Jennings 111).

In *Tar Baby* (1981), Morrison creates both background and narrative from the effulgence of "witchcraft" as it spreads into the natural world. The animistic behavior of trees and land, waters and skies in her fourth novel, set primarily in the Caribbean, brought these seemingly separable evidences of the spirit world to a mysterious reality. Again, Jennings notes that the predominant Catholicism there merged with the strong influence of Voodoo (Voudoun). In the novel, the *loa* (the freed souls of the cosmos) reside in "trees, stones, streams," which serve as vessels for their existences. "The preponderance of African traditional religions and their diaspora mutations are grounded in the belief that nonmaterial 'spirit' animates matter; therefore natural objects, natural phenomena, and the universe itself possesses a consciousness. Originating from a number of sources, divinities and spirits of the natural elements animating trees, stones, and other material objects characterize animistic religions" (Jennings 127–8).

Given that Morrison's fifth novel, *Beloved*, appeared to be the site of a great many manifestations of these, and other, African beliefs – crystallized in the strangely evocative and ghostly figure of Beloved herself – the presence of elements of African belief systems and other folkloric superstitions before that novel may have gone largely unnoticed. For Morrison, however, because she insisted that the writer must draw from all parts of her experience, her knowledge of African life and, perhaps more significantly, of African spiritual beliefs, would be integral to her more visible aims. As she had said in the Le Clair interview,

My work bears witness and suggests who the outlaws were, who survived under what circumstances and why, what was legal in the community as opposed to what was legal outside it ...Whenever I feel uneasy about my writing, I think: what would be the response of the people in the book if they read the book? That's my way of staying on track. *These are the people for whom I write.* (Con I, 121)

Teresa Washington notes in her study of the importance of African belief to, especially, women writers, "Morrison taps into her reservoir of re-memory and finds that the reality of the Ancestors – complex, pan-geographic, and resilient – are truth enough beyond what 'science' can validate or philosophy can justify. ... Morrison makes it clear that the gentle ... and anonymous force was instrumental in her life and the lives of Africana women." She summarizes what she sees as Morrison's greatest gift as novelist: "With both outer and ever-open spiritual eyes, she re-members the historical, mythical and literal in her subtly critical art to help ancestral and contemporary audiences re-envision the past and better hone the potential of the future" (Washington 102–4).

Washington focuses in her scholarship on the feminine spirit, the Aje, and on its manifestations in Hoodoo, which she calls "the African American spiritual system that includes cosmology, divination, root-work, conjuring, power of prayer, the ability to heal, and the power to curse .... the African cult." She also studies "Oro, power of the word," which makes her reading of works by women writers especially apt. As she summarized, "Like Aje, most dislocated Africans were simultaneously human, superhuman, and divine, despite their slave status" (Washington 80–1).

A time of investigation and, in some respects, of creating community, the American 1970s were, particularly for Toni Morrison, a period of reaching out to other women who were writing seriously. She had diligently promoted the works of Gayl Jones and Toni Cade Bambara (as both their editor and their friend), and Jones was to write later, about Morrison's fiction, that she "lifted out of the early confines of mere comedy and pathos ... the oral tradition." Jones, writing as critic, compared Morrison's first novels with the work of both Carlos Fuentes and Gabriel García Márquez (Jones 171, 173). In 1977, Morrison joined with Alice Walker and June Jordan to form "The Sisterhood," a group of African American women writers. The intention, according to critic Pearl McHaney, was "to create a space for black women writers to honor each other, to know each other, so that nothing from outside could make us fight over anything. Or even feel competitive" (McHaney 138). Forming such a group was a signal move, in the midst of the still male-dominated African American literary world. Morrison would take from those friendships with women the kind of confidence and support she had previously never known.

What Toni Morrison had known, seemingly instinctively, was that any writer's life was one of essential loneliness. She said much later, speaking in retrospect

> I never played it safe in a book. I never tried to play to the gallery. For me, it was this extraordinary exploration. You have to be willing to think the unthinkable. ... I always think I'm at some archaeological site and I find this shard, this little piece of pottery and then I have to invent the rest. But first I have to go to the place, move the dirt, find why I am there. What's interesting here, why are you frightened, what is it that keeps nagging you? Then you see something, it may be a color, an image, a voice, and you build from it. (Lanker 36)

1
Song of Solomon: One Beginning of Morrison's Career

Morrison's immersion in the world of African belief systems and its centuries of lore fueled her decision to attempt a novel about the multi-generational "Dead" family. She kept them American, and African American; she started this third novel, *Song of Solomon*, with the families of both Macon Dead and Pilate Dead living in Michigan, a state still segregated in the 1940s but (probably) less racist than would have been a state located in the deep South. Reifying the experiences she had known as she grew up close to Lake Erie at the northern edge of Ohio, Morrison created the "better" part of this Michigan town as the site of Macon Dead's large home, and set it in contrast to "Darling Street," where Pilate and her unconventional family of women lived a seemingly less stable life. (Pilate did not believe in either paying for, or having, modern technology such as electricity or city water; she was announcing to the world that she was a creature from a different culture, whether a griot, an ancestor, or a witch; her brother Macon, in contrast, had assimilated to the point that he took on the persona of a successful white business man, though he behaved cruelly to his fragile wife and daughters.)

By setting up this visible dichotomy of the siblings, Morrison drew from her principles about creating character. As she had said:

we pretend there was no past, and just go blindly on, craving the single thing that we think is happiness ... The ideal situation is to take from the past and apply it to the future, which doesn't mean improving the past or tomorrow. It means selecting for it ... The novel has to provide the richness of the past as well as suggestions of what the use of it is. I try to create a world in which it is comfortable to do both, to listen to the ancestry and to mark out what might be going on sixty or one hundred years from now. (Con I, 112–13)

It would be a much bigger book, Morrison's third novel, and it would attempt to replicate what she described as the already existing "black mythology ... in music, gospels, spirituals, jazz." She paired this description of information sets with what she called "a kind of village lore. The community had to take on that responsibility of passing from one generation to another the mythologies, the given qualities, stories, assumptions which an ethnic group that is culturally coherent and has not joined the larger mainstream keeps very much intact for survival" (Con I, 112). As the title of this third novel announced, *Solomon* was to be the primary ancestor – and the primary act of Solomon was his flying back to Africa. Jennings notes about Morrison's aims here: "Although discredited knowledge that Blacks embraced was unbelievable, Morrison felt it was impossible not to write about their knowledge as an authority and authentication of Blackness" (Jennings 127).

Recent criticism finds importance in the gender differences. Valerie Loichot points to the novel's offering "a mode of reconstruction of the masculine through a necessary female intervention .... Morrison explicitly rejects a genealogical model based on the legacy of the father or the inverted revenge of the daughter. She calls for horizontal openness in which the foundation is important, but in which also open spaces – windows and doors – demand a relation with the outside" (Loichot 158, 164). Echoing Yaeger's earlier commentary about the importance of land in African American (and Native American cultures), Loichot sees both subversion and strength in Morrison's narrative. Yaeger's commentary stems from this idea: "ownership, in the African American context, often supplants personhood, in a world in which persons turned into things were deprived of the right to possess. Owning becomes 'not only the right to possess things but of the right to possess personhood'" (Yaeger 210). From an even broader perspective, Craig Werner notes that Morrison's use of the ancient/the folk "suggests the multiplicity of repressed historical experience. Morrison's point in *Song of Solomon* ... is that while Afro-American history may be repressed by the reifying myths, it is not destroyed. Where *Song of Solomon* emphasizes Milkman's developing understanding of this repressed history, *Tar Baby* expands the focus to involve a multitude of individuals engaged in similar processes" (Werner 72). In Loichot's summary, "Morrison romances the feminine shadows in male texts ... [Pilate] and her nephew Milkman perform interlocking masculinity and femininity, male and female ancestry, orality and writing, childhood and old age, womb and mind" (Loichot 158).

Much of the positive critical response to this novel rested on the gendered complexity, as well as on the visibility of black folklore. Finally, critics seemed to say, an *African American* novel that is filled with *African American* lore – whether stemming from Africa itself or from what Morrison referred to as "the folk" or, in other contexts, the "village." Reynolds Price, in his *New York Times Book Review* essay, emphasized that what makes *Song of Solomon* such a good piece of writing is that it is not basically realistic, but rather that it is memorable for "its negotiations with fantasy, folk, song and allegory." He calls it a "full novel – rich, slow enough to impress itself upon us like a love affair or a sickness," and notes that it encompasses many lives and nearly a hundred years of a family. He sees Morrison's purpose as equally large – "communication of painfully discovered and powerfully held convictions about the possibility of transcendence within human life" (Price). Summarizing that *Song of Solomon* is "a wise and spacious novel," Price also points out that "The end is unresolved ... (no big, good novel has ever really ended)" (Price).

Nervous as Morrison had been about attempting this book, saddened and for a time numbed by the loss of her father (*Song of Solomon* is dedicated, simply, to "Daddy"), she knew that writing such a book would stretch her abilities. As she said in an interview,

> Writing about male characters when you are female ... it takes some relaxed sensibility ... Trying to imagine it. I look at my children – boy children – and they are different from me. And they are impelled by different things. Instead of saying something general about it, I would say, "I wonder what that is" and then try to see the world the way they might see it. So that you enter the world instead of hovering over it and trying to dominate it and make it into something. You have to have that kind of absence of hostility –

absence of anything. You should do it for every character, and if a character is very old or very young or very rich or very poor or black or white or male or female, your ability to do it is the marked difference between writing on the surface and writing underneath. (Con I, 91–2)

Years later, in the "Foreword" that was published in 2004 with a new paperback edition, she explained that "Writing *Song of Solomon* ... I had no access to what I planned to write about until my father died. In the unmanageable sadness that followed, there was none of the sibling wrangling, guilt or missed opportunities ... Each of his four children was convinced that he loved her or him best." As Morrison tried to envision her father's life as a boy and man, she felt privy to new knowledge. She mentions that she asked him to tell her what the men he had known were "really like." She said that he answered, and she followed his advising ("Foreword" xi).

Thinking back to the start of her career as a novelist, Morrison told an interviewer,

the first two books were beginnings. I start with the childhood of a person in all the books, but in the first two, the movement, the rhythm is circular, although the circles are broken. If you go back to the beginnings, you get pushed along toward the end. This is particularly so with *The Bluest Eye*. *Sula* is more spiral than circular. *Song of Solomon* is different. I was trying to push this novel outward; its movement is neither circular nor spiral. The image in my mind for it is that of a train picking up speed. (Con I, 124)

She emphasizes this change again in the "Foreword": "The challenge ... was to manage what was for me a radical shift in imagination from a female locus to a male one. To get out of the house, to de-domesticate the landscape that had so far been the site of my work. To travel. To fly. In such an overtly, stereotypically male narrative, I thought that straightforward chronology would be more suitable than the kind of play with sequence and time I had employed in my previous novels" ("Foreword" xii).

Because this novel was to be a bildungsroman, to tell the story of Macon Dead the younger (named "Milkman" for his late suckling from his mother's breast), Morrison consciously drew on what she called "Old-school heroic, with other meanings ... A journey, then, with the accomplishment of flight, the triumphant end of a trip through earth, to its surface, on into water, and finally into air" ("Foreword" xii). In her own family as well as in families of others she knew, the flying African – leaving slavery, leaving modern life – who can return to his ancestral roots through his individual act of flight is omnipresent. More than mythic, the flying Solomon exists – still exists – in imagination and, perhaps, in reality. As novelist Gayl Jones explains, "The African myth was that black people could fly until they ate salt, introduced by the white man ... . Flying is wide-ranging topos in African American lore – in North America, in the Caribbean, and in Latin America – as a symbol of freedom" (Jones 172).[1] Jones links the letter of the failed flyer, Robert Smith, whose story – both writing and act – opens *Song of Solomon*, with the best uses of folklore. She describes it as shaped by "clarity, directness, assurance and double-edge realistic humor," as if it were folktale (Jones 171).

Song of Solomon begins with the red, white, and blue of the insurance agent's attempt to fly – beginning from the elevation of the hospital roof and looking down into the red rose petals covering the snowy ground, scattered there by Ruth Foster Dead and her two daughters and marked by the unnamed woman in the crowd singing the "Sugarman done fly away" folk song. Pilate is the singer. When Ruth goes into labor at the start of Milkman's birth, the young nurse sends Guitar Bains for help. Robert Smith's flight takes place in 1931, Morrison's birth year. Under the crushing weight of the Depression, the Bains family can barely rent their living space from Macon Dead (and Guitar, as the adult best friend of Milkman, later points out that his father, Macon Dead, is "a very strange Negro ... He behaves like a white man, thinks like a white man") (*Song* 223).

Some of the best-described scenes in the novel relate to the friendship between Guitar and Milkman, perhaps a stylistic improvement over the scantily sketched scenes within *Sula*, where Morrison left unspoken the intimate pairing of the children, Nel and Sula, who grew into womanhood together – their voices speaking as if from one throat. Before *Song of Solomon* opens in the present time, when Milkman is 32, Guitar and he have gone through various stages of adolescence. As Milkman says to himself as he searches the town for

Guitar, "He needed to find the one person left whose clarity never failed him ..." (*Song* 79).

When he finds Guitar, it is in Tommy's barbershop, where African American men are clustered around the radio, listening to news of the murder of a black boy in Mississippi. Here the reader first learns of Guitar's involvement with the Seven Days, the radical black organization that takes a white life for every black death that goes unpunished (see the later passages on pp. 155–7). (It is in this context that Morrison's lament for the murder of Emmett Till in 1955 begins to dominate much of her fiction. As she told an interviewer, "I always felt that the civil rights movement really began with the murder ... but nobody could rally around him because there were so many buried and unspeakable issues ... One was sexual aggression, the other was violence, the other was black manhood, so that they couldn't, or they didn't, organize behind him" [Bigsby 270]. Linden Peach's description of Till's murder stresses that the child was only fourteen, that he was "flogged, lynched, shot in the head, and thrown into the Tallahatchie River with a 70-pound cotton gin fan round his neck" [Peach, *Toni* 7]. (In this scene, the cause of death is the boy's being "stomped.").

No criticism of *Song of Solomon* includes scenes from Tommy's barbershop, but it is there that the young African American men are united in their sorrow over the murder of the boy from the North who whistled at a white woman. Dead in Sunflower County, Mississippi, the unnamed black boy is clearly meant to be Till. In Guitar's purposely crude language, Morrison charts the absence of either attention or mourning: "Dead, aint' he? Cause he whistled at some Scarlett O'Hara cunt."

Freddie jibes, "What'd he do it for? He knew he was in Mississippi. What he think that was? Tom Sawyer Land?"

"So he whistled! So what!" Guitar was steaming. "He supposed to die for that?"

"He from the North," said Freddie. "Acting big down in Bilbo country. Who the hell he think he is?"

"Thought he was a man, that's what," said Railroad Tommy.

"Well, he thought wrong," Freddie said. "Ain't no black men in Bilbo country."

"The hell they ain't," said Guitar.

"Who?" asked Freddie.

"Till. That's who."

"He dead. A dead man ain't no man. A dead man is a corpse. That's all. A corpse."

As tempers intensify, the other men crowd into the conversation. Porter interjects, "South's bad. Bad. Don't nothing change in the good old U.S. of A. Bet his daddy got his balls busted off in the Pacific somewhere," reminding Morrison's readers of the thousands of African American men killed in each war of the twentieth century – disproportionately so.

Questioning the likely outcome for the killers of Emmett Till, Guitar pointedly notes that there will be no punishment – more likely a parade. "You stupid, man. Real stupid. Ain't no law for no colored man *except* the one sends him to the chair." Freddie answers Guitar, "They say Till had a knife." But Guitar knows his history as he replies, "They always say that. He could have had a wad of bubble gum, they'd swear it was a hand grenade" (*Song* 80–2).

As Morrison often does, she writes this scene as originary, serving as an unfolding of both men's lives – Milkman's assault on his father for his brutality to his mother teaches him that he cannot return home. He will stay with Guitar. Guitar in turn is frustrated with his aimless life – that life of many African American men whose promise has been stifled through poverty and racism. A turning point for particularly Milkman, this barbershop scene sets the bildungsroman in motion.

Such a scene also reinforces the importance of community. As Justine Baillie notes, *Song of Solomon* parallels the earlier *Sula* as Morrison privileges the community as a site of understanding, "its myths, folklore, history and language" (Baillie 93). Morrison crafts this male story about "the rites of passage," by juxtaposing many voices, and Baillie adds that Morrison never writes "a monolithic narrative." She instead tries to show the differences that exist within even a seemingly homogenous group of African American characters (Baillie 95).

Emphasizing the male community, as Morrison does here, allows her to foreground gender. The author acknowledged early, "There's a male consciousness and there's a female consciousness. I think there are different things operating on each of the sexes. Black men

... frequently are reacting to a lot more external pressures than Black women are. For one thing they have an enormous responsibility to be *men*" (Con I, 7). From a more personal perspective, Morrison comments later that her own "first responsibility is as a mother to Dino and Slade." She speaks candidly about the difficulties a single woman has raising two male children: "initially you're afraid that you're going to give your children, whether they're girls or boys, a one-sided education because you can't be that other parent. Then after a little bit it occurs to you that it wouldn't make any difference. All you can be in any case is the most complete human being possible, and that not only must suffice, it does ..." "A long time ago it occurred to me that I had never been a little boy, so I could never know what that meant, ever. Certainly I could not be a father ... So my best shot was to be a person, and then they'd have to take it from there" (Con II, 4).

In the barbershop scene, for example, as Milkman and Guitar leave their friends and walk toward a bar, Guitar tells his younger buddy about the day he inadvertently killed a doe. (His narrative is meant to complement Milkman's story of his hitting his father, and implies the mistaken action of sometimes faulty male pride.) Guitar rehearses what a natural hunter he was: "I could hear anything, smell anything, and see like a cat ... And I was never scared – not of the dark or shadows or funny sounds, and I was never afraid to kill. Anything." In the boy's bragging, Morrison also enumerates a number of "male" qualities – but the point is, eventually, deflating because Guitar as storyteller has to admit, "I killed a doe ... Not a young one; she was old, but she was still a doe. I felt ... bad" (*Song* 85). As Milkman looked at Guitar "with the wide steady eyes of a man trying to look sober," he reifies those male qualities that are universal. Again, Morrison says, "All I'm saying is that the root of a man's sensibilities are different from a woman's. Not better, but different" (Con I, 7).

Critic Daniel Worden notes that no one "has" masculinity but rather "acts masculine ... an acting that involves negotiation of a complex set of signs." The trait is, in his words, "multiple, historical, and social." (Worden 1; see also Halberstam). Here Morrison lets readers see both Guitar and Milkman using the guise of the masculine to maintain their longstanding friendship. In Philip Page's critique, Morrison's narrative choices overlay simple gender emphases with the recognition that the history of African Americans has made personality formation difficult: her novels show the use of "divisions, displacements and pressures that skew the formation of African American identities ... Morrison has the courage to open these issues and the skill to hold them open, not to fall back on the closure of fixed positions" (Page 26).

Page translates Morrison's methodology into the schema for entire novels. He views *Song of Solomon* as the working out of such skewed histories: "Because the African-American (and therefore the American) cultural past has been only partially recognized and inadequately absorbed, Morrison's characters have difficulty finding what they need from their pasts" (Page 29). The hegira that Milkman chooses to take is much more than his relinquishing his father's world and finding meaning in his aunt Pilate's – it becomes part of this much larger quest, to unearth both history and meaning.

In drawing their earlier years, Morrison has prepared the reader for this relentless friendship. She writes that Milkman was "with his friend, an older boy – wise and kind and fearless" (*Song* 47). One comic central scene that Morrison uses to show both the powerful friendship between Guitar and Milkman and the isolation of these young black men from the culture that surrounds them is set in Feather's pool hall. Milkman is only 13; he and Guitar have skipped school, but Feather will not serve them beer because of who Milkman is – Feather hates and fears his father, who is his landlord. From their being turned away by Feather, the monologue Railroad Tommy composes for Guitar outside the barber shop takes on a dozens tone: Tommy's theme is a listing of all the things Guitar will *never* have:

"You ever pull fourteen days straight and come home to a sweet woman, clean sheets, and a fifth of Wild Turkey? Eh?" ... Well, don't look forward to it, cause you not going to have that ... You not going to have no private coach with four red velvet chairs that swivel around in one place whenever you want 'em to. No. And you not going to have your own special toilet and your own special-made eight-foot bed either. And a valet and a cook and a secretary to travel with you and do everything you say ... That's something else you not going to have. You ever have five thousand dollars of cold cash money in your pocket and walk into a bank and tell the bank man you want such and such a house on such and such a street and he sell it to you right then? Well, you won't ever have it. And you not going to have a governor's mansion ... you never going to have four stars on your shirt front, or even three. And you not going to have no breakfast tray brought in to you early in the morning with a red rose on it and two warm croissants and a cup of hot chocolate. Nope. Never. And no pheasant buried in coconut leaves for twenty days and stuff with wild rice and cooked over a wood fire so tender and delicate it make you cry. And no Rothschild '29 or even Beaujolais to go with it .... And *no* baked Alaska! None! You never going to have that.

"No baked Alaska?" Guitar opened his eyes wide with horror and grabbed his throat. "You breaking my heart!"

"Well, now. That's something you will have – a broken heart ... And folly. A whole lot of folly. You can count on it." (*Song* 60–1)

So quickly Morrison changes the import of this scene, of any scene. After Guitar tells Milkman what this dessert is, Guitar becomes ill and then further explains that he cannot eat sugar or sugary desserts because after his father had been "sliced up in a sawmill," the boss had brought home-made divinity candy to the Bains' house. As if in exchange for his father's life, the candy had permanently sickened Guitar on whiteness, sugar, and the suffocating sympathy from the higher classed.

This fast-paced scene in itself shows the gamut of emotion Morrison can evoke – the comedy of the deprivation African American men must face set alongside their actual dead bodies – and underscores how condemnatory *Song of Solomon* is intended to be. It is not only Emmett Till who lives a life filled with risks. Placing the journey of Milkman Dead into this context creates real urgency for readers. A streetwise novel, *Song of Solomon* remains admonitory. It has been approached as a mythic book and as a bildungsroman in which the childishly named protagonist has no hope of living unless he matures. It is, perhaps more convincingly, a generational novel that fits one generation's existence into the histories of the ancestors who came before.

Stelamaris Coser compares this novel to Gabriel García Márquez's *One Hundred Years of Solitude*, stressing that the lineage that Milkman eventually discovers is hybrid, not pure. Solomon represents an African source, but Sing is Native American. Coser states:

"Cultural resistance through the creative 're-Africanization' of a nation's texts and rituals is a major theme in African struggles for liberation, although Franz Fanon and others, such as Amilear Cabral, leader for the independence of Guinea and Cape Verde, who was assassinated in 1973, warned against the idealization of a 'pure' African source" (Coser 213, n14; 214, n21). Coser notes that both Morrison and García Márquez draw from their own mixed family histories, and place vast confidence in folk wisdom to undermine the more visible presence of mainstream history (Coser 82, 85). This critic, in fact, finds the impetus toward their fine writing – their essential genius – to lie in their "deep preoccupation with affirming and reinforcing popular culture against models inspired or imposed by the dominant culture ... [these novels show] how cultural roots can be deep and strong enough to cross borders, hemispheres, and oceans; can erase the usual East–West and North–South divisions; and finally, can meet in the far recesses of human myth" (Coser 85).

Aoi Mori too finds significant differences between Morrison's first two novels – *The Bluest Eye* and *Sula* – and *Song of Solomon*. About this third novel Mori notes, "the movement displays a much more powerful and robust motion that departs from the spiral, inducing an out-thrusting impetus that escapes circularity, like a train increasing speed. In *Song of Solomon*, Morrison redirects the circular and spiral motions toward a linear thrust, guiding her characters to a recovery of their last history, culture and values" (Mori 122). She links the motion of Sula's spinning Chicken Little – that is, flight – to Robert Smith's attempt to fly in the opening of *Song of Solomon*. She forces the reader to remember how Chicken Little's body looked once it was returned to his family, calling that disfigurement a "parable" of the way "society diminishes and discredits African American experience." This is the connection Mori makes: "As observed in Chicken Little's death, the inability to fly is closely associated with the social-cultural limitations imposed by African Americans. Those who are unable to repel the burden which prevents them from expressing themselves are inevitably led to destruction" (Mori 124).

Morrison's *Song of Solomon*, however, makes conventional readings inadequate. Just as the reader focuses on Milkman – either as the son of Macon Dead or as the friend of Guitar Bains – the narrative and its layered structure makes those considerations seem secondary. The dynamic, and dramatic, character from this novel becomes Pilate Dead, the outcast ("outlaw") woman, forbidden to spend time with her nephew because of her magical, witchlike and perhaps "snake-like" qualities. Although never as fully developed as Milkman in the number of pages given to her characterization, Pilate embodies "the magic of conjure" in her dealings with other people; she becomes the route for Morrison to "establish cultural continuity with Africa" (Billingslea-Brown 55). *Song of Solomon* itself becomes the author's way of presenting what this critic calls "alternative epistemologies and discredited forms of knowledge."

In Morrison's own retrospective commentary about writing this novel, she consistently draws Milkman as a male character who needs to learn from women: their strengths will be the tools he needs to complete his quest for human understanding, which will come only through his own development as a man. As she said in one interview, "I realized how much he had to learn from women ... [he] has to walk into the earth – the womb – in that cave, then he walks the surface of the earth and he can relate to its trees – that's all very maternal." Morrison justified using Milkman in the first place thus:

> it had to be a man. Men have more to learn in certain areas than women do ... I wanted ... a character who had everything to learn, who would start from zero, and had no reason to learn anything; because he's comfortable, he doesn't need money, he's just flabby and pampered. Well, that kind of character, a sort of average person who has no impetus to learn anything – to watch that person learn something was fascinating to me as opposed to watching the man who already was that perfection ... And the men have more places they can hide and not learn. They don't have to learn anything, they can always be men. (Con I, 75–6)

Judging *Song of Solomon* to be Morrison's first attempt at a conventional epic telling a male story, the quest in this case being Milkman's discovery of his family's origin myth – long ignored by his father, and only hinted at within Pilate's family – Africanist scholar Kokahvah Zauditu-Selassie comments that the addition of a female character to the male hero is unusual. Agreeing with Morrison that the discovery of the true family name is crucial to Milkman's search, this critic also points out that a legitimate quest seldom ends – the journey must serve as both an ending and a beginning (Zauditu-Selassie 69, 71). She personalizes Pilate's characteristics as relating to the Yoruba idea of *oju inu* (inner eye) which refers to that woman's being born without a navel: the feature of the inner eye suggests "the ability to look beyond the present moment" (Zauditu-Selassie 217, n6). Pilate also radiates "spiritual energy," and becomes Milkman's *ndoki*, his spiritual guide and double. (Zauditu-Selassie 79, 81).

When Morrison later discussed the role of Pilate, she admitted that the narrative hinged on this female character:

> Pilate is the ancestor. The difficulty that Hagar has is how far removed she is from the experience of her ancestor. Pilate had a dozen years of close, nurturing relationships with two males – her father and her brother [Macon Dead as child and adolescent]. And that intimacy and support was in her and made her fierce and loving because she had that experience. Her daughter Reba had less of that and related to men in a very shallow way. Her daughter [Hagar] had even less of an association with men as a child, so that the progression is really a diminishing of their abilities because of the absence of men in a nourishing way in their lives. Pilate is the apogee of all that: of the best of that which is female and the best of that which is male, and that balance is disturbed if it is not nurtured, and if it is not counted on and if it is not reproduced. (Nonfiction 63)

Pilate is the means by which Morrison is able to "blend the acceptance of the supernatural and a profound rootedness in the real world at the same time with neither taking precedence over the other. It is indicative of the cosmology, the way in which Black people looked at the world. We are very practical people, very down-to-earth, even shrewd people. But within that practicality was also accepted what I suppose could be called superstition and magic, which is another way of knowing things. But to blend those two worlds together at the same time was enhancing, not limiting ... That kind of knowledge has a very strong place in my work" (Nonfiction 61).

The magic of the *Song of Solomon* narrative has at its core the reverence for the ancestor figure (whether that figure be living or dead). Morrison explains, in this same essay, that the presence or absence of that figure determined the success or the happiness of the character. It was the absence of an ancestor that was frightening, that was threatening, and it caused huge destruction and disarray in the work itself. That the solace comes, not from the contemplation of serene nature as in a lot of mainstream white literature, not from the regard in which the city was held as a kind of corrupt place to be. Whether the character was in Harlem or Arkansas, the point was there, this timelessness was there, this person who represented this ancestor. (Nonfiction 60–2)

For Susan Neal Mayberry, who studies Morrison's treatment of the masculine, she begins with *Song of Solomon* (with a look back at Shadrack from *Sula*). For all Morrison's attention to Milkman, Mayberry states, she grounds him within a feminine circle (Pilate). She also, throughout her fiction, remains even-handed about the male and the female characters – there is never a man in a Morrison novel who is outright despicable. It is Mayberry who builds a paradigm of "free" characters – a shape that includes some women – to show a kind of disdain for the social morality that tends to dominate human lives. In this critic's words, "Morrison provides us with complex and compassionate constructions of black masculinity in tandem with her powerful and complicated explorations of black femininity" (Mayberry 136). She also cites Morrison's saying in an interview that she "applauds the incredible amount of magic and feistiness in black men that nobody has been able to wipe out [although] everybody has tried." Considering both Cholly Breedlove and Sula's Ajax, Morrison noted that "through neglect of the fact that someone was not there, [they] made up themselves ... Cholly was a 'free man,' not free in the legal sense, but free in his head ... This is a man who is stretching, you know, he's stretching, he's going all the way within his own mind and within whatever his outline might be. Now that's the tremendous possibility for masculinity among black men" (Con I, 19).

Barbara Christian's observations about *Song of Solomon* see the male characters enfolded with the female:

Song of Solomon is structurally based on the conflict between the preoccupation with earthly matters and the need to fly, that is by nature a part of each of us. The novel is divided into two parts. Part I emphasizes the tension between these two poles within Milkman's natal community in the North, while Part II traces the resolution of this tension as a result of Milkman's quest in his Southern community. But in every section of this novel, these two thrusts are woven together, for there is a continual interplay between the community of the North and the South, the past and the present, and Macon's and Pilate's respective point of view. In developing the relationship of Milkman to these two communities, Morrison uses the elements as her structural guides. (Christian, *Black* 89)

Christian begins by attaching Morrison's development of the male characters – Macon, Milkman, and Guitar – to their community ethics, saying, "The relationship between Nature and a particularly human community is the kernel of the contemporary fable as Morrison has wrought it ... Like many oral storytellers, Morrison spins tales about how the characters' conduct of their lives is connected to their community's value system. Her novels present worlds that are very much like villages in which kinship ties are woven into the dreams, legends, the subconscious of the inhabitants. Like the ancestral African tradition, place is as important as the human actors, for the land is a participant in the maintenance of the folk traditions ..." (Christian, *Black* 76).

Christian too sees Pilate as separate from her generalized observations: that character "is as landless as the birds." She is also "a tall black tree," much like the four pines that border her back yard (Christian 90). Immune from the social pressures that have ruined the spirit she remembers from Macon Dead's boyhood, Pilate comes to represent what Zauditu-Selassie calls the highly stylized performance and ritual: she cooks food for Guitar and Milkman, making every dish a ceremonial offering; she frightens casual suitors to her daughter by threatening them with death; she weaves narratives that are in themselves life lessons; she creates a dynamic ceremony at her beloved granddaughter's funeral (Zauditu-Selassie 72). In the words of Genevieve Fabre, "the celebratory spirit of Africans accompanied them to the Americas, where the Africans reinvented both ritual and forms to alter the time space framework prescribed or suggested by whites" (Fabre 72).

Rebelling against the conventional African American characters set against the dominant white ethos, Morrison placed her emphasis here on the flying myth – the African belief in shape-shifting, that a person could fly through being transformed into a bird. To fly back to Africa was, finally, to escape bondage within a hostile culture (Zauditu-Selassie 217, n8). Aside from choosing this particular folktale, Morrison noted that in *Song of Solomon* she

> wanted to use black folklore, the magic and superstitious part of it. Black people believe in magic. Once a woman asked me, "Do you believe in ghosts?" I said, "Yes. Do you believe in germs?" It's part of our heritage ... That's why flying is the central metaphor in *Song* – the literal taking off and flying into the air, which is everybody's dream. My children used to talk about it all the time – they were amazed when they found they couldn't fly. They took it for granted that all they had to do was jump up and flap their arms. I used it not only in the African sense of whirling dervishes and getting out of one's skin, but also in the majestic sense of a man who goes too far, whose adventures take him far away. (Con I, 46)

For critic Fritz Gysin, that Morrison imbues the myth with shades and levels of unexpected meaning is characteristic of the way the author often writes. Gysin notes, "these different forms of flying combine and fuse in ways that obscure the clear distinctions ... so that the success of the magic flight as the central determinant of the male monomyth is called into question." He continues to point out that neither "pseudo-Daedalus Robert Smith" or Milkman's own "death leap into the arms of Guitar, his friend and enemy ... is directly related to black resistance. Furthermore the objects of his quest, the legend of his flying great-great-grandfather, is full of paradoxes: the revealing song addressed to Sugarman/Solomon contains in its center his wife's wail *not* to leave her and her twenty-one children back in bondage, and there is a report of the mother going mad when Solomon does fly off, so that his children have to be brought up by neighbors" (Gysin 184–5).

As she considers her first writing here about a masculine protagonist, Morrison found that men interested me in a way I hadn't thought about before, almost as a species. I used what I knew, what I'd heard. But I had to think of becoming a whole person in masculine terms, so there were craft problems. I couldn't use the metaphors I'd used describing women. I needed something that suggested dominion – a different kind of drive. I think *Song* is more expansive because of that; I had to loosen up. I could not create the same kind of enclosed world that I had in previous books. (Con I, 45–6)

To signal to readers that reading *Song of Solomon* would be a different kind of experience – as had been her writing of it – Morrison chose the epigraph, "The fathers may soar and the children may know their names." This phrasing was at odds with the more common pattern of children's losses (in the disappearance of the father, the loss of family cohesion – or even family information). In the usual aftermath of a man's flying back to Africa, his woman and children would be, necessarily, bereft. Morrison here points to a different kind of narrative.

According to critic John Roberts in his study of the trickster figure, all Africans have a mystical capacity ("the quest for mystical knowledge and power constitutes an on-going activity") but using such capacity for individual gain can be judged a "punishable evil. Such behavior is viewed as a violation of taboos that threaten the well-being of the entire group" (Roberts 128). Many of the trickster qualities common to the definition are more evident in Morrison's creation of Son Green (in *Tar Baby*) than in Milkman, who appears to be at the nascent edge of his quest. As Morrison plots the changes that Milkman will need to make, she transfers him from his normal life circumstances in middle-class Michigan through a literal journey that takes him from Michigan to Pennsylvania and into Virginia.

Morrison's familiarity with the environs of both Michigan and northern Ohio did not lead to an easy transference to "the South." She recalled, "I remember how long it took me to write about the town that Milkman goes to, when he finally gets there. It took me months, and I could not begin. I could see it, but I wanted to write without going through long, involved descriptions of that village. Then I remembered the women walking without anything in their hands, and that set the scene" (Con I, 99). In translation, a truly small community means a woman does not need to carry her purse – she has not locked her house, she does not need keys; and she is most likely walking, not driving. (For Morrison the city dweller, such an image showed a free culture, filled with positive and reliable people.) For Barbara Christian, the Virginia town of Shalimar bespeaks the fact that the land is "not owned but lived with. The people are so much a part of it that they know the language that was before language, the language of the animals, of the earth itself. Milkman learns through the music of the earth, the rivers, and the folk, the name of his ancestor, the one his father had glimpsed in his imagination years before" (Christian 90).

Before Morrison begins what she labels "Part II," she tries to conclude various narrative strands. Much of the dialogue between Milkman and Guitar is about the Days' work and the fact that Guitar is the "Sunday" killer: the strange irony of marking that holy day with what Guitar insists *is* holy work does not convince Milkman. As he lies in Guitar's bed waiting for the angry Hagar's next attempt to murder him, Milkman realizes, "He felt like a garbage pail for the actions and hatreds of other people. He himself did nothing" (*Song* 120). He also follows his mother's middle-of-the-night trip to her father's grave; on the return, she explains to him that Macon had murdered her father and was attempting to kill him, once Pilate had given her the charm that brought Macon back into her bed long enough to impregnate her. The events that lead to Milkman's leaving home are not, in themselves, mystical. He again becomes a tool of his father as he searches for what he surmises is gold in Pilate's unkempt house. He then learns part of his childhood history from his vehement sister Lena, who tells him about his history of pissing on her. Unexpectedly, she warns him to leave. "You have pissed your last in this house ... get out of my room" (*Song* 216).

Part II sets Milkman on his journey east, inappropriately weighed down with a heavy suitcase. He finds Reverend Cooper, who directs him to Circe, living with her ménage of large, frightening dogs – the human link with the animal world no longer hidden. It is the kindly aged Circe who tells him about Singing Bird, his grandmother known only as "Sing," who looked white but was "Mixed. Indian mostly. A good-looking woman, but fierce, for the young woman I knew her as. Crazy about her husband too, overcrazy. You know what I mean? Some women love too hard. She watched over him like a pheasant hen. Nervous. Nervous love" (*Song* 243). Acting out the folk song about Solomon's flight leaving his wife and children bereft, Circe acknowledges that this Solomon, Milkman's grandfather, had left abruptly: Sing's dilemma (though reminiscent of Hagar's grief over losing Milkman) stemmed from that all too mystical experience. Milkman endures several quest-type tests. He survives a knife fight; he finds friends among the Southern men (many of whom are named "Solomon"); he hunts – carefully avoiding the killing of any does. He does not kill the bobcat but he helps dress it by removing its heart and metaphorically linking his male act with Hagar's eventual suicide.

His ritual hunting advances Milkman "to the next phase of his soul journey," says Zauditu-Selassie:

> Milkman's ability to be exhilarated by simply walking the earth is an indication of his new status. His walking is analogous to his being part of the earth. Like a tree "his legs were stalks, tree trunks, a part of his body that extended down down down into the rock and soil, and were comfortable there" (*Song* 284). Milkman experiences the ritual meal that follows the successful hunt, and the ritual bath with Sweet. "Through water imagery, an archetypal idea, Milkman is transported from his singular life and is initiated into his new status as a member of the African collective" (Zauditu-Selassie 93–4).

He also listens carefully as Circe explains to him that the murdered Macon Dead did not stay in the grave his son and daughter had dug for him – instead, his body was thrown into a cave, where it remains. She gives him directions to the cave and insists, "Tell your daddy you buried him properly, in a grave-yard. Maybe with a headstone. A nice headstone ... The dead don't like it if they're not buried" (*Song* 245).

Milkman manages to stay alive. Increasingly, single words hold the key to his family's history, but those words are dulled and sometimes inaudible: Is the name "Jay" or "Jake"? "Crow" or "Crowell"? "Sing" or "Singing" Byrd? "Solomon" or "Sugerman" or "Shalimar"? The twists in spoken language, the import of tribal tales, can change established history as quickly as can the most accomplished narrator. What Milkman learns is to trust his instinctual ear rather than his literal one. He learns to trust a conglomerate of images in place of any single genealogical system. And he also learns to trust the good, if simple and probably poor, people who befriend him. He especially learns to share his love with Sweet, doing her dishes, cleaning her bathtub, absorbing some of the work her life – and her kindness to him – creates for her.

The rapid closing of the novel has left some readers bewildered. Pilate is shot by the deranged Guitar, who has come to believe that Milkman has found the gold and is cutting him out of his share. As Milkman and Guitar "fly" toward each other in mid-air, there is no factual outcome – no one dies, or both die, or the single important metaphor is that the men trust each other, that they recognize their love for each other.[2] In her last moments of life, Pilate murmured, "I wish I'd a knowed more people. I would of loved 'em all. If I'd a knowed more, I would a loved more." (Her last words seem to echo what Guitar had told Milkman in his confession about joining the Days: his motivation is not about hating white people. "It's about loving us. About loving *you*. My whole life is love.") (*Song* 336, 159). Cheryl Wall repeats this positive emphasis when she calls *Song of Solomon* "a singing book," opening as it does with Pilate's singing "O Sugarman done fly away" and ending with Milkman's repeating that song to Pilate as she dies (Wall, *Worrying* 27).

For Justine Baillie, Morrison's ending emphasizes "an alternative masculinity that embraces both 'surrender' and 'domination,' that in effect does not erase gender but builds upon difference as a positive force" (Baillie 96). In a larger consideration, Keith Byerman links Morrison's *Song of Solomon* with works by Leon Forrest, Ernest Gaines, Alice Walker, and Toni Cade Bambara in creating what he terms "novels of the post-civil rights period." He describes those works as fiction that

> engages African American history and folk culture, but combines that material with a commitment to a high level of artistry, learned from whatever sources work best for them ... They construct fictions that employ folk characters, music, tales, rituals, and verbal expression (signifying, dozens, sermons). More important, they articulate a folk sensibility that embraces both survival and resistance. They go beyond merely offering a contemporary version of local color narrative; instead they engage in social and cultural critique through the device of the worldview of the oppressed. They reject a binary of victim and hero, avoid the rhetoric of nationalism and protest, or accommodation, examine the positive and negative aspects of black community, and construct sophisticated and artistically successful fictions. (Byerman, "African" 92).

2
Tar Baby and Other Folktales

Morrison's fascination with building novels around a folktale continued as she wrote her fourth book, *Tar Baby*, published in 1981. Many of her comments about the folktale appeared separate from the novel, however. She described a kind of fear she felt when the concept of that "baby" – a girl child – made from sticky tar by a white man was used to lure, and catch, the necessarily black Br'er Rabbit character. The tale became a narrative of men pitted against each other, the black man less powerful, in the attempts to capture the desirable, but false, "baby." As she explained,

> I use that old story because, despite its funny, happy ending, it used to frighten me. The story has a tar baby in it which is used by a white man to catch a rabbit. "Tar baby" is also a name, like nigger, that white people call black children, black girls, as I recall. Tar seemed to me to be an odd thing to be in a Western story, and I found that there is a tar lady in African mythology. I started thinking about tar. At one time, a tar pit was a holy place, at least an important place, because tar was used to build things ... For me, the tar baby came to mean the black woman who can hold things together. (Con I, 122)

Even though Morrison dedicated this novel to a widely inclusive list of women, many of them family members that she credits with her own development, as *Tar Baby* developed, it seemed to be less about Jadine, the beautiful African American female protagonist, than it was about Son Green, the rootless "water" man who appears in the opening section of the book. As Son leaves ship and swims across water to reach the island that will become the site of much of the narrative, he grasps the reader's attention immediately. As one critic notes, Son Green is "instinctively aligned with nature" (Billingslea-Brown 71).

Perhaps a more pervasive theme of this novel is the life-giving spirit of the natural world – not only the world of oceans and rivers – a spirit that could overcome many more dramatic conflicts when the elements of that natural world were properly cared for and reverenced. The second segment of *Tar Baby* begins with Morrison's personification of the land. She describes the Isle des Chevaliers as the island with the power to strike blind slaves who had come to it three hundred years before. For two thousand years before that time, the island was covered with rain forests – "the sea-green green of the sea and the skyblue sky of the sky" made a home for the wild parrots, the diamondbacks, and the champion daisy trees (*Tar* 8–9). The destruction of the forested lands occurred when the river lost its bearings.

"Evicted from the place where it had lived, and forced into unknown turf, it could not form its pools or waterfalls, and ran every which way. The clouds gathered together, stood still and watched the river scuttle around the forest floor, crash headlong into the haunches of hills with no notion of where it was going, until exhausted, ill and grieving, it slowed to a stop just twenty leagues short of the sea." Crippled by the behavior of what Morrison called "the scatterbrained river," the trees "broke in two and hit the ground." In the abyss of the natural melee, "houses instead grew in the hills." Prosperous whites had taken over not only the island but all parts of its natural habitat, and the river was considered only poor and "brokenhearted" (*Tar* 9–10).

Critics quickly saw that Morrison's emphasis on the "tar baby" legend was going to be more complex than expected. Trudier Harris decades ago had coined the term "literary folklore" to suggest the ways in which African American writers change these oral narratives to suit their often ironic or duplicitous purposes. Harris notes of Morrison's adaptations that "she has solved the problem of warring genres ... She may begin with a joke or superstition in its recognizable, traditional form, but she then takes fictional license in making the lore into something that has never circulated in any folk community ... We recognize folkloric patterns in her work, but she constantly surprises us in the reconceptualization and restructuring of these patterns" (Harris, *Fiction* 7–8). Similarly, Craig Werner stated that "numerous potential meanings coexist in Toni Morrison's use of this myth." He adds that readers might think of a "continuum" as she brings in one character after another, white as well as black: "Morrison's panoramic presentation of the complex *is*-ness of Afro-American experience focuses on the way individuals – both blacks and the whites who frame their world – express and reflect on the tar baby myth, in the process reasserting its historical genealogy and renewing its *mascon* energy" (Werner 71–2).

For critic Philip Page, *Tar Baby* is "pivotal" because it looks ahead to Morrison's later books. In this novel, the narrative is no longer set in the United States; the Caribbean becomes a larger, deeper mythic source. Morrison creates layers of social and racial classes, so that a reader is as bewildered as Jadine seems to be (Page, *Dangerous* 108–9). Page stresses that, by the time of her fourth novel, Morrison is comfortable with blending the realistic with the mystical/mythical, so that *Tar Baby* is "quintessentially postmodern, American, and African-American." In it she privileges "polyvocalism, stretched boundaries, open-endedness, and unraveled binary opposites." As in other of her novels, "time is nonlinear, the forms are open, multiple voices are heard, and endings are ambiguous ..." (Page *Dangerous* 33–4).

Harris has also seen the ways in which Morrison replaced traditional ideas of heroism – deeds of bravery performed by male characters – with women's acts. (In *Tar Baby*, Tiresias of *The Waste Land* fame has become Marie Thérèse, for example.) By linking Morrison's treatments of gendered figures with an understanding of the African beliefs underlying many folk beliefs, this critic and others, such as John Roberts and Charles Scruggs, emphasize the possibility of the heroic and some combinations of the magical/mystical with the real – in both women and men. In Roberts's assessment, "Africans are not so much threatened by the possession of mystical power, since they believe that all individuals are born with mystical power or a life-force, as they are by the consequences of behaviors that individuals adopt to increase their share of it ... For Africans, no threat is posed by the efforts of individuals to enhance their life-force to achieve full ontological being by observing the forms of behaviors recognized by the group as ideal. However, efforts to enhance one's own life-force using magic or witchcraft is a punishable evil. Such behavior is viewed as a violation of tabus that threatens the well-being of the entire group" (Harris, *Fiction* 185; Roberts 128).

These premises about the uses of folklore underlie the dichotomy Morrison sets up in *Tar Baby* between native and white cultures. Whites like the wealthy Valerian Streets knew nothing of the Caribbean world – neither its culture nor its customs. They called every local woman who worked in their household "Mary" rather than learn native names; "Yardman" was similarly labeled. They used up whatever prosperity they reached. The Isle des Chevaliers had become an envelope for the swamp that had once been the river, now known as the witch's tit (Sein de Vieilles). Now broken and ineffectual, the river – like the natural world it had once encircled – seeped "with a thick black substance that even mosquitoes could not live near" (*Tar* 10). LaVinia Jennings traces this location to Haiti, the first independent black republic in the Western hemisphere, and attributes Morrison's use of historical background to the maroon history there (Jennings 129).

Wasted and depraved, the beauty of this Caribbean island surrounded the Streets, their servants Ondine and Sydney Childs and their ward, Jadine, and a few select friends – but as it diminished, the native islanders could only mourn. The mainlanders did not seem to realize what was being destroyed. As Africanist Zauditu-Selassie wrote, "For the Yoruba, places where land and trees converge with water are thought to be sites of great spiritual energy." Setting most of the *Tar Baby* narrative on the Isle des Chevaliers "illustrates an African-derived idea of the natural world as a primary dwelling for the divine" (Zauditu-Selassie 98, 100). The primary spiritual force (Aje) represents "the potential for self-realization as well as for ecological and spiritual balance." That force is based on "ancient properties."

Morrison explains her belief that nature governs much human behavior:

It's an animated world in which trees can be outraged and hurt, and in which the presence or absence of birds is meaningful. You have to be very still to understand these so-called signs, in addition to which they inform you about your own behavior. It always interested me, the way in which black people responded to evil. They would protect themselves from it, they would avoid it, they might even be terrified of it, but it wasn't as though it were abnormal. I used the line "as though God had four faces instead of three" .... Evil was a natural presence in the world. What that meant in terms of human behavior was that when they saw someone disgraced, they would not expel them in the sense of tarring and killing. I think that's a distinct cultural difference, because the Western notion of evil is to annihilate it. That may be very cleansing but it's also highly intolerant. (Con I, 100–1)

Constructing Morrison's commentary about her path to writing *Tar Baby* means including this body of non-Western knowledge. She explains the progression within her first four novels: "from a book that focused on a pair of very young black girls, to move to a pair of adult black women, and then to a black man, and finally to a black man and a black woman is evolutionary. One comes out of the other" (Con I, 142). "All the books I have written deal with characters placed deliberately under enormous duress in order to see of what they are made ... It's the complexity of how people behave under duress that is of interest to me – the qualities they show at the end of an event when their backs are up against the wall ..." (Con I, 143, 145). To translate this fictional aim into some commentary about African American characters in search of a valid, honest identity might be over-simplification. Readers know, however, that Morrison intends to write – as she has from the start of her career – about *African American* characters, leading lives in often-inimical situations.

One variation in *Tar Baby* is that she *dis*places these characters. If the United States provided a known quantity – urban, raced, sophisticated in terms of education and religion – then the Caribbean provided only questions. Valerian Street used up much of a base of natural resources in the manufacture of his profitable candy; he planted lush flowers within his home greenhouse rather than search his environs for flowers that grew naturally. He was content to burn through the resources that surrounded him in his extravagant residence with little concern for the circumstances of the people who served him and his household. When Street welcomes Son Green, the unknown and unkempt black man – a Vietnam veteran traumatized by war – who hides in his wife's closet, Morrison sets in motion the *tar baby* situation: Street is pulling the strings for his two black puppet characters, one female (the light-skinned Jadine) and one male, and completely unknown to the powerful white man. It is not simply loneliness that makes Valerian Street want the young black man's companionship; it is in part the older white man's desire to become a puppeteer.

Whereas some readers found *Tar Baby* different from Morrison's first three novels, more recent critics have found the author's choices in this fourth book broadening and deepening the accomplishments of her first novels. As Stelamaris Coser points out, *Tar Baby* shows an impulse "toward a new art," a move which "goes beyond mere aesthetic concerns to reveal a deep preoccupation with affirming and reinforcing popular culture against models inspired or imposed by the dominant culture" (Coser 85).

The narrative patterning suggests that readers should pay more attention to the lives of Gideon and Thérèse, and other of the native characters, rather than setting up the more predictable duality of the Streets' profitable white culture juxtaposed with the dependent African American culture of the Childs's. Both families are, in the Caribbean islands, displaced from their sources, so that no matter how frequently Valerian Street tries to "Americanize" his life there, he remains adrift and unmoored.

One of the results of this displacement is the fact that the Streets have lost their son and therefore any chance of being able to pass down their inheritance. Michael Street has taken as his career the study of Native Americans ("Cultures in danger of extinction"). As an anthropologist he is drawn to the fragility of maintaining genera-tions of folk life when that life is surrounded by a hostile mainstream culture.

Valerian Street has set up himself, and Margaret, to *be* the main-stream culture. Yet his vapid and increasingly weak responses to per-sonal situations show the impact of his rootlessness in this Caribbean habitat. Unlike Street, Gideon has returned to his homeland after more than 20 years in Quebec and then the United States: he has realized that leaving home to make his fortune was futile and when he returns to the island, wearing a suit and bringing Thérèse only apples in his pockets, he relinquishes prosperity for personal fulfill-ment based in part on ancestral wisdom. Gideon brings new energy to the Edenic image of a loving couple existing in an isolated land with the apple as the crystallization of desire, an image Morrison uses again in *Jazz* with similarly great effect.

Gideon provides a different set of choices for the truly itinerant Son, the damaged quest figure, traumatized into inept violence after his military service in Vietnam. Repressed by the American (i.e., Floridian) culture into a normalcy that his wartime life has made impossible, Son – William Green – carries on the natural male existence surrounded by the worlds of physical sensation. Linked with water, with sensuality, with the basic premises of supporting life (here, with water and with chocolate as he plunders the Streets' pantry), Son has become linked with clear and unadorned survival.

Morrison connects the character of Son Green here with Milkman Dead in *Song of Solomon*. The latter is much more advantaged: he has middle-class privileges and education. He will not go hungry. But ironically Son Green is much further along in his personal journey to maturity (and perhaps in his search for a viable identity) than Milkman is, even as *Song of Solomon* ends. The connections between the two books are clear: the cultural narrative that Pilate inscribes in *Song of Solomon*, which may seem partial because so few of the book's characters understand the living and the "living-dead" worlds she represents, can easily become a way of reading *Tar Baby*. Pilate stands alone in the earlier narrative; in *Tar Baby*, the native wisdom of the Aje, the folk, the voodoun, is shared by a number of characters – Gideon, Marie Thérèse Foucault (though blind, she is otherwise reminiscent of Pilate), the Marys, Alma Estee, and the unnamed woman in yellow, who carries the three eggs. About the latter symbolic figure, Morrison noted that she is "somehow transcendent ... the one who authenticates everything. The one that is very clear in some deep way about what her womanhood is" (Con I, 194). Morrison also said in another comparison of the novels, "the lore is there [in *Tar Baby*] but in a more direct, bold way .... I ran the risk of having nature itself bear witness" (Con I, 109).

As the book's title suggests, Jadine is the object of desire: courted by wealthy Europeans, her light skin color (so different from the blackness of the woman in yellow and Alma Estee) places her on an indiscriminate border between the Streets and her aunt and uncle, Ondine and Sydney Childs. African Americans from the United States, the Childs are very different from the island blacks – and while they yearn to be back in the States, they still enjoy the luxurious Caribbean life. In this fourth novel, Morrison has finally created white characters – splendidly wealthy, proud of their possessions, only marginally respectful of their African American retainers who travel to the Caribbean with them. But as hidden malice becomes exposed – that Margaret Street had abused their only child, Michael, from childhood on – Morrison leaves realism and makes this evil a kind of self-punishment. Valerian's second wife, a former beauty queen and a young white American woman, loathes both her spouse and her life, and bonds with Jadine over their superiority as beautiful females. (Coser remarks that Margaret's having been a beauty queen echoes Márquez's Fernanda del Carpio, seen by Aureliano Segunda during her triumphal parade; neither woman is well-classed and their changes in status create "hysteria"; Coser 201, n81).

The women are seriously flawed, too, in that they have never known true maternal loving. Jadine has no children, and Margaret has driven her son from her – he is perpetually expected for Christmas but he will never come. He does not come this season either, but the carnival that their house contains, at least in part because of Son Green's presence, is a kind of substitute merriment. Truly carnivalesque, the dinner table conversation with its participants both white and African American reveals the hidden currents of the Streets' relationship. The dis-ease that mars Margaret's behavior is, later, transferred to Jadine when the circumspect African American aunt warns her about her cold behavior to the Childs, her older and immediate ancestors. Ondine begins apologetically, "well, I never told you nothing ... and I take full responsibility for that. But I have to tell you something now."

Jadine, a girl has got to be a daughter first. She have to learn that. And if she never learns how to be a daughter, she can't never learn how to be a woman. I mean a real woman: a woman good enough for a child; good enough for a man – good enough even for the respect of other women. No you didn't have a mother long enough to learn much about it and I thought I was doing right by sending you to all them schools and so I never told you and I should have. You don't need your own natural mother to be a daughter. All you need is to feel a certain way, a certain careful way about people older than you are. (*Tar* 281)

(The progression in Ondine's serial list above suggests that being a mother is the primary role, followed by being a lover or wife. But coming at the end of the sequence is the woman as friend to other women, the woman as object of respect from other women, and that position seems to equate with mothering a child.)

For Jadine, whose entire focus has been on herself as love object, surrounded as she has been by men of all types and skin colors, to be told about the *ancient properties* of the maternal so abruptly is disturbing. Ondine ends her admonition by saying, "A daughter is a woman who cares about where she came from and takes care of them that took care of her ... I don't want you to care about me for my sake. I want you to care about me for *yours*" (*Tar* 281). Ondine herself falls short of this desired role. Only the unnamed women of Eloe (and this island) and Marie Thérèse Foucault, whose earlier life as wet nurse continues through the lactation of her aging breasts, carry the ancient properties into the future. Conversely, Margaret drinks alone in her palatial house and Jadine flies back to the European lover who has given her the present of a sealskin coat made of 90 baby sealskins.

In many ways, Morrison places Son Green in the novel to reify what Ondine tells Jadine: Son and his insistence that Eloe is the heartland of his life – despite his having killed his wife there – makes Jadine attempt to understand the allure of the small, natural all-black Florida town. She travels there with him, only to find herself ostracized by the (for her) unappealing women of the community. This same kind of separation has occurred when the swamp women (Native American women who originally married the slaves brought to the island) also rejected her, after trying to molest her. These women represent the wisdom of the "passed-on ancestors," and in their inarticulate expressions, they echo Ondine's caveats – certain behaviors become the sources of earthly power. It is only through bringing forward the African past into the American present that characters can avoid the extinction of "a Black social, political, and religious consciousness in the American diaspora" (Jennings 136). More pragmatically, Jennings describes the animistic natural world of the Caribbean as an outgrowth of the Catholicism that dominates their world, as well as the strong influence of Voudoun. One tenet is their belief that the *loa* (the freed souls of the cosmos) reside in "trees, stones, streams," which serve as vessels for their existences. "The preponderance of African traditional religions and their diaspora mutations are grounded in the belief that non-material 'spirit' animates matter; therefore natural objects, natural phenomena, and the universe itself possesses a consciousness. Originating from a number of sources, divinities and spirits of the natural elements animating trees, stones, and other material objects characterize animistic religions" (Jennings 127–8). As Susan Willis wrote decades ago, "The problem at the center of Morrison's writing is how to maintain an Afro-American cultural heritage once the relationship to the black rural South has been stretched thin over distance and generations" (Willis, "Eruptions" 34). Moving *Tar Baby* to Eloe, Florida, allows a less sophisticated scrutiny of the cultures that seem exotic to the Americans attempting to live in the Caribbean.

Son Green's function in *Tar Baby* is not only to contrast with Jadine. He becomes a prototype for the black man who has not followed white paths to prosperity or acceptability. In terms of profession, the African American William Green seems to be a bum. What does he *do*? What is his occupation? Morrison places him in what she called "that great underclass of undocumented men ... an international legion of day laborers and musclemen, gamblers, sidewalk merchants, migrants, unlicensed crewmen, part-time mercenaries, full-time gigolos, or curbside musicians" (*Tar* 166). The dialogue Morrison creates between Margaret Street and Jadine, soon after they have discovered Son, shows how quickly any lack of assimilation to mainstream culture becomes a kind of sin. Margaret refers to Son as "Nigger," as does Jadine:

" ... instead of throwing him right out of here."
"Maybe we're making something out of nothing."
"Jade. He was in my closet. He had my box of souvenirs in his lap."
"Open?"
"No. Not open. Just sitting there holding it. He must have picked them up from the floor. Oh, God, he scared the shit out of me. He looked like a gorilla!" Jadine's neck prickled at the description. She had volunteered nigger – but not gorilla. "We were all scared, Margaret," she said calmly. "If he'd been white we would still have been scared." (*Tar* 129)

Ironic as this description is, with Jadine feigning criticism of the word "gorilla," Morrison had just a few pages before shown Jadine herself using scathing language to talk with Son – at least partly because of her erotic response to the man. Much of the conversation Jadine has with Son focuses on his smell, the essence of an unbathed refugee, and perhaps as well of the racial smell she wants to deny. Filled with Son's sheer lust for Jadine, whom he has watched sleeping night after night, her response to him evokes a natural sexual reply.

More significant to the author's incremental descriptions of Son are his thoughts about his displacement here, and his contrast between the Caribbean island with his hometown of Eloe. As he watched Jadine sleep, he tried to force upon her "the dreams he wanted her to have about yellow houses with white doors which women opened and shouted Come on in, you honey you! And the fat black ladies in white dresses minding the pie table in the basement of the church and white wet sheets flapping on a line, and the sound of a six-string guitar plucked after supper while children scooped walnuts up off the ground and handed them to her" (*Tar* 119). All that remains positive in Son's memory is the commonplace heterosexual living in the small Florida town, and the "pie ladies" center that memory.

As Morrison draws Son as the erotic and exotic refugee, he takes on qualities of the trickster figure. Not particularly androgynous as in some legends, Morrison's trickster in *Tar Baby* is smart, cunning, and fixed on the objective of winning Jadine – as well as keeping himself in a social construct that makes the latter possible. As John Roberts points out, tricksters were not magical or other-worldly: they used the power of their intelligence, and they often acted in self-protective ways. "Trickster's acts were accepted as beneficial since Africa lived at such a minimal subsistence lever ... Necessity justified trickery. The trickster takes on people but also the 'Sky-God'" (Roberts 28–9).

Many of the stories that illustrate the trickster's exploits have to do with food. Son Green certainly is marked by his wily hunger throughout the early chapters of *Tar Baby* – he is known as "the chocolate eater" to the native population. But Morrison's embroidery of the man's physical hunger with its overlay of hunger for the beautiful, which Jadine represents, moves him out of the stereotypical category as a conqueror of the rebellious. And the central and expressly moving section, as Son convinces his dream woman that he does truly love her, and that he has the capacity to care for her, makes his relinquishment at the conclusion of the novel a kind of nobility (among the most famous tricksters in African history are, of course, Br'er Rabbit – along with Stackalee, John Hardy, Railroad Bill, and Daniel Winston, black folk heroes completely unknown to Valerian Street) (Roberts 173).

Tar Baby is the most "African" of Morrison's fictions to this time. Her insistence that the world is more than its global existence – that it must stem from the still-living ancestors and lead its living generations into future lives – expands what she saw as a "jubilant" ending for *Song of Solomon.* In that 1977 novel, for Milkman and Guitar to find a love that did not depend on their alliance against white culture was admirable, but it did not salvage others from their American environs (and it did not save Pilate). In her open-endedness which acts as closure for *Tar Baby*, Morrison creates an entirely separate existence for her protagonists – Jadine observes the soldier ants living their proud matriarchal existence while she flies off to a European culture that will deny her any further knowledge of her self, or of her primary culture.

Morrison creates several scenes of Jadine's being rejected by the women characters who are themselves firmly rooted in both the lore of mothers and daughters and the ancient properties. The first rejection comes as she and Son find love on the island, and the swamp women create a hostile atmosphere that surrounds them: "Thérèse and an assemblage of living women (Son's Aunt Rose, his best friend Soldier's wife Ellen, Jadine's aunt by marriage Ondine, dog-ravaged Francine, and the woman in yellow) and living-dead women" [living vs. 'living-dead']" (Jennings 124).

The second manifests itself when Jadine goes to Eloe with Son, as much committed to him as she will ever be. When she has a nightmare there, it is "Son's mother, his past wife Cheyenne, Cheyenne's mother Sally Brown, and Jadine's mother [who] bare their breasts to her." All these women knew "how to nurture, to be daughters, to be soldier ants." (Jennings 124). They not only observe Jadine's lovemaking with Son, they want to join in:

Pushing each other – nudging for space, they poured out of the dark like ants out of a hive ... "I have breasts too." she said or thought or willed, "I have breasts too." But they didn't believe her. They just held their own higher and pushed their own farther out and looked at her. All of them revealing both their breasts except the woman in yellow. She did something more shocking – she stretched out a long arm and showed Jadine her three big eggs. (*Tar* 258–9)

Relying on the narrative of a romance,[1] Morrison reminds her readers that inversion is often the mark of any borrowing of myth. As she had said in "Unspeakable Things Unspoken,"

> I was interested in working out the mystery of a piece of lore, a folk tale, which is also about safety and danger and the skills needed to secure the one and recognize and avoid the other. I was not, of course, interested in re-telling the tale; I suppose that is an idea to pursue, but it is certainly not interesting enough to engage me for four years. I have said, elsewhere, that the exploration of the Tar Baby tale was like stroking a pet to see what the anatomy was like but not to disturb or distort its mystery. Folk lore may have begun as allegory for natural or social phenomena; it may have been employed as a retreat from contemporary issues in art, but folk lore can also contain myths that re-activate themselves endlessly through providers – the people who repeat, reshape, reconstitute and reinterpret them. The Tar Baby tale seemed to me to be about masks. Not masks as covering what is to be hidden, but how masks come to life, take life over, exercise the tension between itself and what it covers. For Son, the most effective mask is none. ("Unspeakable" 30)

Despite a commentary which is both a kind of disclaimer and an insight, in *Tar Baby* Morrison played the dozens with the *tar baby* story, ending with a comic exaggeration of Son's run for freedom. By giving the reader the phrase "lickety-split," repeatedly, she has made the displaced black man into a kind of loose-jointed human doll, in himself illustrative of mainstream culture's view of the way black people can sometimes embody animal traits.

She has given the reader no such comedy in connection with Jadine. Indeed, by placing her in a first-class seat on the luxurious jet to Europe, Morrison has removed her so far from the Caribbean island that readers do not care about her outcome. With another customary trick of her narrative, however, Morrison has made Jadine's last thoughts of her American roots (though damaged through the colonization she has herself undergone) into her description of the tough, matriarchal soldier ants:

> Straight ahead they marched, shamelessly single-minded, for soldier ants have no time for dreaming. Almost all of them are women and there is so much to do – the work is literally endless. So many to be born and fed, then found and buried. There is no time for dreaming. The life of their world requires organization so tight and sacrifice so complete there is little need for males and they are seldom produced. When they are needed, it is deliberately done by the queen who surmises, by some four-million-year-old magic she is heiress to, that it is time. So she urges a sperm from the private womb where they were placed when she had her one, first and last copulation.

Here Morrison underscores that the life of the good woman, the willing and capable mother and queen, is filled with "literally endless" work. She also makes clear that the province of the queen is the death of her lover, limited to giving her "Sperm which she keeps in a special place to use at her own discretion when there is need for another dark and singing cloud of ant folk mating in the air" (*Tar* 290–1). Even as Jadine remembers the "star" quality of Son's lovemaking, she has those thoughts against the backdrop of Ondine's lecture about what it means to be a daughter. By flying to Europe, Jadine walks away from those responsibilities.

Prior to this clear recognition scene, however, in the airport, Jadine has recognized Alma Estee in her new, garish wig, and has condescendingly tipped her. But she has also reverted to the Streets' demeaning practice of calling the girl "Mary." The Caribbean has made no positive impression on Jadine: all women exist to serve her, even though Alma Estee demands to know what she has done with Son, the man she calls "the chocolate eater" because of the way he lived in secret before he was discovered.

> "'You kill him?' asked the girl in a very matter-of-fact tone ...
> 'Thérèse said you kill him,' the girl insisted."
> "'Tell Thérèse *she* killed him'" (*Tar* 289).

Jadine has understood all along that the native beliefs have both changed and sanctified Son Green. As a traumatized returning veteran, eviscerated by his memories from Vietnam, the diffident man she has come to love brought her only temporary solace. By returning to Paris, she relinquishes him ("No more shoulders and limitless chests.

No more dreams of safety") (*Tar* 290). As simple as the two strokes of her emery board to repair her fingernail, Jadine moves away and on. The last chapter of the novel, suitably, is given to the way Son Green attempts to deal with his loss of Jadine. He is here thrown back to his angry misbehavior in Vietnam, the time and place where he began feeling that "It was all mixed up" (*Tar* 299). Loving Jadine with a kind of synesthesia – "a woman who was not only a woman but a sound, all the music he had ever wanted to play, a world and a way of being in it" – he could not hear either Alma Estee or Gideon. Thérèse did not wait for him to hear her. She woke him during the night and, blind as she was, led him to her boat: "The feel of the current was what she went by" (*Tar* 303). More obviously than in many of Morrison's drawings of disabled women, Thérèse represents the outsider status of the female. Critic Rosemarie Garland-Thomson calls these powerful women (Pilate, Sula, Eva Peace, and the women of *Beloved* to come) "pariah figures" and notes that "their disabilities and anomalies are the imprints and the judgments of social stigmatization – rejection, isolation, etc." They find their force "outside culturally sanctioned spaces" (Garland-Thomson, "Disability" 99–100).

In this scene as in many others, Morrison fuses the realistic with the mystical. Sitting in the small boat, Son relies on his own calm and on Marie Thérèse. It is she who tells him to join the ancient properties that men acknowledge. Marie Thérèse voices what the reader has come to believe: "take a choice," she tells Son bluntly. "Forget her. There is nothing in her parts for you. She has forgotten her ancient properties." Referring to the myth of the three-centuries-old horsemen, blinded by the ophthalmia that came to the Caribbean through the Middle Passage journey, Thérèse Foucault speaks of her literal ancestors. She commands Son, "Don't see, feel ... The men [are waiting]. You can choose now. You can get free of her. They are waiting in the hills for you. They are naked and they are blind too ... But they gallop; they race those horses like angels all over the hills where the rain forest is, where the champion daisy trees still grow. Go there. Choose them" (*Tar* 304–6).

As Morrison explained in an interview,

I ... wanted to suggest that this journey is Son's choice although he did not think it up. *Thérèse* did. He said he had no choice, so she manipulated his trip so that he had a choice. On his way back to Valerian's house in order to get the address so he can find Jadine, there is a strong possibility that he joins or is captured by the horsemen – captured by the past, by the wish, by the prehistoric times. The suggestion in the end when the trees step back to make way for a certain kind of man, is that Nature is urging him to join them.

Morrison also makes the point that the scenes of Son's arrival in water bracket the novel – and are not given chapter titles – so that in the first scene, the water fights him but in the concluding scene he is being urged by the water to go ashore (Con I, 150). As he stumbles from Thérèse's boat, moving as if the act of walking is unknown to him, he gradually straightens, gains poise, and then runs. "Lickety-split. Lickety-split. Looking neither to the left nor to the right, Lickety-split. Lickety-split. Lickety-lickety-lickety-split" (*Tar* 306).

Like most of Morrison's other endings, this concluding scene of *Tar Baby*, though it privileges Son's return to the fraternal and to the animal, does not truly conclude. Morrison has here, near the closing, introduced a young Caribbean girl – not known as "Mary" but rather as "Alma Estee," whose attraction for Son has been made clear. *Alma*, the soul, may prove to lead readers away from the temptation to use either/or endings that Morrison has so far avoided. Her presence confirms Page's reading of the strength available in both Thérèse (and through her, Gideon), as they "embody what is absent in the other characters. Living genuine lives, in harmony with themselves, each other, their community, and nature ... distinguishes them from the highly simplified existences of not only the Streets but of all their household" (Page, *Dangerous* 118). In the dissatisfaction readers find when they focus only on Jadine or only on Son, Morrison confirms Loichot's conclusion that, once again, this author's privileging of genealogy "subverts linear legacies and transmissions, goes beyond racial divides to create an interracial family marked by violence, dissonance, disruption, and ambivalence." (Loichot 163). Stelamaris Coser broadens that commentary to note that Morrison's answers in *Tar Baby* are "tentative and plural ... *Tar Baby* presents a conflicting dialogue of individual consciences, not a monologic, finished theory about the issues it raises ... [the questions] address many issues related to our time and place in this world" (Coser 118).

3
Beloved, Beloved, *Beloved*

Morrison's mining of the dimensions of folktale that appeared so prominently in both *Song of Solomon* and *Tar Baby* had proved less expansive than she had hoped. She found that many of her readers were still caught up in an all-too-frequently bifurcated world, and much of that world's bifurcation was premised on a black–white racial division that seemed to come naturally to readers' minds because Toni Morrison was herself black. Even if Morrison had considered some of her uses of the folk ironic, readers seemed incapable of finding that irony when the African American author was drawing characters who were similarly African American.

The author's puzzled reaction to the various readings of both her third and fourth novels might have led to her spending more time finishing the fifth novel, *Beloved* (1987). Taking on the subject of American slavery, she had, in the process of working through myriad issues about slavery – escape from bondage, beginning with the history of the Middle Passage, family deconstruction, parent–child or more significantly mother–child relationships, and resettlement – unearthed narratives that were new to the history of slavery. Critic Charles Scruggs comments that Morrison told the story of slavery in an "epic" manner, intent on making readers identify with Sethe's need to establish "a heavenly city within" (Scruggs 185). A. S. Byatt, similarly, compares what Morrison has achieved with the novels of Tolstoy – "she gives you no option but to inhabit her world. You can't read it as though you were looking on" (Byatt 222). Gina Wisker takes the impact of *Beloved* beyond slavery, saying, "*Beloved* is an intensely social and psychologically political book. It engages the reader with the everyday lived horrors of slavery and the race memory of the slave crossing, each equally felt as real, and it also engages the individual, black or white, with the complex consuming pain, and guilt, of the everyday lived memory of slavery" (Wisker, "Remembering" 278).

During the six years between the publication of *Tar Baby* and *Beloved,* Morrison was, in some respects, stumped (and then, later, stunned) by trying to discern enough about slavery that she could write Sethe's narrative. "The problem was the terror," she said in retrospect. "I wanted it to be truly *felt.* I wanted to translate the historical into the personal. I spent a long time trying to figure out what it was about slavery that made it so repugnant, so personal, so indifferent, so intimate and yet so public" (Con II, 76). Defending her choices to write such a difficult narrative, Morrison continued her explanation: "life was infinitely worse than I describe it" (Bigsby 257). Breaking up the story was intended to "enable the reader to understand. You have to look at it through the eyes of people who are shocked by it ... [otherwise] it would be too anguished. I needed a non-threatening narrator. I had to move the camera around from place to place, so that you see this terrible thing from the outside and you have to permit the reader to go through the horror as an outsider" (Bigsby 258).

In Claudine Raynaud's careful analysis of *Beloved,* she notes the way Morrison "initially [uses] a broken syntax and later an increasingly more complex grammar ... the daughter attempts to translate the experience of abomination. This necessary progression goes from flesh to body to voice, from matter to language, from abjection to subjecthood ...." Raynaud also focuses on the fact that Morrison rewrites the Middle Passage "as a ritual, the enactment of Beloved's conjoining with the mother," and that "the return to beginnings leads to a revisiting of the original – that is, total fusion with and possession of the mother" (Raynaud 72, 83; see also Christol, Konen). Some of Morrison's difficulty in writing the core narrative of Sethe's killing her child comes through as she speaks about the process in her *Paris Review* interview:

> It seemed important to me that the action in *Beloved* – the fact of infanticide – be immediately known, but deferred, unseen. I wanted to give the reader all the information and the

consequences surrounding the act, while avoiding engorging myself and the reader with the violence itself. I remember writing the sentence where Sethe cuts the throat of the child very, very late in the process of writing the book. I remember getting up from the table and walking outside for a long time – walking around the yard and coming back and revising it a little bit and going back out and in and rewriting the sentence over and over again ... each time I fixed that sentence so that it was exactly right, or so I thought, but then I would be unable to sit there and would have to go away and come back. I thought that the act itself had to be not only buried but also understated, because if the language was going to compete with the violence itself it would be obscene or pornographic. (Con II, 81)

Even as most readers found themselves sympathizing with the slave mother's justifiable act of killing her child, regardless of how much convolution Morrison used to convey that description, a few critics charged her with sentimentalism, with inflating atrocity, with subversion of the tropes of the historical slave narratives. Others pointed to those earlier patterns – Tim Spaulding, for example, discusses the way the original slave narratives drew from "the sentimental novel, spiritual autobiographies, captivity narratives, and abolitionist political tracts" and determines that Morrison bases much of her novel on the gothic but still relies on earlier patterning (Spaulding 61). The review Margaret Atwood wrote for the *New York Times Book Review*, characterizing the novel as about the family in slavery, is largely descriptive, whereas Stanley Crouch's "Aunt Medea" in *The New Republic* uses surprisingly sharp criticism about Morrison's portrayal of vindictive motherhood (Atwood 49–50; Crouch 38). Many critics moved quickly to choices about style rather than focusing on the moral meanings of the novel: for Carl Malmgren, the book is "unusually hybridized ... part ghost story, part historical novel, part slave narrative, part love story." He sees *Beloved* as "both a tragedy, involving a mother's moment of choice, and as a love story, exploring what it means to be be-loved" (Malmgren 190; see also Williamson 147–85 and Wagner-Martin, *Maternal* 67–83). Judith Thurman, in her *New Yorker* review, says that *Beloved* is not an historical novel, and that Morrison "does not attempt ... to argue the immorality of slavery on rational grounds .... As the reader struggles with its fragments and mysteries, he keeps being startled by flashes of his own reflections in them" (Thurman 75).

For Maisha Wester, in her study of the African American Gothic, "*Beloved* implies that the absolute horror of slavery lay not just in its dehumanization of individuals, but how this dehumanization inevitably impacts and disrupts the African American family beyond the era of slavery." The existence of slavery, in African American lives,

> continues to destroy black bodies and futures indefinitely. Morrison reveals the loss of family as the primary issue for blacks and their descendants, all of whom, the text warns, can be reensnared by oppressive rac(ial)isms at any given moment lest they beware. In addition, Morrison insinuates that continuing to privilege and mimic patriarchal family structures will only reproduce the oppressions suffered under racist culture and, therefore, aggravate the haunting. Salvation, consequently, lies in constructing a familial system that is not based in gender dominance. (Wester 32)

As if an echo of Terry Otten's early religiously based reading of Morrison's first five novels, Wester stresses the novel's "moral authority." As Otten had said, *Beloved*'s authority "resides less in a revelation of the obvious horrors of slavery than in a revelation of slavery's nefarious ability to invert moral categories and behavior and to impose tragic choice" (Otten, *Crime* 82). The complications of readers having sympathy with one or another of the book's characters lead to such moral attitudes: "Sethe cannot evade the consequences of her act" – and as Morrison frequently suggested, killing a child is never "the right thing to do" (Otten 83).

When Kristine Yohe writes about the novel, she pairs it with Morrison's later opera, *Margaret Garner* (Morrison wrote the opera because, as she had included in *The Black Book,* the thread of Sethe's story was taken from Margaret Garner's killing of one of her children). In the opera, unlike the novel, Margaret is raped by her white owner, following his daughter's wonderfully staged, costly marriage. Yohe notes, "self-protection involves maintaining a sense of oneself separate from the abuse and the abuser"; she also quotes Morrison's having said that she intended to take a "narrow and deep" approach to the story of slaves, which was based, in fact, on "their very ordinary, unheralded lives. It's extraordinary what they did just to get through sixty years of existence" (Yohe 110, 107).

That Morrison would eventually write about slavery seemed in keeping with her pervasive focus on black people, their culture, their being divided – both historically and psychologically – between the United States, with its dominant white culture, and Africa, the incomparable source of so many black beliefs and customs. As she said in an early interview, "When I view the world, perceive it and write about it, it's the world of black people. It's not that I won't write about white people. I just know that when I'm trying to develop the various themes I write about, the people who best manifest those themes for me are the black people whom I invent" (Con I, 157). Critic Linden Peach attributes Morrison's preference to some vestigial influence of her father, who gave whites little credit for their accomplishments. "He thought Africans were superior to Europeans because they were morally superior." Says Peach, somewhat like Guitar Baines in *Song of Solomon*, George Wofford believed that "harmony could never exist between the races" (Peach, *Toni* 5).

Governing the narratives of slavery, the dominance of white culture naturally inscribes slaves' behaviors. The persistence of Sethe's guilt and atonement becomes the gist of *Beloved*'s downward spiral (and if readers literally cannot finish the novel, it is the truth of Sethe's disintegration that saddens them). What absorbs more and more of any reader's attention, however, is the presence of the quasi-human, ghostly character named Beloved. Morrison was unsure that the novel *Beloved* as it now exists was itself a separate book (taking it to her editor apologetically), because what she was conceiving of as her novel had fallen into three parts – parts she later called a trilogy, and later accepted the existence of both *Jazz* and *Paradise* as parts of her initial narrative.

Most of the reviews of *Beloved* included commentary about the figure of the title: most readers could not get past that fragile waterlogged girl who appeared as soon as Paul D had returned from his own, and Sethe's, past at Sweet Home. Originally, the character of Beloved seemed *not* to be a part of the novel. As Morrison explained to an interviewer, about a quarter of the way through her writing of the book "I realized that the only person really in a place to judge the woman's action would be the dead child. But she couldn't lurk outside the book." To include the child, dead for these 20 years, "was like an earthquake in the book. " Believing as she consistently had in the existence of an other world, whether it was expressed through dreams or through visible presences, Morrison continued, "I could use the supernatural as a way of explaining, of exploring the memory of these events. You can't get away from this bad memory because she [the character of Beloved] is here, sitting at the table, talking to you. No matter what anybody says we all know that there are ghosts" (Bigsby 259, 278). As Gina Wisker points out, however, the literary world in the mid-1980s seldom acknowledged the ghostly; she notes how *new* Anne Rice was. *Beloved* did not find a ready readership (Wisker, "Remembering" 270).

Beloved might have given readers a new glimpse of Morrison's belief system – so that the novel *Beloved* felt very different from her earlier four novels. But Morrison had not shied away from ghostly presences in her other books. The continuing conversations between Nel and Sula seem to be taking place even some 20 years after Sula's early death: no spectral visitation, but the permeation of Nel's consciousness by the spirit of Sula leads to the striking climax of *Sula*. Similarly, though given more embodiment, Milkman finds throughout his hegira in *Song of Solomon* – whether in the persona of Circe or the hovering wisdom of Pilate or the unspoken dialogue among all those Southern men named Solomon – some essential knowledge that he had not previously had. In *Tar Baby*, the unspoken wisdom of Gideon and Marie Thérèse gives Son some of the same insight that Milkman seems to have acquired, but it is Valerian Street, one of the most un-emperor like figures Morrison draws, who experiences visitation by the ghost of his ex-wife. She has died soon after his own retirement, and later, when he moves with Margaret, his second wife, to the Caribbean, Morrison explains, "He began to miss her at precisely that point – terribly – and when he settled in the Caribbean she must have missed him too for she started visiting him in the greenhouse with the regularity of a passionate mistress. Funny. He couldn't remember her eyes, but when she came, flitting around his chair and gliding over his seed flats, he recognized her at once ... He was not alarmed by her visits" (*Tar* 143). (Morrison also gives Valerian the repeated experience of seeing two-year-old Michael, hiding under the sink until his father's return – and thereby escaping Margaret's brutality.)

The unnamed wife/ghost has no impact on the story of the Streets, except that Valerian may spend more and more time secluded in the greenhouse. Beloved, in contrast, comes to dominate the narrative of Morrison's fifth novel – besides the book's carrying her name as title – so the use of the ghostly presence is vastly different. Such recent critics as Washington, Jennings, and Zauditu-Selassie explain the physical presence of the Beloved character as a visible link to African beliefs, whereas Melanie Anderson studies Morrison's reliance on spiritualism, with overtones of Central American ghostliness. In addition to these important readings, one of the most helpful among recent theorists is Kathleen Brogan. Her *Cultural Haunting, Ghosts and Ethnicity in Recent American Literature* allows a more psychological slant to such unquantifiable textual evidence. For Brogan, remembering that Morrison had taken the text of *Beloved* to Robert Gottlieb thinking it not yet a novel, the author's motivation itself seemed incomplete. Brogan notes, "In the literature of cultural haunting, such haunting potentially leads to a valuable awareness of how the group's past continues to inhabit and inform the living. The exorcism of all forms of ghostliness could result in a historical amnesia that endangers the integrity of the group." In Morrison's *Beloved*, says Brogan, she does not accomplish this purpose smoothly. In fact, "the curious disjunction between the novel's reclamation of the past and its characters' flight into amnesia" might instead show a "powerful resistance of trauma to the consolations of ritual, or to any attempt to limit and contain suffering by establishing a continuity between the traumatic and the ordinary …. trauma names a disastrous alternative to history, one that leaves the traumatized highly vulnerable to revictimization" (Brogan 71).

While Morrison so thoroughly depicts the stages of Sethe's memory and rememory, ignoring Denver as she does, hanging onto just a thread of self while she, robotlike, goes to the restaurant every morning and comes home every evening (there appears to be no variation during those 18 years of Sethe's mourning), she makes the reader look back to Shadrack's commemorating every year with National Suicide Day and, more purposefully, ahead to the kind of tragic trauma Frank Money will carry on his shoulders once he has returned – alone – from Korea. Twenty-five years after Morrison completed *Beloved*, she seems in her 2012 novel *Home* to understand why people could *not* be comforted by ritual, any more than their emotions could be honed into acceptance by someone else's version of "history."

In Brogan's words, Sethe feels that her mind is "homeless" because of the disjunction of the times – what Morrison creates for her readers is "the tortured internal world of those traumatized by slavery" (Brogan 204, 79). Even the structure of *Beloved* lends a kind of irony to the trauma that Sethe endures: "Throughout the novel we find in its many scenes of story telling, a straining toward a narrative ordering of the past that is repeatedly thwarted by the unspeakable nature of the events the telling would organize" (Brogan 77).

By seeing that the damaged human psyche provides the undergirding of much twentieth- and twenty-first-century life, Morrison moves beyond what some critics have seen as her reliance on key historical events from African American history. Slavery as the paramount block that underlies *Beloved*, of course, cannot be erased; but with the Northern migration to city life, which *Jazz* describes, or the westward migration to independent and separable existences, which *Paradise* limns, Morrison is not categorizing herself as the chronicler of African American history. Morrison is a *writer*, keenly involved in all elements that comprise the human heart. She knows her readers can look in many other places for historical accounts. What Morrison wants to do with the history she knows is make her readers understand how futile the search for happiness can be, how firmly lodged in the human psyche are the slights and injuries of people throughout the range of cultures.

In 1987, Morrison began the arc that would take her through the crucial narratives of the next 25 years. That arc begins with *Beloved*. It runs through the trilogy of novels but it also goes beyond those books. Whereas *Love* and *A Mercy* have sometimes bemused readers, they fit with deft structural placement into the patterning of characters broken by their times – or *nearly* broken by their times. The changes Morrison evokes in the books that follow *Beloved* often have to do with *how* the stories are conveyed – conveyed in contrast to merely *told*. How does the author equip her readers to apprehend what the novel says, what the characters in that novel experience (and what they are able to survive)? The explanations for Violet Trace's endurance (in *Jazz*), for L's murderous act (in *Love*), for Florens's becoming voice and conscience (in *A Mercy*) are found more regularly in the way Morrison creates their stories than in the events of any actual history. *Fact* in the latter part of Morrison's writing career has been subsumed by a voice that belongs at times to the author but more often to some disembodied spirit. Morrison comes more and more often to rely on the spiritual, and the spirited, world. Her fiction gains dimension through her acknowledgment of those spirits. In contrast to the treatment she gives to the character of Beloved, if her ghosts are only suggested, or only privately visible, readers can ignore or fabricate or obfuscate their existences.

Keith Byerman discusses the expansion of a consideration of history in his book *Remembering the Past in Contemporary African American Fiction*:

> "History" can also be understood as the stories of ordinary people in times of stress rather than hero or victim narratives, but in the all-too-common context in human history of violence, dehumanization, abjection, and invisibility, this experience is comparable to holocaust. The writers ... are in this sense generating a historical rather than an essentialist idea of black experience ... a shared experience of suffering rather than a genetic or geographical connection that shapes group identity. (Byerman 8)

This critic reads *Beloved* as "about repression and its relationship to oppression; it is also about the return of the repressed and about the need to bear witness. [Morrison] creates narratives that reveal the past by breaking through the repression, by revealing the distorting effects of the 'white word' ... they do this through the expansion of individual memory into communal history." Byerman notes, I think rightly, that Morrison does not ignore the realities of slavery but that the author is "most interested in the psychological and cultural effects of such history" (Byerman 28, 33).

Dana A. Williams' study places *Beloved* at the forefront of the reaction to the Black Arts movement – a movement she calls "unsympathetic to both the novel and women writers." She quotes Paul Gilroy's saying that *Beloved* was "not a manifesto, but it insists on an entirely new aesthetic and political agenda" (Gilroy 176 in Williams, "Dancing" 93–4). As do many recent critics, Williams groups the Morrison novel (as well as her *Paradise*) with Gayl Jones's *Corregidora* and Toni Cade Bambara's *The Salt Eaters*, in order to discuss not only their engagement with feminist themes but also their affinity to modernist narrative strategies; a corresponding "highly participatory quality between the book and the reader," which attempts to obviate the alienation between the book and the reader caused by the modernist techniques; a corresponding invocation of the ancestor and use of multiple perspectives to reconstruct the stability modernity disturbed; and a final impetus to move beyond binaries and categories to suggest a more humanistic approach to the (re)construction of the self. (Williams 95)

Williams is also alert to the fact that while Morrison worked as an editor at Random House, she was intent on neutralizing that male-oriented preference that carried over from Black Arts days. Whatever the topics of the books she sponsored, Morrison saw the field of African American literature as a means of encouraging both black readers and writers: she felt that if she were interested in a book, other African Americans would also want to read that work (Williams 94).

Considering the decades-old tradition that African American writing should be focused toward "uplift," Morrison's characters in *Beloved* might have been somewhat difficult in themselves. Just as some readers of *Tar Baby* may have objected to the somewhat aimless character of Son Green, Michael D. Hill suggests that *Beloved's* protagonists – Sethe and Paul D – "represent two of the black community's more controversial members – the single mother and the ex-convict," comprising what Hill terms "a pariah community" (Hill, *Ethics* 28). Given that Morrison's narrative of slavery predetermines some of the characteristics she attributes to Sethe and Paul D, and that she makes clear that Halle and Sethe were dedicated to each other, this objection may not have struck most readers.

Readers during the mid-1980s had only just begun to accept African American characters as complex individuals – especially African American *women* characters – when in *Beloved* Morrison presents them with the enigmatic and largely inexplicable Sethe, a woman who appears to be the essence of good mothering. But then Morrison abruptly shatters that characterization and gives the readers Sethe as murderer.

The circumstances leading up to the killing of the "crawling already?" daughter have in no way prepared the reader for this demonized Sethe. Morrison places the reader in the position of Baby Suggs, the child's grandmother. It is Baby Suggs and her maternal generosity – "Baby Suggs holy" – who has in part created the deep bonds within the Ohio community of escaped and freed slaves. Her loving welcome to African Americans who come to the Clearing for her ministry bespeaks the harmony possible when people can live together unafraid. When Sethe and Halle's children arrive at her home, 124 Bluestone Road, Baby Suggs is ecstatic. Her joy is increased when Stamp Paid delivers Sethe and the new baby Denver. During the 28 days of the family's shared happiness, a female marker that suggests the menstrual cycle and also foreshadows the 28 parts into which *Beloved* is structurally divided, Sethe and Baby Suggs – in spite of Halle's absence – know joy.

The fact that Morrison creates a trilogy of women's life experiences also inscribes *Beloved* as a woman's narrative. The book initially pivots between the early scene of Sethe's opening her body to the engraver of her daughter's burial stone ("Ten minutes, he said. You got ten minutes I'll do it for free;" *Beloved* 5) and the later flashback to Sethe's giving birth to the premature Denver, barely breathing as Sethe crawls into the rowboat on the Ohio River. Aided by Amy Denver, the white runaway, "two throw-away people, two lawless outlaws – a slave and a barefoot whitewoman" succeed in keeping the baby alive (*Beloved* 84). As the narrator commends them, "There was nothing to disturb them at their work. So they did it appropriately and well" (85).

The third leg of women's experience is the anticipated death of Baby Suggs, lying on her bed and finding her only joy (once Sethe has killed her daughter and then been imprisoned for that crime) in the faint colors of life still available to her. Reading *Beloved* means focusing on Morrison's key scenes: other than these scenes, the disparity of language and memory is sometimes confusing to readers. According to the above-mentioned scenes, the roles of women are to provide sexual comfort, to give birth and thereby assume nurturing roles for children, and to create coherence for other human beings within a community. In the fact of Baby Suggs' death, Morrison also implies the stridency of moral judgments: Baby Suggs' denunciation of Sethe's violent act is her choice to die.

Poised in the early and mid-1980s, a decade awash in feminist ideology, Morrison in her natural role as an African American woman held herself aloof from women's liberation. When she was asked by an interviewer to confirm that the 1960s were "about race" and the

1970s and 1980s were "about gender," she answered that she felt "an equal commitment to both. Because making children out of black people, or making children out of women, in an effort to dominate and control the economy and the bodies of these people, whether it is a racial domination or a patriarchal domination, seemed to me to go hand in hand, historically" (Bigsby 288). Morrison's economic emphasis here is surprising: the ownership of a woman's body, and its power to give birth, becomes the primary concern. To the particular point of the anguished life of the slave mother, Morrison contends, "Slavery asserted that she had no responsibility to her children, that she had nothing to say about them; whether they lived or died was not her business. She was a breeder, not a mother, not a parent" (Bigsby 278). In *Beloved,* Baby Suggs and such other women of the community as Ella illustrate the bitterness of their having lived lives of loss and deprivation: their children taken from them to be sold as slaves, the women could only persevere on their own. In Ella's case (as in the experience of Sethe's mother), to let a child die rather than becoming a means of making profit for their owners was an efficacious way of challenging ownership.

Narratively, how does the woman writer make plausible infanticide – or other means of claiming power over her owner? As Morrison said, "I thought I knew all I needed to know about it [slavery], and I didn't. I didn't know. I had not imagined .... I had not known what it had felt like and it was so painful I had to write differently, slowly. I had to be free *not* to write for long periods of time in order to be able to write simply and clearly about it" (Bigsby 256). She also described how frightening she thought immersion in this story was: "I could imagine slavery in an intellectual way, but to feel it viscerally was terrifying. I had to go inside. Like an actor does. I had to feel what it might feel like for my own children to be enslaved. At the time, I was no longer working at any office, and that permitted me to go deep."

With *Beloved,* I wanted to say, "Let's get rid of these words like 'the slave woman' and 'the slave child,' and talk about people with names, like you and like me, who were there. Now, what does slavery feel like? What can you do? How can you be? Clearly, it is a situation in which you have practically no power. And if you decide you are not going to be a victim, then it's a major risk. And you end up doing some terrible things ... the risk of being your own person, or trying to have something to do with your destiny, is one of the major battles in life." (Con II, 105–6)

Among the effects Morrison had created for *Beloved* was the quickly paced juxtaposition among both scenes and voiced transitional sections; the creation of the difficult reading process was a part of her calculations. "It is abrupt and should appear so … The reader is snatched, yanked, thrown into an environment completely foreign, and I want it as the first stroke of the shared experience that might be possible between the reader and the novel's population. Snatched just as the slaves were from one place to another, from any place to another, without preparation and without defense" ("Unspeakable" 31).

In "Unspeakable Things Unspoken," Morrison's first major lecture/essay about her writing process as it is aligned with the history of American letters, she makes the choice to explain carefully and in great detail her reasoning for the beginnings of each of her five novels. Speaking at the University of Michigan in 1988, well aware that critics – as well as readers – were finding it difficult to read her novels easily, she added to the wider discussion of Americanisms, of the newly colonized country seeking to separate its voice from the centuries of traditional British literature, five distinct sections. In each one she located the importance of the openings of her works from *The Bluest Eye* through *Beloved*. Insistent that every word was a carefully chosen mandala for the system of a single text's meaning, Morrison shows her readers how the paradigm of language works:

'124 was spiteful. Full of a baby's venom.'

"Beginning *Beloved* with numerals rather than spelled out numbers, it was my intention to give the house an identity separate from the street or even the city; to name it the way "Sweet Home" was named; the way plantations were named, but not with nouns or "proper" names – with numbers instead because numbers have no adjectives, no posture of coziness or grandeur or the haughty yearning of arrivistes and estate builders for the parallel beautifications of the nation they left behind, laying claim to instant history and legend. Numbers here constitute an address, a thrilling enough prospect for slaves who had owned nothing, least of all an address. And although the numbers, unlike words, can have no modifiers, I give these an adjective – spiteful (There are three others). The address is therefore personalized, but personalized by its own activity, not the pasted on desire for personality.

Also there is something about numerals that makes them spoken, heard, in this context, because one expects words to read in a book, not numbers to say, or hear. And the sound of the novel, sometimes cacaphonous, sometimes harmonious, must be an inner ear sound or a sound just beyond hearing, infusing the text with a musical emphasis that words can do sometimes even better than music can. Thus the second sentence is not one: it is a phrase that properly, grammatically, belongs as a dependent clause with the first. Had I done that, however (124 was spiteful, comma, full of a baby's venom, or 124 was full of a baby's venom) I could not have had the accent on *full* (/ u u / u / u pause/ u u u u / u).

Whatever the risks of confronting the reader with what must be immediately incomprehensible in that simple, declarative authoritative sentence, the risk of unsettling him or her, I am determined to take. Because the *in medias res* opening that I am so committed to is here excessively demanding ... ("Unspeakable" 31– 2).

The careful skill with which Morrison explains her choices about these half dozen words and numbers gives readers the sense that her fiction operates as if it were a poem. Word by word, section by section, silence by silence as the juxtaposed parts are moved from an early page to a later, Morrison carefully chooses not only white spaces but each and every digit that interrupts the silences. The author crafts each sentence, each page, because she is dedicated to transmitting both an African American language and an African American culture. She is intent on creating what she calls "the serious study of art forms that have much work to do, ... already legitimized by their own cultural sources and predecessors" ("Unspeakable" 33).

Throughout the African images and symbols that pepper the novel (from the bisected circle that brands Sethe's mother's body to the various "antelope" designations, as well as Sethe's name itself read as Seth/ Set representing Egyptian art gods), Morrison maintains her focus on the female. When Denver creates a solitude for herself in the "emerald hide-away" near 124 (experiencing her developing sexuality in that isolation), Morrison underscores the woman who can stand alone: this is not only a paean to nature. Similarly, the narrative line of *Beloved* – which grows from countless interactions between Sethe and Paul

D – shows Morrison's intention to describe trauma as *different* in the two characters. The characterization of Sethe as a vessel of the trauma of having killed her child differs radically from Paul D's trauma of himself as he escapes death; admittedly, his memories are frequently bloodstained, but for Sethe's indelibly inscribed memory Morrison creates the coined word *rememory*. As alive as it had been 20 years earlier, *rememory* in this novel signals the convoluted, erased, re-membered, and finally reclaimed story that so wraps Sethe in its shroud that she cannot even think of living a normal life. As Justine Tally notes, quoting from Shoshana Felman and Dori Laub, "so-called 'traumatic memory' is not, in fact, 'memory' as we normally understand it, but the actual reenactment of the original trauma" (Tally, *Beloved* 48).

For Brogan, too, as she studies the psychological phenomenon of "haunting," Sethe's state of mind shows the marks of irreparable damage. Even without titling the novel *Sethe*, Morrison makes clear that her interest in guilt and pain is centered on the mother rather than on the victimized child. For Sethe, her flight into amnesia is the telltale move, and once the figure of Beloved appears, the existence of actual or remembered history undergoes "a disastrous alternative" and may leave the traumatized mind "highly vulnerable to revictimization" (Brogan 71). Morrison makes abundantly clear that Sethe cannot ever forget her killing of her older daughter.

For critic Gurleen Grewal, Sethe's condition as Morrison presents it shows the African belief that "the dead ... not finished with the living because the past (the dead), present (the living), and future (the unknown) are coexistent ... Such a world view posits a fluidity and continuity between the past and the present" (Grewal 106). Grewal also states hopefully that Paul D and Sethe, as survivors of Sweet Home, will eventually communicate: "The narrative represents fragmented bodies, psyches, stories and memories gradually become whole through telling ... The circular movement of the narrative both repeats and makes whole" (Grewal 104). Late in 2013, however, as novelist Junot Diaz questioned Morrison about the intentionality of her choices in writing *Beloved*, she explained to him that Paul D does *not* understand the horror of Sethe's undergoing the mammary rape by schoolteacher's nephews: it is clear that Paul D cannot move past the fact that, in his words, "They used cowhide on you?" Because Sethe sees that he thinks her being beaten is a greater crime than having her milk taken by force, she answers him with "They took my milk." But when Paul D repeats his question about the cowhide, she refuses to hear his – to her – irrelevant question. Even though she repeats the real indignity to him, Paul D does not comprehend what her words tell him. It is in this interview, too, that Morrison says, somewhat disdainfully, that *Halle* does not survive what she calls Sethe's *milking*. In contrast to Halle's breakdown, Sethe takes control of all aspects of her life; in Morrison's words, "But *she* does" (Live from NY Public Library). As critic Jan Furman had noted years earlier, "Morrison's implicit contrast of Sethe and Paul D is not a faultfinding mission against Paul D or against men in general … She uses Paul D in much the same way she does the community: to set Sethe's extraordinary strength in relief" (Furman 76).

It was Furman early on who explained that Morrison had never capitalized the name "schoolteacher," in order to "reflect the scholarly way in which racism was pursued in theology and in biology in the Darwinian theory of evolution" (Furman 70). In a recent essay, Morrison describes her hatred of what she calls "ideological whiteness. I hate when people come into my presence and become white." She uses this illustration to show the ways people attempt to disclaim their race. "I had just been elected to the American Academy of Arts and Letters and a man whom I used to read in anthologies came up to me and said, 'Hello, welcome to the Academy.' Then his third sentence was about his splendid black housekeeper. This little code saying 'I like black people or I know one" is humiliating for me – and should have been for him" (Lanker 36).

Again and again, Morrison must answer critics and readers about the characterization of Sethe, and about the infanticide. The conundrum lay, as Furman and other critics had noted, in the fact that Morrison had rendered "Sethe, then, almost completely, as mother … a woman whose love for her children has absolutely no limits" (Furman 70). The novel is studded with Sethe's comments to that effect; one of the key scenes between Paul D and Sethe has her explaining to him, "I was big, Paul D, and deep and wide and when I stretched out my arms all my children could get in between … there wasn't nobody in the world I couldn't love if I wanted to" (*Beloved* 162).

Repeatedly, Sethe is the mother supreme. But many of the questions Morrison fielded had to do with Beloved. Here she described her intentions, speaking about what she calls "the levels on which I wanted Beloved to function."

> She is a spirit on one hand, literally she is what Sethe thinks she is, her child returned to her from the dead. And she must function like that in the text. She is also another kind of dead which is not spiritual but flesh, which is, a survivor from the true, factual slave ship. She speaks the language, a traumatized language, of her own experience, which blends beautifully in her questions and answers her preoccupations ... with the desires of Denver and Sethe. So when they say "What was it like over there?" they may mean – they do mean – "What was it like being dead?" She tells them what it was like being where she was on that ship as a child. Both things are possible, and there's evidence in the text so that both things could be approached, because the language of both experiences – death and the Middle Passage – is the same. Her yearning would be the same, the love and yearning for the face that was going to smile at her. (Con I, 247)

Part of the stylistic experimentation that Morrison creates for the prose-poem segments that come toward the end of the novel helps to blur the speakers' identities as well as their historical contexts.

In a larger sense, Morrison focuses on the roles mothers play, adding,

> This story [*Beloved*] is about, among other things, the tension between being yourself, one's own Beloved, and being a mother. The next story [*Jazz*] has to do with the tension between being one's own Beloved and the love. One of the nicest things women do is nurture other people, but it can be done in such a way that we surrender anything like a self. You can surrender yourself to a man and think that you cannot live or be without that man; you have no existence. And you can do the same thing with children. (Con I, 254)

When the conditions of slavery and slave lives were added in to these homiletic ideas, Morrison herself realized how bleak the fiction might become. She was of necessity focusing on "generation after generation ... [of the] expendable. True, they had the status of good horses, and nobody wanted to kill their stock. And, of course, they had the advantage of reproducing without cost" (Con I, 258). But finally, as Morrison admitted, "Nobody will want to read this: the characters don't want to remember, I don't want to remember, black people don't want to remember, white people don't want to reminder. I mean, it's national amnesia" (Con I, 259).

Morrison in another interview points out that Beloved's being pregnant by Paul D means that "she is real, [that] ghosts or spirits are real ... one purpose of making her real is making history possible, making memory real ... it was not at all a violation of African religion and philosophy; it's very easy for a son or parent or neighbor to appear in a child or in another person" (Con I, 249).

She also glosses the fact that Sethe had continued to live for those 18 isolated and isolating years as personified strength, toughness:

> One of the things that's important to me is the powerful imaginative way in which we deconstructed and reconstructed reality in order to get through. The act of will, of going to work every day – something is going on in the mind and the spirit that is not at all the mind or the spirit of a robotized or automaton people. Whether it is color for Baby Suggs, the changing of his name for Stamp Paid, each character has a set of things their imagination works rather constantly at, and it's very individualistic ... an interior life of people that have been reduced to some great lump called slaves. (Con I, 253)

Critic Michael Hogan points out that 124 (which might well be known as "the house of Sethe") is "both safe house and slaughter house," and should serve as a tribute to the brave mother. It is also as filled with tragedy as any Greek edifice. As Morrison draws her, in this critic's eyes, Sethe comes to represent the "heroic struggle between the claims of community and individual hubris" (Hogan 128–9). Teresa Washington reminds readers that – in that all-important face-off with the community 18 years before – both Baby Suggs and Sethe trespass on the law of Aje, "one must not display wealth" (Washington 233). For Bernard W. Bell, Paul D represents both that community and a striving male character: "The arrival, departure, and return of Paul D ... provide the frame story for Sethe's realization of personal wholeness in the community" (Bell, *Bearing* 238). Tina

Groover makes the community the primary antagonist for Sethe's continuing life: "Rather than judging Sethe's action, Morrison judges the community that condemns and shuns Sethe for the next eighteen years" (Groover 105). As the novel draws to its climactic ending, with Sethe resting in the small space of Baby Suggs' bed while Beloved grows larger and larger – pregnant, explosively fat, succubus-like filled with matter that had once belonged to Sethe, Denver has of necessity conquered her fears of people and reached out to that hostile community. She has found food; later she finds work, and a sense of her own self-identity. It is through the story of *Denver's* actualization that Morrison has written her mother's story (Ramah Willis Wofford becomes the center for *Beloved* just as George Wofford centered *Song of Solomon*).

Seemingly unnecessary pieces of Sethe's story shape the last few pages of the book. The character of Sethe has been in no way fulfilled by her reunion with the ghostly Beloved. She is anguished, wrung out, leaning on the desperate quiet of the release of death. Accordingly, Morrison begins the last segment of the novel with the repetition of "124": "124 was quiet" (*Beloved* 281). The quiet does not reinscribe the earlier beauty of the three women – Sethe, Denver, Beloved – trying to ice skate on their shoddy equipment, or trying to exist alone and unattended as the weeks pass. Morrison has, finally, used those peaceful scenes ironically. Here the quiet is that of desperation, of approaching death, and what appears to be Sethe's last valiant act – to quell the men/man arriving to take away her children – only a representation of her madness. But that act occurs in what Roynon calls

a gothic but effective exorcism. The women gather "at three in the afternoon on a Friday," a time recalling the crucifixion of Christ. As they pray and, most importantly, sing, there is a sudden transition from past to present. Sethe rushes with the ice pick at the unsuspecting Mr. Bodwin because, in a flashback to the hummingbird-beak moment of the infanticide, she believes that he has come to do harm either to her children or to her. At this moment the naked, hugely pregnant, vine-haired Beloved senses Sethe and Denver's disappearing from her view, while in the eyes of the others, it is she who disappears from the porch. (Roynon 54)

To Roynon's capable analysis Justine Tally adds not only Egyptian and classic lore, but numerology. She notes, for instance, that Morrison's use of the 3, a sacred number, often pairs with the 7 (1 and 2 and 4 gives 7, as there are seven letters in the words *slavery* and *Beloved*, and small facts such as Baby Suggs' losing seven children before Halle, Denver's starting school at seven, seven on-lookers when the sheriff finds Sethe, Paul D's walking for seven years). Tally also adds a gloss to the number 28 by noting that the present action of *Beloved* occurs in 1873 and that 18 and 7 and 3 are 28. (Tally, *Beloved* 77–83).

Morrison's *Beloved* is likely to give critics that read the novel from highly specialized or otherwise intricate perspectives information adequate to publish many extended critical writings. What remains for readers of the novel itself is the author's own deft presentation of a mother, a grandmother, children, and a spirit world that attempts to bring together wrong-doers as well as beneficence. Morrison creates a final scene that returns the reader to the maternal world of women who love. As the 30 neighbor women come to 124, Morrison states,

> the first thing they saw was not Denver sitting on the steps, but themselves. Younger, stronger, even as little girls lying in the grass asleep. Catfish was popping grease in the pan and they saw themselves scoop German potato salad onto the plate. Cobbler oozing purple syrup colored their teeth. They sat on the porch, ran down to the creek .... Baby Suggs laughed and skipped among them, urging more. Mothers, dead now, moved their shoulders to mouth harps. (*Beloved* 258)

The novel needed nothing more: a tapestry of girls and women, varied in tastes and sizes and roles, here focused on "mother and child, where the child was the identity of the mother" but as well, beneath the ostensible story, a narrative aimed to "make some sense out of personal and interpersonal relationships, the effort to discover how we do what we were born for, which is, to know and to love" (Bigsby 286–7).

4
Jazz and Morrison's Trilogy: New York in the 1920s

James Baldwin's death in 1987, the year *Beloved* was published, made the African American literary community more sensitive than usual to the fact that very few African American writers – poets, novelists, dramatists, critics – ever won the truly prestigious prizes of the academic world. Accordingly, when *Beloved* was nominated for the National Book Award, but then lost out to Larry Heinemann's *Paco's Story*, readers who knew the Morrison novel were incensed. Other novels nominated for that prize seemed to be non-contenders – Alice McDermott's *That Night*, Philip Roth's *The Counterlife*, and Howard Norman's *The Northern Lights*. Led by poet June Jordan and critic Houston A. Baker, Jr., nearly 50 African American writers signed an extensive letter of protest which appeared in the *New York Times*. It was an unusual mark of unified support for both *Beloved* and for Morrison.

Although Morrison had never won an award as consequential as the National Book Award, she had appeared on the cover of *Newsweek* magazine when *Tar Baby* was published. *Song of Solomon* had been a Book-of-the-Month Club selection, and had won several prizes, among them the National Book Critics' Circle Award, the American Academy Award, the Institute of Arts and Letters Award, the Cleveland Arts Prize, and the Oscar Michaeux Award; before that time, *Sula* had won the Ohioana Award and had been similarly nominated for the National Book Award. It was on the basis of book sales of *Song of Solomon* and *Tar Baby* that Morrison felt financially able to give up her Random House job. According to Junot Diaz, in his December 2013 interview with Morrison, had she still been working in New York publishing, she would not have been able to undergo what became her flawless immersion in her slave mother's story. (Morrison does not specifically concur with Diaz but she does explain that she had first cut back her hours in New York, and then realized she would have to end that work. She also said that concentrating on the novel usurped much of her energy; Live, NY Public Library.)

After *Song of Solomon* had received such a strong reception, Morrison served on the National Council on the Arts – appointed by President Jimmy Carter. In 1981 she was elected to the American Academy and Institute of Arts and Letters, and in 1984 she accepted an endowed chair as the Albert Schweitzer Professor of the Humanities at the State University of New York at Albany. She also was a visiting lecturer at Bard College, at Bowdoin College, and at the University of California at Berkeley.

Once *Beloved* had appeared, she was honored with the National Organization for Women's Elizabeth Cady Stanton Award, as well as the Modern Language Association's Commonwealth Award in Literature. In 1988 *Beloved* won the Pulitzer Prize for Fiction. Recently, Morrison has written about receiving that prize, particularly after the letter which appeared in the *New York Times*. "When the Pulitzer was awarded, the response in many quarters – white, black, male, female, young and old – was 'we.' 'We did it!' It had a sense of hallelujah about it. But it's foolish to surrender to that because it interferes with work. I'd begin to think of myself in my sleep as Toni Morrison comma Pulitzer Prize, and never get anything done" (Lanker 36).

Morrison then presented the Tanner lecture at the University of Michigan and followed that with the three William E. Massey, Sr. lectures at Harvard University (these became the basis for her 1992 book, *Playing in the Dark: Whiteness and the Literary Imagination*). From 1989 through 2006, Morrison held the Robert E. Goheen Chair of Humanities at Princeton University.

The reader must keep in mind the fact that this is only a partial list of the exploding bevy of honors that overtook Morrison in her ongoing life and work: fueled by the unexpected support in 1987 from her African American colleagues, support that helped the whole readerly world acknowledge the superior achievement of the difficult *Beloved*, Morrison again resumed writing the principal parts of the trilogy of novels that she had come to consider her essential life work.

Readers easily accepted the ostensible setting and timing of *Jazz*, published in 1992. True to the premise that Morrison enjoyed working in African American history, bringing new information and understanding into play, her focus on the story of Violet and Joe Trace (both poor, both Southerners) was in part on the migration of Southern blacks to Northern, urban areas. As she had explored slavery in *Beloved*, Morrison was poised to explore the Northern migration in *Jazz*. As she had written about mother-love in *Beloved*, she saw *Jazz* as having "to do with the tension between being one's own Beloved and the love" (Con I, 254). She gives a fuller explanation of her purposes in fiction several years later, in her essay titled "Home."

> In writing novels the adventure for me has been explorations of seemingly impenetrable, race-inflected, race-clotted topics. In the first book I was interested in racism as a cause, consequence, and manifestation of individual and social psychosis. In the second [*Sula*] I was preoccupied with the culture of gender and the invention of identity, both of which acquired astonishing meaning when placed in a racial context. In *Song of Solomon* and *Tar Baby* I was interested in the impact of race on the romance of community and individuality. In *Beloved* I wanted to explore the revelatory possibilities of historical narration when the body–mind, subject–object, past–present oppositions, viewed through the lens of race, collapse. In *Jazz* I tried to locate American modernity as a response to the race house. It was an attempt to blow up its all-encompassing shelter, its all-knowingness, and its assumptions of control ... In *Jazz* the dynamite fuse to be lit was under the narrative voice – the voice that could begin with claims of knowledge, inside knowledge, and indisputable authority ("I know that woman ...") and end with the blissful epiphany of its vulnerable humanity and its own needs. ("Home" 9)

(In later sections of this essay, Morrison creates bridges between the 1992 novel *Jazz* and the third book of the trilogy, *Paradise*, which would not appear until 1998.) For her readers in 1992, the chief conduit to their successful reading of *Jazz* was its relationship to the highly visible *Beloved*.

In contrast to *Beloved*, *Jazz* is a much more complicated narrative. For Morrison to allow herself to move even further into the convolutions that had disturbed some readers about the process of their accurately comprehending Sethe, Denver, Paul D, Baby Suggs, and Beloved may have seemed an ill-chosen gamble. Morrison often repeated the story that she was mesmerized by the photograph of a dead black girl, taken by James Van Der Zee, the famous Harlem photographer (he recounts the girl's lying down and saying nothing about who had shot her – telling her friends she would tell them later. He adds, "For the picture, I placed flowers on her chest"). Linking the story of *Beloved*, set in slavery, with the modernist urban story that *Jazz* represents, Morrison asked her readers to think of more than literal connections. She said in the Gloria Naylor interview that she wanted to use Beloved "as a filter [and] extend her life, you know, her search, her quest all the way through as long as I care to go, into the twenties where it switches to that other girl ... But Beloved will be there also" (Con I, 208).

She had stated in "Home" that the choice of narrator for *Jazz* was one of the book's intriguing problems. Why give readers this mysterious narrator (or narrators)? Why refuse reasonable or predictable behavior for such seemingly normal characters as Violet and Joe? Why interlard present-day happenings with detailed histories from childhoods experienced decades earlier, or histories of characters not previously included in the story? More specifically, why does the transgendered figure of Golden Gray take over the narrative that should by all rights belong to Joe Trace? Does titling the novel "jazz" – a word that appears nowhere else within the book's pages – give Morrison some esoteric right to digress, and repeat, and then repeat with variations, and then create a narrative bridge that appears to lead nowhere, and then digress again, in this profound and apparently unsettled account of a restless man's infidelity?

If readers of *Beloved* liked to pretend that Morrison's 1987 novel was not a dramatically sentimental rendering of motherhood during slavery, but was instead a story that created for readers the same kind of moral interrogation that Dostoyevsky's *Crime and Punishment* evoked, that was their choice. Admittedly, taking a life is serious moral business.

Similarly, Joe Trace in *Jazz* (somewhat inexplicably) also takes a life. The morality of his act in *Jazz*, however, does not seem to have any relationship to the anguished morality or immorality of Sethe's act in *Beloved*. Whereas Sethe believes earnestly and without quali-fication that her children will "live" if they have died (rather than being returned to slavery), Morrison does not give the reader much insight into why Joe Trace feels compelled to kill Dorcas (and, in another conundrum, why Dorcas keeps his identity as killer secret). What Morrison attempts to probe in the comparatively brief *Jazz* is a range of motivations for an equally wide range of characters. She is attending to the historically based issue of the Northern migration, when African Americans from Southern states traveled north, lured by better opportunities and higher wages in railroads, slaughter-houses, factories, and sales, at least in comparison to their working poor farms. Advertising and news items in *The Chicago Defender* led to the black population of Chicago being quadrupled between 1916 to 1920; labor agents from the North were also sent south to recruit workers.

More vividly portrayed in *Jazz* is the allure of urban life: the busy-ness of the city, the fact of entertainment and of music itself, the physical satisfaction of dancing, which paralleled the satisfaction of the body, the appearance, the sexual. "A city like this one makes me dream tall and feel in on things. Hep. It's the bright steel rocking above the shade below that does it. When I look over strips of green grass lining the river, at church steeples and into the cream-and-copper halls of apartment buildings, I'm strong" (*Jazz* 7). The visual fuses with the aural: "clarinets and lovemaking, fists and the voices of sorrowful women." African Americans arriving in a city such as New York or Chicago were conscious of themselves as *people of value*: when Joe Trace and Violet train-danced into New York, they saw themselves as important, good-looking enough to *be* New Yorkers. The paltry gray identities and lives that marginal farming had pro-vided gave way to the vivid colors of dark skin, bodies fashionably clothed, the abilities (however compromised) to earn some kind of a living. "Here comes the new. Look out. There goes the sad stuff. The bad stuff. The things-nobody-could-help stuff ... History is over, you all, and everything's ahead at last" (*Jazz* 7).

Being New Yorkers meant walking on paved sidewalks, listening to radios for the sensual and satisfying music of the times, having pets (in Violet's case, her beloved birds), and taking part in the urban energy. Moving to New York, however, in the cases of both Violet and Joe, meant uprootednesss. Leaving behind their families, friends, and ways of life put the Traces in conflict with what Morrison in her 1984 essay had claimed was essential – "Rootedness," a re-naming of "ancient properties." It is a designed riddle – that Joe Trace carries no family name, rather the hurtful memory of his being told that when his mother left abruptly, there was no "trace." Within the riddle, too, lies the word *race*, and even in the environs of other African American people in their strata of New York, the dark-skinned new city dwellers are handicapped. If "knowledge" stems from experience, then the experiences need not be one's own – they might be *narrative* experiences, existing in stories passed down from ancestors, from family, from mystical voices. Just as Joe Trace falls out of the tree he has chosen as "his" sleeping place, so he has been abandoned, cut off from his family tree, his experiential knowing. And Violet, too, after her mother's suicide, has also lost the memories that she shared with her siblings of that woman both alive and dead: where are the lines of knowledge that each person has a right to expect to have? Part of the complicated narration in Morrison's novel *Jazz* stems from her trying to include these lost tendrils of both Violet's and Joe's uprootedness.

As she explained in the "Rootedness" essay,

> when the peasant class, or lower class, or what have you, confronts the middle class, the city, or the upper classes, they are thrown a little bit into disarray. For a long time, the art form that was healing for Black people was music. That music is no longer *exclusively* ours; we don't have exclusive rights to it. Other people sing it and play it; it is the mode of contemporary music everywhere. So another form has to take that place and it seems to me that the novel is needed by African-Americans now in a way that it was not needed before – and it is following along the lines of the function of novels everywhere. We don't live in places where we can hear those stories anymore; parents don't sit around and tell their children those classical, mythological archetypal stories that we heard years ago. But new information has got to get out, and there are several ways to do it. One is in the novel ….
>
> It should be beautiful, and powerful, but it should also *work*. It should have something in it that enlightens; something in it that opens the door and points the way. Something in it that suggests what the conflicts are, what the problems are. But it need

not solve those problems because it is not a case study, it is not a recipe. (Nonfiction 58–9)

Morrison goes on in this essay to discuss what she elsewhere calls the "aural" in her writing. She says here that a text can be read in silence, of course, but one should also be able to hear the words:

> having at my disposal only the letters of the alphabet and some punctuation, I have to provide the places and spaces so that the reader can participate. Because it is the affective and participatory relationship between the artist or the speaker and the audience that is of primary importance, as it is in these other art forms that I have described.
>
> To make the story appear oral, meandering, effortless, spoken – to have the reader *feel* the narrator without *identifying* that narrator, or hearing him or her knock about, and to have the reader work *with* the author in the construction of the book – is what's important. (Nonfiction 59)

As Morrison said in an interview, "The Black mythology has existed in music, gospels, spirituals, jazz …. and in a kind of village lore. The community had to take on that responsibility of passing from one generation to another the mythologies, the given qualities, stories, assumptions which an ethnic group that is culturally coherent and has not joined the larger mainstream keeps very much intact for survival" (Con I, 112). The author sees her role in that process, as author, in this way: "The novel has to provide the richness of the past as well as suggestions of what the use of it is. I try to create a world in which it is comfortable to do both, to listen to the ancestry and to mark out what might be going on sixty or one hundred years from now" (Con I, 113).

A great deal of commentary about *Jazz* has been about the characteristics of African American jazz music. Perhaps more to the point, a recent study by Andrew Scheiber about the blues adds in qualities germane to the literary use of those musical rhythms (whether considered *jazz* or *blues*). Even though Morrison was a bit of a music critic herself, she never split the hairs of definition to the extent that some of her critics have. Gene Bluestein and Robert B. Stepto early on saw African American jazz as the premier music form throughout the United States, moving as it had from New Orleans throughout the country, roughly following the Northern migration of African American people. Both critics suggest parallels with call-and-response patterns. Bluestein, himself a folk singer and archivist, says that Morrison does *not* improvise (contradicting what has been the most common assessment of her prose style in *Jazz*). Noting that jazz never exists as a solo mode, he concentrates on the skill paramount in a jazz ensemble: "[T]he will to achieve the most eloquent expression of idea-emotion through the technical mastery of their instruments ... the give-and-take, the subtle rhythms, shaping and blending of ideas, tone and imagination demanded of group improvisation. The delicate balance struck between individual personality and the group during those early jam sessions was a marvel of social organization" (Bluestein 135–6).

For this critic, another significant quality of jazz is its impression of sexuality (and part of the reason young mainstream listeners were often forbidden from going to jazz places). Bluestein suggests that the music threatens sexual danger – that is, "stereotypes of the Negro as fantastically virile and barbarously effective in his sex life" (Bluestein 119). As this critic's language choices indicate, the foreignness of jazz as a mode added to an impression of "Negro" dangerousness.

When Andrew Scheiber assesses the difference between jazz and the blues, he emphasizes that the latter does not work toward achieving an ending. Rather, the blues serve "as a form of disclosure, through repetition, of the terms of the hero's *Gewarfenbeit* ... The blues narratives suggest a human condition defined as continuing engagement without possibility of a definitive victory" (Scheiber 37). Blues creates a "narrative projection" in a language that captures "an African American poetics." He discusses what he calls "blues narratology" – using repetition, chance, and descant, elements that are usually "related in sequence." Perhaps less intricate than a jazz performance, the blues seems to be tied in with character (Scheiber 35). Scheiber refers to Stepto's early definition of the descant, also termed "the immersion narrative .... a ritualized journey into a symbolic South in which the protagonist forsake[s] highly individualized mobility in the narrative's least oppressive social structure for a pasture of relative stasis in the most oppressive environment, a *loss* that is only occasionally assuaged by the newfound balms of group identity" (Stepto 167).

For Scheiber, descant is not "a moment." Rather, it is "a potentiality within every moment. It can manifest at any time." According to this reading, "one soars by getting down, and the recursive path to the future always involves a transversing of the depths of the past" (Scheiber 43). He relates this personification to Morrison's ancient figure: "The presence of such guide-ancestors ... suggests the aspects of historical memory and cultural preservation entwined in the descent figure; especially in novels that deal with post-slavery black life in the Northern metropolis; the ritualized journey into the South is also a foray into the past" (Scheiber 43). He chooses from the actual language of *Jazz* the narrator's metaphor of life as "an abused record with no choice but to repeat itself at the crack" (*Jazz* 220; Scheiber 39).

In Scheiber's exposition, "Part of the descant is the experience of being taken 'way back' – often to a place one never knew existed or would rather not go – by a guide-elder whose cure for the ills of life is a controlled (or sometimes not so controlled) homeopathic dose of the very things the hero most fears or abjures ...." As he discusses Morrison's novel itself, he uses "the Golden Gray episode" to illustrate the way she "rends the fabric of the modern cityscape to reveal the tangled roots of the Southern past that lies below" (Scheiber 43–4). Less specifically, "What changes, what passes for progression in blues narrative, is the hero's or heroine's increasing ability to play the changes, to enter, negotiate, and even sometimes subvert the recursive patterns of experience that present themselves" (Scheiber 37).

This critic's more generalized commentary (about Ralph Ellison and August Wilson, as well as Morrison) leads him to conclude that using a blues format

> does not represent a rational or a planned world. The appropriate form of mastery in this world is not *predict and plan* but *bob and weave*, and success comes through ... a readiness of response that understands the broken guitar string, the natural disaster, the chance juxtaposition of numbers in a lottery ... the course of events turns for no apparent reason (and often with no apparent preparation) toward encounters with repeated paradigmatic figures or situations. (Scheiber 40–2)

Bernard Bell identifies Morrison's narrator in *Jazz* as "an inner-city, street-smart, transplanted southern narrator in Harlem"; he notes that Morrison, while she does not use the word *jazz*, mentions a "Trombone blues" and several blues lyrics (e.g., 'ain't nobody going to keep me down,' 'you got the right key baby but the wrong keyhole,' 'you got to get it, bring it, and put it right here, or else'). He summarizes, "the theme, characters, and mood of *Jazz* are *bluesy*. And insofar as jazz, like the blues, constructs a traditional melody or harmonic framework as the base for both subtle and strident improvisational flights, either solo or collective, then the structure, and much of the style of [*Jazz*] ... is derived from the jazz tradition" (Bell, *Bearing* 220). Justine Tally puts forth much detail to support her claim that *Jazz* is meant to reflect the music's divisive claims. Because jazz was considered a representation of "low life" and was performed chiefly for white audiences (people looking to scandalize their own friends and families), it was often considered a popular form rather than "true folk art" (Tally, *Story* 67). In contrast, Gurleen Grewal identifies Morrison's use of African American jazz and blues as giving her fiction the indelible stamp of authentic black life: "Morrison takes the novel home to the intimate address of the rural and urban African American tradition from which she came, back to the blues with its longstanding traditions of voicing pain, registering complaint and comfort. The unrelenting lyrical pressure of her prose aims to unsettle as well as to heal" (Grewal 1). Toward the end of this discussion, she notes that, collectively, Morrison's novels often "subvert dominant middle-class ideology" (5).

When Morrison discusses the significance of African American music in relation to this novel, she is less specific about form. In the "Foreword," added more than a decade after the original publication of *Jazz*, she noted, "I was interested in rendering a period in African American life through a specific lens – one that would reflect the content and characteristics of its music (romance, freedom of choice, doom, seduction, anger) and the manner of its expression. I had decided on the period, the narrative line, and the place long ago ..." ("Foreword" xv). Recognizing that *Jazz* was itself a different kind of fiction, she continued, "I had written novels in which structure was designed to enhance meaning; *here* the structure would *equal* meaning. The challenge was to expose and bury the artifice and to take practice beyond the rules. I didn't want simply a musical background, or decorative references to it. I wanted the work to be a manifestation of the music's intellect, sensuality, anarchy; its history, its range, and its modernity" (xix). In a later interview, she continued, "I was always conscious of the constructed aspect of the writing process, and that art appears natural and elegant only as a result of constant practice and awareness of its formal structures .... I was very conscious in writing *Jazz* of trying to blend that which is contrived and artificial with improvisation" (Con II, 81–2).

As early as her first interviews, Morrison had explained:

> Classical music satisfies and closes. Black music does not do that. Jazz always keeps you on the edge. There is no final chord. There may be a long chord, but no final chord. And it agitates you. Spirituals agitate you, no matter what they are saying about how it is all going to be. There is something underneath them that is incomplete. There is always something else that you want from the music ... [Jazz comes from European harmonies and African rhythms] ... I want my books to be like that – because I want that feeling of something held in reserve and the sense that there is more ... They will never fully satisfy – never fully. (Con I, 155)

Recently, Justine Baillie joined this conversation by emphasizing that, "for Morrison, the novel must retain the healing function of music and the oral, collective, and oppositional elements expressive of black experience in America. Orality and the tradition of storytelling are transferred into the novel form and this, for Morrison, is an important political act, narrating being, for her, in her Nobel Lecture, 'one of the principal ways in which we absorb knowledge'" (Baillie 3).

Baillie, too, sees the incorporation of different belief systems as Morrison's way of expanding the reach of her fiction. "Through a process of appropriation, mastery, and inversion, Morrison improvises on European and American literary forms and employs them to foreground stories yet untold. She engages closely with romance narrative forms, Greek myths or the Bildungsroman and takes from them what is needed, as 'found objects,' to be reshaped and decoded in order to recover the presence of blackness in the narrative of American nation building" (Baillie 4). From a somewhat different perspective, Jennifer Heinert echoes Baillie's reading:

> In the tradition of the American novel, the relationship between genre and race has been largely determined by the dominant culture. By rejecting and revising conventions, especially to account for race, Morrison rewrites the genres in American literature. By resisting "resolution," Morrison also rewrites the role of "narrative truth"; rather than a political message inherent in the text or an interpretable message dependent on conventions, the "truth" of Morrison's novels is left in the reader's hands. (Heinert 5)

At a deeply embedded point in the novel, too, *Jazz* began to be the narrative of a young couple, Ramah Willis and George Wofford. When Morrison's mother was 20 and her father 19, they were courting. One of the treasured items from the family chest, mentioned here at the close of the novel's "Foreword," was her mother's chic "evening purse, tiny, jeweled with fringe dangled in jet and glass." Nostalgic and redolent with the "Jazz Age,"

> The moment when an African American art form defined, influenced, reflected a nation's culture in so many ways: the bourgeoning of sexual license, a burst of political, economic, and artistic power; the ethical conflicts between the sacred and the secular; the hand of the past being crushed by the present. Primary among these features, however, was invention. Improvisation, originality, change. Rather than be about those characteristics, the novel would seek to become them. ("Foreword" xviii)

As if to question her own abstractions here, Morrison deftly closed that "Foreword" with the recollection of her mother and her mother's voice – an aural image perhaps more striking than the visualization of the fragile evening bag:

> She sang, my mother, the way other people muse. A constant background drift of the beautiful sound I took for granted, like oxygen. "Ave Maria, gratia plena ... I woke up this morning with

an awful aching head / My new man has left me just a room and a bed ... Precious Lord, lead me on ... I'm gonna buy me a pistol, just as long as I am tall ... L'amour est un oiseau rebel ... When the deep purple falls over hazy garden walls ... I've got a disposition and a way of my own / When my man starts kicking I let him find a new home ... Oh, holy night ..." Like the music that came to be known as Jazz, she took from everywhere, knew everything – gospel, classic, blues, hymns – and made it her own. ("Foreword" xix)

Few readers would have ferreted out this acutely personal source, however. *Jazz* begins with the riff of an unnamed speaker: "Sth, I know that woman. She used to live with a flock of birds on Lenox Avenue. Know her husband too" (*Jazz* 3). The voice of the narrator begins with the pre-colloquial, and plunges directly into the story of Violet (to be known as *Violent* from the moment of Dorcas's funeral, when Violet brings a knife along so that she might damage the dead girl's face). What Morrison tells us immediately – about Violet's birds – is a key positive image. As an aging woman, she has become a caring woman: childless biologically, she has assumed the care of the grateful birds. (In African lore, a person such as Violet is linked to "Eleye, Owner of Birds.") Africanist Teresa Washington also glosses the aesthetic of Oro – said to be traditionally African – that shares traits with jazz and blues music: "art forms that are at once *tito*, enduring, lasting, and genuine, and *sisi*, open to revision and reinterpretation and open to welcoming new Oro that reconceive and complement existing art forms" (Washington 273, 277).

The novel, then, so announced, is to be Violet's story (with a secondary nod to her husband – who, in terms of relative space, takes over much of the narrative with his behavior, both past and present). Difficult to claim a reader's attention with Violet's feeding her birds and building an eventual friendship with Dorcas's aunt, Alice Manfred, over their loss of Dorcas, Morrison's *Jazz* builds its evocative structure from long plateaus of calm – moving slowly and idiomatically through simple conversation. The distortions in that calm come chiefly from Joe Trace, but once in a while, Violet disrupts the tenor of the fiction. She does this initially as she tries to cut the dead Dorcas. She does this later that day when she turns out her birds into the winter night – and does not reclaim even the parrot whose mantra has been that he loves her:

> There he sat, outside her window: "He forgot how to fly and just trembled on the sill ... She tried not to look at him as she paced the rooms, but the parrot saw her and squawked a weak 'Love you' through the pane."
>
> All night long Violet watched for Joe to return but no one appeared except for the parrot, "shivering and barely turning his green and blond head." The bird each time told her "Love you."
>
> "'Get away,' she told him. 'Go on off somewhere!'"
> And the second morning he had." (*Jazz* 93)

Violet has never named the parrot, nor has she ever told him that she too loves him, but he is the center of her womanly affections. Her casting off her erstwhile children, once she has discovered Joe's affair with Dorcas – complicated then by his killing her – is Violet's relinquishment of all that is good about her in her primary character as mother.

Morrison creates the plot strand that emphasizes the Violet–Alice friendship through scenes of what she calls "mother-hunger." Morrison describes Violet's yearning: "hunger hit her like a hammer. Knocked her down and out .... Violet was drowning in it, deep-dreaming" (*Jazz* 108–9). She mourns even as she undergoes abortions; she loses consciousness at times; she sleeps with a doll; she eventually tries to steal a baby in a carriage, in plain sight of neighbors. All that happens, however, is that she ages, travels through Harlem to work on her clients' hair, and shows symptoms of her own mother's loss through painful suicide. (She also has difficulty seeing Dorcas as someone other than her own possible daughter.) The trauma that marked characters from Morrison's earlier novels recurs here in Violet.

More effectively, perhaps, that same trauma marks Joe Trace. Surrounding himself with compatible friends – men enjoying their exploits and their indulgences in the citified life of Harlem – Joe is seldom far removed from his anguished memories of his desperate, unsuccessful searches through the Virginia woods for his mother,

Wild. Less compatible with the city than Violet is, Joe had in boy-hood been the prize pupil of Hunter's Hunter. (Linguistically, both Violet and Joe are marked by the unsatisfied *hunger/hunter* miasma of the child's search for parents.) Just as they are *not* parents, so too have they never regularly *known* parents. Early in her writing career, Morrison had explained to Robert Stepto the difficulties of parenting – and of not parenting. Taking her questioner's interest past simple gender categories, Morrison noted, "there's the black woman as parent, not as a mother or father, but as a parent, as a sort of umbrella figure, culture-bearer, in that community with not just *her* children but *all* children" (Con I, 27).

Joe Trace at first seems less damaged than Violet by his having grown up alone, but part of a reader's sense of this man as independ-ent and in control accrues from the fact that Morrison does not introduce him for nearly a hundred pages. Violet, and then Violet and Alice, absorb the reader's attention. Initially, Joe Trace seems to be in the spirited line of Guitar Baines, Sixo, Paul D, even Cholly Breedlove. He is not a man to be pitied. As critic Susan Neal Mayberry states, Morrison in creating Joe "confronts the limitations and celebrates the power of authentic, multifaceted, African American masculinity and welcomes the androgyny and the humanity that establishes the griot." She also reminds the reader of Guitar's admo-nition to Milkman Dead, that any black man's life is no good "unless he can choose what to die for" – and the pivotal choice of Joe Trace's later life has been to love (and then to kill) Dorcas (Mayberry, *Can't I Love* 14).

The reader tries to unearth Joe's story from the assortment of nar-ratives Morrison shapes around him. But for a further understanding of Violet, Morrison creates a lengthy, intimate stream of conscious monologue. Besides identifying this woman with birds and their care, then, Morrison gives the reader Violet's voice in its inchoate despair. In the angry recesses of her mind, stunned as she is by Joe Trace's betrayal, and self-identified herself with the young Dorcas, Violet fuses her anger with her love for Joe:

> Violet is me! The me that hauled hay in Virginia and handled a
> four-mule team in the brace. I have stood in cane fields in the
> middle of the night when the sound of it rustling hid the slither
> of the snakes and I stood still waiting for him and not stirring a

speck in case he was near and I would miss him, and damn the snakes my man was coming for me and who or what was going to keep me from him? Plenty times, plenty times I have carried the welts given me by a two-tone peckerwood because I was late in the field row the next morning. Plenty times, plenty, I chopped twice the wood that was needed into short logs and kindling so as to make sure the crackers had enough and wouldn't go hollering for me when I was bound to meet my Joe Trace don't care what, and do what you will or may he was my Joe Trace. Mine ..." (*Jazz* 96)

Unlike anything in Morrison's earlier fiction, Violet's speech act here becomes a soliloquy. She moves fluidly if tersely from concept to concept, finally tormenting herself with the fact that Joe must have preferred Dorcas' light skin color:

What did she see, young girl like that, barely out of high school, with unbraided hair, lip rouge for the first time and high-heeled shoes? And also what did he? A young me with high-yellow skin instead of black? A young me with long wavy hair instead of short? Or a not me at all. A me he was loving in Virginia because that girl Dorcas wasn't around there anywhere. Was that it? Who was it? Who was he thinking of when he ran in the dark to meet me in the cane field? Somebody golden, like my own golden boy who I never ever saw but who tore up my girlhood as surely as if we'd been the best of lovers? Help me God help me if that was it, because I knew him and loved him better than anybody except True Belle who is the one made me crazy about him in the first place. Is that what happened? Standing in the cane, he was trying to catch a girl he was yet to see, but his heart knew all about, and me, holding on to him but wishing he was the golden boy I never saw either. Which means from the very beginning I was a substitute and so was he. "I got quiet because the things I couldn't say were coming out of my mouth anyhow ..." (*Jazz* 97).

Morrison gives Violet many irrepressible images – Dorcas's hand reaching into the popcorn box or under the table at a bar, brushing up against Joe's thigh "drumming out the rhythm on the inside of his thigh, his thigh, his thigh, thigh, thigh and he bought her underwear with stitching done to look like rosebuds and violets, VIOLETS, don't you know" (*Jazz* 95). The monologue as blues here conveys the pain no woman could pretend.

In the poignance of Violet's assumption that she had (perhaps) been a substitute lover all her life comes an unfamiliar kind of recognition. Had Morrison written such an interior reverie for Sethe, readers would have had fewer questions about *Beloved*. It is the fulcrum of Violet's amazing speech that pushes the narrative to its concluding scenes of reconciliation.

In Morrison's "Foreword" to *Love*, a later novel, she notes, "People tell me that I am always writing about love. Always, always love. I nod, yes, but it isn't true – not exactly. In fact, I am always writing about betrayal. Love is the weather. Betrayal is the lightning that cleaves and reveals it" ("Foreword" ix). In her "Foreword" to *Jazz* she further qualifies that interest in emotional rapport: "Following *Beloved*'s focus on mother-love, I intended to examine couple love – the reconfiguration of the 'self' in such relationships, the negotiation between individuality and commitment to another." She concludes this essay by pointing specifically to *Jazz*: "Romantic love seemed to me one of the fingerprints of the twenties, and jazz its engine" ("Foreword" xviii).

With a digressive and strangely truncated prose in hand, Morrison loops what might have been a Joe Trace narrative (something on the order of Milkman Dead's trek south) into a multi-layered set of romances, affairs of the heart that wrench all color from the participants. Just as some critics have speculated that Joe Trace, son of Wild, is really Joe, son of Paul D and Beloved (and that Wild is the Beloved character after she has run away from 124 Bluestone Road), others have settled for Joe as the lost black searcher – victim of his mother's abandonment (Tally, *Beloved* 2–3). But Morrison brings Wild more prominently into the plot, along with the cumbersome and not quite steady saga of Golden Gray – child of the elite white Vera Louise Gray – whose support is the servant True Belle, Violet's grandmother – and Hunter's Hunter, Henry "Lestory or LesTroy or something like that, but who cares what the nigger's name is" (*Jazz* 148).

It is Golden Gray, helping to rescue Wild, who literally delivers Joe Trace into the world. And it becomes Hunter's Hunter, training both Joe and his foster brother Victory in his own hunting skills – and the ways of the world, who seems to be a pivot for the countryside's accumulated knowledge. (Hunter's Hunter may also be half-brother to his love, Vera Louise Gray.) One of the few critics to unravel these elements of Morrison's *Jazz*, Michael Nowlin begins with the epigraph from *The Nag Hammadi*, "The Thunder: Perfect Mind." He links Wild as a primal goddess into this patterning, and emphasizes the powerful set of images that lead to Golden Gray's understanding that he has a black father – the missing arm, an appendage he mourns but finds less than essential. As he becomes the black son, Golden Gray takes on feminine traits for himself, which Morrison signals by having him wear clothing that belongs to Wild.

Jazz, like *Beloved*, has not been divided into chapters. The segments of prose lie juxtaposed to one another, color blocks laid into a quilt-like arrangement, and – as in *Beloved* – the reader faces reorientation with every new segment. In the midst of the separate elements of story that Morrison creates runs the still-unidentified voice of the observing narrator. As if these various storytelling agents have not proved effective, Morrison creates an entirely new voice, that of Dorcas's girlfriend, Felice. In a strange symmetry (both Dorcas and Felice are near-orphans), Felice becomes a third person in the Joe Trace–Violet Trace coupling. It is Felice who carries the narrative weight of the ending of the novel. It is also Felice who shares with a somewhat recovered Joe the last words she had heard Dorcas say. Lying quietly in the bedroom, keeping Joe's identity secret from her friends and her new lover, Dorcas has asked Felice to tell him, "'There's only one apple.' Sounded like 'apple.' 'Just one. Tell Joe'" (*Jazz* 213). The Edenic imagery, complete with its apples and snakes, comes to a positive stasis, and Violet (who finds herself in the process of becoming a woman her mother would have enjoyed knowing), Joe, and Felice are comfortable dancing together in the Trace living room.

Sleeping together again, Joe and Violet find immense physical comfort in the "nice wool blanket with a satin hem. Powder blue, maybe." A literal blues relic transformed into acceptance as the old is reinvented once again, Morrison gives Violet a new bird to care for, and she creates a concluding image for her and Joe – exhausted after his three days of searching for Dorcas as if she were Wild, using his hunting skills to erase the girl's presence from all these Harlem lives. Joe sees "darkness taking the shape of a shoulder with a thin line of blood. Slowly, slowly it forms itself into a bird with a blade of red on the wing. Meanwhile Violet rests her hand on his chest as though it were the sunlit rim of a well and down there somebody is gathering gifts ..." (*Jazz* 224–5). The primacy of the bird as emblematic of expressed love, the death line of seeping blood, the sunlight above the depths of the dark well where Violet's mother has died – "love" as a composition of all these fragments of emotion finds an almost mystical peace within these closing scenes.

In the spring "sweetheart weather" that New York brings to the characters, Felice has one of the final monologues – and in it she forgives her own mother for stealing the silver ring, and being the absent mother. But then the unknown narrator takes over, a speaker who says wise things about lovers' talk under covers, about "When I see them now they are not sepia, still, losing their edges to the light of a future afternoon," returning Joe and Violet Trace to the annals of sharp-edged photographs, letting their story continue writing itself.

In "Home," Morrison's 1997 essay, she backs up to quote from the now-placid narrator's voice here at the close of *Jazz*. Without any signal to the reader, the narrator speaks, "I want to be in a place already made for me, both snug and wide open. With a doorway never needing to be closed, a view slanted for light and bright autumn leaves but not rain. Where moonlight can be counted on if the sky is clear and stars no matter what. And below, just yonder, a river called Treason to rely on" (*Jazz* 221).

In the case of what Morrison achieved in *Beloved*, drawing largely on "history" that was shared with thousands of other people, readers, slaves, survivors, her attempt and her accomplishment in *Jazz* was somewhat more limited. There is much more personal family history, and one assumes more of Morrison's own history, in this novel of the 1920s – and following. The piecing together of both spoken and sung stories, the seemingly effortless collection of narratives that share and shed their intrinsic meaning with every reader, show a keen effort on Morrison's part to bring real emotions and lived lives into a tapestry that is only partly historical.

5
Morrison as Public Intellectual

Morrison's ability to immerse herself in the writing of intricate fiction – a talent which had become more visible with the completion of both *Beloved* in 1987 and *Jazz* in 1992 – was even more remarkable as her life grew full to the brim with an amazing range of cultural and political interests. Had she been able to do nothing but write, her quality of dwelling in the fiction, of becoming one with the characters and the places of the novel, might seem a natural consequence of her thorough preparation for each work – a preparation that was emotional as well as factual.

Morrison's life, however, had become nearly kaleidoscopic. Even though she liked to rise early and take her coffee along as she began writing, welcoming the sunrise was far from mind-clearing if that mind could not be fooled: there was a class to be taught within a few hours. Or an interview to be given in her Random House or her Princeton office. Or a trip to the airport so that she would arrive in France the day before she had agreed to speak for an international literary meeting. If anyone had warned Morrison that such accolades make terrible inroads on a person's writing time, she might not have believed them. (She might also have turned down more invitations than she accepted.) This painful separation from her work seemed to be a steadily growing accouterment, now looming so large that she wondered *when* she could finish another major piece of writing.

Many of her friends and colleagues remembered her important essays for the *New York Times*, dating from the early 1970s, and suggested that she could play a similar role here in the late 1980s and

early 1990s. It was obvious that the supposed "gains" in issues of
race and gender made 20 years earlier were eroding, and that few
people from the mainstream culture understood the continuous (if
changing) problems that faced African Americans. Morrison had frequently written about the frustration of being a black person in the
United States: her extensive work in compiling *The Black Book* made
her a pioneer of social consciousness, and the subsequent essays she
wrote about producing that book added to its historical importance.
In 1985 she had written about being an African American woman
("A Knowing So Deep" opened, "I think about us, black women, a
lot. How many of us are battered and how many are champions";
Nonfiction 31). There she lamented the existence of what she termed
"a gender/racial war" that needed to stop battling and instead
put forth answers about "the distribution of money, the manage-
ment of resources, the way families are nurtured, the way work is
accomplished and valued, the penetration of the network that connects these parts." Moving beyond the aesthetic considerations she
frequently brought into her essays and interviews, here Morrison
demands that women of color pay attention to their resources in the
real, and immensely varied, world.

In 1992 appeared the first book that reflected Toni Morrison's interest in speaking broadly about the world's circumstances. Compiled
and edited by Morrison, *Race-ing Justice, En-gendering Power: Essays
on Anita Hill, Clarence Thomas, and the Construction of Social Reality*
consisted of previously unpublished essays, many of them written
by Morrison's Princeton colleagues such as Nell Irvin Painter, Claudia
Brodsky Lacour, Cornel West, and others. The book also included
essays by Christine Stansell, Nellie Y. McKay, Patricia J. Williams,
Wahneema Lubiano, Homi K. Bhabha, Andrew Ross, Margaret A.
Burnham, Kendell Thomas, Kimberle Crenshaw, Manning Marable,
Gayle Pemberton, Paula Giddings, Michael Thelwell, and Carol M.
Swain, alongside the long introductory essay by Morrison.

Published by Pantheon (as was the second book in this series), the
title as designed for the jacket emphasized the words *Race*, *Justice*,
Gender, and *Power*. Morrison stressed in the introduction that her
collection was to establish "new conversations in which issues and
arguments are taken as seriously as they are. Only through thought-
ful, incisive, and far-ranging dialogue will all of us be able to appraise
and benefit from [such an exchange of views]" (Introduction xxx).

As her friend Paul Gilroy had earlier written, "Morrison's work is continually focused by a concern with how blacks, living amidst the stresses of racial terror, can first acquire and then maintain emotional and sexual intimacy with each other" (Gilroy 176). There need be no mandate that Morrison could write effective fiction; her opinions about real-world life, however, often had no predictable venue. The stroke of real brilliance as she assembled this book was her using A. Leon Higginbotham, Jr.'s "An Open Letter to Justice Clarence Thomas from a Federal Judicial Colleague" to open the book. Sent to Thomas in November 1991, and then published in the *Law Review* at the University of Pennsylvania (vol. 140, 1992), Higginbotham congratulated Thomas and also warned him – the Supreme Court seat he was taking had been held for decades by Thurgood Marshall, a great African American court justice. Higginbotham includes a listing titled "Measures of Greatness or Failure of Supreme Court Justices" as he reminds Thomas of the history, that this appointment "is the culmination of years of heartbreaking work by thousands who preceded you … you have *no* right to forget that history."

After Clarence Thomas had been nominated for this vacancy, the process had become complicated because Anita Hill, a young lawyer who worked for Thomas, had charged him with sexual opportunism. Therefore, the title of Morrison's collection included both the names *Anita Hill* and *Clarence Thomas*. Gender issues, among them sexual impropriety – with both parties securely placed within the African American community – had turned the announced appointment into a media carnival. Morrison speaks obliquely in her introduction about relative power, raced power, by using as title and reference "Friday on the Potomac." The charges from Anita Hill had appeared on a Friday, but Morrison's real metaphor links Thomas's nomination with the subservient position held by the "Friday" who served Robinson Crusoe. Almost too far-reaching in its application, Morrison's essay said bluntly that the charges by Hill and the subsequent countercharges by Thomas were of interest to news media only because both people were African American. As critic Jan Furman assessed, the media created "two black stereotypes with which the country is familiar, even comfortable: the sexually aggressive black male and sexually easy black female" (Furman 111). By using these stereotypes, judgments about both the appointment and the controversy were questioned.

Morrison's focus is on "Friday," October 11, 1991, when Thomas defended himself from Hill's charges. Her essay opens with statements from both speakers as the first and second epigraphs to the essay. The third epigraph is from *Robinson Crusoe*, evoking the scene of Friday's putting Crusoe's foot on his head, making the sign "of subjugation, servitude, and submission ... to let me know that he would serve me as long as he lived" (Introduction vii). Forcing the elements of the court hearing into a space that derives from the fawning icon of black service – our man Friday – Morrison signals that this collection comprises a cultural commentary.

She explains her title by saying that both Clarence Thomas and Friday were black. They were so far outside their cultures that they had no power at all. Neither man, says Morrison, will ever "utter a single sentence understood to be beneficial to their original culture" (Introduction xxviii). (She will make essentially this same statement in describing O. J. Simpson in her second essay collection.)

When Morrison writes about the range of different viewpoints about both Thomas's hearing and Hill's accusations, she comments first on the uniform intensity of the varied opinions – "The points of the vector were all the plateaus of power and powerlessness: white men, black men, black women, white women, interracial couples ..." (Introduction ix). Knowing full well that only privileged views found space in the media, Morrison attempted in this book to give voice to different speakers. (As she had written in "The Site of Memory," any person who is black, or who belongs to any marginalized category ... [these] were seldom invited to participate in the discourse even when we were its topic" Nonfiction 111). She repeated in her introduction that, hopefully, the collection would draw attention to "the consequences of denial or distortion:" "what is at stake during these hearings is history itself" (Introduction x).

Morrison had carefully pointed out that the contretemps between Hill and Thomas showed the way that race and gender routinely provide categories on which the nation can displace its problems. She continued, "As in virtually all of this nation's great debates, non-whites and women figure powerfully, although their presence may be disguised, denied, or obliterated." One should not be surprised that "serious issues of male prerogative and sexual assault, the issues of racial justice and racial redress, the problematics of governing and controlling women's bodies, the alternations of work space into (sexually) domesticated space" occur. "That these issues should be worked out, on, and inscribed upon the canvas/flesh of black people should come as no surprise to anyone" (Introduction xix–xx). Historian Nell Irvin Painter notes in the conclusion to her essay that "More, finally, is at stake here than winning a competition between black men and black women for the title of ultimate victim as reckoned in the terms of white racism, as tempting as the scenario of black-versus-white tends to be. Anita Hill found no shelter in stereotypes of race not merely because they are too potent and too negative to serve her ends" (*Race-ing* 213).

Michael Thelwell approached the controversy anthropologically: "Among the men, politicians and powerful bureaucrats alike there is a syndrome of the phallic mystique of candidacy and power ... In this ambience women become the legitimate spoils of victory and office and, where the woman is malleable enough, sometimes a small change of political favors" (*Race-ing* 119).

Carol M. Swain spoke for a somewhat larger issue: "For African Americans generally, the issue was not so much whether Hill was credible or not; she was dismissed because many saw her as a person who had violated the code of censorship, which mandates that blacks should not criticize, let alone accuse, each other in front of whites" (*Race-ing* 225). Taking attitudes back to the minority perspective – that whenever a person of a minority group has success, his peers must support that position – Swain echoed much of the public news commentary. But for Paula Giddings, regardless of race, the issue remained gender, and she says firmly, "The issues of gender and sexuality have been made so painful to us in our history that we have largely hidden them from ourselves, much less the glaring eye of the television camera. I am convinced that Anita Hill, by introducing the issues in a way that could not be ignored, offered the possibility of a modern discourse on these issues that have tremendous, even lifesaving import for us" (*Race-ing* 442).

Stefanie Mueller thinks Morrison's editing of this collection, and the second to follow in 1997, enhanced her worldwide reputation immensely. She describes the author's political stances as "more open, more decided, as her position becomes more secure and more independent" (Mueller 256). She adds in details about the Thomas–Hill interchange, repeating that Clarence Thomas had referred to

Anita Hill's charges by calling them "a high-tech lynching for uppity Blacks. " In this exploration of the cultural moves necessary to ensure Thomas's approval after his nomination, Mueller points out that Morrison's use of Friday was meant to suggest that when Thomas was introduced to the Senate Judiciary Committee, he was linked with his approachability and his warm laughter. In playing this stereotype – the smiling "darky" – both Thomas and Morrison showed how well they understood their culture (Introduction xiii; Mueller 257).

Critics Jill Matus and Karen Carmean had both, earlier, insisted that Morrison's fiction, too, was often political – that, in Carmean's words, Morrison's "interest in using her novels to 'bear witness' in the process of retrieving and recovering the lost history of black Americans" gave what she wrote a broadly political thrust (Carmean 17). Matus emphasizes that Morrison takes seriously the act of "witnessing" for African American lives and history. "Bearing witness to the past, Morrison's novels can also be seen as ceremonies of proper burial, an opportunity to put painful events of the past in a place where they no longer haunt successive generations ... The experience of Morrison's novels is never simply curative" (some of the past trauma may be shaken loose.) Because Morrison's writing is "attentive to historical specificity," she involves her readers "to see how identities are constructed temporally, relationally and socially" (Matus 2–4).

Assessing Morrison's fiction as well as her essays, and now including *Race-ing Justice*, was a difficult, time-consuming job. Many readers were unaware of this 1992 essay collection: important as it was, definitive in providing new materials for readers, *Race-ing Justice* had only a tenuous impact. Morrison's role was still seen primarily as that of novelist, and even though she would announce clearly that all her opinions came from a fusion of the inward with the external, that "the personal ... is always embedded in the public" ("Home" 12), she was not yet seen to be the kind of cultural spokesperson that Cornel West had become.

Since Morrison had featured the African American barbershop scene in *Song of Solomon*, replete with the men's conversation about the murder of Emmett Till, that element of black history – the mainstream misuse of young black men, the eventual murder of those people – kept surfacing in Morrison's fiction. Finally, in 1985, she wrote a play about Emmett Till. *Dreaming Emmett* represented

Morrison's deepest-held convictions, intensified as she watched her own two sons grow through adolescence and into manhood, that being an African American boy/man in the United States was inherently dangerous. She discussed her observations with Bigsby:

> I always felt that the civil rights movement really began with the murder of Emmett Till, but nobody could rally around him because there were so many buried and unspeakable issues. One was sexual aggression, the other was violence, the other was black manhood, so that they couldn't, or they didn't, organize behind him. But a few years later, when Rosa Parks refused to go to the back of the bus in Montgomery, Alabama, that was a rallying cry. Here was a woman, a servant, who had already done her work and simply wanted to move and sit where it was comfortable for her. It has never been resolved, not in the national psyche and not in fact, but it touched every young black man in the country. That is what the play [*Dreaming Emmett*] was supposed to be about, a young man dreaming of the heroism of Emmett Till. (Bigsby 270)

It is to Bigsby, too, that Morrison gives a hint as to her interest during the mid-1970s in creating the story of Milkman Dead in *Song of Solomon*. As she explained, "they [young black men] had seldom seen themselves treated seriously in an art form. They were there as entertainment, an expression of violence or jokes, but never treated as complex individuals" (Bigsby 270). In Morrison's obvious attention to characters that are young and African American and male, she writes a prolegomenon for black male readers: Son in *Tar Baby* does not fit the mainstream culture's script for macho success; Paul D and Sixo come closer to finding ways to make hard choices in *Beloved*; Joe Trace in *Jazz* is not unredeemed. But it is in *Dreaming Emmett* that Morrison created a representative African American boy, visiting the South from his customary home in the North, bringing his naive independence into the unintentionally aggressive scenario that will kill him.

She wrote the play while she was teaching as a chaired professor at State University of New York-Albany. Commissioned by the New York State Writers Institute, it was produced by the Albany Capital Repertory Theater, to commemorate the first nationwide celebration of the birthday of Martin Luther King, Jr. It premiered at Albany's

Marketplace Theater on January 4, 1986: once it had closed, Morrison collected all video records and all print texts and they have never been seen again. She explained to the *New York Times* critic Margaret Croyden, "I'm not interested in documentaries. I'm not sticking to facts. What is interesting about the play is the contradiction of fact. *Dreaming Emmett* is really about that." In another interview, Morrison continued, "There are these young black men getting shot all over the country today, not because they were stealing but because they're black. And no one remembers how any of them looked. No one even remembers the facts of each case" (Sanna 23).

In Croyden's coverage of the play, she quoted Morrison as saying that she "wanted to see a collision of three or four levels of time through the eyes of one person who could come back to life and seek vengeance. Emmett Till became that person" (Croyden 6H). Directed by Gilbert Moses, a friend of Morrison's, *Dreaming Emmett* centers on, in Morrison's words, "an African-American boy murdered thirty years before. Dreaming, he summons up his murderers, his family, and his friends – but these ghosts refuse to be controlled by his imagination. All see the past from their own perspective" (Croyden 6H) In her discussion of the play, Ellyn Sanna quotes from a sponsor of the play: "Morrison has been able to take one of the toughest themes, child murder, and make it the subject of a retrospective history. It puts Till's death in a totally different context" (Sanna 24).

Writing after having seen *Dreaming Emmett* in rehearsal, Croyden describes it as a play within a play: "the characters and the action shift back and forth in time and place ... The nonlinear story involves an anonymous black boy who was murdered." "At one point he is challenged by a member of the audience, a black woman who rejects his dream" and confronts him on sexual issues (Croyden H6). Roynon adds that in places the actors – or at least some of them – wear masks (Roynon 88).

Knowing that Morrison works by immersing herself in the characters and context of her fiction, the reader assumes that her immersion in the life and death of Emmett Till was a sorrowful period for her. Just as she had repeatedly mourned the death of one of her Random House writers, Henry Dumas, whose poems she placed throughout *The Black Book* and whose collections of both poetry and fiction she published posthumously, Morrison never feared grieving for people lost to her. Her 1988 essay about Dumas opens,

In 1968, a young Black man, Henry Dumas, went through a turnstile at a New York city subway station. A transit cop shot him in the chest and killed him. Circumstances surrounding his death remain unclear. Before that happened, however, he had written some of the most beautiful, moving, and profound poetry and fiction that I have ever in my life read. He was thirty-three years old when he was killed, but in those thirty-three years, he had completed work, the quality and quantity of which are almost never achieved in several lifetimes. He was brilliant. He was magnetic, and he was an incredible artist. (Nonfiction 83)

Morrison published the works of a number of African American men while she was a senior editor at Random House, but the biographical details of Henry Dumas's life seem to be reflected in what she provided as background for Milkman Dead in her 1977 novel, a novel – interestingly enough – about hundreds of African American men who carried the name *Solomon* in their lineage. Macon Dead, Jr., known as "Milkman," was faced with learning how to assimilate into that generous body of male humanity, from the wise ancients through his contemporaries.

Morrison's explanation for the way she created the worlds – and characters – of her fiction helps with this assessment:

In order to get at the thing at once, I have to see it, to smell it, to touch it. It's something to hold on to so that I can write it. What takes longest is the way you get into the heart of that which you have to describe. Once I know, then I can move. I know that if the action is violent, the language cannot be violent; it must be understated. I want my readers to see it, to feel it, and I want to give them things even I may not know about, even if I've never been there. (Con I, 99)

What Morrison knew about, even as early as her first years as a New York editor, was that being a mother to children was relentlessly demanding. She seldom talked about her frantic schedule as a single mother, but when she did her statements rang with authenticity. In a discussion about the fact that a mother who was also a writer would be interrupted:

There was never a place I worked, or a time I worked, that my children did not interrupt me, no matter how trivial – because it was never trivial to them. The writing could never take precedence over them. Which is why I had to write under duress, and in a state of siege and with a lot of compulsion. I couldn't count on any sustained period of free time to write. I couldn't write the way writers write, I had to write the way a woman with children writes. That means that you have to have immense powers of concentration. I would never tell a child, "Leave me alone, I'm writing." That doesn't mean anything to a child. What they deserve and need, in-house, is a mother. They do not need and cannot use a writer. (Con I, 238)

In an interview in spring 2012, Morrison recalled how long her sons' adolescent years seemed to stretch: "There were instances, when they were teenagers. Being stopped in the car, and given a ticket because you had tinted glass or something. Little bits and pieces of police harassment that happened to be light because we were not living in New York and also – and I did not even tell them this, because I didn't know to – but they always said 'sir' to the police. Yes sir, no sir. I don't know where they got that from, but it worked" (Brockes).

On being asked about the United States' reaction to the Trayvon Martin killing (and more recently, that of Michael Brown, Jr.), Morrison notes the institutional racism in the United States.

They keep saying, we have to have a conversation about race in this country. Well, this is the conversation. We'll see if it plays out, if it makes a difference in terms of not just the hate crime thing, but the law. It's not like it is on television. The police are ill-trained and they're corrupt, and they're protected, and that's what they do. All over. I don't mean all police, but the system itself is protective. So yeah, they're going to lie ... And now we're getting the demonization of the kid [Trayvon Martin]. He was this, he was that, he wore his pants down. (Brockes)

Still apparently hopeful, Morrison finished her interview with Emma Brockes by noting that "The real thing is how we move forward. I was describing that thing of a mixed neighborhood, of shared misery and shared joy. We were citizens. I mean we, African-Americans, were second-class citizens, but anyway, hopeful people. And then after the war we became consumers. Happiness in acquisition. And now we are only taxpayers. I'm going to give *my* tax dollars to *those* people? ! If I'm only a taxpayer, I'm very upset. That's a different deal. A citizen has some connection to his neighborhood, or his state or his country. The taxpayer doesn't."

Morrison reflected back to the several decades of sanity that followed World War II ... but then after Barack Obama's election, the viciousness of racism took over again: "from the stump Newt Gingrich refers to Obama as the 'food-stamp president'; Mitt Romney accuses him of wanting to turn America into a 'welfare state' ... Oh, that's very deliberate. Welfare, food stamps; gangs. They have a whole vocabulary of code. Some overt, some covert." Morrison tells the interviewer she finds this language both "hateful" and embarrassing – "Really embarrassing for my country" (Brockes).

Morrison's second essay collection, co-edited with Claudia Brodsky Lacour, attempted again to break through – and interrogate – the complacency of strident racist attitudes. *Birth of a Nation'hood: Gaze, Script, and Spectacle in the O. J. Simpson Case* followed the format of the *Race-ing Justice* book. Based on the 1994 murders of Nicole Brown Simpson and Ronald Goldman, with the accused O. J. Simpson, former Heisman Trophy winner and pro football star, movie actor, and corporate mogul, Morrison's introduction presented the reader a layered set of assumptions. It took the reader from the heights of O. J. Simpson's celebrity to the enormity of his driving his white Bronco on a well-lit highway in view of millions of observers. A police chase, writ large, to allow time for those millions of observers to draw conclusions based on nothing except their television screens. Morrison's phrase was "a chase, a cuffing, a mob, name calling, a white female victim" (Introduction xiii). She titled her essay "The Official Story: Dead Man Golfing" and began it by calling out to all viewers of both the arrest and the trial: "We have been deceived. We thought he loved us. Now we know that everything we saw was false ... Not only did he not love us, he loathed and despised us. All the time he was planning to kill us" (Introduction vii).

Apparently writing to a liberal community, Morrison established a number of similarities in the national (read "official") narrative of Simpson's trial and all other race-based judgments in post-Civil

Rights America. She called the trial "the Simpson spectacle ... a discourse on black deviance"; she called it "gargantuanism" in its garish (and monolithic) story (Introduction xxvii, xiii). She referred to the way this *official* narrative "limited his biography to an insolent, womanizing golf life," forgetting that he had for years been seen as an "affable athlete" (viii).

Just as learning to play a piano was a marker for rising into the middle class a century ago, so learning to play golf – with its separation from the domestic, its expensive equipment, its increasingly high skill level – became a similar marker in the mid-twentieth century. For Simpson, the American pro football star, excelling in golf was easy, and his athletic skills gave him automatic entry into mainstream social circles. Having a beautiful white wife, and children who shared some of that woman's characteristics, also enhanced a less racial image for Simpson. The contradictions of this celebrity trying to lose some of his African American identifiers added layers of suspicion to the roles that his minority race *obviously* played in his acts, according to the official narrative.

For her exploration of the ways in which Simpson had been portrayed, Morrison built analogies with Herman Melville's *Benito Cereno* on the *San Dominick* to illustrate the blacks' pretense and the captain's naivety. In her echo of many of the points she made in the "Friday" essay about Clarence Thomas and Anita Hill, Morrison emphasizes again "the denial of black cognition by the 'official story'" (Introduction ix). In media accounts Simpson is a monster, a wild dog in his ravaging, murderous behavior. Where, asks Morrison, is the attention to any rational motivation? She asks, early on, "Even when permitted to enter the kingdom of *Homo sapiens*, blacks have historically been viewed as either submissive children, violent men, or both at once ... What might be illogical for a white is easily possible for a black who has never been required to make [or] assumed to make ... 'sense'" (Introduction xi).

Taking away the celebrity of O. J. Simpson, and the reasons for that celebrity, Morrison places him – again, on the basis of media coverage – as a man being used to "stand in for the entire race." All African American men can be judged, in miniature, by the behavior of "a living, black man repeating forever a narrative of black inferiority" (Introduction xxviii).

By echoing the early film *The Birth of a Nation* (drawn from *The Klansman*) in their title, Morrison and Lacour flip the image:

"Nation'hood" retitles the often overused "neighborhood," shortened in some black vernaculars to "hood." Again drawing – often ironically – on stereotypes of the young black men who live within their geographic neighborhoods, Morrison draws the reader in to a memory of the virulently racist film (Introduction xxvii). Race is the nexus of both the Simpson trial and the film. As Mueller explained, "like *Birth of a Nation*, the Simpson official narrative is ruled by race. Like *Birth of a Nation*, the case has generated a newer, more sophisticated national narrative of racial supremacy. But it is still the old white sham supremacy forever wedded to and dependent upon faux black inferiority" (Mueller 259).

Morrison's introduction led intentionally to George Lipsitz's own parodic essay, "The Greatest Story Ever Sold: Marketing and the O. J. Simpson Trial." Pricing the cost of months of publicity into the event of the Simpson trial, Lipsitz made readers re-identify with the power of media as well as the underlying echoes of the murder of the Christ. Several other lengthy essays – those by Kimberle Williams Crenshaw, Armond White, Nikol G. Alexander and Drucilla Cornell, and Higginbotham (with his colleagues Linda Y. Yueh and Aderson Bellegarde Francois) – explored the machinations of justice, and the trial by jury concept, in toto. Because these detailed and insightful essays were to be included, Morrison did not need to focus on legal processes in her introduction. Essays by Patricia J. Williams, Ann duCille, and Claudia Brodsky Lacour also exposed legal concerns.

Ann duCille's essay, "The Unbearable Darkness of Being: 'Fresh' Thoughts on Race, Sex, and the Simpsons," recharacterized the media involvement as not the exploration of the "Othello Syndrome." Rather, says this critic, despite what good might have come from describing Simpson as a wife abuser (as well as a wife murderer), the trial shows "the browning of Nicole Simpson." Referring to the "one-drop" rule, duCille points out that "It's not so-called black blood that is the issue ... it's black semen. And the operative 'psychosis' isn't the Othello Syndrome but what I am calling here the 'Mandingo Syndrome': white women's penchant for and willing submission to black men and the national anxiety that even the possibility of such consensual coupling has traditionally evoked" (*Birth* 304).

For Leola Johnson and David Roediger, writing in "'Hertz, Don't It?' Becoming Colorless and Staying Black in the Crossover of O. J. Simpson," his more celebrated role in American culture is his role as a "corporate icon" for Hertz Rental Cars. Their essay forces attention to the fact that Simpson's meteoric rise to fame and fortune depended on the adulation of a "white male target audience." Enhanced by the slow-motion replays of his early football career, the Simpson body (though deformed as a child because of "a largely untreated case of rickets") imaged fertile male prowess – "slow-motion supermanhood." These critics see the trial as an illustration of "the transcendence of concern about race via class mobility" (*Birth* 213–30).

In another essay, Ishmael Reed uses Richard Wright's *Native Son* as his scaffolding. In "Bigger and O. J.," he sees that the truths of Wright's novel from half a century earlier played out here in what he calls the 1995 "trial of the century." While society has changed little, says Reed, the circumstances that Simpson's life created for him differed immensely – but only as long as he stayed in his appropriate role (*Birth* 195).

In the midst of Morrison's more overtly political writings, she still expressed her beliefs about modern literature – the work she was both writing herself and publishing, the work she knew would remain valuable for her target audience of African American as well as mainstream readers. Late in the 1980s she accepted invitations to create a true hierarchy of the traits in literature that she valued. In 1988, she gave the Tanner Lecture on Human Values at the University of Michigan. Titled "Unspeakable Things Unspoken: The Afro-American Presence in American Literature," this lecture, published the following year in the *Michigan Quarterly Review*, rehearsed the evolution of written literature from Egyptian times to the present. It foreshadowed in different ways the set of three lectures Morrison gave in 1989 at Harvard University. It is the texts of the three William E. Massey, Sr., Lectures in the History of American Civilization which appeared in 1992, in a publication from Harvard University Press, entitled *Playing in the Dark: Whiteness and the Literary Imagination*. This book in many respects would change the way readers viewed race in American letters. It would, in effect, change the way readers *read* American literature. In some respects, and surprisingly, Morrison's first book of literary criticism overshadowed both her 1992 novel *Jazz* and her 1992 essay collection.

One of the things *Playing in the Dark* initially did was to make critics, writers, and educators understand that "whiteness" was itself a definitional term: all literature heretofore had been *unc*ategorized because it was written as *white.* Yet for Morrison who had been an English major at Howard University and, following that, had gotten a two-year MA degree at Cornell University, her understanding of the usual monolithic approach to the study of English and American literature had deep and sometimes contradictory roots. She sometimes mentioned that her idea at Howard to write a paper on Shakespeare's black characters (in a Renaissance course) was not encouraged. As she told Claudia Tate, "Critics generally don't associate black people with ideas. They see marginal people; they just see another story about black folks. They regard the whole thing as sociologically interesting perhaps but very parochial. There's a notion out in the land that there are human beings one writes about, and then there are black people or Indians or some other marginal group. If you write about the world from that point of view, somehow it's considered lesser. It's racist, of course ... [Black people] are people, not aliens" (Con I, 160).

Throughout Morrison's comments about her writing, it is clear that she objects – and has long objected – to the *sociological* reading of African American literature. But it is also clear that, here in 1992, more than 20 years after Morrison had herself become a writer of note (*The Bluest Eye* published in 1970s, followed by many of her *New York Times* essays and reviews), she remained frustrated with the lack of deference to her *mind*: "Critics generally don't associate black people with ideas."

She is also taking on both the publishing community (while she works hard as an editor at Random House to find and bring to readership such African American writers as Leon Forrest, James Alan McPherson, James Baldwin, Toni Cade Bambara, Paule Marshall, Henry Dumas, Albert Murray, Gayl Jones and others) and the community of literary critics, on which she sees how dependent the receptions of these writers are. Through the 1980s, Morrison had worked to express her literary ideas, and when she was invited to give the Tanner Lecture at Michigan, she knew it would be an important address. In that 1988 essay, she traced through a studied description of canon issues choices beginning with the shift from the dominance of Egypt to that of Greece, using *They Came Before Columbus*, Ivan van Sertina's book (which she had helped to publish) in conjunction with Edward Said's *Orientalism* and Martin Bernal's *Black Athena*. She began "Unspeakable Things Unspoken: The Afro-American Presence in American Literature" not by emphasizing that she had been a classics minor but by noting

that much of Greek tragedy parallels "Afro-American communal structures (the function of song and chorus, the heroic struggle between the
claims of community and individual hubris) and African religion and
philosophy" (Tanner 3, 6–7). Then she laid out a scaffolding for what
would become her text in *Playing in the Dark*, warning that critics risk
the "orphanization" of Afro-American literature if they do not allow
critical theory to *accommodate* that writing.

More to the point of the Massey lectures, Morrison insists here
that the astute and observant critic must assume the role of "exami-
nation and re-interpretation of the American canon, the founding
nineteenth century works, for the 'unspeakable things unspoken';
for the ways in which the presence of Afro-Americans has shaped
the choices, the language, the structure – the meaning of so much
American literature." She then moves away from the nineteenth
century into "contemporary or non-canonical literature" for the
Afro-American presence. Here she says, "I am always amazed by the
resonances, the structural gear-shifts, and the *uses* to which Afro-
American narrative, persona, and idiom are put in contemporary
'white' literature" (Tanner 11). Morrison continues to emphasize
that the blackness of literature depends on its "language – its unpol-
ished, seditious, confrontational, manipulative, inventive, disrup-
tive, masked and unmasking language."

Providing as illustration a deft reading of Melville's *Moby-Dick*,
Morrison repeatedly stresses the dimensions of whiteness. She then
posits the fact of her own (gendered and raced) absence from these
male-oriented and largely white texts: "We can agree, I think, that invisible things are not necessarily 'not-there': that a void may be empty, but
is not a vacuum." She draws the reader in with a sophistry of defending
both "universal" and "race-free" critiques" (Tanner 11, 13).

A substantial part of her Tanner lecture is a series of lengthy and
incisive essays about the opening of each of her five novels, beginning with *The Bluest Eye* and including *Beloved*. Before she comes
to this revealing section, however, Morrison lists the white authors
whose work should be given these more widely inclusive readings
(readings that do not create voids where Afro-American characters
might exist). Besides Melville, Edgar Allan Poe, Nathaniel Hawthorne
and Mark Twain, she enumerates "Willa Cather, Ernest Hemingway,
F. Scott Fitzgerald, and William Faulkner," closing her list with the
comment that "Canonical American literature is begging for such

attention" (Tanner 18). Strident as she has been in discussing canon issues (saying "Canon building is Empire building. Canon defense is national defense"), she also repeats that intellectual prowess is never innocent: "All of the interests are vested" (Tanner 8). Coining the word "whitemale" early in her discussion, Morrison repeats that "race" has always been masked. If ever a critic does consider race, "the basis of Western civilization will require re-thinking ... 'race' is still a virtually unspeakable thing" (Tanner 3).

Surprising critics the following year as she gave the three Massey lectures, in that she omitted mention of the canon, Morrison's less formal comments at Harvard gave her more opportunity to engage her audience. She began by discussing Willa Cather's last novel, *Sapphira and the Slave Girl*, in which she fuses the author's own childhood with the presentation of the slave girl, Nancy. She spent considerable time in a discussion of Ernest Hemingway's posthumously published, unfinished novel, *The Garden of Eden*, a book vexed in several ways (since Hemingway had not finished the book, the choices made by editor Tom Jenks had sent critics scurrying to the manuscripts – and to writing mountains of critical commentary). Morrison's discussion of Hemingway's novelist figure David Bourne and his two beloved women, Catherine and Marita, vying with each other to become darker and darker, relinquished psychobiography and made her emphasis on the skin colors of the three protagonists something of value. As Morrison explained, in this novel as in his *To Have and Have Not*, "ideological Africanism is extended metaphorically to function as a systematic articulation ... of an entire aesthetics. Africanism – the fetishizing of color, the transference to blackness of the power of illicit sexuality, chaos, madness, impropriety, anarchy, strangeness, and helpless, hapless desire – provides a formidable field for a novel that works out the terms and maps a complete, if never formalized, aesthetics" (*Playing* 80–1).

As Morrison had insisted in the early pages of this book, "literary 'blackness' and its study reveals literary 'whiteness'" (*Playing* 9). Setting her principles in line with the expectations of a white reader, Morrison notes that there can be no 'white' culture without a 'black' and there can be no overall premise that does not interrogate the meaning of whiteness as a literary and cultural designation (*Playing* 6). Her belief that recognizing the Africanist presence is crucial becomes the driving force of the lectures:

The contemplation of this black presence is central to any understanding of our national literature and should not be permitted to hover at the margins of the literary imagination ... These speculations have led me to wonder whether the major and championed characteristics of our national literature – individualism, masculinity, social engagement versus historical isolation; acute and ambiguous moral problematics; the thematics of innocence coupled with an obsession with figurations of death and hell – are not in fact responses to a dark, abiding, signing Africanist presence.

Morrison continues:

It has occurred to me that the very manner by which American literature distinguishes itself as a coherent entity exists because of this unsettled and unsettling population. Just as the formation of the nation necessitated coded language and purposeful restriction to deal with the racial disingenuousness and moral frailty at its heart, so too did the literature, whose founding characteristics extend into the twentieth century, reproduce the necessity for codes and restriction. Through significant and underscored omissions, startling contradictions, heavily nuanced conflicts, through the way writers peopled their work with the signs and bodies of this presence – one can see that a real or fabricated Africanist presence was crucial to their sense of Americanness. (*Playing* 5–6)

Difficult to summarize as Morrison weaves her expositions of texts in and through her radical pronouncements, the ideas in *Playing in the Dark* have unsettled any strict adherence to ideas about "good" literature, inherited from the United Kingdom and other English-speaking countries. Morrison's ideas were so influential that it might be said that her being awarded the Nobel Prize for Literature in 1993 might have stemmed partly from the critical importance of *Playing in the Dark: Whiteness and the Literary Imagination*, when that text was considered along with *The Bluest Eye, Sula, Song of Solomon, Tar Baby, Beloved,* and *Jazz.* A global audience had been enriched with an understanding of the ways in which African American – and African – and American – imaginations had shaped much of the world's literature. In the case of twentieth-century American literature, it had never been enclosed within its national borders. It had always seen *beyond.*

6
The Nobel Prize in Literature and Morrison's Trilogy

Morrison survived the year 1992 with its three books (*Jazz*, *Race-ing Justice*, and *Playing in the Dark*) but it was difficult. She got very little new writing done. In fact, since *Beloved* had won the 1988 Pulitzer Prize for Fiction, Morrison had been on the reading and lecturing circuit – and she had also been the recipient of important literary prizes in addition to the Pulitzer. In 1990, for instance, she was asked to deliver the first Chazen Lecture at the University of Wisconsin, the Charter Lecture at the University of Georgia, and the Clark Lectures at Trinity College in Cambridge. That same year she received the Chubb Fellowship at Yale University, and the Chianti Ruffino Antico Fattore International Literary Prize. Perhaps it should have come as no surprise, then, that in 1993 she was awarded the Nobel Prize in Literature – the first United States African American writer to be so honored, and the first United States woman to be a recipient since Pearl Buck had received the award many decades earlier.

News media stressed the unexpectedness of the award. That same news media tried to suggest this was an honor given for the exceptionalism of race and gender. The long list of United States authors who had previously been so honored included dramatist Eugene O'Neill, poet T. S. Eliot (after he had become a British citizen), Sinclair Lewis, Pearl Buck, William Faulkner, Ernest Hemingway, John Steinbeck, Saul Bellow (though a Canadian), and Isaac Bashevis Singer. On the basis of the global acclaim *Beloved* was already achieving – not to mention the oeuvre of her distinguished fiction and opinion writing – Morrison had no reason to be humble about the prize. As she told Claudia Dreifus in a 1994 interview,

> I felt a lot of "we" excitement. It was as if the whole category of "female writer" and "black writer" had been redeemed. I felt I represented a whole world of women who either were silenced or who had never received the imprimatur of the established literary world. I felt the way I used to feel at commencements when I'd get an honorary degree: that it was very important for young black people to see a black person do that; that there were probably young people in South-Central Los Angeles or Selma who weren't quite sure that they could do it. But seeing me up there might encourage them to write one of those books I'm desperate to read. And that made me happy. It gave me license to strut. (Con II, 99)

In a recent essay, Morrison repeated that conviction – as an aside to the issue of the *universality* of her writing: "any artist wants to feel that there is something in her work that all peoples of the world are receptive to. On the other hand, *I* did not want to be erased. I didn't want my femininity to be erased. I wanted it to be very clear that 'universal' is *not* for me a buzz word for *not* political or *not* ethnic" (Lanker 36). In that same essay, as a coda to this statement, Morrison said with her usual passionate conviction, "I want to write better. THINK better. I don't know how not to want that ..." (36).

Morrison rehearses the difficulty she had had with saying outright that she was a writer. She attributes her reticence to gender. "I said, 'I am a mother who writes' or 'I am an editor who writes.' ... it's the difference between identifying one's work and being the person who does the work. I've always been the latter. I've always thought best when I wrote. Writing is what centered me. In the act of writing, I felt most alive, most coherent, most stable and most vulnerable" (Con II, 99–100).

The voice in Morrison's 1993 Nobel Prize Acceptance Speech might well be "the mother who writes" (one remembers Morrison's metaphor in a 1986 interview that she writes that, regardless of risk, "You take your womb, and then after your children are born, you just stretch it to include the house, then the neighborhood, then the town ... 'til the whole world becomes a part of that"; Con II, 40). Critic Valerie Smith had said early on, "children occupy a central role in Morrison's fiction" (Smith, *Toni* 99); it seemed a natural expression of Morrison's persona that she would choose that recognizable voice for the Nobel lecture.

The lecture is disguised as a story, a narrative about an old woman – man – guru – griot, who is blind. She is a citizen of several countries, several cultures. She is the mythic ancestor robbed of sight so that only the *sound* of language remains. The process of listening to the children's language, of deciphering their difficult question, becomes the griot's test.

The blind persona who hears is "an old woman. Blind. Wise ... a daughter of slaves, black, American, and lives alone in a small house outside of town. Her reputation for wisdom is without peer and without question. Among her people she is both the law and its transgressor" (Nonfiction 198). Morrison does not relinquish the sense of "outlaw woman" that she has employed throughout her fiction. The children, to trick her, carry to her an object – a bird – and ask whether it is living or dead. She is candid: "'I don't know,' she says. 'I don't know whether the bird you are holding is dead or alive, but what I do know is that it is in your hands. It is in your hands.'" (The bird is also the African metaphor for language.)

Morrison's parable of responsibility in this Babel of tongues centers on the bird. "For parading their power and her helplessness, the young visitors are reprimanded, told they are responsible not only for the act of mockery but also for the small bundle of life sacrificed to achieve its aims." In a voice so digressive as to encapsulate all listeners, so warm as to seem welcoming rather than admonitory, Morrison's "old woman – Blind. Wise" transforms the voice to context and the bird to language. She moves it through a tundra of the very abstractions that most of the previous American Nobel laureates had listed, changing the elevated words of Faulkner, of Steinbeck, of Bellow into her own modest story.

She digresses into a parable about President Abraham Lincoln, attempting to nurse his war-inscribed country back to health as he speaks modestly at Gettysburg, thinking about "the graveyard his country had become" with 600,000 men already dead including the early slaves, "in a cataclysmic race war." Not the invited speaker for the occasion, the sorrowful Lincoln gave the world "life-sustaining properties" in his simple invocation, acknowledging his words "poor power to add or detract." It is his deference that moves her, that recognition that language can never live up to life: "Nor should it.

Language can never 'pin down' slavery, genocide, war ... Word-work is sublime ... because it is generative, it makes meaning, that secures our difference, our human difference – the way in which we are like no other life .... We die. That may be the meaning of life. But we do language. That may be the measure of our lives" (Nonfiction 203). Morrison invokes the children in a picturesque traveling caravan, "a girl and a boy ... The boy will have a gun in three years, but now he carries a lamp and a jug of warm cider. They pass it from mouth to mouth. The girl offers bread, pieces of meat and something more: a glance into the eyes of the one she serves. One helping for each man, two for each woman. And a look. They look back. The next stop will be their last. But not this one. This one is warmed."

In the quiet broken only by the old woman's pacifying voice, she admonishes the group to congratulate themselves: the bird is gone, it is no longer in their hands, it has become a fragile remnant of something *their* words have created. "'Look,' says the woman – 'Blind. Wise.' – with no irony at all, 'How lovely it is, this thing we have done – *together*'" (Nonfiction 207).

Morrison closed her remarks with the image she had often chosen to explain the way the act of reading enlivens the thing written, the dual responsibility for effective literature. She had crafted an inclusive meditation that makes her listeners, like those unruly children, respond to her very language, the simplest presence of deeply felt and deeply honored words.

Morrison had invited both President Clinton and novelist Salmon Rushdie to accompany her to Sweden; neither could attend. But her son Harold did, and her sister Lois and two nieces, and critics John Leonard, Henry Louis Gates, Jr., Nobel-recipient Wole Soyinka, and others (Li 90). After returning, she recounted that "The award itself is fine but it is not going to help you with the things that really challenge you. You have to deal with your children and your friends, and that is what makes life original and interesting" (Con II, 228). One of the family stories Morrison then tells was that of her son's asking, "'The person who got the Nobel Prize, does she walk behind you or in front of you? Do you like her, or don't you?'" Morrison answers, "I do like her, and she walks ahead of me, so that I can see her and warn her before she does anything foolish" (Con II, 227).

Despite the large monetary prize (something over $800,000) and having Sweden issue a Toni Morrison postage stamp, the author recalled the terrific exhaustion of the prize's being awarded, choosing suitable clothes, traveling to Sweden – and once she had returned home, the burning of her house on the Hudson River where she had lived for 15 years. In the loss of her manuscripts, photographs, her sons' possessions, and various curios from her own travels, Morrison was truly devastated: "I think I may not ever, ever, ever get over it. And it isn't even about the *things*. It's about photographs, plants I nurtured for twenty years, about the view of the Hudson River, my children's report cards, my manuscripts" (Con II, 103). (Later, she had the house rebuilt, but nothing could bring back her valuables.) Within her immediate family, too, she suffered great losses: in 1992 one of her younger brothers, George Wofford, died after only a brief illness; in 1993 her other brother Raymond died of cancer. Early in 1994, just a day before Morrison's birthday, she lost her mother.

Life continued – even more publicly than before. In 1993 she was awarded Commander of the Order of Arts and Letters; she returned to France. In 1994 she received the Pearl Buck Award as well as the Condorcet Medal (along with the award of the International Condorcet Chair, Ecole Normale Superieure and College de Prance, at which occasion she delivered the Condorcet Lecture). She also received Premio Internazionale, "Citta dello Stretto," Rhegium Julii, Reggio Calabria, Italy. In 1996 she was named the Jefferson Lecturer in the Humanities by the National Endowment for the Humanities; she also received the National Book Foundation Medal for Distinguished Contribution to American Letters. *The Dancing Mind*, her National Book Foundation Lecture, was published as a book by Knopf.

Reminiscent in some respects of Morrison's 1987 "Site of Memory" essay, "The Dancing Mind" explains that the essence of peace has nothing to do with war or its absence: it is rather "the dance of the open mind when it engages another equally open one" (Nonfiction 186). One prizes – and privileges – "the reading/writing world we live in." Morrison includes two narratives. One describes a young man who has been given the best intellectual resources possible – education, travel, conversation. But this man had been so well cared for that he had never found the joy of reading alone for hours, "without any companionship but his own mind." The second is her account of being a speaker at an international writers meeting and realizing how desperate many of the world's intellectuals are, living as they must in totalitarian circumstances. Morrison concludes by pointing out that "the life of the book" is crucial (Nonfiction 188–9).

In "The Site of Memory" she takes a more historical tack, aligning herself as writer with African American autobiographers, especially those who wrote the slave narratives. Saddened by the reticence some of these earlier writers had to adopt, Morrison announces, "My job becomes how to rip that veil down over 'proceedings too terrible to relate'" (Nonfiction 70). A corollary to what Morrison sees as the demand for writing *truth* is her anger that earlier public opinion focused on the lie that "blacks were incapable of intelligence" (Nonfiction 69). For her, "[w]riting is thinking and discovery and selection and order and meaning. [I]t is also awe and reverence and mystery and magic" (Nonfiction 71).

Morrison's "Dancing Mind" essay also foreshadows "Peril," the preface she wrote for her edited book in 2009, *Burn This Book* (PEN). There she laments the powerful injustices occurring throughout the supposedly literate world, mourning "efforts to censor, starve, regulate, and annihilate us." She describes knowing which regimes are corrupt by "the flight of writers from their shores, noting [t]he alarm, the disquiet, writers raise" ("Peril" 2). Trying to speak in such locations violates the writer's very self. "Certain kinds of trauma visited on peoples are so deep, so cruel, that ... only writers can translate such trauma and turn sorrow into meaning, sharpening the moral imagination" (4).

When Morrison looked ahead to the third book in her often-interrupted trilogy, she could not avoid seeing the same disquiet, the trauma, of much twentieth-century life – particularly as it affected women and minorities. Even though she had once speculated that the third book would have to do with women's choices, including love, or possibly with twentieth-century warfare (she used the title *War* throughout much of her writing of the novel that was to become *Paradise*), she finally settled on a continuation of providing history of, largely, African Americans in America. Just as *Beloved* had focused on slavery and escapes from it and *Jazz* on the migration to Northern cities, so *Paradise* drew the narrative of all-black towns in western states.

Once again, reviewers were puzzled by the lack of stable narrative voices – who *are* these characters in this carefully imagined world, a world unrecognizable to most readers? Just as some critics had earlier speculated that Morrison's vaunted realistic descriptions of places were less than realistic – were, in fact, fantasy locations – the sites of Ruby and the Convent assumed qualities more than a little metaphorical.

James Clifford terms this kind of postmodern use of place "translocal," a means authors may use to help readers envision a global setting – or, more likely, "a global domestic sphere" where "the culture is a complex articulation of the local and global processes in relational, non-telelogical ways" (Clifford 210). Corollaries to this concept take on women writers' means of "embracing space," writing texts more ecological and yet less geographically specific than traditional descriptions. If one can see that the realistic presentations Morrison achieved in both *The Bluest Eye* and *Sula* give way as soon as her work in *Song of Solomon* and *Tar Baby* moves to a more staged inclusion of events and characters from generations past, then the fantasy she must draw on in giving readers the various *places* in *Beloved* – Sweet Home, the settings for Paul D's tortures, the Ohio River bank, 124 Bluestone Road – is understandable. Archival records do not exist for historical place markers in minority cultures: history is written by the conquerors, not the conquered.

Without emphasizing how fanciful the sites of Joe Trace's life – both past and present – are, Morrison draws from the same stream of license to create a translocal milieu for the entire story of *Jazz*. Despite her discussion of the all-black towns in the American West, she follows that format as well for *Paradise*. Roberta Rubenstein describes the setting here as "a spiritual home, with strong maternal associations, located in a liminal space where past and future converge" (Rubenstein 8). Morrison also calls attention to the fact that *Paradise* was her first investigation of religion and its practices. She said, "I went into a place I had never gone before, which was into religion and into the Bible. I am a Catholic; some of my family is Catholic, some of them are Protestant, some of them are all sorts of things" (Con II, 254). After the book was published, she asked that the word always be written with a lower-case *P* (she closes her New York Public Library interview with that request, saying the idealization of life occurs where it occurs. It can happen on earth as well).

Readers have assumed that the locations described in *Love* and *Home* are reasonably factual, but they do not expect that kind of facticity for the settings of *A Mercy*. An acceptance of James Clifford's "translocal" would cut through the difficulties such as reality versus myth and allow the fact that Morrison uses "invented locations" as a way of enlarging reality and – through hybridity – "decentering white privilege." "'Home' can then be located through national and global political contexts."

Morrison in that same New York Public Library interview admits to salting the novel with the false clue about skin color: *Paradise* opens: "They shoot the white girl first. With the rest they can take their time." She compares what she is attempting here with the tour de force she created in her only published short story, "Recitatif," a narrative in which the races of the two young (and then mature) women are never revealed. In *Paradise*, the emphasis on skin color occurs within the African American culture, so that the very dark men constitute a clan that is in itself as dangerous as the black–white antagonisms in the United States that gave rise to the Ku Klux Klan.

Throughout her writing and publishing career, Morrison had pledged herself to narrating stories of and from African American life that would otherwise be lost; she had remarked in her Lincoln Center comments, "What is overwhelming is the silence, the absence of those stories, when you realize no one's going to write that book but you, because history, as well as fiction, has elided and avoided those stories. They have been told seldom and mistold frequently. So there's this absence and you want to fill it" (Lincoln Center 21). Jill Matus sees in this emphasis a stand for Morrison's "reclamation of erased or occluded history," yet she points out that Morrison does her best to "avoid any easy sense of reparation for past losses and oppressions; indeed, they imply the impossibility of restoration or redemption" (Matus 35).

As she often did, for *Paradise* too Morrison used a familiar and personal analogue to reach through to what might have been difficult characterizations. Her recent comments about the novel show that some of the men of Ruby, Oklahoma, bore similarities to her maternal grandfather:

We called him Big Papa. He stood in the vegetable garden peeling a yam with his pocketknife. Then he ate the raw slices slowly, carefully. If he wanted the chair you were in, he stood there, silent, looking at the sitter until you got the message and got up.

He was too religious for any church. He drew pictures of my sister and me and gave us the gift of chewing gum. Wherever he was – on the porch, at the kitchen table, in the garden, in the living room reading – that's where the power and deference were. He didn't exert power: he assumed it. And it was in part from knowing him that I felt I could understand and create the men in Ruby.

For all the novel's apparent attention to its women characters from both the Convent and Ruby, with chapter titles derived from women's names, it is the murderous acts of the threatened men who inhabit Ruby that force the action the novel records. Men of Ruby are the actors. Morrison told an interviewer that the novel began when she was in Brazil; there she heard a story about young black schoolgirls living in a convent who practiced *candomblé* (an African Brazilian religion based on the soul of nature). The enraged police shot the girls when they were found "not doing the Catholic thing. I saw them in my mind running away from the convent, running through the fields, running away from the bullets, running from men ... so I cast it as a question: Who would shoot a bunch of women and why?" ("I Start with an Image" 123). Forceful as the image is, Morrison immediately gave context to the story per se, by telling the interviewer, "Usually there is a 'what if' that might resolve the narrative, but the narrative is less interesting to me than the architecture, the language, all the other things that I can bring into the so-called story" (ibid.)

The "architecture" of naming chapters after women figures is one of the choices Morrison makes; another is the confusion in narrative voices. As she had written carefully in "The Site of Memory,"

As for point of view, there should be the illusion that it's the characters' point of view, when in fact it isn't; it's really the narrator who is there but who doesn't make herself (in my case) known in that role. I like the feeling of a told story, where you hear a voice but you can't identify it, and you think it's your own voice. It's a comfortable voice, and it's a guiding voice, and it's alarmed by the same things that the reader is alarmed by, and doesn't know what's going to happen next either. So you have this sort of guide. But that guide can't have a personality; it can only have a sound, and you have to feel comfortable with this voice, and then this voice can easily abandon itself and reveal the interior dialogue of a character. So it's a combination of using the point of view of various characters but still retaining the power to slide in and out, provided that when I'm "out" the reader doesn't see little fingers pointing to what's in the text.

Morrison summarized, "What I really want is that intimacy in which the reader is under the impression that he isn't really reading this: that he is participating in it as he goes along. It's unfolding, and he's always two beats ahead of the characters and right on target" (Nonfiction 78).

There seems to be little reason for Morrison to mislead her readers – she had previously created this prototypical unnamed narrator throughout *Jazz*. In *Paradise*, however, there are many ministers (and characters such as Patricia Best, historian of Ruby, who claim authoritative voices), and some unidentified narrators, but were the reader to demand "stories" for the men of Ruby, those would have to concern Steward and Dovey Morgan, Deacon and Soane Morgan, Nathan and Mirth DePres, and Jeff and Sweetie Fleetwood. Scattered throughout the novel are the pieces of the twin Morgan boys' lives. Married to sisters Dovey and Soane, the Morgans are less marked by infertility than are some of Ruby's couples – notably the Fleetwoods' four disabled children. Glimpsed as the site of death (Deacon and Soane's boys killed in Vietnam, for example), the parents of Ruby remain dominated by patriarchal law. Their suspicion of the Convent women hinges partly on their fear of homosexuality, and of women who are both self-sufficient and "unclean."

The Paradise Morrison creates is bifurcated. Ruby represents the traditional – male, patriarchal, exclusive, protestant. The Convent is maternal and inclusive; its inhabitants believe in "something that verges on magic" (Mihan 160). In Mihan's description, Ruby "epitomizes the ideas connected with the traditional paradise: It is available only to a small and select group of people [through] their purity and moral rectitude .... it is oppressive toward internal dissidents."

The Convent differs in most respects. It represents a paradise that is "heterogeneous, multifaceted space ... made available to everybody ... a multicultural society that is liberating, empowering" (Mihan 158). The events of the novel show how "endangered" such a liberatory space will usually be.

The men of Ruby have power but as Morrison creates them they seldom have voices. Finally, after the killings, they are given speech so that they can create their competing – and false – descriptions. Deacon Morgan, however, tells the truth: "My brother is lying. This is our doing. Ours alone. And we bear the responsibility" (*Paradise* 291). Except for this and the words of the nephew K. D., we seldom see men in compatible conversation/discussion. Perhaps some of the men's belligerence grows from the frustration of their natural outlet of speaking. Morrison hints that they are all silently stifled – even in scenes with their wives – when she speaks about the human dilemma in an interview, "no one speaks, no one tells the story about himself or herself unless forced. They don't want to talk, they don't want to remember, they don't want to say it, because they're afraid of it – which is human. But when they do say it, and hear it, and look at it, and share it, they are not only one, they're two, and three, and four, you know? The collective sharing of that information heals the individual – and the collective" (Con I, 248).

Morrison uses the voice of Reverend Misner here in the manner of a chorus, in this scene saying to himself about Deacon, "the man's life was uninhabitable" (*Paradise* 302). Featuring Misner and his partner Anna, who have been absent during the killings, Morrison gives this couple the role of being emissaries from higher powers. After the murders of the five Convent women, Anna finds five "warm, umber eggs" in the Convent's chicken coop; and it seems that both she and Misner are visited by the women's spirits. Misner sees an open window; Anna, an open door. Connected as they are with the spiritual world, this couple serves to center – if not ameliorate – the disquiet of Ruby and its residents (*Paradise* 304–5).

Hard as it is to accept that Ruby is, in Lone's words, "A backward noplace ruled by men whose power to control was out of control and who had the nerve to say who could live and who not and where," she mourns the killings of those "lively, free, unarmed females" who lived in the Convent (*Paradise* 308). In Morrison's words, the "beloved" part of the self "is what is reliable, that never betrays us, that is cherished by us, that we tend to cover up and hide and make into a personality" ("Why Did the Women" 2). This inner being – real or spiritual, male or female – links the works in Morrison's oeuvre, just as it links the three novels she describes as her trilogy.

All three of these books are about common American characters – what Morrison names "detritus – throwaway people that sometimes blow back into the room after having been swept out the door" (*Paradise* 4). Beyond this focus on the commonest of characters – writing against the recuperation of personal heroism – Morrison creates in *Beloved*, *Jazz*, and *Paradise* a triptych of past ages of African American life. What is most visible in Morrison's wall of paneled portraits is the dominance of women figures. Sethe is the protagonist of *Beloved*, and even as she dwindles into a death mask of her former self, Morrison does not claim that she is heroic. In *Jazz*, Violet, Alice, Dorcas, and Felice balance against Joe Trace and Golden Gray, offering their questing voices as grace notes to the strident and searching bass the men provide. But it is most obvious in *Paradise*, where Morrison has chosen to draw men as reticent – even the powerful men who kill women for no apparent reason – that women's stories drive both the narrative and the eventual life available to the divided community.

Decades ago, Marianne Hirsch asked a key critical question: "Where are the stories of women in men's plots?" Intent as she was on finding evidence of "women-centered mythologies" in modern literature, Hirsch chose Morrison's *Beloved* as a text that might accompany *Oedipus*: the mother–daughter plot needs to be seen as equally valuable and far-reaching (Hirsch 4–5). Her emphasis in her 1989 book, *The Mother/Daughter Plot: Narrative, Psychoanalysis, Feminism*, was on the heretofore absent emphasis. According to Hirsch, when narrative has women as protagonists, it is limited in that it is "always repetitive, literal, hopelessly representational" (Hirsch 185).

A decade later, Caroline Rody draws from more texts by women and creates, in *The Daughter's Return*, a more inclusive paradigm. She finds nothing limited about chronicles of daughterhood, "suggesting at once legacy and youth, inheritance of culture and self-conscious membership in a generation with a new agenda." What she has found is that many of these contemporary fictions render "history in a symbolic structure of daughterly engagement with the maternal past." The approaches are richly varied; many create "the unconventional feminist story of a daughter's return to repair a severed matrilineage." Within those books, says Rody, "The scene of childbirth, for example, appearing again and again ... becomes the signature trope for contact with historical origins" (Rody 6–7).

Rody reminds her readers of Denver's role in *Beloved*; of Felice's (and Violet's) role in *Jazz*, and of the multiple women's roles in *Paradise*. Rody insists, too, that "to tell history in a vocabulary derived solely from female experiences is to claim the past as a female realm, owned and made meaningful by the women who lived it" (ibid.) Morrison published *Paradise* in 1998 but it was as if she was foreshadowing Rody's critique about women protagonists in contemporary fiction by women writers. What *Paradise* accomplishes is precisely this nexus of *women*'s stories creating meaning for all realms of story, even if the historical acts are still seen as being the actions of *men*. From the perspective of critic Andrea O'Reilly, Morrison's novels, including *Paradise*, repeat the importance of her belief that the well-being of African Americans depends upon their "preserving the funk and ancient properties of the African American motherline." She reads the ending of *Paradise* as hopeful – "women are healed ... The women have survived and triumphed over the Town" (O'Reilly, *Toni* 169–70). Morrison herself said, "I thought the end of *Paradise* was transcendent! Beautiful! Everyone got to see who they were mad at. What could be better than that?" ("I Start with an Image" 124).

Morrison's choices as author, then, fold into new critical directions in important ways. If a reader sees the stories of Mavis, representative of bereaved and abused women throughout history; of Gigi, who learns to use her sexuality but never for her own happiness; of Seneca, brutalized throughout her existence; and others – as centering the narrative, that narrative becomes the tracing of men's horrible misuses of their power. Violent in the language of that abuse, Morrison is able to create scenes such as Mavis's being forced into sex with her threatening spouse just after her twin babies have suffocated in her car ("When he pulled her nightgown up, he threw it over her face, and she let that mercy be. She had misjudged. Again ... Would it be quick like most always? or long, wandering, collapsing in wordless fatigue? It was neither. He didn't penetrate – just rubbed himself to climax while chewing a clump of her hair through the nightgown that covered her face. She should have been a life-size Raggedy Ann," *Paradise* 26).

The exact centering of *Paradise* occurs through the character of Connie, renamed Consolata Sosa. Raped at nine, she has cared for the Mother Superior of the convent for 30 years of her life. Once Mother dies, she breaks down, becomes an alcoholic, engages in a frightening affair with Deacon Morgan – frightening to him – but then recovers her sense of who she might become and renames herself. (She saves Morgan's son, using her otherworldly powers – powers that will lead to the climactic ending of the novel.)

Having learned that self-abnegation and sacrifice alone is not a complete answer, Consolata learns how to teach these broken refugees, the women cared for at the Convent, to become themselves, some people of value. As critic Kelly Reames has noted, "her purpose is to return the women to their bodies. She instructs them never to let their soul be separated from their bodies again, asserting that 'Eve is Mary's Mother. Mary is the daughter of Eve' (*Paradise* 263). Consolata thus insists on the union of the two parts into which woman has been divided in Western culture: the sinning flesh and the immaculate soul" (Reames 57).

It is no accident that the murder of Consolata occurs in full view of the people involved in her killing – including those people from Ruby who may have come to try to keep the violence under control – whereas most of the killing occurs in the fields and is not witnessed. Consolata, who sleeps with Pallas's baby, Divine, leaves him to go into the kitchen because she hears noises – she finds the body of the white woman, near death, but as she holds her, absorbing her shed blood, Steward Morgan shoots her in the forehead, despite Deacon's efforts to stop him. This is Morrison's re-enactment of Jesus' crucifixion:

> Consolata narrows her gaze against the sun, then lifts it as though distracted by something high above the heads of the men. "You're back," she says, and smiles. Deacon Morgan needs the sunglasses, but they are nestled in his shirt pocket. He looks at Consolata and sees in her eyes what has been drained from them and from himself as well. There is blood near her lips. It takes his breath away. He lifts his hand to halt his brother's and discover who, between them, is the stronger man. The bullet enters her forehead.

As throughout the Gospels, Morrison spends time on the white woman's and on Consolata's dying: during this time the Convent is filled with confusion, blame, the wounded Ruby men, acrimony:

> Meanwhile Soane and Lone Du Pres close the two pale eyes but can do nothing about the third one, wet and lidless, in between.

"She said, 'Divine,'" Soane whispers.

"What?" Lone is trying to organize a sheet to cover the body.

"When I went to her. Right after Steward ... I held her head and she said 'Divine.' Then something like 'He's divine he's sleeping divine.' Dreaming, I guess."

"Well, she was shot in the head, Soane."

"What do you think she saw?"

"I don't know, but it's a sweet thought even if it was her last."

Dovey comes in, saying, "She's gone." [the white woman, still unnamed]

"You sure?" asks Lone.

"Go look for yourself."

"I will."

The sisters cover Consolata with the sheet.

"I didn't know her as well as you," Dovey says.

"I loved her. As God is my witness I did, but nobody knew her really."

"Why did they do it?

"They? You mean 'he,' don't you? Steward killed her. Not Deek."

(*Paradise* 291–2)

When Dovey asks why Soane is blaming everyone for the act of one man, the sisters' closeness is torn irretrievably (just as Lone never recovers from the experience of these killing fields). The twins are never truly brothers again. (Just as Mavis has lost her twins, so here Morrison shows the consequences for the most sacred of African pairings: evil distorts even twin relationships.)

Leaving the Bible, Morrison ends the narrative of the Ruby killings with reference to Melville's "Billy Budd," a story that had itself to evoke several endings.

However sharp the divisions about what really took place ... the big and agreed-upon fact was that everyone who had been there left the premises certain that lawmen would be happily swarming all over town (they'd killed a white woman, after all), arresting virtually all of Ruby's businessmen. When they learned there were no dead to report, transport or bury, relief was so great they began to forget what they'd actually done or seen. Had it not been for Luther Beauchamp – who told the most damning story – and Pious, Deed Sands and Aaron – who corroborated much of Lone's version – the whole thing might have been sanitized out of existence … The difficulties churned and entangled everybody: distribution of blame, prayers for understanding and forgiveness, arrogant self-defense, outright lies, and a host of unanswered questions …. (*Paradise* 298)

To these various strands of narrative, Morrison creates the quasi-mystical ending of the Ruby story, making it in fact the *Convent* story. Even as the bodies of the murdered women have disappeared, what remains is a resonant dark-skinned maternal image, holding an adult-sized "child" as if it were the Pietà writ large. Morrison's term for this maternal figure is Piedade, and she is "a woman black as firewood." She sings. "Next to her is a younger woman whose head rests on the singing woman's lap." This image of two dark-skinned women, existing in "this solace which is what Piedade's song is about … of speech shared and divided bread smoking from the fire: the unambivalent bliss of going home to be at home – the ease of coming back to love begun" (*Paradise* 318).

In discussion with a young critic, Morrison stated:

> Love of God is what the book is about. It's about spiritual love – how it gets played out and how it gets corrupted … The idea of Paradise is based on boundaries, on exclusion, which is not love …. I chose to use the New Testament motif of resurrection. After his resurrection, Jesus appears to those who want to see him. Vision is a kind of life. The women of the convent in Paradise are not deified, but after death they appear to those who want to see them … The person who has the vision, converses with it, becomes larger than themselves. The language of these passages in the novel is not just lyrical, but transitional, as between two realities. (Con II, 197–8)

When critic Michael Wood discusses this ending, he begins with Morrison's use of the Gnostic epigraph, "They will live / and they will not die again." He does not give one single interpretation for the Piedade scene, instead saying, "Much depends on our own actual beliefs about death and what follows death. At the very least we are being asked not to solve a difficult puzzle, but to reflect on the way fiction and memory resemble and reinforce each other, and the way both of them, inestimable consolations that they are, will also betray us if we let them" (Wood 124). Wood reads the younger woman as "Connie dead and reborn." Roberta Rubenstein sees that figure as linked with Beloved and, the imaged other "dead girl," Wild and perhaps Dorcas, calling the three foci in the three books of Morrison's trilogy, "the psychic core of collective loss and mourning" (Rubenstein 122; see also Gauthier). Rebecca Ferguson notes that "The self is, for Morrison, necessarily relational" (Ferguson 15). She then quotes Morrison's words from an interview: the author wants to inscribe "how we are able to love, how we balance political and personal forces, who survives in certain situations and who doesn't and, specifically, how these and other universal issues relate to African-Americans. The search for love and identity runs through most everything I write" (Con I, 278).

In Magali Michael's study of the ways in which women authors use "community," she chooses *Paradise* as the most radical of current texts. Set intentionally in 1976, so as to mark the two hundred years of American democracy, the book absorbs the deaths of Malcolm X, Medgar Evers, Martin Luther King, Jr., John F. Kennedy and Robert Kennedy, and the questionable successes of the Civil Rights movements of the 1960s. She points out that men control everything, even reproduction, and that, in contrast, women "live by a more communal sense than do the men of Ruby" (Michael 163). Michael emphasizes that important scenes of food production, as well as the intense sharing of life stories ("lost dreaming"), insulate the women characters to some extent from the savage behavior that surrounds them. Finally, however, nothing can insulate them.

Replaying the scene of Jesus' death lends credence to critic Lucille Fultz's comment about what she calls Morrison's "life work – the conviction that African American lives have literary value and, therefore, deserve center stage" (Fultz, *Playing* 102), and in the larger sense, that Morrison aims to show "the centrality of the marginalized" (103). Few characters in fiction of any race are more marginalized than Connie could have remained – yet she is the savior in that closing image.

Morrison wrote in a *New Yorker* essay, taking morality in its broadest sense, of "the power of embedded images and stylish language to seduce, reveal, and control" within any literature, to bring to fruition the force of books' "capacity to help us pursue the human project – which is to remain human and to block the dehumanization of others" ("Strangers" 70). A reader can align this comment with what she had told interviewer James Marcus about the fact that *Paradise* was originally titled *War*:

> War was off-putting. Besides the novel wasn't about war as we know it, with armies, navies, and so on. I was interested in the kind of violent conflict that could happen as a result of efforts to establish a Paradise. Our view of Paradise is so limited: it requires you to think of yourself as the chosen people – chosen by God, that is. Which means that your job is to isolate yourself from other people. That's the nature of Paradise: it's really defined by who is not there as well as who is ... the book was an interrogation about the very idea of Paradise ... It has a sort of question mark implied behind it" (Marcus in Mueller 47).

7
Morrison and the Twenty-first Century: *Love*

If Morrison saw the title of *Paradise* as, in her words, "interrogative" or ironic, with the word possibly followed by a question mark, she surely would have moved those descriptors onto the title of her 2003 novel, *Love*. *Love?* *Love?* Critic Anne Mihan called *Paradise* a book with "a decidedly political impetus" (Mihan 24). For critic Missy Kubitschek, *Paradise* exemplifies such dominant African beliefs as that the common and the communal is the sacred; that distinguishing between the "living" and the "dead" is often (as here) arbitrary; and that the self and other selves are frequently inseparable (Kubitchek 22–3). In *Paradise*, the ramifications of Morrison's African beliefs are less obtrusive. Instead, what comes across are the emphases on what Rebecca Ferguson calls "mother–daughter relationships" – it is this critic who comments "there is very little about relationships between mothers (or fathers) and living sons ... much more about mothers and daughters: Connie and Mary Magna, Mavis and Sal, Delia and Patricia and Billie Delia, Pallas and Dee Dee, Seneca and Jean" (Ferguson 97, 240). Much evidence of this compatibility occurs after the women have been killed, and then are (presumably) resurrected.

Morrison here also traces the motherline in her own family. She dedicates *Paradise* to her remaining sibling Lois (and the sisterhood within the book – of the Convent women as well as the bond between Dovey and Soane who are sisters – reinforces that dedication) and she dedicates *Love* to her maternal grandmother, using the phrase "For and with Ardelia." Long dead when *Love* appears in 2003, Ardelia Willis is the remarkable figure Morrison created in her 1976

New York Times essay, "A Slow Walk of Trees (as Grandmother Would Say), Hopeless (as Grandfather Would Say)." One of Morrison's most important essays, this dual portrait of female and male "ancestors" posits a contemporary history of African Americans in the United States, and deifies Ardelia who "believed that all things could be improved by faith in Jesus and an effort of the will" (Nonfiction 4). She also believed that the fortunes of African Americans were improving, and would continue to do so. Despite events that captured media headlines, the slow and steady progress of *good* was like the movement of the seemingly immobile trees as suburbs took over hillsides.

In contrast, her grandfather, John Solomon Willis, provided the cynical side to the couple's dialogue – largely because he had no faith in the capacity of white people to improve. So long as whites occupied majority positions, he thought that any progress would be limited.

Ardelia, however, joins the best of Morrison's listing of black Americans "whose work is real and pointed and clear in its applications to the race. The ones who refuse to imitate, to compromise, and who are indifferent to public accolade. Whose work is free or priceless. They take huge risks economically and personally. They are not always popular, even among black people, but they are the ones whose work black people respect. They are the healers" (Nonfiction 12).

In the Ardelia Willis mold, then, Morrison crafts the narrative voice of L, a woman who seemingly loved all the characters described in *Love*. She observed, she worked – first as Bill Cosey's cook when the resort was running well; then in an independent café – and she eventually murdered Cosey so as to keep his inheritance intact for the young second wife whose life he had usurped. L died in 1976, the year Morrison wrote the "slow walk of trees" essay; L had killed Cosey in 1971.

As far removed from any traditional use of point of view as was possible, Morrison's convoluted telling of the various strands of *Love* pushes her past the patterns she had created for *Beloved, Jazz,* and *Paradise*. Experimental Morrison began a reign of postmodern excellence that left pieces of narrative cast this way and that across the landscape of Cosey's Hotel and Resort on Sooker Bay, on the Florida Atlantic coast. An unequalled haven for the newly prosperous black middle class in the 1940s, Cosey's Resort was an acknowledged mecca for postwar fun – "The best good time" (*Love* 33). License for whatever needed doing seemed possible. The family mansion, in the village of Silk, stood on Monarch Street.

The chapter titles in this novel all relate to Bill Cosey: Husband, Father, Friend, Stranger, Lover, Benefactor, Guardian; the engraving on his tombstone stays unchallenged, "Ideal Husband, Perfect Father." Using his father's blood money from his days of serving as an informer for the white police, Cosey thought little of his saddened wife, who died young, though his son Billy Boy, who also died young, was much beloved. Living his American dream of success, Cosey is of necessity one center of the novel, the assumed protagonist of the book. Aside from his magisterial portrait hanging in the Monarch Street mansion, he does not appear anywhere in the novel, except in people's memories.

Morrison gives the reader a male businessman center in a script written and spoken by a seemingly inconsequential cook – and the reader's work is to unravel the story lines. The author remembers working hard to create Cosey as the center of the narrative:

> I had diagrams for groups of people and rooms and streets, but the structure basically was how to reveal this responsibility that this man Bill Cosey was given, all these roles. And how his life and his entrepreneurship affected, destroyed, helped, re-made a set of people who lived in that community. So he is sort of not really on stage. Everything had to accrue around him. And to describe how and whether and what was possible in terms of the range of kinds of love in this book, I had this collection of people who knew him and each other in different ways and had a terrible time trying to articulate this. (Con II, 217)

It is as if the farther into the twenty-first century Morrison moved, the more her fiction illustrated crucial remarks critic Barbara Rigney had made in the 1990s. In *The Voices of Toni Morrison*, Rigney assessed what Morrison was able to do: "Toni Morrison's vantage at the intersection of race and gender [gives her a means to exempt her voice] from phallocratic law: her own language and her theory of language ... reflect a consciousness that she writes both from and about a zone that is "outside" of literary conventions … and modifies patriarchal inscriptions" (Rigney, *Voices* 1). In *Paradise*, Morrison invalidates the successful men of Ruby by showing their heinous acts; in *Love*, she rewrites the mainstream American dream by showing its disastrous underbelly. The novels differ but in each, the plots extend what Rigney had early on seen as Morrison's superb, meaningful craft with language. As she wrote, "Morrison implies the primacy of the maternal and the semiotic, in the economy of language, in order to achieve signification and a higher form of poetic (and also political) truth" (Rigney, *Voices* 12).

Difficult as it is to stay outside of commonly held narrative conventions, Morrison had come to rely on her ingenuity with structure and character. It might have looked as if Cosey was the protagonist of *Love*, but once various events and speakers were given credence, little admirable about him remained. L announced several times that Cosey was "a good bad man, or a bad good man." "He didn't have an *S* stitched on his shirt and he didn't own a pitchfork. He was an ordinary man ripped, like the rest of us, by wrath and love" (*Love* 200). Brief as L's opening and closing sections are, the reader has confidence in her judgments. Morrison repeated in interviews that the affection people searched for was "the sort of wide-spirited love that L has for them all … she obviously is not going to abandon them." This is not only a sexual or a "carnal" feeling, but "that human instinct to care for somebody else" (Con II, 219–20).

Morrison has designed L's sections to work through indirection. They are dominated by her careful, and accepting, *hum*, the almost soundless compatibility she has shown to other characters throughout the novel. (Her *hum* closes the book; *Love* 202.) It is in her concluding monologue that L refers to 1 Corinthians, chapter 13, the famous definition of love as "charity … And now abideth faith, hope, charity, these three; but the greatest of these is charity." A means of silencing more audible voices in the novel, L's reliance on the Bible helps the reader see why she thinks as she does. Chapter 13 opens, "Though I speak with the tongues of men and of angels, and have no charity, I am become as sounding brass, or a tinkling cymbal… .Charity suffereth long, and is kind; charity envieth not; charity vaunteth not itself, is not puffed up … ." Whether or not Morrison is hearing her grandmother's recitation of these familiar words, she may be remembering that her grandfather had read through the King James Bible at least five times: Bible reading was foundational in the Willis–Wofford household.

Earlier chapters in 1 Corinthians apply to a conjectural reading that Cosey himself might have come across. Chapter 7 has to do with sexual satisfaction. There, Paul exhorts, "to avoid fornication, let every man have his own wife." A few verses later, he continues, "I say therefore to the unmarried and widows, It is good for them if they abide even as I. But if they cannot contain, let them marry: for it is better to marry than to burn." Used ironically in this novel, since Cosey's marrying the 11-year-old friend of his granddaughter appears to be far from his following any religious mandate, Morrison continues her postmodern questioning of accepted conventions. (The experimental Morrison in these instances becomes the irreverent, postmodern Morrison.)

It is within L's last monologue that she confesses to her murdering Cosey with hemlock, prepared in her kitchen according to her recipe – and she also provides full justification for her managing to keep his last will, leaving everything to the "sweet Cosey child," hidden and then destroyed.

This mélange of significations – words from the Bible juxtaposed with the confession of the murderer who has been linked with boundless love for her fellow men and women – brings to mind Morrison's demand that readers participate in her act of creating fiction. If the involved reader follows the sometimes oblique references, only to arrive at mixed answers, then the further sorting through the site, the condition, the speaker, and the event involves that reader even more deeply.

In *Love*, Morrison creates a different kind of foil for Cosey – a man necessary since Cosey and L are both already dead. Sandler Gibbons is a poor sidekick, too proud to benefit much from his friendship with Cosey, although they often fish together. Sandler is happily married, and he and his wife Vida care for their grandson, Romen, whose parents serve in the military. The teenaged Romen becomes a key player in the second set of narratives that Morrison creates to move the lives of characters past their actual deaths.

The novel begins with Sandler, in fact, getting his snow equipment readied in the garage for an unexpected cold snap. After she stops to inquire of him, he tells the very young (and pretty) Junior how to find the Cosey mansion, thinking to himself that – for all her attempt at sophistication – the woman looked to him "like a sweet child, fine-boned, gently raised but lost" (*Love* 14). Sandler here stands in for Cosey, always overly attracted by the many sweet girls that surrounded him, and Morrison's use of the adjective "sweet" brings to mind Cosey's similar description of the person – "the sweet Cosey child" – to whom he, unexpectedly, planned to leave his estate.

Morrison's narrative structure, then, makes the reader focus on the second and third generations of the Cosey family. Sandler and Vita and Romen talk at supper about the unfamiliar young woman, speculating that she might be a child of one of Heed's many siblings. They talk as well about the mysterious death of Bill Cosey, with Vida warning Romen not to eat any food Christine cooks in the Cosey kitchen. "Somebody killed him as sure as I'm sitting here. Wasn't a thing wrong with that man," Vida says. "You forgive that old reprobate anything" comes her husband's accusation. "He paid us good money, Sandler, and taught us things, too. Things I never would have known about if I'd kept on living on a swamp in a stilt house .... Bill Cosey took us off of it" (*Love* 18). Vida, who had herself been "a little Up Beach girl," consistently defends Cosey (whether or not he had initiated her into sex remains unclear – she marries Sandler and they have their daughter, Romen's mother) (*Love* 35). If Cosey didn't molest Vida, she was one of the few who escaped – having been a fishing buddy of Cosey's, Sandler understands his voracious, and deadly, appetites for female children. His fishing boat was often the site for their sexual uses.

As an introduction to both the Cosey history and the current situation in the mansion, this scene exists for several reasons: it provides Sandler legitimacy as narrator/observer; it leads to an unexpected and grim gang-rape scene in which Romen's failure to participate in the rape of "Pretty Fay" – or "Faith"[1] – makes him a target for the other teenaged boys; and it places Junior within the Monarch Street house, hired by Heed to help her write her book about Cosey. As Junior falls asleep in her new (and luxurious) bedroom, her mind focuses on the imposing portrait of Bill Cosey hanging in Heed's room. Her description of the likeness gives the reader an image of Cosey at his charming best and connects him with another of Morrison's "outlaw" charmers, Joe Trace from *Jazz*: "A handsome man with a G. I. Joe chin and a reassuring smile that pledged endless days of hot, tasty food; kind eyes that promised to hold a girl steady on his shoulders while she robbed apples from the highest branch" (*Love* 30). Readers remember Joe Trace's passion as he makes love to Dorcas; they remember her last words to Felice – that Joe was right, there was only one apple to be cherished – so the image of the young "girl" rather than "woman" robbing the apples has both biblical significance and the echo of the obsessive love affair in *Jazz* between the much older man and his young lover.

Morrison speaks to this theme in her "Foreword" to *Love*, describing the young girl she had known in Lorain whose father molested her – robbing her, infecting her smile with "mournful sympathy" (*Love* ix). The betrayal of trust in the "father" – a role Cosey played to everyone around him – is the most sorrowful condition known, especially when it occurs from the acts of "a friend, a trusted one." Standing outside the "fathering and mothering" that should have been their right, these young and naive people were subject to the worst kind of abuse (*Love* xi–xii). (As she had in her prefaces to both *Jazz* and *Paradise*, Morrison here segues into her personal reliance on what she calls "a feisty mother, a supportive father, and insatiable reading habits" to distance herself as a young, vulnerable girl from these kinds of psychological damages. Reminiscent of the betrayal she writes about in *The Bluest Eye*, this "fatherly" abuse has its separate place in Dante's circles of hell; *Love* xii).

Not all of Bill Cosey's affairs, or his enjoyment in his role as sexual predator initiating young girl after young girl, appear in *Love*. The dominant presence, after his wife Julia dies, is that of Celestial, the beach prostitute who remains loyal to him even in his old age – it is Celestial who visits his grave, along with the spirit of L. (And it is Celestial that gave its working title, "The Sporting Woman," to the novel in process.) The core narrative of the novel, in fact, is less focused on Cosey than it is on the damage his choice – to marry Heed-the-Night when she turns 11, destroying her deep friendship with his lonely granddaughter, Christine – does to the two little girls who had found such solace in each other. Their resulting lifetime enmity over Cosey's choice wastes both lives – and brings nothing of good into either the family or the African American culture.

As a work of fiction, then, *Love* does not develop as a reader might expect. It is, after all, a book about Christine Cosey and her playmate-now-stepgrandmother Heed. There is comparatively little evidence of Cosey's presence in the two little girls' lives. There is the two-part sexual scene, in which Cosey touches the places Heed's breasts will grow and then goes into his granddaughter's bedroom to masturbate (and is seen there, in that act, by Christine). There is the grotesque wedding night scene, when Cosey does not penetrate Heed but instead undresses her, bathes her, and gives her a pleasantly stable definition for the emotion of "love." A few months later, however, he spanks his wife in the presence of Christine and her mother May: such outright betrayal of his promised affection alienates Heed from him for years.

Critic Stefanie Mueller sees *Love* as a kind of sequel to *Paradise* in that it focuses on "domination within the African American community .... it is Morrison's boldest exploration of the complex reverence that the dominated cannot fail to give their dominators" (Mueller 157). As Andrea O'Reilly had quoted from Morrison, "Patriarchy is assumed but women have to agree to the role. You have to say, 'This is the most important person in my life.' It's not that [Cosey] gobbles them up, but they allow themselves to be eaten ..." (O'Reilly, *Toni* 176).

For one of the first times in her novels, Morrison describes issues of class – here, again, within the African American community. The wealth that drives action belongs to Cosey, an African American man, rather than to a white Valerian Street. In *Tar Baby*, Sydney and Ondine Childs were servants to the Streets: they were the stereotypical black poor, asking the white man of wealth to support Jadine, their orphaned charge. Class was inextricably raced. But in *Love*, Morrison reverts to the patterns of her first three novels and sets her narrative *within* African American culture. Bill Cosey and his family are wealthy; nearly everyone else works hard for a living, as the song goes. (Morrison will intensify these class differences once she introduces the young ex-convict, Junior, marked by not only extreme poverty – signaled here by her constant hunger for both food and sex – but also crime.)

By making Sandler into one of the dominant narrators for *Love*, Morrison lets his speaking voice have a powerful reach. The reader hears him talking, in memory, to Cosey. He also speaks, repeatedly, to his grandson Romen (and his voice in these scenes parallels that of Ondine Childs as she tries to educate Jadine). Sandler's speech is recognizable as courteous, well enough educated, and clear. It is not marked by any erosion from extreme poverty.

How to represent classed speech accurately was one of Morrison's pervasive concerns. As she had written for a film about Southern novelist Reynolds Price.

There is the assumption – it's a funny kind of elitism – that lower or middle-class people are functionally illiterate and don't have complicated thoughts and complicated language and complicated images. I find it just hopeless to try to persuade anybody differently, and probably one of the reasons that Reynolds and I have always loved one another is because in this area of black–white relations, having to do with the language of black people and the language of poor people who are black and white, he never patronizes his characters, you never pity those people ... And their language is powerfully articulated, whether or not the grammar is the grammar of standard English .... you can really have tragedy that belongs to people who are not in the so-called aristocracy or the upper class. (Nonfiction 97–8)

Because Heed's family is so poor, and because Bill Cosey has the audacity to offer her parents $200 (and a pocketbook her mother wants) so that he might marry Heed, the trades that seem equitable to the "money man" are early on damned in the reader's view. But as the narrative voice is careful to point out, Heed was always smart, perhaps smarter than Christine, despite the latter's years of private schooling. (Christine was also "stupid about men, unequipped for real work and too lazy to do it anyway; a parasite feeding off men until they dumped her and sent her home to gnaw the hand she ought to be licking.") Heed, in contrast, had a "flawless memory ... like most nonreaders she was highly numerate. She remembered how many gulls had come to feed off a jellyfish ... . Money she grasped completely. In addition she had hearing as sharp and powerful as the blind" (*Love* 75).

Much of *Love* is a record of skirmishes between the now-widowed Heed and the returned Christine (whose saga of abortions, short-lived romantic involvements, and general displeasure with the world makes the quietly passive life on Monarch Street seem appealing). Running parallel with the later months of the women's relationships is a narrative about the quick intellect, and cagey subterfuge, Junior evinces as she lives with the two once-loyal friends. In retrospect, when Morrison tells an early interviewer that "Women generally love something other than themselves," and readers assumed she was talking about heterosexual love, *Love* shows clearly that the single passion in the lives of pre-adolescent Christine and her deepest friend, Heed, was for each other (Bigsby 279). "It's like that when children fall for one another. On the spot, without introduction ... If such children find each other before they know their own sex, or which one of them is starving, which well fed; before they know color from no color, kin from stranger, then they have found a mix of surrender and mutiny they can never live without. Heed and Christine found such a one" (*Love* 199). Set at the end of L's closing monologue, Morrison editorializes that "Most people have never felt a passion that strong, that early" (*Love* 199).

The task of *Love*, then, is to allow the two girls/women to reach a meaningful concluding rapport. Morrison interjects a comment about the fact that the title of this novel fluctuated until almost the end of her process. Finally it was called *Love*. Then, says Morrison, she went through the manuscript carefully "and removed every word every time 'love' appeared so that it would be raw when the first time those women say it, is the only time they could say it" (Con II, 220). It is toward that exchange of long-buried sympathy that the closing section of the novel builds.

The machinations that Morrison creates to reach the women's declaration of love seem comparatively innocuous. They begin with the scheming Junior, infatuated with the man in the Cosey portrait, taking Heed back to the storage attic in Cosey's Resort (in the chapter titled "Phantom"). Once upstairs in the attic, Heed and Junior are surprised when Christine appears. (Heed's desire to return stems from her realization that she has no will; she thinks using the aged paper from the attic will help her create such a document.)

Junior, deciding her fortunes might be better aligned with Christine than with Heed, lures the latter to the edge of the attic trap – and Heed falls through:

> the falling is like a silent movie and the soft twisted hands with no hope of hanging on to rotted wood dissolve, fade to black ... and the feeling of abandonment loosens a loneliness so intolerable

that Christine drops to her knees peering down at the body arching below. She races down the ladder, along the hall, and into the room. On her knees again, she turns, then gathers Heed in her arms. In light sifting from above each searches the face of the other. The holy feeling is still alive, as is its purity, but it is altered now, overwhelmed by desire. Old, decrepit, yet sharp. (*Love* 177)

Listening to Junior's heels clicking, followed by the sound of the car engine, the women know they cannot escape Cosey's Resort. Instead, they talk. As Morrison replays the Pietà scene that closes *Paradise*, its import here is less reconciliation than it is the destruction of Heed's still, small body.

All the hidden histories of Bill Cosey are laid bare: not only the various, and many, women he took on his fishing boat, but the loss of his fortune to unwise loans, outright blackmail, and the complicity of his "friend," the police chief and then the even less scrupulous son of that police chief. In the midst of Heed's recital of all the years of Cosey's adultery, her sense of humor and her acceptance of herself (and her own wiliness) come through plainly. Christine can retell a more glamorous history, but it too is only painful. In their consolation of each other, the women speak their childhood language, which includes the phrase "Hey, Celestial" (their most private code which acknowledges any "bold, smart, risky thing"), but they also – after years of enmity – level with each other. Missing L, taking some of their phrasing from her language, the women near both exhaustion and pain-shrouded closure:

"Jesus, I miss her.
Me too. Always have.
We could have been living our lives hand in hand instead of looking for
Big Daddy everywhere.
He was everywhere. And nowhere.
We make him up?
He made himself up.
We must have helped.
Uh-uh. Only a devil could think him up.
One did.
Hey, Celestial." (*Love* 189–90)

Interrupting the women's slowing conversation, Heed suffused with pain, Morrison replays the scene of Cosey's both touching Heed's chest and then masturbating: both the women, here recreated as young girls, are made to recognize the shame of their own desires. *His* behaviors have instilled that squalid shame in them, and they have been hounded by that egregious miasma all these decades. What they collectively remember, at the close of their hours in Cosey's Resort, are the fireflies and the stars that always mesmerized them. "You're crying" is answered with "So are you ... I can barely hear you." "Hold my ... my hand" is answered with "He took all my childhood away from me, girl." And that is answered with "He took all of you away from me."

A few lines later, as they remember the stars, Christine said "Pretty. So so pretty" and Heed answered, "Love. I really do" (*Love* 194). Morrison almost loses the word that she has tried so hard to include. As it appears without any context, the word *love* assumes its no-longer-understated force. *Love.* "Love. I really do," Heed's declaration of her genuine sought-for dependence resonates through the still air. The reader hears again their earlier interchange, "I wanted to be with you. Married to him, I thought I would be," comes from an 11-year-old Heed, and the 12-year-old Christine answers, "I wanted to go on your honeymoon" (*Love* 193). In the bleak, mournful silence, the women hold each other. They do not speak.

Then Romen arrives, horrified that Junior has left the old women alone and injured in the deserted building. He does what he can in his unbelieving state, carrying the dead Heed down the stairs and placing her in the back seat of the car; Christine rides beside him. After they reach Silk, Christine instructs Romen to lock Junior into L's old rooms, telling him that she will be punished appropriately. Then Christine directs him to drive Heed's body to the mortuary. And then she says, "Thank you, Romen. Everything left in me thanks you" (*Love* 198).

The somber loneliness that closes the novel reflects some of the anguish that had enveloped the United States after the terrorist attacks on September 11, 2001. Even as Morrison had maintained her heavy schedule of accepting awards and giving talks,[2] she too was bowed under the sorrow of the three thousand Americans dead. In her November 2001 essay she called them "the September dead." Specifying their countries of origin – "Asia, Europe, Africa, the Americas, Australia; born of ancestors who wore kilts, obis, saris, gelees, wide straw hats, yarmulkas, goat-skin, wooden shoes, feathers and cloths to cover their hair" – the parade of "The Dead of September 11" sets forth a long stream of mourning. The author of the essay announces, "Speaking to the broken and the dead is too difficult for a mouth full of blood." Morrison claims instead an apt silence – "no words stronger than the steel that pressed you into itself; no scripture older or more elegant than the ancient atoms you have become" (Nonfiction 154–5).

In some respects, *Love* partakes of that stream of mourning. Though gendered, the narrative about men and women, young and old, shows the way patterns of life repeat and, even in their redrawing, culminate in the same endings, the same pains. Misleading readers to expect the canny Junior to remain a quick-witted survivor, Morrison even within that later generation's characterization shows the tendency for a person to be a spoiler. Whether or not the "phantom" of Bill Cosey has had some influence, the girl has become a devil figure: Heed would not have fallen were it not for Junior's taking advantage of her poor eyesight. Junior's efforts to harm the woman can be neither excused nor forgiven.

Within the mood of the destroyed promise of America, Morrison drew in part on her belief about the relationship between readers and book. As she had once written,

What informs my books is the quality of the response. Being in church and knowing that the function of the preacher is to make you get up, you do say yes, and you do respond back and forth. The music is unplanned and obviously not structural, but something is supposed to happen, so the listener participates. The chorus participates both by meddling in the action and responding to it, like the musical experience of participating in church. (Con I, 101)

The tragedy of Morrison's *Love* is that the two perfect halves of the young girls' love became diminished by one. Heed's death stamped "cancelled" on the promise of their possibly long and enduring friendship.

8
Morrison and Various Mercies

Morrison reminded her readers frequently that she did not write autobiographical fiction. She also did not draw characters who represented all African Americans (or all whites); rather, her figures were distinct individuals. Bill Cosey in *Love* might have been a womanizer bordering on a pedophile, proud of his money-making ability, but Morrison never intended Cosey to represent all wealthy African American men. As she wrote,

> My books are frequently read as representative of what the black condition is. Actually, the books are about very specific circumstances, and in them are people who do very specific things. But more importantly, the plot, characters are part of my effort to create a language in which I can posit philosophical questions. I want the reader to ponder these questions. I want the reader to ponder these questions not because I put them in an essay, but because they are part of a narrative. ... I would like my work to do two things: be as demanding and sophisticated as I want it to be, and at the same time be accessible in a sort of emotional way to lots of people ... That's a hard task. But that's what I want to do. (Con I, 106)

The active narrative lines of *Love,* then, which lead to and culminate in the death of Heed Cosey, memorialize not only this character's existence but the tragedy that she was "married" to Bill Cosey while still a child. That she endured through sheer will was a tribute to her native intelligence – and her sad recognition that her family was willing to sell her for a very small price. (As she would much later tell Christine, "Mind you, at eleven I thought a box of candied popcorn was good treatment"; *Love* 186). In reality, her death resulted at least partly from the decades of unhappiness she spent as Mrs. Bill Cosey – and her guilty need to immortalize him in writing.

The novel was another illustration of Morrison's statement about the nature of love as emotion: "I'm trying to get at all kinds and definitions of love. We love people pretty much the way we are. I think there's a line, 'Wicked people love wickedly, stupid people love stupidly,' and in a way we are the way we love other people" (Con I, 106). It was also an oblique illustration of the power of music – not only in people's lives but in the creative world's underlying symbiosis.

At Princeton, Morrison had developed an arts program that drew from fields far from the literary, as well as the literary. Known as the Atelier program, this interdisciplinary workshop placed at its center such artists as Maria Tucci, Lars Jann, Yo Yo Ma, Jacques d'Amboises, A. S. Byatt, Louis Massiah, Richard Danielpour, Roger Babb, Gabriel García Márquez and others. Just as she had years before written the story and lyrics for *New Orleans: The Storyville Musical* (in 1981, working with Donald McKayle and Dorothea Freitag), in 1995 she helped to create *Degga*, an interdisciplinary work with composer Max Roach and choreographer, dancer Bill T. Jones. She had also been writing lyrics for songs performed by Sylvia McNair, Jessye Norman, and Kathleen Battle (with André Previn; with Judith Wier); her work toward both *Margaret Garner* and, to come, *Desdemona*, first performed in 2012, directed by Peter Sellers with Rokia Traore, was an extension of her interest in musical composition.

She had commented to an interviewer that "writing lyrics for André Previn and Kathleen Battle ... experts at what they did, and I was an expert at what I did; but I was a novice in what *they* did. I didn't know anything about it, so working with them was just amazing. So I started to shape language to do other things. Not to *be* the music, but to just sit there and hold it, so that somebody else could do what they did" (Con II, 251). And she often made aesthetic comments that tied literature to music; as she noted to Diana Cooper-Clark, "the way in which one arrives at the idea in a book is via the words and the sentences and the dialogue. It's like knowing what the notes are in the last chord in music" (Cooper-Clark 201).

Just as Morrison fused a number of creative strategies, she found new ways to present themes that had been pronounced in both *Paradise* and *Love*. Uppermost in her recent themes was that of the dominant patriarchy – personified as Bill Cosey in *Love* more so than the powerful men of Ruby. Working against the power dynamic between women and men, Morrison explained that *Love* began with the image of Pretty-Fay and her "little white-mitten hands" as she was being raped by Romen's friends. Morrison notes that "her aim in writing about the act of rape is to 'sabotage' the 'male pride ... in the language' that characterizes rape scenes from the rape of Lucretia onward." She writes in the novel about "naked male behinds" and the more sympathetic victim, "face ... turned to the wall and hidden beneath hair undone by writhing" (Morrison, "Start" 76; *Love* 49, 46). Stefanie Mueller sees *Love* as a sequel to *Paradise* in that it focuses on "domination within the African American community ... . it is Morrison's boldest exploration of the complex reverence that the dominated cannot fail to give their dominator" (Mueller 157).

Five years later, much to the surprise of readers who were assuming that Morrison would once again return to African American history as the site of her fiction's plot and setting, Morrison published *A Mercy*. Set in the seventeenth century, before the United States existed, this novel is an amalgam of varied racial lines, people in diverse economic circumstances, and settings that prompted unique kinds of reader response. In terms of what *A Mercy* contributed to Morrison's interest in African American history, it gave readers a chance to see that slavery (or indenture) was not necessarily equated with skin color. In this novel, Morrison did her best to present a race-free canvas. There is plenty of male dominance, however, given the power of land-holding in the seventeenth century.

Justine Tally points out that *The Black Book*, edited in part by Morrison in 1974, included several documents about indentured servitude. Whereas this element of human ownership had occurred earlier in the person of *Beloved*'s Amy Denver, Morrison's fiction had seldom been focused on such servitude – largely because her novels were set much later. In *A Mercy*, however, prominent characters like Scully and Willard Bond (referred to ironically as "Mr. Bond" by the free blacksmith) are indentured; Rebekka is sold by her English father to become Vaark's wife (once she has painfully crossed the Atlantic); Florens is taken by Vaark from her enslaved mother as partial repayment for her master's debt; Lina is a spoil of war with the Native Americans; and Sorrow is everybody's chattel. Of these people, only the homosexuals Scully and Willard, and Vaark and his wife Rebekka, are white. Sorrow is mixed race, Lina is Native, and Florens is Caribbean black.

The Black Book includes the English "Act XVI," dated 1691, relevant to the free white persons considered: "it is further enacted, that if any English woman being free shall have a bastard child by a Negro she shall pay fifteen pounds to the church wardens, and in default of such payment, she shall be taken into possession by the church wardens and disposed of for five years ... The child shall be bound out by the church wardens until he is thirty years of age." Seventy-four years later, in 1765, the law was modified: children should "be bound out, the males to serve until twenty-one ... females until eighteen" (*Black* 88; Tally, *Beloved* 56).

As Morrison shows within the novel, the settlers are both repulsed and attracted by Florens's skin color; the only other black character is the illiterate blacksmith, a healer as well as a craftsman. Yet for all the centrality that Florens comes to assume in the novel – she is the one who writes, the "historian" of the period, filling the walls and floors of Vaark's unfinished house with her words – other story lines appear to be equally important. As Melanie Anderson suggests, in *A Mercy* Morrison revisits earlier themes: "the destruction of the family unit by slavery; mother and daughter relationships; obsessive love; degrees of freedom; the importance of community; class, gender, and race conflicts; and patriarchal dominance. *A Mercy* can be read as a companion piece to *Beloved*, and the two novels haunt each other in conversation about the effects of slavery" (Anderson 17).

To legitimate Anderson's emphasis on the difficulty of maintaining family within slavery means that Florens's being taken away from her enslaved mother becomes the main narrative line. Saving her pre-adolescent daughter from the sexual abuse she has herself known (often, and from predators of both sexes) is her mother's clear – and only – motive: Morrison gives the reader that scene, and the mother's words, at the end of the novel where, in repetition similar to what Morrison in *Love* had achieved with the word "love," the mother pleads with Vaark to take Florens: "Because I saw the tall man see you as a human child, not pieces of eight. I knelt before him. Hoping for a miracle. He said yes. It was not a miracle. Bestowed by God. It was *a mercy.* Offered by a human" (*Mercy* 166–7). Yet Morrison insists, as the novel closes, that the repetition of the title word *not* be the sound that rests in her reader's mind but instead, the blessing sent by Florens' mother, "Oh Florens. My love. Hear a tua mae" (ibid.). The powerful sorrow that suffuses this novel is rare in the Morrison oeuvre. *A Mercy* becomes a long lament, for the horrors of human treatment of other human beings. Florens's mother's words do not reach her daughter; when Florens dreams of her mother, she sees that the woman is speaking – but she can never hear or interpret her words. Instead the child is wrenched by her belief that she was not so well loved as was her brother, that her mother asked Vaark to take her not because she saw in him some vestige of kindness but because she wanted to be rid of her daughter. In *Love*, Morrison had not emphasized the trauma Heed Cosey felt because her parents had allowed her to be bought by Cosey. In *A Mercy*, however, she gives the reader a thoroughly traumatized Florens. No amount of love and care from Lina can erase Florens's memory of her mother's act, and her lament for her mother – even in an unfamiliar language – becomes one voice of the novel: *minha mae* echoes through passage after passage, even if the girl's call does not sound aloud.

A Mercy is the beginning of Morrison's depiction of trauma that had marked so many of her characters from earlier books – whether or not their trauma was the fulcrum of the novel. In *The Bluest Eye*, Pecola and her damaged life show the effects of abuse, but the reader is given only the image of that waste, not the child's recognition or the internalization of the horror. In *Song of Solomon*, the childhoods of both Macon and Pilate Dead are not the primary canvas for Morrison's working through the importance of knowing the ancient wisdom of African and African American life. In *Beloved*, most visibly, Sethe cannot escape from the memory of her murdering her child or her recognition of what sin means to a mother. In *Paradise*, the women of the Convent are similarly traumatized – some from childhood, others later in their lives – but their deaths/lives beyond deaths seem to provide a tranquil escape. What Morrison achieves in the central characterization of Florens in this 2008 novel will continue to shape the ways in which she draws the figures of both Frank Money and his younger sister Cee in her 2012 novel *Home*.

Florens is Morrison's illustration of the far-reaching effects of childhood trauma. Having been forced to leave her mother when she is only seven or eight, the child must live among strangers in a colder, wilder environment, bereft of language as well as love. As Judith Herman stated, such children "face the task of grieving not only for what was lost but also for what was never theirs to lose. The childhood that was stolen from them is irreplaceable. They must mourn the loss of the foundations of trust" (Herman 193). Herman quotes from the American Psychiatric Association's *Diagnostic and Statistical Manual of Mental Disorders* (fourth edition): children so traumatized experience "recurrent and intrusive recollections of an event ... or recurrent distressing dreams." They are marked as well by "social withdrawal, shame, despair, hopelessness" (424–5).

Ventriloquist that she is, Morrison lets Florens's voice permeate all parts of *A Mercy*. She does this through an intricate 12-part structure: Florens's speaking opens the novel; then she is the speaker in five more sections, alternating with others (Florens speaks in parts 1, 3, 5, 7, 9, and 11; the alternating voices are those of Vaark, then Lina, then Rebekka, then Sorrow, and finally the joint narrative of Scully and Mr. Bond). Even though other characters are speaking, some of what they say has to do with Florens.

The ending sections of *A Mercy* are spoken as if in counterpoint, first by Florens (part 11) and in answer by her mother (the conclusion). As she had from *Beloved* on, Morrison no longer used chapter divisions. So important were the speech patterns of her characters that each separate section began with some figure's characteristic idiom. No chapter divisions, no section titles: Morrison trusted her involved readers to ferret out who was speaking and what the speaking really managed to say.

A Mercy is dedicated to Morrison's editor of long standing, R. G. (Robert Gottlieb), and she thanks him on the dedication page "For decades of wit, insight and intellect." There is a tone of leave-taking in that phrasing. In 2008, when *A Mercy* appears, Morrison is already in her mid-seventies. She has lost many friends, family members, and fellow writers; she knows that her work will eventually cease. It seems as if Morrison in her novels of the twenty-first century puts more and more responsibility on her readers. She had written that one of her aims as a writer was

to try to put the reader into the position of being naked and quite vulnerable, nevertheless trusting, to rid him of all of his literary experience and all of his social experiences in order to engage him in the novel. Let him make up his mind about what he likes and what he thinks and what happened based on the very intimate acquaintance with the people in the book, without any prejudices, without any prefixed notions, but to have an intimacy that's so complete, it humanizes him in the same way that the characters are humanized from within by certain activity, and in the way in which I am humanized by the act of writing.

She continued about her writing – for her, "It's a haven, a place where it can happen, where you can react violently or sublimely, where it's all right to feel melancholy or frightened, or even to fail, or to be wrong, or to love somebody, or to wish something deeply, and not call it by some other name, not to be embarrassed by it. It's a place to feel profoundly ..." (Con I, 109).

Morrison rarely uses the word "profoundly" but in assessing what she has accomplished in *A Mercy*, that word seems apt. The book's similarity to *Beloved* is also clear: Florens begins her first segment, the start of the novel, with a description of haunting:

Don't be afraid. My telling can't hurt you in spite of what I have done and I promise to lie quietly in the dark – weeping perhaps or occasionally seeing the blood once more – but I will never again unfold my limbs to rise up and bare teeth. I explain. You can think what I tell you a confession if you like, but one full of curiosities familiar only in dreams and during those moments when a dog's profile plays in the steam of a kettle. Or when a corn-husk doll sitting on a shelf is soon splaying in the corner of a room and the wicked of how it got there is plain. Stranger things happen all the time everywhere. You know. I know you know. One question is who is responsible? Another is can you read? (*Mercy* 3)

Stated more clearly in the Scully and Willard section (segment 10): "Jacob Vaark climbed out of his grave to visit his beautiful house."
"As well he should," said Willard.
"I sure would," answered Scully.
It was still the grandest house in the whole region and why not spend eternity there? When they first noticed the shadow, Scully,

not sure it was truly Vaark, thought they should creep closer. Willard, on the other hand, knowledgeable about spirits, warned him of the consequences of disturbing the risen dead. Night after night they watched, until they convinced themselves that no one other than Jacob Vaark would spend haunting time there: it had no previous tenants and the Mistress forbade anyone to enter... (*Mercy* 143)

Known for her creation of narratives that sometimes mislead the reader, Morrison here may attribute the "haunting" that Florens does in the uninhabited house to Vaark as owner. It seems likely that the two "Europes," indentured white men who reverence the material success of Vaark, the Anglo-Dutch farmer, would look no further for a source of capable haunting. Underlying the surface narrative, however, runs the fact that the educated Florens will not acquiesce to her role as dependent servant girl. As she had asked at the close of her first monologue about ghostly presences, "Another [question] is can you read?" (*Mercy* 3).

The literacy her mother had secured for them through the services of the Catholic priest in Maryland is Florens's only weapon. Though Lina tries to teach her about nature, living in the wild, observing other human beings, Florens is a child fascinated by language. She calls her opening section a "confession" and despite her reference to "seeing the blood once more," Morrison leaves open the outcome of the girl's attack on the blacksmith. In the novel, that vengeful act stops abruptly just before Scully and Mr. Bond begin their section of narration (with the speculation about Vaark as ghost). That segment of Florens' speech there ends, "Feathers lifting, I unfold. The claws scratch and scratch until the hammer is in my hand" (*Mercy* 142).

That Florens must harm the illiterate blacksmith stems not only from his calling her "slave" and preferring a young boy to her company. It also evidences her childhood trauma, again seeing herself replaced by the baby brother at her mother's breast. In the words of psychologist Kali Tal, using the term "bearing witness" to describe such acts:

Bearing witness is an aggressive act. It is born out of a refusal to bow to outside pressure to revise or to repress experience, a decision to embrace conflict rather than conformity, to endure a lifetime of anger and pain rather than to submit to the seductive pull of revision and repression. Its goal is change ... If survivors retain control over the interpretation of their trauma, they can sometimes force a shift in the social and political structure. (Tal 7)

Otherwise, it goes without saying, their state of mind will not change. Given this extreme reaction to the blacksmith's turning her away, Florens may have unleashed her creative abilities in her writing. As Lina had seen, the Vaark family was heading toward destruction. With her untutored but acute observational skills, she saw "the disruption, the shattering a free black man would cause. He had already ruined Florens, since she refused to see that she hankered after a man that had not troubled to tell her goodbye. When Lina tried to enlighten her, saying 'You are one leaf on his tree,' Florens shook her head, closed her eyes and replied, 'No. I am his tree" (*Mercy* 61). In the distant third person Morrison uses for Lina's section, she then concluded, "Florens had been a quiet, timid version of herself at the time of her own displacement. Before destruction. Before sin. Before man" (*Mercy* 61). When Lina was raising the little girl, telling her stories at night before they slept as a pair, Florens preferred her stories about good and brave mothers. Lina refers to this as "Mother hunger – to *be* one or *have* one – both of them were reeling from that longing which, Lina knew, remained alive, traveling the bone" (*Mercy* 63). Within the complicated narrative lines of this novel, Morrison uses the multiple stories connected with Sorrow to bring *this* hunger to a close. After Sorrow's second baby is born safely – amid some suggestion that Lina, perhaps, had killed her first baby – she expresses the joy that motherhood brings her, telling her new daughter that she no longer needs her spirit "Twin" but instead has changed her own name from "Sorrow" to "Complete" (*Mercy* 134).

Using the historical background of the 1676 Bacon's Rebellion as a setting for *A Mercy*, Morrison emphasizes *class* rather than *race*. When Vaark travels through Virginia, he describes the rebellion as being "against hereditary privilege ... the people's rebellion." Goulimari uses this expansion to claim that *A Mercy* might be considered the fourth book of Morrison's trilogy, since the other three also traced "alternative historiography." She sees that the reference to rebellion "decenters the role of New England Puritans" and provides "a Babel of nations, languages, religious denominations and classes"

(Goulimari 127–8). Morrison confirmed this historical connection in her 2013 interview: "After Bacon's War, any white man could kill any black people, and blacks could have no power." There existed many separate groups "but the master controlled everybody" (Live, NY Public Library).

Morrison is intent on "getting the history straight" (ibid.), as well as creating a "pre-racist" world, a place where "very little separates enslaved Africans, white indentured servants, and poor unmastered women." Much of the friendship that seems to exist in *A Mercy* is improbable – perhaps this is "virtual reality" rather than historical – as is the treatment that the homosexuals Scully and Willard Bond receive. (Striking as examples of Vaark's friendship, for instance, are his sharing liquor with Bond, and sharing an apple – cut with his personal knife – with the blacksmith.) "*A Mercy* confirms and displays the linguistic and cultural dispossession, nomadism and pluralism of the American colonies in the seventeenth century" (Goulimari 128–9, 142).

Whereas *A Mercy* may be – for many reasons – termed "political," it could also be linked with the author's autobiography. Morrison has revered language and the recording of it for almost her entire life. As she once said, "I don't remember myself being in the world before I could read. I just don't remember what that was like … I was about three, because my sister was four and a half, and I remember writing on the cement sidewalks with her; it was an early thing. And I don't remember myself before forming and understanding language, so that is the way I entered the world" (Con II, 255). She also felt comfortable with mixed-race cultures: "I went to school with white children – they were my friends. There was no awe, no fear. Only later, when things got … sexual … did I see how clear the lines really were. But when I was in first grade nobody thought I was inferior. I was the only black in the class and the only child who could read" (Strouse).

For Tessa Roynon, Morrison's recounting of "America before it was America" – the author's phrase – is apt in showing "the multicultural nature of the country before monocultural narratives of nationhood were imposed upon it" (Roynon 80). This critic explains that the language Morrison created for the novel, illustrated through Florens's telling as "a hybrid text," draws from "Portuguese-inflected pidgin English that only colonialism and the transatlantic slave trade could have produced – a non-Anglo speech" that calls attention to these sources. The language of *A Mercy*, then, bears "a palimpsistic relationship with texts that precede it – the Bible; the canonical histories and literary works about colonial America; the slave narratives; the writings of Milton, of Blake, and of Wordsworth, to name a few" (Roynon 82).

Erudite as this fusion of language may seem to be, the reader takes the cue from Florens in her first monologue, when she admits, "At first when I am brought here I don't talk any word. All of what I hear is different from what words mean to a minha mae and me. Lina's words say nothing I know. Nor Mistress's. Slowly a little talk is in my mouth and not on stone ..." (*Mercy* 6). Cut off from dominant language, Florens makes her way into adulthood slowly, and perilously. But she survives. In critic Farah Griffin's assessment, calling this novel Morrison's "meta-statement,"

> she presents a world, as yet untamed, with pliable boundaries. A world, filled with birds, bugs, natural beauty, disease, passion, pestilence, and utter chaos ... [and] a household of three 'unmastered' women, but this time they are the white Rebekka, the Native American Lina, and Sorrow, who is of mixed heritage ... This is a new American narrative. The moment of what might have been. The moment of when those who would possess power turned away from one set of possibilities: a family of orphans, needing and clinging to each other in spite of emerging hatreds. (Griffin 126)

(To complete the paradigm of being motherless, Morrison emphasizes that Vaark is himself an orphan.)

Griffin also calls attention to the fact that in *A Mercy* the natural world is almost another character:

> The topos Morrison describes is so distant from our own that it appears magical and magnificent ... Here we get a land more ancient than Eden. The land (not Founding Fathers, sacred documents, religious exiles, or settler colonists) sits at the beginning of this history. And to that land came the dangerous, superstitious theologies of the Baptists, Anabaptists, and the Catholics. The so-called Pagan beliefs of the Native American Lina honors the sacredness of the landscape far better than the newcomer Christians. (Griffin 127)

Morrison herself underscores the affinity between Lina and her Native sensibilities and the natural world – and it is Scully who manages to survive there as well. Being outside the rule-bound patriarchal and religious cultures has its advantages in seventeenth-century America. As many critics have pointed out, *A Mercy* includes Morrison's first treatments of homosexual men, as well as the wise, even if incredibly bereaved, Native American woman. (Much of Lina's wisdom comes from her mother as she dies of the smallpox; here, *not* being orphaned has made this character understand the ancient properties.) Among the author's descriptions are these: "Sudden a sheet of sparrows fall from the sky and settle in the trees. So many the trees seem to sprout birds, not leaves at all." The moose, observing Rebekka as she bathes in the river, "turns slowly and walks away. Like a chieftain" (*Mercy* 70–1). The trapped partridge attracts the sow bear, always famished in early spring:

> the smell washed over them at the same moment the sow crashed through the laurel clicking her teeth .... Scully, certain he felt hot breath on his nape, leaped for the lowest branch and swung up onto it. Unwise. Herself a tree climber, the bear had merely to stand up to clamp his foot in her jaws .... Scully snatched out his knife, turned and, without even aiming, rammed it at the head of the agile black hulk below. For once desperation was a gift. The blade hit, slid like a needle into the bear's eye. The roar was terrible as, clawing bark, she tumbled to the ground on her haunches ... Snarling, standing straight up, she slapped at the stuck blade until it fell out. Then down on all fours she rolled her shoulders and wagged her head from side to side. It seemed ... a very long time before the grunt of a cub got her attention and, off balance by the blinding that diminished her naturally poor sight, she lumbered away to locate her young. (*Mercy* 147–8)

Readers might not attribute such scenes and their descriptive power to Morrison's admiration for William Faulkner, but comparisons with "The Bear" and much of *Go Down, Moses* (as well as the novels she used in her Cornell thesis, *The Sound and the Fury* and *Absalom, Absalom!*) are obvious. As she said when she spoke in the mid-1980s at the Faulkner Conference, "William Faulkner had an enormous effect on me, an enormous effect ... My reasons, I think, for being interested and deeply moved by all his subjects had something to do with my desire to find out something about this country and that articulation of its past that was not available in history" (Con II, 25). She continued, "There was in Faulkner this power and courage – the courage of a writer, a special kind of courage ... something else which I can only call 'gaze.' He had a gaze that was different. It appeared, at that time, to be similar to a look, even a sort of staring, a refusal to look away ... [this] appeared in his writing that I found admirable" (ibid.)

As she had also told an interviewer years ago, she likes Faulkner "a great deal. He was heavily influenced by black people, by their concept of time as a circle, as a spiral, by their rhythms, their perception of things. The cultural exchange is insidious. They [people of white culture] were erecting these very, very careful barriers, but at the same time there was this incredible seepage and leakage." She refers particularly to *Absalom* and "The Bear": "you have this sense of Faulkner's being affected in some extraordinary sense by a black population." She continues, "This is not *Gone with the Wind*; this is the white South's nightmare, which is the search for the black figure which no one can recognize" (Bigsby 284).

In Morrison's *Paris Review* interview she comments on his treatment of "the insanity of racism." She uses a personal anecdote to explain her fascination with his style: "Faulkner in *Absalom, Absalom!* spends the whole book tracing race, and you can't find it." She describes the hours she spent studying the book for mentions of race (or non-mentions), "all the moments of withheld, partial, or disinformation, when a racial fact or clue *sort* of comes out but doesn't quite arrive ... I was so fascinated technically ... The structure is the argument ... No one has done anything quite like that ever" (Con II, 74).

Many critical books and essays relate Morrison to Faulkner: John N. Duvall, placing both *Love* and *A Mercy* in line with Faulkner's "brinksmanship," adding in the existence, in *Jazz*, of Golden Gray and Wild replicating Charles Etienne Bon in his marriage (Duvall, "House" 23). In *Love*, Duvall reads Cosey as Sutpen, with Christine and Heed as parallels to Rosa and Clytie. Both David Cowart and Justine Baillie read *Song of Solomon* as influenced by *Go Down, Moses*; Karla Holloway sees that *Beloved* follows *As I Lay Dying* in being memoirs, if not spirituals (Cowart 97; Baillie 105; Holloway,

"Narrative Time" 93). Cheryl Wall finds a much wider pattern of influence by suggesting that Morrison plays and replays what she calls "Faulknerian themes and topoi: the past that is not past, the mixed bloodlines of African, Europe, and native America, the hunt as existential ritual" (Wall, *Worrying* 26).

Difficult as it has been for Morrison to escape the charges from very political twenty-first-century critics that Faulkner was more of a racist than he might have been, she explained that, even though her mother had very limited spending money, she belonged to a book club. Those books were precious in the Wofford household: Morrison devoured them all. If writers – such as Hemingway and Faulkner – used a racial stereotype, she explained that she just "Read over it. Because I loved those books. I loved them. So when they said these things that were profoundly racist, I forgave them. As for Faulkner, I read him with enormous pleasure. He seemed to me the only writer who took black people seriously. Which is not to say he was – or was not – a bigot" (Con II, 101).

9
Morrison and the Definitions of *Home*

Morrison's last two novels – *A Mercy* in 2008 and *Home* in 2012 – are comparatively short books. One of the reasons for their brevity is the author's use of innovative and unusual structures. By choosing to center the reader's attention on the language of each character, as she does in *A Mercy*, Morrison strips the narrative movement down to still focus points. Sometimes told by one of the other half dozen narrators but more often by Florens herself, the story of her great love for the blacksmith – as well as her enraged punishment of him – provides continuity that spins outward from a vortex of emotion. In Florens' six sections of the 12-part narrative, over a third of the novel, she repeatedly provides for the reader the scene of her mother's giving her away, as well as the account of what the blacksmith has done to her life. (No reader could distill the fabric of such earlier Morrison novels as *Song of Solomon* or *Beloved* into such a brief summary.)

Morrison's *Home* is another intricately fashioned structure; the way Frank Money's story reaches the reader differs dramatically from the organization the author had created for *A Mercy*. Rather than the alternating of Florens's sections with the narratives of other characters, in *Home* Morrison stays more often within several levels of Frank Money's mind, along with several sections told by an omniscient voice. Obscured in part by Frank's wandering quest for a safe home, his personal center – like that of his narrative – is the search for masculine integrity and purpose. *Home* is a novel that draws more visibly from Morrison's early love for the novels of Virginia Woolf than from her continuing interest in William Faulkner's works: as she had earlier insisted, "Good prose is poetic ... good prose has to have this underground life. The metaphor is a way of energizing it. And absolutely – absolutely – the sounds of the sentence, the choice of words" (Con II, 31).

The most visible difference between *A Mercy* and *Home* is the seemingly oblique opening for the latter novel. Metaphor takes on its force in the opening three sentences: "They rose up like men. We saw them. Like men they stood" (*Home* 3). Calling attention to the stream-of-consciousness import of this several-page section, titled simply "One," the italics of this segment will recur at key places in the novel. The immediate impact of italicization is obscure. What resonates from the scene of the beautiful, sweating horses is their fierce masculine force – "So brutal. And they stood like men." Morrison told one interviewer that the image of these horses came from nowhere:

> I thought to myself, *What am I talking about? I've never seen horses fighting. Do they even stand up?* So I ran around and got some films, and of course horses bite a lot when they fight, but they do stand up .... I don't know where it came from – this picture of the horses – but once it was there, I knew the kid, this character who is a child, who is black and vulnerable and living in the '50s in a place where race circumscribes him. And the look of the horses is one thing – and the violence involved – but the other thing is the "like men" part of the sentence, the "how to be a man" part. That notion is what is important to the boy. ("I Start with an Image" 123)

Morrison also spoke in her New York Public Library interview about what she called the "thin line" between the animal and the human, saying, "I find the intimacy of humans with animals, birds, etc., is a way of extending the human" (Live, NY Public Library). In countless scenes of *Beloved*, for instance, the reader is asked to stretch across that line – Paul D's competing with Mister the rooster, Sethe's being charged with having four feet instead of two. In *Jazz*, similarly, Violet Trace's intimacy with birds lessens some of her anguish, and some of the reader's anguish observing that character's behavior.

Besides the image of the fighting horses, Morrison opens *Home* with lines from one of her own early poems – searching for a house where her key would fit the lock, a dream-like sequence that posits lostness as miasma. In contrast to the "house" of *her* dreams – "another, sweeter, brighter / With a view of lakes crossed in painted boats" – *this* "house is strange. Its shadows lie." Its spirit does not calm the speaker; it rather *erases* calm from her.

All parts of the opening of *Home* suggest the importance of not only Woolf's emotionally charged novels (Morrison had used *Mrs Dalloway* in her Cornell thesis, and some hint of both Clarissa Dalloway's powerful interior life and Septimus Smith's damaged war nerves carry into *Home*) but also of Emily Dickinson's poems (Morrison owned several editions of Dickinson's work). Capturing readers with suggestions of the unknown in this opening to *Home* makes them sensitive to the events from Frank's childhood – even those happenings he seems not to "remember." What he *does* remember is his fear – he has brought his little sister Cee with him to the neighboring farm where not only do they see the fighting horses, they also see strange men and trucks, the men taking "a body from a wheelbarrow." This form they throw "into a hole already waiting. One foot stuck up over the edge and quivered, as though it could get out, as though with a little effort it could break through the dirt being shoveled in" (*Home* 4).

"Two" brings the disoriented Frank Money, Korean War veteran, into the mental hospital in Seattle where he is incarcerated. Drugged, ravaged by PTSD (post-traumatic stress disorder), he carefully plots his escape, aiming to reach the *AME Zion* yard sign visible from his window. He is not only hiding; he has received a note about Cee from Sarah Williams of Atlanta, warning him to "Come fast. She be dead if you tarry" (*Home* 8). The spur for action, this note shows the reader a capable Frank – his year of wasted life after leaving the service, broken only by his time with Lily. But he is no longer with her, the successful woman of his dreams, so traveling back to Georgia in order to help his sister gives him a purpose.

Unlike *A Mercy*, *Home* is spoken largely by Frank, though some of his words challenge the reader. It is as Morrison described as she considered the tricks memory plays, "The memory is long, beyond the parameters of cognition. I don't want to sound too mystical about it, but I feel like a conduit. I really do. I'm fascinated by what it means to make somebody remember what I don't even know" (Con II, 13). As if Morrison was immersing herself once more in the context she drew from as she wrote *Song of Solomon*, finding accuracies in her knowledge of Milkman Dead at least partly through her mourning for her father, here she fought through the unspeakable sorrow of having lost her son, Slade. (The novel is dedicated to "Slade.") While the son, who was a very talented writer – with whom she had written a series of children's books – died from pancreatic cancer, Morrison put the novel away. Months after his death in December of 2010, she resumed work on the book, but she spoke – as if her personal losses were related – about the *Song of Solomon* experience in an interview: "I was unable to finish the novel until my father died. I was very depressed …. I knew that I no longer had a life that way: the way that I lived in his mind" (Con II, 12). In that vein, Morrison also explained to an interviewer that Slade's death left her wordless: "What do you say? There really are no words for that. There really aren't. Somebody tries to say, 'I'm sorry, I'm so sorry.' People say that to me. There's no language for it. Sorry doesn't do it. I think you should just hug people and mop their floor or something" (Brockes). The mourning that the author-as-mother creates occurs in the *writing* she resumes, through the story of Frank when he is "a child, who is black and vulnerable and living in the '50s in a place where race circumscribes him."

The town is Lotus, Georgia. When Morrison gives Frank's family the name *Money*, she makes readers recall the murder site of Emmett Till (Money, Mississippi), another black and vulnerable male child. Frank's family history has been even more racially mangled than was Till's. Run out of their Texas home by the KKK (where they saw their neighbor Crawford hanged – eyeless – from his mother's prized magnolia tree: a black man who did not leave town), Frank's family history has been desperate. At four, Frank watches his mother, pregnant with Ycidra, forced to give birth in a church basement; he becomes his little sister's safety net, protecting her from Lenore, the step-grandmother who did not like taking in her husband's Texas family. Years later, by the time Frank and his friends Stuff and Mike enlist (largely to escape Lotus), he has given up his role as Cee's protector. She runs away to Atlanta with Prince, a boy interested only in her grandparents' car. He soon dumps Cee.

Sometimes reviewed as a novel about the returning, damaged veteran, *Home* casts a wider net of meaning. It is a psychological study of the damages of homelessness for all children: Frank is marred and marked not only by the warfare he has experienced, losing his best friends on a brutal battlefield; he is scarred as well from the moment he is forced to run from Texas. His disorientation is deepened when he and Cee witness the naked man's rude burial.

Except for the omniscient sections, Frank narrates most segments of *Home*. One speaker is the damaged boy – his words are italicized. Another is the falsely contrived narrator of experiences that might have occurred (but, as the reader finds out later, have not). Usually the italicized sections are very short, working as if they were prose poems. For a time the sections alternate – parts 1, 3, 5, 7, 9, and 11 are italicized. Then two sections interrupt the italicization: sections 12 and 13 form one unit. Similarly, sections 15 and 16 form another unit, and finally, the briefest part of all – section 17, which is a dialogue between Cee and Frank, resumes the italics once again. It is this section that – reminiscent of the emphasis Morrison gave to the word *love* (in *Love*) and the word *mercy* (in *A Mercy*) – ends with the word *home*. It is Cee, speaking "Lightly" and touching his shoulder, who utters the novel's last line, "Come on, brother. Let's go *home" (Home* 147).

The center of the novel is given over to deep mourning. In sections 10 and 11, Frank sorrows for not only the deaths of his friends but for the part of himself that he has stifled. The story that the false narrator Frank tells everyone, including himself, is that the dead Korean girl was shot by an unknown soldier. The eventual realization that Frank comes to is that his screen memory is self-protective: *he* shot the child, seeing her in her innocence as a kind of tempting sexual threat. He realizes then that, rather than mourning inconsolably for his two dead friends, he is only pretending: instead, his life is filled with "people I didn't save" (*Home* 103). This realization occurs as he approaches Buckhead, Georgia, home of the wealthy doctor for whom Cee works (and serves as a guinea pig for illegal eugenics experiments on women's wombs). With his action – taking Cee away from the threatening and armed doctor, hiring a cab to take her home to Lotus where he asks Miss Ethel Fordham to care for her (and save her), finding a job so he can support himself and his sister, and living with truths rather than fabrications during the long months of Cee's healing – Frank takes his first steps toward survival. During section 14, Frank gives the reader his full confession: "I have something to say to you right now."

The process Morrison has so carefully and vividly limned reflects contemporary research into trauma (and not only war-inflicted trauma). Judith Herman describes any child "trapped in an abusive environment [who] must find a way to preserve a sense of trust in people who are untrustworthy, safety in a situation that is unsafe, control in a situation of helplessness" (Herman 102). The anxiety that a tall, strong man (Frank is six feet three) feels when he finds himself powerless is even greater than psychological studies suggest.

As a result of such trauma, events "shatter the construction of the self that is formed and sustained in relation to others" and "cast the victim into a state of existential crisis" (Herman 51). Kali Tal, speaking of military victimization, adds that the soldier in combat is not simply a victim. He is "both victim and victimizer, dealing death as well as risking it. These soldiers carry guns; they point them at people and shoot to kill. Members of oppressed groups, by contrast, almost never control the tools of violence" (Tal 10). As Morrison peels away the layers of Frank's story, the deepest injury done to his psyche seems to have been his killing of the Korean girl. Observing the frightening burial on the farm gives a deep and long-lasting injury to Frank's moral behavior. He is not guilty of that man's death or burial, though. He is, however, completely guilty of the Korean child's murder.

Tal also formulates the stages of dealing with trauma – what she calls "mythologization," "reducing a traumatic event to a set of standardizing narratives, which become the 'story' of the trauma." It then becomes "a contained and predictable narrative" (Tal 6). The repetition of Frank's stories, albeit his periods of great depression that block attempts at normal living, falls into this pattern. It also accounts for the go-between dialogues as Frank seems to be talking to a secondary writer, or perhaps a therapist.

Frank's ability to heal reflects in some ways the time that the "mean" loving women of Lotus were giving to their healing the wounded Cee. His little sister was harmed physically as well as psychically, though the eventual outcome – her being barren and hallucinating about seeing an unborn child – shows that no wounding remains entirely physical. Kali Tal's definition of trauma is more inclusive than some: "An individual is traumatized by a life-threatening event that displaces his or her preconceived notions about the world. Trauma is enacted in a liminal state, outside of the bounds of 'normal.' human experience, and the subject is radically ungrounded" (Tal 15). Recovery is often unpredictable:

> Because the theory of a literature of trauma is based on the reintegrative process – a series of discrete events that occur over a period of time – we can reasonably assume that a chronological approach would provide the clearest picture of this development. Shifts in theme, voice and subject can then be plotted along a time line ... [But] this is no simple project ... since there are several separate chronologies that must be maintained ... Retellings appear at different stages, and it is essential to consider each retelling as a part of the larger process of revision. (Tal 18)

Herman adds that post-traumatic recovery must entail the "empowerment of the survivor and the creation of new connections.." She points out that contact with "a single, caring, comforting person may be a lifeline ... The reward of mourning is realized as the survivor sheds her [his] stigmatized ... identity" (Herman 133, 194).

Home is close to being a memory play. There are very few characters, and those that exist are chosen, for the most part, to provide context for Frank's experiences. The reader needs also to remember Morrison's insistence that humor is valuable. (*Home* does not have many moments that could be described as humorous: perhaps when Salem Money feigns poor hearing to avoid listening to his bedfast wife.) Throughout Morrison's writing career, however, the author privileges humor: "it keeps one from dramatizing and over reacting; it keeps you from romanticizing yourself. It's the most important thing in the world, particularly in parenting and writing because delusions are destructive. Humor provides a frame and a distance and a kind of stability ... you need the proscenium ... High tragedy is not possible, the only other recourse is irony" (Con II, 9).

In *Home*, Morrison somewhat unexpectedly includes section 6, giving the reader the character of Frank's lost love, Lily Jones. Reminiscent structurally of Morrison's inclusion of Geraldine in *The Bluest Eye*, the narrative about Frank's lost Lily works indirectly as background for Frank's story. The story of the talented African American seamstress, prevented by race from buying a house in a location she wants, represents Morrison's continuing interest in strong women. As the author had told an interviewer, "I just like for women to do interesting stuff .... I know they're going to be very lonely ..." (Con II, 189). In critic Jan Furman's expansion of her study of Morrison's oeuvre, she notes that "Morrison is never far from an interest in the historical and social evolution of female identity and relationships" (Furman 2014 135).

The independent Lily Jones breaks off her romance with Frank, who clearly experiences PTSD symptoms, when she can no longer cope with his bouts of depression, his inability to work, and his running from the interchange with the young girl with "slanty" eyes (*Home* 76). At the end of the Lily section, Morrison creates a heavily ironic episode: Lily "finds" a leather coin purse filled with money. She will consequently be able to open her own tailoring shop, a scene that seems to replay both the erroneous message of Frank's name and William Faulkner's equally ironic scene of finding money so the illicit lovers can escape their hometown in *If I Forget Thee, Jerusalem.*

Working as she has in theater circles, Lily's involvement with the group producing proletarian writer Albert Maltz's *The Morrison Case* introduces more than black–white prejudices. Morrison was trying to suggest the exclusionary temper of post-World War II times. As she told Lisa Shea about wanting to give readers an accurate portrait of that decade,

> I was interested in the 1950s because we associate it with the postwar Doris Day decade, when it really wasn't like that. Forty thousand Americans died in the Korean War, which wasn't called a war – it was called a police action. It was the time of the McCarthy hearings and a lot of medical apartheid, the license of [eugenics practitioners] preying on black women, the syphilis trials on black men. The '50s were a highly violent race period. Emmett Till was murdered in 1955. There were a lot of moments like that. The seeds of the '60s and '70s were already being planted. (Shea 236)

More trenchantly, Morrison remarked, "*Mad Men.* Oh please" (Brockes).

It is in the Shea interview as well that Morrison remarks that *not* relying on some strand of the romance plot was freeing. In *Home*, Morrison explained, she was "trying to think of when a man would love a woman without the baggage. Who is the female figure that he could love selflessly. Not a mother, not a lover, not a wife – only a sister" (Shea 236). She had meditated about the other side of the Frank–Cee relationship in a different interview, saying "I have lots of questions in the novels. I was very much interested, not in the male–female love relationship, which is ubiquitous, but in other relations of the women with the idea of what maleness is in their lives. As father, as brother, they are not just guys; they are all these other things" (Con II, 235).

Michael D. Hill has recently pointed out that Morrison often wrote about "cooled affections," beginning with Cholly and Pauline in *The Bluest Eye* and continuing through various pairings in *Love*. Reflecting some of Morrison's impatience with choosing narratives that may have become predictable, Hill's comment provides insight into her moving to narratives – such as those of *Paradise* as well as *A Mercy* and *Home* – that expand definitions of family and community love (Hill, *Ethics* 114, n50).

To balance Morrison's primary metaphor – the horses standing tall as men, striking each other – she borrows a metaphor from her first novel, *The Bluest Eye*, which plays here as the "melon" scene between Cee and Sarah, a seemingly happy closing to section four. As critic Barbara Rigney had pointed out about the well-crafted melon scene in the early novel, melons consistently represent female sexuality (Rigney, *Lilith's* 83–4). In *Home*, perhaps more in keeping with this book's heavily ironic tone, Morrison describes Cee's first few weeks working for Dr. Beau in Buckhead as idyllic.

> This was a good, safe place, she [Cee] knew, and Sarah had become her family, her friend, and her confidante. They shared every meal and sometimes the cooking. When it was too hot in the kitchen, they ate in the backyard under a canopy, smelling the last of the lilacs and watching tiny lizards flick across the walkway.
>
> "Let's go inside," said Sarah, on a very hot afternoon that first week.
>
> "These flies too mean today. Besides, I got some honeydews need eating before they soften."
>
> In the kitchen, Sarah removed three melons from a peck basket. She caressed one slowly, then another. "Males," she snorted.
>
> Cee lifted the third one, then stroked its lime-yellow peel, tucking her forefinger into the tiny indentation at the stem break.

"Female," she laughed. "This one's a female."
"Well, hallelujah." Sarah joined Cee's laughter with a low chuckle.
"Always the sweetest."
"Always the juiciest," echoed Cee.
"Can't beat the girl for flavor."
"Can't beat her for sugar."
Sarah slid a long, sharp knife from a drawer and, with intense anticipation of the pleasure to come, cut the girl in two. (*Home* 65–6)

Linked to other Morrison novels – in *Tar Baby*, the unnamed woman in yellow, so carefully carrying her three eggs, in *Beloved*, Sethe's metaphorically splitting open in the birth of Denver – in *Home*, the misunderstandings that both Cee and Sarah labor under (that this is a *safe* place, that the splitting open here prefaces the morbid experimentation Dr. Beau will begin with young Cee's uterus) are almost unbearable. But the beautiful poise in the dialogue between Cee and Sarah discounts the terror to come: rhythmically, this scene acts as a placid mirror to the women's friendship.

Morrison links section four, which ends with the joyful eating of the female melon, to Lily Jones's narrative in section six, through the most personal and the most sexual of Frank's screen memories – in section five, the full account of all his sexual experiences, and his mourning for what might have existed with Lily. Frank's section returns the reader to the realization that no matter what occurs to the remaining members of the Money family, it is Frank's burden to sort through the fragments of that family's life – he has no calm, restful moments in his consciousness. The melon scene that closes section four – which does not include any mention of Frank – seems to be an illustration of the kind of stillness Morrison was describing in her short essay, "Peril," when she explained to readers: "Certain kinds of trauma visited on peoples are so deep, so cruel, that unlike money, unlike vengeance, even unlike justice, or rights, or the good-will of others, only writers can translate such trauma and turn sorrow into meaning, sharpening the moral imagination" ("Peril" 4).

Morrison draws *Home* to its close by returning the reader to the secret burial on the farm. The momentary stasis that Cee's friendship with Sarah created was short-lived (though it was Sarah who wrote to Frank about the danger his sister was living in). Implicit in the novel is the concept that the fighting horses, sold for meat during wartime, signaled what ideal masculine behavior was to be. But as Frank learns from his grandfather Salem and his cronies, all venerable men, the degradation on the horse farm went far beyond civilized behavior. It had early been a site of prostitution and gambling, but then it became known for its human battling – black sons and fathers shipped in from other states, so that the rules of the betting observers was that either the son died, or the father. The odds were on which of the pair would kill the other.

In Morrison's scene of Salem and his friends retelling the horrible narrative to Frank, the reader recalls the barbershop scene from *Song of Solomon*. Speech among men is not for effect: it is heart-felt, and it also serves as chorus.

"You want to know about them dogfights?" asked Fish Eye ...
"More like men-treated-like-dog fights."
Another man spoke up. "You didn't see that boy come through here crying? What did he call himself? Andrew, you 'member his name?"
"Jerome," said Andrew. "Same as my brother's. That's how come I remember."
"That's him. Jerome." Fish Eye slapped his knee. "He told us they brought him and his daddy from Alabama. Roped up. Made them fight each other. With knives."
"No sir. Switchblades. Yep, switchblades." Salem spat over the railing.
"Said they had to fight each other to the death."
"What?" Frank felt his throat closing.
"That's right. One of them had to die or they both would. They took bets on which one." Salem frowned and squirmed in his chair.
"Boy said they slashed each other a bit – just enough to draw a line of blood. The game was set up so only the one left alive could leave. So one of them had to kill the other." Andrew shook his head.
The men became a chorus, inserting what they knew and felt between and over one another's observations.
"They graduated from dogfights. Turned men into dogs."
"Can you beat that? Pitting father against son?"
"Said he told his daddy, 'No, Pa. No.'"

"His daddy told him, 'You got to.'"

"That's a devil's decision-making. Any way you decide is a sure trip to his hell."

"Then, when he kept on saying no, his daddy told him, 'Obey me, son, this one last time. Do it.' Said he told his daddy, 'I can't take your life.' And his daddy told him, 'This ain't life.' Meantime the crowd, drunk and all fired up, was going crazier and crazier, shouting, 'Stop yapping. Fight! God damn it! Fight!'"

"And?" Frank was breathing hard.

"And what you think? He did it." Fish Eye was furious all over again. "Come over here crying and told us all about it. Everything. Poor thing. Rose Ellen and Ethel Fordham collected some change for him so he could go on off somewhere. Maylene too. We all pulled together some clothes for him. He was soaked in blood."

"If the sheriff had seen him dripping in blood, he'd be in prison this very day."

"We led him out on a mule."

"All he won was his life, which I doubt was worth much to him after that." (*Home* 138–40)

For Frank, a survivor of war and its death-dealing battles, hearing the savage story of these "dogfights," set as they were in the pastoral farm country nearby, Lotus, Georgia took on appreciable depth. The town was no longer the innocuous site of boring existences. Although Frank had not been privy to the wisdom Cee was learning from the older women who were saving her life, bringing her back to health during months of care, the reader has heard the soliloquies about gardening, the instructions about quilting: the truly pastoral spirit of the small Georgia town has already made inroads on the reader's mind and heart. Having lost her son to violence in Detroit, Michigan, Miss Ethel saved as much of Lotus as she could physically get her hands around: she "blocked or destroyed enemies and nurtured plants. Slugs curled and died under vinegar-seasoned water. Bold, confidant raccoons cried and ran away when their tender feet touched crushed newspaper or chicken wire placed around plants. Cornstalks safe from skunks slept in peace under paper bags ... Her garden was not Eden; it was so much more than that" (*Home* 130).

Toward the end of Cee's stay in Miss Ethel's home, the tough love the community women had subjected her to had melded into tenderness – but then Miss Ethel reverted to the toughness she thought Cee needed to hear:

"Look to yourself. You free. Nothing and nobody is obliged to save you but you. Seek your own land. You're young and a woman and there's serious limitations in both, but you a person too. Don't let Lenore or some trifling boyfriend and certainly no devil doctor decide who you are. That's slavery. Somewhere inside you is that free person I'm talking about. Locate her and let her do some good in the world." (*Home* 126)

It takes subsequent conversations between Cee and Frank (who has managed to rent the house in which their parents had lived – both now dead from overwork and illness) to show how independent a spirit Cee has developed. She lives happily with Frank, but she does not *need* to live with him: she accepts everything that has happened to her and attempts to work past the physical damage she will always carry.

The climactic resolution of *Home* occurs in section 16, when Frank tells Cee to bring her first finished quilt to use for a purpose they both must share. Returning to the abandoned farm, they dig up the grave – "Such small bones. So few pieces of clothing. The skull, however, was clean and smiling" (*Home* 139–40). Wrapping these fragments in Cee's quilt, Frank takes the shovel and heads for a better burial site. But Cee has her moment of realization during this somber process: "Cee bit her lip, forcing herself not to look away, not to be the terrified child who could not bear to look directly at the slaughter that went on in the world, however ungodly. This time she did not cringe or close her eyes" (*Home* 141). It is the clear-sighted Cee who ferrets out the zoot-suited spirit across the stream (a figure that earlier haunted Frank as he traveled from Seattle to Chicago, a male imago in stylish urban postwar clothing). But it is Frank who digs the grave under the huge sweet bay tree – a tree split, "hurt right down the middle / But alive and well." After the quilt-wrapped body is buried, Frank takes a sanded piece of wood from his pocket. Pounding nails with a rock, he secured the marker: "Here Stands A Man." The memorial to a man long dead, killed in an unspeakably brutal way by a loved one, stood in quiet repose, as did his bones. Morrison's metaphor has come full circle.

The metaphor of horses standing tall like men has been given incremental force in the process. The genuine man of Lotus, Georgia, has all along been Salem Money, friend of birds and animals, humbly asking little and providing support to whatever townsperson needed him. As regular in his habits "as a crow," Salem visited his friends' porches at certain times, avoiding the grasp of Lenore's power (but still caring for her in her illness). His was a life of quiet, and careful, observations. As Cee told Frank, "He don't say nothing but he knows everything going on" (*Home* 136).

Morrison's 2012 novel also does its best to expand definitions of "home." Critics had used the author's earlier definition of that word in her 1997 essay titled simply "Home." In discussion that focused on race – attempting to reach the idyllic condition of "raceless-ness" – Morrison drew sharp lines between "house" and "home." In an opening section of this essay, the author says commandingly, "I have never lived, nor has any of us, in a world in which race did not matter" ("Home" 3). She makes promises to the reader. She tells the reader that she would never, as a writer, "reproduce the master's voice and its assumptions of the all-knowing law of the white father." Instead she would rebuild typical structures so that she could launch "a moveable feast that could operate, be celebrated, on any number of chosen sites." She would not stay within some "windowless prison ... a thick-walled, impenetrable container." Rather, her home would be "an open house, grounded, yet generous in its supply of windows and doors" ("Home" 4).

In addition to the building's physical appearance, Morrison's *house* in its transformation to *home* would allow people to consider

> legitimacy, authenticity, community, belonging. In no small way, these discourses are about home: an intellectual home; a spiritual home; family and community as home; forced and displaced labor in the destruction of home; dislocation of and alienation within the ancestral home; creative responses to exile; the devastations, pleasures, and imperatives of homelessness as it is manifested in discussions on feminism, globalism, the dias-pora, migrations, hybridity, contingency, interventions, assimi-lations, exclusions. The estranged body, the legislated body, the

violated, rejected, deprived body – the body as consummate home. ("Home" 5)

The overwhelmingly simplified reaches of Morrison's narrative of Frank and Cee Money's effort draws in much of this assumptive text: gender, law, religion, war, family, and the visible transgressions against those implied principles. In its sometimes bare prose – some stretches given as terse dialogue, other scenes implied but omitted entirely from the novel – *Home* carries the reader from the family's lost home in Texas, bloodied with the neighbor's unnecessary death; to the hostile surroundings of the grandparents' house in Georgia; to the inhuman conditions of war, poverty, addiction, and medical trespass. Morrison's closing resolution as she finds a means of placing Frank and Cee, as newly formed family, within the safe household that had once sheltered their parents, makes clear the ways in which community laves its attention and its promise on two lost people.

The quest that Frank and Cee have undertaken, whether consciously or unconsciously, is, at its simplest, the search for home. Critic Evelyn Schreiber has long read Morrison's novels *Love* and *A Mercy* as parts of this quest, pointing out the appropriateness of Heed Cosey's dying in Cosey's Hotel and Resort, since that had been for decades "a site of black personal and collective memory" as well as "a physical and a psychic space tied to self-concept and adequacy for the community and family members." In Schreiber's analysis *A Mercy* continues these narrative threads of the "dispossessed and transplanted people" who initiate a similar search for home (Schreiber 29–30). Furman adds, "*Home* concludes on a buoyant note, and Frank and Cee emerge scarred but optimistic: they have acquired new, liberating knowledge, a loving, transformative relationship, and a place in community" (Furman 2014 141). In Morrison's words, again from "Home," "My efforts were to carve away the accretions of deceit, blindness, ignorance, paralysis, and sheer malevolence embedded in raced language so that other kinds of perception were not only available but were inevitable" ("Home" 7).

Never accusatory but always aware, Morrison views the compilation of history – whether it be the untold story of a seemingly murdering slave mother or the depiction of black lives in small Southern towns, unnoticeable and unimportant to the observing eye – as one of her primary responsibilities, as both writer and public intellectual.

In the words of critic Jill Matus, as she draws on a metaphor apt for this 2012 novel, "Bearing witness to the past, Morrison's novels can also be seen as ceremonies of proper burial, an opportunity to put painful events of the past in a place where they no longer haunt successive generations ..." (Matus 2–3). For Justine Baillie, Morrison's novel *Home* was always intended as allegory. Despite the fact that the advance contract was for Morrison's memoir, she wrote the Frank Money narrative, choosing "to represent black experience in 1950s America in a novel that echoes twenty-first century, post 9/11 anxieties" (Baillie 197). This critic draws analogies with today's climate:

> The allegorical nature of *Home* is clear as America continues to send men home from war, Morrison concerned to project the present onto the imaginings of the past "to yield up a kind of truth." The war in Korea is remembered lest America slip further into amnesia or nostalgia for the prosperity of the Eisenhower years and *Home* is written to redress the ideological distortions of political discourse. (Baillie 198)

Whereas the quality of the house that shelters the home may be "this gothic, mendacious nightmare," in Baillie's words, the act of *making* the home is positive, and the house maintains its "healing possibilities." It does, by the ending of Morrison's 2012 novel, become a *home* (Baillie 199).

Coda

Toni Morrison identifies herself consistently and emphatically as an African American woman writer. She prides herself on being a part of this forceful, intelligent, adaptive population, and she frequently writes praise songs to her people. For example,

> what Black people did in this country was brand new ... These people were very inventive, very creative, and that was a very modern situation. It was, philosophically, probably the earliest nineteenth-century modernist existence. And out of thrown things they invented everything: a music that is the world's music, a style, a manner of speaking, a relationship with each other, and more importantly, psychological ways to deal with it. And no one gives us credit for the intelligence it takes to be forced into another culture, be oppressed, and make a third thing. Other cultures who get moved like that die or integrate; or because they're White, they don't even integrate, they disappear into the dominant culture. That never happened to us ... this is a whole new experience – and it is a modern experience. (Con II, 193)

This same sense of proud heritage comes through in the "Foreword" she was asked to write in 2007 for a reissue of August Wilson's play, *The Piano Lesson*. Praising him because he "confines his themes to African American culture," and he writes his plays with "vigor and coherence," Morrison emphasizes that in some places his scenes read "like lyrics. He teases from African American vernacular its most salient elements: loaded metaphor, nuance, clever use of the unsayable ... And the music – hear the percussive staccato of these lines" ("Foreword" vii, x). Of Wilson's work collectively, she notes, "It is very like living in a war zone where alertness is all, where fear is simply one element of breathable air. That is the tension that roils under the humor, the storytelling, the ferocity with which the characters hold their positions, the efforts at reconciliation" ("Foreword" xiii).

Assuming that Wilson's writing stemmed from the same kind of identification as has hers, Morrison writes an essay that also relates to her work. Here in 2015, watching as the fact that her fiction appears in more than 30 different languages, and that her 1987 novel *Beloved* was chosen by the *New York Times* in 2006 as the most important literary work of the previous 25 years, a critic can only attempt to summarize the accolades that have accumulated since 1993, when she won the Nobel Prize in Literature.

Early in the twenty-first century, Morrison was awarded the "Arts and Communities" prize from the Academy of Culture in Paris, France, as well as the NAACP Image Award for Outstanding Literary Work in Fiction. She traveled to Scotland to give the Amnesty International Lecture. She was invited to join the Universal Academy of Cultures, the International Parliament of Writers and Artists, and the African and Helsinki Watch Committee on Human Rights. She received the Coretta Scott King Award from the American Library Association, a Doctor of Letters Degree from Oxford University in England, and an Honorary Doctorate of Letters from The Sorbonne, Paris, France. She was invited to give the Leon Forrest Lecture at Northwestern University. She was chosen a Radcliffe Medalist by the Radcliffe Institute at Harvard, and was given the Lifetime Achievement Award from *Glamour* Magazine, as well as the Ellie Charles Artist Award from the African Institute at Columbia University.

Her community of Lorain, Ohio, had named the reading room of the public library for her, and the abstract sculpture at Lorain County Community College, entitled "The Gift," consisted of three figures bearing a stone upon which appear quotations by both Aristotle and Morrison. The lines from Morrison are: "We die. That may be the meaning of life. But we do language. That may be the measure of our lives."

Four of Morrison's novels – *Paradise, Beloved, Sula,* and *Song of Solomon* – were chosen for discussion more than a decade ago by the

Oprah Winfrey television book club during the years when those selections were printed with the gold Oprah seal and sold in separate sections in bookstores. Throughout the years there have been large celebrations for Morrison's birthdays, her retirement from Princeton University, and similar occasions.

After *A Mercy* appeared in 2008, she was awarded the Norman Mailer Prize for Lifetime Achievement, and chosen Officier de la Legion d'Honneuer and given the Medaille Vermeil Grand Prix Humanitaire de France/Honor Medal of the City of Paris, as well as Honorary Doctorate of Letters awards from both Rutgers University and the University of Geneva.

In 2012, *Home* was published. That year Morrison received the Presidential Medal of Freedom from President Barack Obama. In 2013, she was awarded the Nichols-Chancellor's Medal from Vanderbilt University. For the past 25 years, the Toni Morrison Society has had biennial meetings – and has placed a dozen of the commemorative "Bench by the Road" memorials in honor of people who experienced slavery. In 2014, on September 12, Morrison honored her friend of 40 years at the Maya Angelou Memorial service at Riverside Church in New York City. Morrison is said to be working now on a new novel about, among other things, the cosmetics industry.

Notes

Introduction

1. Morrison as editor was something of a chameleon. She said, "When I edit somebody else's book no vanity is involved, I simply want the writer to do the very best work he can do. Now if that means letting him alone, I'll do that. If it means holding hands, I'll hold hands. If it means fussing, I'll fuss" (Con II, 8). As she later wrote, "Editing sometimes requires re-structuring, setting loose or nailing down: paragraphs, pages may need re-writing, sentences (especially final or opening ones) may need to be deleted or re-cast; incomplete images or thoughts may need expansion, development. Sometimes the point is buried or too worked-up. Other times the tone is 'off,' the voice is wrong or unforthcoming or so self-regarding it distorts or mis-shapes the characters it wishes to display. In some manuscripts traps are laid so the reader is sandbagged into focusing on the author's superior gifts or knowledge rather than the intimate, reader-personalized world fiction can summon" (Nonfiction 86–7).

1 *Song of Solomon*: One Beginning of Morrison's Career

1. Toni Cade Bambara's best-known novel, *The Salt Eaters*, illustrates the pervasive belief that white conquerors destroyed this ability. As Morrison said in an interview about the dangers of freedom, "The salt tasters ... They express either an effort of the will or a freedom of the will" (Con I, 164).

2. As Morrison explained, "I really did not mean to suggest that they kill each other, but out of a commitment and love and selflessness they are willing to risk the one thing that we have, life, and that's the positive nature of the action. I never really believed that these two men would kill each other. I thought they would, like antelopes, lock horns, but it is important that Guitar put his gun down and does not blow Milkman out of the air, as he could. It's important that he look at everything with his new eyes and say, 'My man, my main man.' It's important that the metaphor be in the killing of this brother, that the two men who love each other nevertheless have no area in which they can talk, so they exercise some dominion over and demolition of the other. I wanted the language to be placid enough to suggest he was suspended in the air in the leap towards this thing, both loved and despised, and that he was willing to die for that idea, but not necessarily to die" (Con I, 111).

2   *Tar Baby* and Other Folktales

1. There are some overtones of Shakespeare's *The Tempest*, with a Jadine who is a mere shade of Ariel set in opposition to a much more handsome Caliban. Valerian Street, however, does not even play at being Prospero.

7   Morrison and the Twenty-first Century: *Love*

1. The book of Romans appears just before 1 Corinthians, and some critics have connected the boy's name with this part of the Bible. As Paul instructs, "The just shall live by faith" (chapter 1); later in chapter 16 comes Paul's promise, "And the God of peace shall bruise Satan under your feet shortly." With rape, either by teenaged boys or by Cosey, as the pervasive metaphor, even this incident has relevance.

2. Between 1998 and 2003, Morrison had received the Medal of Honor for Literature from the National Arts Club in New York, the Ohioana Book Award and the Oklahoma Book Award, the National Humanities Medal, the Pell Award for Lifetime Achievement in the Arts, the Jean Kennedy Smith New York University Creative Writing Award, the Enoch Pratt Free Library Lifetime Literary Achievement Award, the Cavore Prize (Turin, Italy), the Fete du Livre, Cite du Livre, Les Escritures Croisees (Aix-en-Provence, France), and the Docteures Honoris Causa, Ecole Normale Superieure (Paris, France). In 1998 the Oprah Winfrey production of *Beloved*, directed by Jonathan Demme with Winfrey as Sethe, premiered; in 2002 the opera *Margaret Garner*, for which Morrison wrote the libretto and Richard Danielpour the score, was produced, and later productions in Detroit, Philadelphia, and elsewhere were planned.

Bibliography

Primary Work

Novels

Morrison, Toni. *Beloved*. New York: Knopf, 1987. Print.
——. *The Bluest Eye*. New York: Holt, Rinehart, & Winston, 1970. Print.
——. *Home*. New York: Knopf, 2012. Print.
——. *Jazz*. New York: Knopf, 1992. Print.
——. *Love*. New York: Knopf, 2003. Print.
——. *A Mercy*. New York: Knopf, 2008. Print.
——. *Paradise*. New York: Knopf, 1998. Print.
——. *Song of Solomon*. New York: Knopf, 1977. Print.
——. *Sula*. New York: Knopf, 1973. Print.
——. *Tar Baby*. New York: Knopf, 1981. Print.

Books for Children

Morrison, Toni. *Remember: The Journey to School Integration*. New York: Houghton Mifflin, 2004. Print.
—— with Slade Morrison. *The Big Box*. New York: Jump at the Sun, 1999. Print.
—— with Slade Morrison. *The Book of Mean People*. New York: Hyperion, 2002. Print.
—— with Slade Morrison. *Little Cloud and Lady Wind*. New York: Simon and Schuster, 2010. Print.
—— with Slade Morrison. *Peeny Butter Fudge*. New York: Simon and Schuster, 2009. Print.
—— with Slade Morrison. *Who's Got Game? The Ant or the Grasshopper?* New York: Scribner, 2003. Print.
—— with Slade Morrison. *Who's Got Game? The Lion or the Mouse?* New York: Scribner, 2003. Print.
—— with Slade Morrison. *Who's Got Game? The Mirror or the Glass?* New York: Scribner, 2004. Print.
—— with Slade Morrison. *Who's Got Game? Poppy or the Snake?* New York: Scribner, 2004. Print.
—— with Slade Morrison. *Who's Got Game? Three Fables*. New York: Scribner, 2007. Print.

Edited Collections

Morrison, Toni, ed. *The Black Book*. Ed. Middleton Harris, et al. New York: Random, 1974, 2009. Morrison's Preface (1974) and Foreword (2009), n.p. Print.

——, ed. *Burn This Book: PEN Writers Speak Out on the Power of the Word.* New York: Harper, 2009. Morrison's introductory essay, "Peril," 1–4. Print.

——, ed. *Race-ing Justice, En-gendering Power: Essays on Anita Hill, Clarence Thomas and the Construction of Social Reality.* New York: Pantheon, 1992. Morrison's introduction, "Friday on the Potomac," vii–xxx. Print.

——, and Claudia Brodsky Lacour, eds. *Birth of a Nation'hood: Gaze, Script, and Spectacle in the O. J. Simpson Case.* New York: Pantheon, 1997. Morrison's introduction, "The Official Story: Dead Man Golfing," vii–xxviii. Print.

Nonfiction Books

Morrison, Toni. *Five Poems* (illustrated by Kara E. Walker). Las Vegas, NV: Rainmaker, 2002. Print.

——. *Playing in the Dark: Whiteness and the Literary Imagination.* Cambridge, MA: Harvard U P, 1992. Print.

——. "Virginia Woolf's and William Faulkner's Treatment of the Alienated." Cornell University, MA thesis, English Department, 1955. Print.

——. *What Moves at the Margin: Selected Nonfiction.* Ed. Carolyn Denard. Jackson: U P of Mississippi, 2008. (Includes several dozen of Morrison's most famous essays.) Print.

Other Writings

Morrison, Toni. Afterword. *The Bluest Eye.* New York: Plume, 1994: 209–16. Print.

——. "Back Talk: Toni Morrison." *Nation* (December 8, 2008). Morrison with Christine Smallwood. Print.

——. "A Bench by the Road." *The World* 311 (1989): 4–5, 37–41. Print.

——. "Black Matters." *Grand Street* 10.4 (1991): 205–25. Print.

——. "City Limits, Village Values: Concepts of the Neighborhood in Black Fiction." *Literature and the American Urban Experience: Essays on the City and Literature.* Ed. Michael C. Jaye and Ann Chalmers Watts. Manchester: Manchester U P, 1981: 35–44. Print.

——. "Clinton as the First Black President." *New Yorker* (October 5, 1998). Print.

——. "Cooking Out." *New York Times Book Review* (June 10, 1973): 4. Print.

——. "Exclusive interview with Toni Morrison." *Oprah.com.* October 10, 2008. http://www.oprah.com/. On line.

——. "'The Foreigner's Home': Introduction." Louvre Museum Auditorium Exhibit, Paris (November 6, 2006). Print.

——. Foreword. *Black Photographer's Annual.* Ed. Joe Crawford. New York: Another View, 1972: i–ix. Print.

——. Foreword. *Jazz.* New York: Vintage, 1999, 2004: xv–xix. Print.

——. Foreword. *Love.* New York: Vintage, 2005: ix–xii. Print.

——. Foreword. August Wilson's *The Piano Lesson.* New York: Theatre Communications Group, 2007: vii–xiii. Print.

——. Foreword. *Song of Solomon.* New York: Vintage, 2004: xi–xiv. Print.

——. Foreword. *Sula.* New York: Vintage, 2004: xi–xvii. Print.

——. "Good, Bad, Neutral Black." *New York Times Book Review* (May 2, 1971): 3+Print.

——. "'Harlem on My Mind': Contesting Memory – Meditations on Museums, Culture and Integration." Louvre Museum Auditorium, Paris (November 15, 2006). Print.

——. "Home." *The House That Race Built: Black Americans, U.S. Terrain.* Ed. Wahneema Lubiano. New York: Pantheon, 1997: 3–12. Print.

——. "Honey and Rue." Lyrics, musical score by André Previn. 1992. Print.

——. "'I Start with an Image.' Interview with Pam Houston." *AARP Magazine* (July 2009): 122–4. Print.

——. "Interview with Melvyn Bragg." *The South Bank Show.* London: Weekend Television, Channel ITV, 1987. Print.

——. "Interview with Maya Joggi." *Brick* 76 (2005): 97–103. Print.

——. "Interview with Monice Mitchell, Toni Morrison Chafes at Being Labeled 'Role Model.'" *Charlotte Observer* (September 2, 1990): 6c. Print.

——. "Interview with Florence Noiville." *Literary Miniatures.* London: Seagull: 112–17. Print.

——. "Interview with Francois Noudelmann." *Black Renaissance* 12.1 (October 2012): 36–51.

——. "Interview with Charlie Rose." Charlie Rose. PBS (January 19, 1998). Web.

——. "Interview with Ntozaka Shange." *American Rag* (November 1978): 48–52. Print.

——. "Interview with Jean Strouse. 'Toni Morrison's Black Magic.'" *Newsweek* (March 30, 1981): 53–5. Print.

——. Introduction. *Adventures of Huckleberry Finn by Mark Twain,* The Oxford Mark Twain. Ed. Shelley Fisher Fishkin. New York: Oxford U P, 1996: xxxii–xli. Print.

——. "Jean Toomer's Art of Darkness" (review of Toomer's *The Wayward and the Seeking). Washington Post Book World* (July 13, 1980): 1. Print.

——. "Letter to Obama." http://firstread.msnbc.msn.com/archive/2008/ 01.27.614795.aspx. On line.

——. "Live from New York Public Library." December 12, 2013 (Junot Diaz interviewing Toni Morrison). Video.

——. *Margaret Garner: An Opera in Two Acts.* Rev. ed. New York: Associated Music, 2004. Print.

——. "Maya Angelou." New York Memorial, September 12, 2014.

——. "Memory, Creation, and Writing." *Thought: A Review of Culture and Idea* 59 (1984): 385–90. Print.

——. "Presentation for 'Roundtable on the Future of the Humanities in a Fragmented World.'" *PMLA* 120.3 (2005): 715–17. Print.

——. Presentation of National Medal in Literature to Eudora Welty. Public Broadcasting System, July 6, 1980 [phonotape, Michigan State University Voice Library, cat. No. M3395, band 11]. Audio.

——. "Race and Literature." Lecture, University of Chicago (March 7, 1997). C-SPAN2. On line.

——. "The Reader as Artist." *Oprah Magazine.* Harpo Productions, July 2006. http://www.oprah.com/omagazine/Toni-Morrison-on-Reading. On line.

——. "Reading." *Mademoiselle* 81 (May 1975): 14. Print.
——. "Recitatif." *Confirmation: An Anthology of African American Women*. Ed. Amiri Baraka and Amina Baraka. New York: Morrow, 1983: 243–66. Print.
——. Review of *Amistad 2*. Ed. John A. Williams and Charles Harris; *The Black Aesthetic*. Ed. Addison Gayle; *New African Literature and the Arts, 2*. Ed. Joseph Okpaku. *New York Times Book Review* (February 28, 1971). 5.
——. Review of *The Black Man in America, 1791–1861*, by Florence Jackson; *Black Politicians*, by Richard Bruner; *Black Troubadour*, by Charlamae Rollins; *Forward March to Freedom: The Biography of A. Philip Randolph*, by Barbara Kaye; *Gordon Parks*, by Midge Turk; *Jackie Robinson*, by Kenneth Ruddeen; *James Weldon Johnson*, by Harold W. Felton; *Jim Beckwourth*, by Lawrence Cortest; *The Magic Mirrors*, by Judith Berry Griffin; *The Making of an Afro-American: Martin Robinson Delany*, by Dorothy Sterling; *Men of Masaba*, ed. Humphrey Harmon; *The Orisha: Gods of Yorubaland*, by Judith Gleason; *The Picture Life of Thurgood Marshall*, by Margaret B. Young; *The Rich Man and the Singer: Folktales from Ethiopia*, by Mesfin Habre-Mariam; *Sidewalk Story*, by Sharon Bell Mathis; *Soldiers in the Civil War*, by Janet Stevenson; *Songs and Stories of Afro-Americans*, by Paul Glass; *Tales and Stories for Black Folks*, by Toni Cade Bambara; *Unsung Black Americans*, by Edith Stull. *New York Times Book Review* (May 2, 1971): Pt. 11, 43. Print.
——. Review of *Con*, by M. E. White. *New York Times Book Review* (September 3, 1972): 6. Print.
——. Review of *Hero in the Tower*, by Hans Hellmut Kirst; *Love Songs*, by Lawrence Sanders. *New York Times Book Review* (October 1, 1972): 41. Print.
——. Review of *Who Is Angela Davis: The Biography of a Revolutionary*, by Regina Nadelson. *New York Times Book Review* (October 29, 1972): 48. Print.
——. "Start the Week: Toni Morrison Special." BBC Radio 4. December 8, 2003. Audio.
——. "Strangers." *New Yorker* 74 (October 12, 1998): 69–70. Print.
——. "This Side of Paradise: Interview with Toni Morrison." James Marcus. Amazon.com. Web. August 17, 2008. http://www.amazon.com/. On line.
——. "Toni Morrison" (essay). *I Dream a World: Portraits of Black Women Who Changed America*, rev. ed. Ed. Brian Lanker. New York: Stewart, Tabori, & Chang, 1999: 36. Print.
——. "Toni Morrison Discusses *A Mercy*." Lynn Neary interview, *Book Tour, National Public Radio*, October 27, 2008. Print, audio.
——. "Toni Morrison: More Than Words Can Say." *Rolling Out* 3.43 (April 29, 2004): 16–17. Print.
——. "Toni Morrison on Cinderella's Stepsisters" [adapted from commencement address given at Barnard College, May 1979], *Ms* 8 (September 1979): 41–2. Print.
——. "Toni Morrison on Theater." *Lincoln Center Theater Review* 40 (Winter/ Spring 2005): 20–2. Print.
——. "Toni Morrison Talks Obama." EURWeb.com (November 7, 2008). On line.
——. "Unspeakable Things Unspoken: The Afro-American Presence in American Literature, The Tanner Lecture in Human Values." *Michigan Quarterly Review* 28.1 (Winter 1989): 1–34. Print.

——. "Why Did the Women Get Shot?" *The Straits Times Interactive* (January 17, 1998): 2. Print.
——. "Writing Lyrics." Louvre Museum Auditorium, Paris (November 26, 2006). Print.

Papers

Firestone Library, Princeton University, Princeton, New Jersey holds the Toni Morrison papers and manuscripts archive.

Secondary, Selected

Abel, Elizabeth. "Black Writing, White Reading: Race and the Politics of Feminist Interpretation." *Critical Inquiry* 19 (Spring 1993): 470–98. Print.
Adell, Sandra. *Double-Consciousness/Double Bind: Theoretical Issues in Twentieth Century Black Literature.* Urbana: U of Illinois P, 1994. Print.
Aguir, Sarah Appleton. "'Passing On' Death: Stealing Life in Toni Morrison's *Paradise.*" *African American Review* 38.3 (2004): 513–19. Print.
Als, Hilton. "Ghosts in the Attic." *New Yorker* (October 27, 2003): 62–73. Print.
Anderson, Melanie R. *Spectrality in the Novels of Toni Morrison.* Knoxville: U of Tennessee P, 2013. Print.
Andrews, Jennifer. "Reading Toni Morrison's *Jazz*: Rewriting the Tall Tale and Playing with the Trickster in the White American and African-American Humor Traditions." *Canadian Review of American Studies* 19.1 (1999): 87–107. Print.
Andrews, William L., Frances Smith Foster, and Trudier Harris, eds. *The Oxford Companion to African American Literature.* New York: Oxford U P, 1997. Print.
Askeland, Lori. "Remodeling the Model Home in *Uncle Tom's Cabin* and *Beloved.*" *American Literature* 64.4 (1992): 785–805. Print.
Atlas, Marilyn Judith. "The Darker Side of Toni Morrison's *Song of Solomon.*" *Society for the Study of Midwestern Literature Newsletter* 10 (1980): 1–13. Print.
——. "Toni Morrison's *Beloved* and the Reviewers." *Midwestern Miscellany* 18 (1990): 45–57. Print.
——. "A Woman Both Shiny and Brown." *Society for the Study of Midwestern Literature Newsletter* 9 (1979): 8–12. Print.
Atwood, Margaret. "Haunted by their Nightmares: *Beloved.*" *New York Times Book Review* (September 13, 1987): 1, 49–50. Print.
Aubry, Timothy. "Beware the Furrow of the Middlebrow: Searching for *Paradise* on *The Oprah Winfrey Show.*" *The Oprah Affect: Critical Essays on Oprah's Book Club.* Ed. Cecilia Konchar Farr and Jaime Harker. Albany: State U of New York P, 2008: 163–88. Print.
Awkward, Michael. *Inspiriting Influence: Tradition, Revision and Afro-American Women's Novels.* New York: Columbia U P, 1989. Print.
Babb, Valerie. "*E Pluribus Unum?* The American Origins Narrative in Toni Morrison's *A Mercy.*" *MELUS* 36.2 (2011): 147–64. Print.
Babbitt, Susan E. "Identity, Knowledge and Toni Morrison's *Beloved*: Questions about Understanding Racism." *Hypatia: A Journal of Feminist Philosophy* 9.3 (1994): 1–18. Print.

Badt, Karin Luisa. "The Roots of the Body in Toni Morrison: A *Mater* of 'Ancient Properties.'" *African American Review* 29 (Winter 1995): 567–77. Print.

Baillie, Justine Jenny. *Toni Morrison and Literary Tradition: The Invention of an Aesthetic.* London: Bloomsbury, 2013. Print.

Baker, Houston A., Jr. *Workings of the Spirit: The Poetics of Afro-American Women's Writing.* Chicago: U of Chicago P, 1991. Print.

Bakerman, Jane S. "Failures of Love: Female Initiation in the Novels of Toni Morrison." *American Literature* 52.4 (1981): 542–63. Print.

Bambara, Toni Cade. *The Salt Eaters.* New York: Random, 1980. Print.

Barnett, Pamela. "Figurations of Rape and the Supernatural in *Beloved.*" *PMLA* 112 (1997): 418–27. Print.

Barrett, Eileen, "'For Books Continue Each Other ...': Toni Morrison and Virginia Woolf." *Virginia Woolf: Emerging Perspectives: Selected Papers from the Third Annual Conference on Virginia Woolf.* Ed. Mary Hussey and Vara Neverow. New York: Pace U P, 1994: 26–32. Print.

Bassett, Reverend P. S. "Interview with Margaret Garner." *Toni Morrison: Beloved.* Ed. Carl Plasa. New York: Columbia U P, 1998: 39–41. Print.

Bearn, Emily. "Toni Morrison: Voice of America's Conscience." *Times Online* (November 9, 2008). On line.

Beaulieu, Elizabeth Ann, ed. *Toni Morrison Encyclopedia.* Westport, CT: Greenwood, 2003. Print.

Bell, Bernard W. *Bearing Witness to African American Literature.* Detroit: Wayne State U P, 2012. Print.

——. *The Contemporary Afro-American Novel: Its Folk Traditions and Modern Literary Branches.* Amherst: U of Massachusetts P, 2004. Print.

Bell, Pearl K. "Self Seekers." *Commentary* 72 (August 1981): 56–60. Print.

Benedrix, Beth. "Intimate Fatality: *Song of Solomon* and the Journey Home." *Toni Morrison and the Bible.* Ed. Shirley A. Stave. New York: Peter Lang, 2006: 94–115. Print.

Bennett, Barbara. *Scheherazade's Daughters, The Power of Storytelling in Ecofeminist Change.* New York: Peter Lang, 2012. Print.

Benston, Kimberly. "I Yam What I Yam: Naming and Unnaming in Afro-American Literature." *Black American Literature Forum* 16 (Spring 1992): 3–11. Print.

——. "Re-weaving the 'Ulysses Scene': Enchantment, Post-Oedipal Identity and the Buried Text of Blackness in *Song of Solomon.*" *Comparative American Identities: Race, Sex and Nationality in the Modern Text.* Ed. Hortense Spillers. New York: Routledge, 1991: 87–109. Print.

Bent, Geoffrey. "Less Than Divine: Toni Morrison's *Paradise.*" *Southern Review* 35.1 (Winter 1999): 145–9. Print.

Berger, James. "Ghosts of Liberalism: Morrison's *Beloved* and the Moynihan Report." *PMLA* 111.3 (1996): 408–20. Print.

Bergner, Gwen. *Taboo Subjects: Race, Sex, and Psychoanalysis.* Minneapolis: U of Minnesota P, 2005. Print.

Berret, Anthony J. "Toni Morrison's Literary Jazz." *CLA Journal* 32 (March 1989): 267–83. Print.

Bigsby, Christopher. "Jazz Queen (interview with Toni Morrison)." *The Independent* (London) (April 26, 1992). Print.

Billingslea-Brown, Alma Jean. *Crossing Borders through Folklore: African American Women's Fiction and Art*. Columbia: U of Missouri P, 1999.

Birat, Kathie. "Stories to Pass On: Closure and Community in Toni Morrison's *Beloved*." *The Insular Dream: Obsession and Resistance*. Ed. Kristiaan Versluys. Amsterdam: V U Univ. P, 1995: 324–34. Print.

Bjork, Patrick. *The Novels of Toni Morrison: The Search for Self and Place Within the Community*. New York: Peter Lang, 1992. Print.

Blackburn, Sara. "You Still Can't Go Home Again." *New York Times Book Review* (December 30, 1973): 3. Print.

"Black Writers in Praise of Toni Morrison," *New York Times Book Review* (January 24, 1988). Print.

Blair, Sara. *Harlem Crossroads: Black Writers and the Photograph in the Twentieth Century*. Princeton, NJ: Princeton U P, 2007. Print.

Blake, Susan L. "Folklore and Community in *Song of Solomon*." *MELUS* 7.3 (Fall 1980): 77–82. Print.

Bluestein, Gene. *The Voice of the Folk: Folklore and American Literary Theory*. Amherst: U of Massachusetts P, 1972. Print.

Bononno, George A. *The Other Side of Sadness: What the New Science of Bereavement Tells Us about Life After Loss*. New York: Basic, 2009. Print.

Bouson, J. Brooks. *Quiet As It's Kept: Shame, Trauma, and Race in the Novels of Toni Morrison*. Albany: State U of New York P, 2000. Print.

Bow, Leslie. "*Playing in the Dark* and the Ghosts in the Machine." *American Literary History* 20.3 (Fall 2008): 556–65. Print.

Boyce Davies, Carole. *Black Women, Writing and Identity: Migrations of the Subject*. London: Routledge, 1994. Print.

Bracks, Lean'tin L. *Writings on Black Women of the Diaspora*. New York: Garland, 1998. Print.

Branch, Eleanor. "Through the Maze of the Oedipal: Milkman's Search for Self in *Song of Solomon*." *Literature and Psychology* 41.1–2 (1995): 52–84. Print.

Brivac, Sheldon. *Tears of Rage: The Racial Interface of Modern American Fiction: Faulkner, Wright, Pynchon, Morrison*. Baton Rouge: Louisiana State U P, 2008. Print.

Brockes, Emma. "Toni Morrison: 'I Want to Feel What I Feel. Even If It's Not Happiness.'" *The Guardian* (April 13, 2012). http://guardian.co.uk. On line.

Broeck, Sabina. *White Amnesia – Black Memory? American Women's Writing and History*. Frankfurt am Main: Peter Lang, 1999. Print.

Brogan, Kathleen. *Cultural Haunting, Ghosts and Ethnicity in Recent American Literature*. Charlottesville: U of Virginia P, 1998. Print.

Brophy-Warren, Jamin. "A Writer's Vote: Toni Morrison on Her New Novel, Reading Her Critics and What Barack Obama's Win Means to Her." *Wall Street Journal Weekend* (November 7, 2008): W5. Print.

Brundage, W. Fitzhugh. *The Southern Past: A Clash of Race and Memory*. Cambridge, MA: Harvard U P, 2005. Print.

Burr, Benjamin. "Mythopoetic Syncretism in *Paradise* and the Deconstruction of Hospitality in *Love*." *Toni Morrison and the Bible: Contested Intertextualities*. Ed. Shirley A. Stave. New York: Peter Lang, 2006: 159–74. Print.

Burrows, Victoria. *Whiteness and Trauma: The Mother–Daughter Knot in the Fiction of Jean Rhys, Jamaica Kincaid, and Toni Morrison.* New York: Palgrave Macmillan, 2004.

Busia, Abena P. A. "The Artistic Impulse of Toni Morrison's Shorter Works." *Cambridge Companion to Toni Morrison.* Ed. Justine Tally. Cambridge: Cambridge U P, 2007: 101–11. Print.

Butler, Robert. *Contemporary African American Fiction: The Open Journey.* Madison, NJ: Fairleigh Dickinson U P, 1998. Print.

Butler, Robert James. "Open Movement and Selfhood in Toni Morrison's *Song of Solomon.*" *Centennial Review* 28–29 (Fall-Winter 1984–85): 58–75. Print.

Butler-Evans, Elliott. *Race, Gender and Desire: Narrative Strategies in the Fiction of Toni Cade Bambara, Toni Morrison and Alice Walker.* Philadelphia: Temple U P, 1989. Print.

Byatt, A. S. *Imagining Characters: Conversations About Women Writers: Jane Austen, Charlotte Brontë, George Eliot, Willa Cather, Iris Murdoch, and Toni Morrison.* New York: Vintage, 1997. Print.

Byerman, Keith. "African American Fiction." *American Fiction after 1945.* Ed. John N. Duvall. Cambridge: Cambridge U P, 2012: 85–98. Print.

——. *Remembering the Past in Contemporary African American Fiction.* Chapel Hill: U of North Carolina P, 2005. Print.

Caldwell, Gail. "West of Eden: Toni Morrison's Shimmering Story of an Oklahoma Paradise That's Asking for Trouble." *Boston Globe* (January 11, 1998): F1. Print.

Callahan, John F. *In the African-American Grain, The Pursuit of Voice in Twentieth-Century Black Fiction.* Urbana: U of Illinois P, 1988. Print.

Campbell, Jane. *Mythic Black Fiction: The Transformation of History.* Knoxville: U of Tennessee P, 1986. Print.

Cantiello, Jessica Wells. "From Pre-Racial to Post-Racial? Reading and Reviewing *A Mercy* in the Age of Obama." *MELUS* 36.2 (2011): 165–83. Print.

Carby, Hazel V. *Reconstructing Womanhood: The Emergence of the Afro-American Woman Novelist.* New York: Oxford U P, 1987. Print.

Carlacio, Jami L., ed. *The Fiction of Toni Morrison: Reading and Writing on Race, Culture, and Identity.* Urbana, IL: NCTE, 2007. Print.

Carmean, Karen. *Toni Morrison's World of Fiction.* Troy, NY: Whitston, 1993. Print.

Century, Douglas. *Toni Morrison* (Black Americans of Achievement series). New York: Chelsea House, 1994. Print.

Charles, Ron. "Toni Morrison's Feminist Portrayal of Racism." *Christian Science Monitor* (January 29, 1998): B1. Print.

Childs, Dennis. "'You Ain't Seen Nothin' Yet': *Beloved*, the American Chain Gang, and the Middle Passage Remix." *American Quarterly* 61 (June 2009): 271–97. Print.

Chinweizu, Onwuchekwa Jemie and Ihechukwu Maduibuika. *Toward the Decolonization of African Literature.* Washington, DC: Howard U P, 1983.

Christian, Barbara. "Beloved, She's Ours." *Narrative* 5 (1997): 36–49. Print.

——. *Black Women Novelists: The Development of a Tradition 1892–1976.* Westport, CT: Greenwood, 1980. Print.

——. "Layered Rhythms: Virginia Woolf and Toni Morrison." *Modern Fiction Studies* 39 (Fall/Winter 1993): 483–500. Print.

——. "'The Past Is Infinite': History and Myth in Toni Morrison's Trilogy." *Social Identities* 6.4 (2000): 411–23. Print.

Christianse, Yvette. *Toni Morrison: An Ethical Poetics.* New York: Fordham U P, 2013. Print.

Christol, Helene. "The African American Concept of the Fantastic as Middle Passage." *Black Imagination and the Middle Passage.* Ed. Maria Diedrich, Henry Louis Gates, Jr., and Carl Pedersen. New York: Oxford U P, 1999:164–73. Print.

Christopher, Lindsay M. "The Geographical Imagination in Toni Morrison's *Paradise.*" *Rocky Mountain Review* (2009): 89–95. Print.

Churchwell, Sarah. "History as a Warehouse of Horrors." *Guardian* (April 28, 2012). 6. Print.

Cliff, Michelle. "Review of Toni Morrison's *Paradise.*" *Village Voice* (January 27, 1998): 85–6. Print.

Clifford, James. *Routes: Travel and Translation in the Late Twentieth Century.* Cambridge, MA: Harvard U P, 1997. Print.

Cohen, Leah Hager. "Point of Return." *New York Times Book Review* (May 20, 2012): 1, 18. Print.

Coleman, James W. "Beyond the Reach of Love and Caring: Black Life in Toni Morrison's *Song of Solomon.*" *Obsidian* II 1.3 (Winter 1986): 151–61. Print.

Collins, Patricia Hill. "The Meaning of Motherhood in Black Culture and Black Mother/Daughter Relationships." *Sage* 4.2 (1987): 3–10. Print.

——. "Shifting the Center: Race, Class, and Feminist Theorizing about Motherhood." *Representations of Motherhood.* Ed. Donna Bassin, Margaret Honey, and Meryle Mahrer Kaplan. New Haven, CT: Yale U P, 1994: 56–74. Print.

Colter, Cyrus. "Review of *Tar Baby.*" *New Letters* 49 (Fall 1982): 112–14. Print.

Conner, Marc C. "Wild Women and Graceful Girls: Toni Morrison's *Winter's Tale.*" *Nature, Woman, and the Art of Politic.* Ed. Eduardo A. Velasquez. New York: Rowman & Littlefield, 2000: 341–69. Print.

Coonradt, Nicole M. "To Be Loved: Amy Denver and Human Need – Bridges to Understanding in Toni Morrison's *Beloved.*" *College Literature* 32.4 (2005): 168–83. Print.

Cooper-Clark, Diana. *Interviews with Contemporary Novelists.* New York: St. Martins, 1986. Print.

Coser, Stelamaris. *Bridging the Americas: The Literature of Paule Marshall, Toni Morrison, and Gayl Jones.* Philadelphia, PA: Temple U P, 1995.

Cowart, David. "Faulkner and Joyce in Morrison's *Song of Solomon.*" *Toni Morrison's Fiction: Contemporary Criticism.* Ed. David Middleton. New York: Garland, 1997: 95–108. Print.

Crouch, Stanley. "Aunt Medea." *New Republic* (October 19, 1987): 38–43. Print.

Croyden, Margaret. "Toni Morrison Tries Her Hand at Playwriting." *New York Times* (December 29, 1985): H6. Print.

192   *Bibliography*

Cummings, Kate. "Reclaiming the Mother('s) Tongue: *Beloved, Ceremony, Mothers and Shadows." College English* 52.5 (1990): 552–69. Print.

Curti, Lidia. *Female Stories, Female Bodies: Narrative, Identity and Representation.* Washington Square, NY: New York U P, 1998. Print.

Cutter, Martha J. "The Story Must Go On and On: The Fantastic, Narration, and Intertextuality in Toni Morrison's *Beloved* and *Jazz." African American Review* 34.1 (2000): 61–75. Print.

Daily, Gary W. "Toni Morrison's *Beloved*: Rememory, History, and the Fantastic." *The Celebration of the Fantastic: Selected Papers from the Tenth Anniversary International Conference on the Fantastic in the Arts.* Ed. Donald E. Morse et al. Westport, CT: Greenwood, 1992: 142–50. Print.

Dalsgard, Katrine. "The One All-Black Town Worth the Pain: (African) American Exceptionalism, Historical Narration, and the Critique of Nationhood in Toni Morrison's *Paradise." African American Review* 35.2 (2001): 233–48. Print.

Daly, Brenda O. and Maureen T. Reddy, eds. *Narrating Mothers: Theorizing Maternal Subjectivities.* Knoxville: U of Tennessee P, 1991.

Daniels, Steven V. "Putting 'His Story Next to Hers': Choice, Agency, and the Structure of *Beloved." Texas Studies in Literature and Language* 44.4 (2002): 349–67. Print.

David, Ron. *Toni Morrison Explained.* New York: Random, 2000. Print.

Davidson, Rob. "Racial Stock and 8-Rocks: Communal Historiography in Toni Morrison's *Paradise." Twentieth Century Literature* 47.3 (2001): 355–73. Print.

Davis, Cynthia A. "Self, Society and Myth in Toni Morrison's Fiction." *Contemporary Literature* 23.3 (1982): 323–42. Print.

Davis, Kimberly Chabot. "'Postmodern Blackness': Toni Morrison's *Beloved* and the End of History." *Twentieth Century Literature* 44.2 (1998): 242–60. Print.

Davis, Thadious M. *Southscapes.* Chapel Hill: U of North Carolina P, 2011. Print.

DeLancey, Dayle B. "Motherlove Is a Killer: *Sula, Beloved*, and the Deadly Trinity of Motherly Love." *Sage* 7.2 (Fall 1990): 15–18. Print.

Denard, Carolyn C., ed. *Toni Morrison: Conversations.* Jackson: U P of Mississippi, 2008. Print.

——, ed. *Toni Morrison: What Moves at the Margin, Selected Nonfiction.* Jackson: U P of Mississippi, 2008. Print.

de Weever, Jacqueline. *Mythmaking and Metaphor in Black Women's Fiction.* New York: St. Martin's P, 1991. Print.

Diu, Nisha Lilia. "*Home* by Toni Morrison: Review." *The Telegraph* (May 10, 2012). Print.

Dixon, Melvin. *Ride Out the Wilderness: Geography and Identity in Afro-American Literature.* Urbana: U of Illinois P, 1987. Print.

Donahue, Deirdre. "Morrison Presents a Profound *Paradise." USA Today* (January 8, 1998): 1D. Print.

Donaldson, Susan V. "Telling Forgotten Stories of Slavery in the Postmodern South." *Southern Literary Journal* 40.1 (2008): 267–83. Print.

Douglas, Christopher. "What *The Bluest Eye* knows about Them: Culture, Race, Identity." *American Literature* 78.1 (2006): 141–68. Print.

Doyle, Laura. "Bodies Inside/Out: Violation and Resistance from the Prison Cell to *The Bluest Eye*." *Feminist Interpretations of Maurice Merleau-Ponty*. Ed. Dorothea Olkowski and Gail Weiss. University Park: Pennsylvania State U P, 2006: 183–208. Print.

Dreifus, Claudia. "Chloe Wofford Talks about Toni Morrison." *New York Times Magazine* (September 11, 1994): Sec. 6, 72–5. Print.

Dubey, Madhu. *Black Women Novelists and the Nationalistic Aesthetic*. Bloomington: Indiana U P, 1994. Print.

——. "The Politics of Genre in *Beloved*." *Novel: A Forum on Fiction* 32.2 (1999): 187– 206. Print.

Durrant, Sam. *Postcolonial Narrative and the Work of Mourning*. Albany: State U of New York P, 2004. Print.

Dussere, Erik. *Balancing the Books: Faulkner, Morrison, and the Economics of Slavery*. New York: Routledge, 2003. Print.

Duvall, John N. "Doe Hunting and Masculinity: *Song of Solomon* and *Go Down, Moses*." *Arizona Quarterly* 47.1 (1991): 95–115. Print.

——. *The Identifying Fictions of Toni Morrison: Modernist Authenticity and Postmodern Blackness*. New York: Palgrave, 2010. Print.

——. "Morrison and the (Faulknerian Dark) House of Fiction." *Faulkner and Morrison*. Ed. Christopher Rieger and Robert W. Hamblin. Southeast Missouri State U P, 2013: 19–35. Print.

Edelberg, Cynthia Dubin. "Morrison's Voices: Formal Education, the Work Ethic, and the Bible." *American Literature* 58 (May 1986): 217–37. Print.

English, James F. *The Economy of Prestige: Prizes, Awards and the Circulation of Cultural Value*. Cambridge, MA: Harvard U P, 2005. Print.

Espinola, Judith. "Woolf, Virginia, Influence of." *The Toni Morrison Encyclopedia*. Ed. Elizabeth Ann Beaulieu. Westport, CT: Greenwood P, 2003: 380–2. Print.

Evans, Mari, ed. *Black Women Writers (1950–1980): A Critical Evaluation*. New York: Doubleday Anchor, 1984. Print.

Eyerman, Ron. *Cultural Trauma: Slavery and the Formation of African American Identity*. Cambridge: Cambridge U P, 2001. Print.

Fabre, Genevieve. "Genealogical Archeology or the Quest for Legacy in Toni Morrison's *Song of Solomon*." *Critical Essays on Toni Morrison*. Ed. Nellie McKay. Boston: Hall, 1988: 105–14. Print.

Fahy, Thomas. *Freak Shows in Modern American Imagination: Constructing the Damaged Body from Willa Cather to Truman Capote*. New York: Palgrave, 2007. Print.

Fallon, Robert. "Music and the Allegory of Memory in *Margaret Garner*." *Modern Fiction Studies* 52.2 (Summer 2006): 524–41. Print.

Faulkner, William. *Absalom, Absalom!* New York: Vintage, 1936. Print.

——. *Sound and the Fury, The*. New York: Vintage, 1929. Print.

——. *Wild Palms, The*. New York: Vintage, 1939. Print.

Felman, Shoshana and Dori Laub. *Testimony: Crises of Witnessing in Literature, Psychoanalysis, and History*. New York: Routledge, 1992. Print.

Feng, Pin-Cha. "'We Was Girls Together': The Double Female Bildungsroman in Toni Morrison's *Love*." *Feminist Studies in English Literature* 15.2 (Winter 2007): 37–63. Print.

Ferguson, Ann. *Blood at the Root, Motherhood, Sexuality, and Male Dominance*. London: Pandora, 1989. Print.

Ferguson, Rebecca Hope. *Rewriting Black Identities; Transition and Exchange in the Novels of Toni Morrison*. New York: Peter Lang, 2007. Print.

Fitzgerald, Jennifer. "Selfhood and Community: Psychoanalysis and Discourse in *Beloved*." *Modern Fiction Studies* 39.3–4 (1993): 669–87. Print.

Fitzgerald, Judith. "Woes Aplenty in this *Paradise*." *Toronto Star* (January 31, 1998): M15. Print.

Fleischner, Jennifer. *Mastering Slavery: Memory, Family, and Identity in Women's Slave Narratives*. New York: New York U P, 1996. Print.

Flint, Holly. "Toni Morrison's *Paradise*: Black Cultural Citizenship in the American Empire." *American Literature* 78.3 (2008): 585–612. Print.

Fraile-Marcos, Ana Maria. "Hybridizing the 'City upon a Hill' in Toni Morrison's *Paradise*." *MELUS* 28.4 (2003): 3–33. Print.

Franco, Dean. "What We Talk About When We Talk About *Beloved*." *Modern Fiction Studies* 52.2 (2006): 415–39. Print.

Frank, Arthur W. *The Wounded Storyteller: Body, Illness, and Ethics*. Chicago: U of Chicago P, 1995. Print.

Freyd. Jennifer. *Betrayal Trauma: The Logic of Forgetting Childhood Abuse*. Cambridge, MA: Harvard U P, 1996. Print.

Frye, Marilyn. "On Being White: Thinking Toward a Feminist Understanding of Race and Race Supremacy." *The Politics of Reality: Essays in Feminist Theory*. Freedom, CA: Crossing, 1983: 110–27. Print.

Fulmer, Jacqueline. *Folk Women and Indirection in Morrison, Ni Dhuibhne, Hurston, and Lavin*. Hampshire, UK: Ashgate, 2007. Print.

Fultz, Lucille P. "Images of Motherhood in Toni Morrison's *Beloved*." *Double Stitch: Black Women Write about Mothers and Daughters*. Ed. Patricia Bell-Scott. Boston: Beacon, 1991: 32–41. Print.

——. *Toni Morrison: Playing with Difference*. Urbana: U of Illinois P, 2003. Print.

——, ed. *Toni Morrison: Paradise, Love, A Mercy*. New York: Continuum Bloomsbury, 2013. "Introduction: The Grace and Gravity of Toni Morrison," 1–19. Print.

Furman, Jan. *Toni Morrison's Fiction*. Columbia: U of South Carolina P, 1993, 2014. Print.

Gallego, Mar. "*Love* and the Survival of the Black Community." *Cambridge Companion to Toni Morrison*. Ed. Justine Tally. Cambridge, MA: Cambridge U P, 2007: 92–100. Print.

Garland-Thomson, Rosemarie. "Disability." *The Toni Morrison Encyclopedia*. Ed. Elizabeth Ann Beaulieu. Westport, CT: Greenwood, 2003: 99–101. Print.

——. *Extraordinary Bodies: Figuring Physical Disability in American Culture and Literature*. New York: Columbia U P, 1997. Print.

Gascuena Gahete, Javier. "Narrative Defusion and Aesthetic Pleasure in Toni Morrison's *Love*." *Figures of Belatedness: Postmodern Fictions in English*. Ed.

Gascuena Gahete, Javier and Paule Martin Salvan. Cordoba, Spain: Servicio de Publicaciones, Universidad de Cordoba, 2006: 259–73.

Gates, Henry Louis, Jr. *Figures in Black: Words, Signs, and the "Racial" Self.* New York: Oxford U P, 1987. Print.

———. *The Signifying Monkey: A Theory of African-American Literary Criticism.* New York: Oxford U P, 1988. Print.

Gates, Henry Louis, Jr. and K. A. Appiah, eds. *Toni Morrison: Critical Perspectives Past and Present.* New York: Amistad, 1993. Print.

Gauthier, Marni. *Amnesia and Redress in Contemporary American Fiction.* New York: Palgrave, 2011. Print.

Gibson, Donald B. "Text and Countertext in The *Bluest Eye.*" *Toni Morrison: Critical Perspectives, Past and Present.* Ed. Henry Louis Gates, Jr. and K. A. Appiah. New York: Amistad, 1993: 159–74. Print.

Gillespie, Carmen R., ed. *Toni Morrison, Forty Years in the Clearing.* Lanham, MA: Bucknell U P, 2012. Print.

Gilman, Sander L. "Black Bodies, White Bodies: Toward an Iconography of Female Sexuality in Late Nineteenth-Century Art, Medicine, and Literature." *"Race," Writing, and Difference.* Ed. Henry Louis Gates, Jr. Chicago: U of Chicago P, 1986: 223–61. Print.

Gilroy, Paul. "Living Memory: An Interview with Toni Morrison." *Small Acts: Thoughts on the Politics of Black Cultures.* London: Serpent's Tail, 1993: 175–82. Print.

Goldman, Anne E. "'I Made the Ink': (Literary) Production and Reproduction in *Dessa Rose* and *Beloved.*" *Feminist Studies* 16 (1990): 313–30. Print.

Goulimari, Pelagia. *Toni Morrison.* New York: Routledge, 2011. Print.

Gray, Paul. "Paradise Found." *Time* (January 19, 1998): 62–8. Print.

Greene, Gayle. "Feminist Fiction and the Uses of Memory." *The Second Signs Reader: Feminist Scholarship, 1983–1996.* Ed. Ruth-Ellen B. Jones and Barbara Laslett. Chicago: U of Chicago P, 1996: 184–215. Print.

Grewal, Gurleen. *Circles of Sorrow, Lines of Struggle: The Novels of Toni Morrison.* Baton Rouge: Louisiana State U P, 1998. Print.

Griffin, Farah Jasmine. "Wrestling Till Dawn: On Becoming an Intellectual in the Age of Morrison." *Toni Morrison, Forty Years in the Clearing.* Ed. Carmen R. Gillespie. Lanham, MA: Bucknell U P, 2012: 116–27. Print.

Groover, Kristina K. *The Wilderness Within: American Women Writers and Spiritual Quest.* Fayetteville: U of Arkansas P, 1999. Print.

Guth, Deborah. "A Blessing and a Burden: The Relation to the Past in *Sula, Song of Solomon* and *Beloved.*" *Modern Fiction Studies* 39.3&4 (Fall/Winter 1993): 575–96. Print.

Gutmann, Katharina. *Celebrating the Senses: An Analysis of the Sensual in Toni Morrison's Fiction.* Tubingen: Francke Verlag, 2000. Print.

Gwin, Minrose C. *Black and White Women of the Old South: The Peculiar Sisterhood in American Literature.* Knoxville: U of Tennessee P, 1985. Print.

Gysin, Fritz. "The Enigma of the Return." *Black Imagination and the Middle Passage.* Ed. Maria Diedrich, Henry Louis Gates, Jr., and Carl Pedersen. New York: Oxford U P, 1999: 183–90. Print.

Haaken, Janice. "The Recovery of Memory, Fantasy, and Desire: Feminist Approaches to Sexual Abuse and Psychic Trauma." *Signs: Journal of Women in Culture and Society* 21.4 (1996): 1069–94. Print.

Halberstam, Judith. *Female Masculinity*. Durham, NC: Duke U P, 1998. Print.

Hall, Alice. *Disability and Modern Fiction: Faulkner, Morrison, Coetzee and the Nobel Prize for Literature*. New York: Palgrave, 2012. Print.

Hamilton, Cynthia S. "Revisions, Rememories and Exorcisms: Toni Morrison and the Slave Narrative." *Journal of American Studies* 30.3 (1996): 429–45. Print.

Handley, William R. "The House a Ghost Built: Allegory, Nommo, and the Ethics of Reading in Toni Morrison's *Beloved*." *Contemporary Literature* 36.4 (1995): 676–701. Print.

Harding, Wendy and Jacky Martin. *A World of Difference: An Inter-Cultural Study of Toni Morrison's Novels*. Westport, CT: Greenwood, 1994. Print.

Harris, Trudier. *Exorcising Blackness: Historical and Literary Lynching and Burning Rituals*. Bloomington: Indiana U P, 1984. Print.

——. *Fiction and Folklore: The Novels of Toni Morrison*. Knoxville: U of Tennessee P, 1991. Print.

——. "Religion and Community in the Writings of Contemporary Black Women." *Women's Writing in Exile*. Ed. Mary Lynn Broe and Angela Ingram. Chapel Hill: U of North Carolina P, 1989: 151–69. Print.

——. *Saints, Sinners, Saviors: Strong Black Women in African American Literature*. New York: Palgrave, 2001. Print.

——. "Toni Morrison." *Oxford Companion to Women's Writing in the United States*. Ed. Cathy N. Davidson and Linda Wagner-Martin. New York: Oxford U P, 1995: 578–80. Print.

Haskins, Jim. *Toni Morrison: Telling a Tale Untold*. Brookfield, CT: Twenty-first Century Books, 2003. Print.

Hassan, Ihab. *The Postmodern Turn: Essays in Postmodern Theory and Culture*. Columbus: Ohio State U P, 1987. Print.

Hawthorne, Evelyn. "On Gaining the Double-Vision: *Tar Baby* as Diasporean Novel." *Black American Literature Forum* 22.1 (1988): 97–107. Print.

Hedin, Raymond. "The Structure of Emotion in Black American Fiction." *Novel* 16.1 (Fall 1982): 35–54. Print.

Heinert, Jennifer Lee Jordan. *Narrative Conventions and Race in the Novels of Toni Morrison*. New York: Routledge, 2009. Print.

Heinze, Denise. *The Dilemma of "Double Consciousness": Toni Morrison's Novels*. Athens: U of Georgia P, 1993. Print.

Heise-von der Lippe, Anya. "Others, Monsters, Ghosts: Representations of the Female Gothic Body in Toni Morrison's *Beloved* and *Love*." *The Female Gothic: New Directions*. Ed. Diana Wallace and Andrew Smith. Basingstoke: Palgrave Macmillan, 2009: 166–79. Print.

Henderson, Carol E. *Scarring the Black Body: Race and Representation in African American Literature*. Columbia: U of Missouri P, 2002. Print.

Henderson, Mae G. "Toni Morrison's *Beloved*: Re-Membering the Body as Historical Text." *Comparative American Identities: Race, Sex, and Nationality in the Modern Text*. Ed. Hortense J. Spillers. New York: Routledge, 1991: 62–86. Print.

Herman, Judith. *Trauma and Recovery*. New York: HarperCollins, 1992. Print.
——. *Trauma and Recovery: The Aftermath of Violence – from Domestic Abuse to Political Terror*. New York: Basic, 1997. Print.
Higgins, Therese E. *Religiosity, Cosmology, and Folklore: The African Influences in the Novels of Toni Morrison*. New York: Routledge, 2001.
Hilfer, Anthony C. "Critical Indeterminacies in Toni Morrison's Fiction: An Introduction." *Texas Studies in Literature and Language* (Spring 1991): 91–5. Print.
Hilfrich, Carola. "Anti-Exodus: Countermemory, Gender, Race, and Everyday Life in Toni Morrison's *Paradise*." *Modern Fiction Studies* 52.2 (2006): 322–49. Print.
Hill, Michael D. *The Ethics of Swagger: Prizewinning African American Novels, 1977–1993*. Columbus: Ohio State U P, 2013. Print.
Hill, Michael. "Toni Morrison and the Post-Civil Rights American Novel." *Cambridge Companion to the American Novel*. Ed. Leonard Cassuto. Cambridge: Cambridge U P, 2011: 1064–83. Print.
Hirsch, Marianne. *The Mother/Daughter Plot: Narrative, Psychoanalysis, Feminism*. Bloomington: U of Indiana P, 1989. Print.
——. "Maternity and Rememory: Toni Morrison's *Beloved*." *Representations of Motherhood*. Ed. Donna Bassin, Margaret Honey, and Meryle Mahrer Kaplan. New Haven: Yale U P, 1997: 92–110. Print.
Hirsch, Marianne and Ivy Schweitzer. "Mothers and Daughters." *The Oxford Companion to Women's Writing in the U. S.* Ed. Cathy N. Davidson and Linda Wagner-Martin. New York: Oxford U P, 1995: 583–5. Print.
Hogan, Michael. "Built on the Ashes: The Fall of the House of Sutpen and the Rise of the House of Sethe." *Critical Insights: Toni Morrison*. Ed. Solomon O. Iyasere and Marla W. Iyasere. Pasadena, CA: Salem, 2010: 127–46.
Hogue, W. Lawrence. "Postmodernism, Traditional Cultural Forms, and the African American Narrative: Major's *Reflex*, Morrison's *Jazz*, and Reed's *Mumbo Jumbo*." *Novel* 35.2–3 (Spring–Summer 2002): 169–92. Print.
Holloway, Karla F. C. *Moorings and Metaphors: Figures of Culture and Gender in Black Women's Literature*. New Brunswick, NJ: Rutgers U P, 1992. Print.
——. "Narrative Time/Spiritual Text: *Beloved* and *As I Lay Dying*." *Unflinching Gaze: Faulkner and Morrison Re-envisioned*. Ed. Carol A. Kolmerten, Stephen M. Ross, Judith Bryant Wittenberg. Jackson: U P of Mississippi, 1997: 91–8. Print.
Holloway, Karla F. C. and Stephanie Demetrakapoulos. *New Dimensions of Spirituality: A Biracial and Bicultural Reading of the Novels of Toni Morrison*. Westport, CT: Greenwood, 1987. Print.
Hoofard, Jennifer. "Thinking about a Story." *Writing on the Edge* 17.2 (2007): 87–99. Print.
Horvitz, Deborah M. *Literary Trauma: Sadism, Memory, and Sexual Violence in American Women's Fiction*. Albany: State U of New York P, 2000. Print.
House, Elizabeth B. "Artists and the Art of Living: Order and Disorder in Toni Morrison's Fiction." *Modern Fiction Studies* 34 (Spring 1988): 27–44. Print.
——. "The 'Sweet Life' in Toni Morrison's Fiction." *American Literature* 56 (1984): 181–202. Print.

——. "Toni Morrison's Ghost: The Beloved Who is Not Beloved." *Studies in American Fiction* 18.1 (1990): 17–26. Print.

Hubbard, Dolan. "In Quest of Authority: Toni Morrison's *Song of Solomon* and the Rhetoric of the Black Preacher." *CLA Journal* 35 (1992): 288–302. Print.

Hull, Gloria T., Patricia Bell Scott, and Barbara Smith, eds. *All the Women Are White, All the Blacks Are Men, but Some of Us Are Brave: Black Women's Studies*. New York: Feminist P, 1982. Print.

Iannone, Carol. "Toni Morrison's Career," *Commentary* 84 (December 1987): 59-63. Print.

Inoue, Kazuko. "'I Got a Tree on My Back': A Study of Toni Morrison's Latest Novel, *Beloved*." *Language and Culture* (1988): 69–82. Print.

Irving, John. "Morrison's Black Fable." *New York Times Book Review* (March 29, 1981): 1, 30–1. Print.

Iyasere, Solomon O. and Marla W. Iyasere, eds. *Understanding Toni Morrison's Beloved and Sula*. Troy, NY: Whitston, 2000.

Jablon, Madelyn. "Rememory, Dream Memory, and Revision in Toni Morrison's *Beloved* and Alice Walker's *The Temple of My Familiar*." *CLA Journal* 37 (1993): 136–44. Print.

Jackson, Chuck. "A 'Headless Display': *Sula*, Soldiers, and Lynching." *Modern Fiction Studies* 52.2 (2006): 374–92. Print.

Jenkins, Candice M. "Pure Black: Class, Color and Intraracial Politics in Toni Morrison's *Paradise*." *Modern Fiction Studies* 52.2 (2006): 270–96. Print.

Jennings, LaVinia Delois. *Toni Morrison and the Idea of Africa*. New York: Cambridge U P, 2008. Print.

Jessee, Sharon. "The Contrapuntal Historiography of Toni Morrison's *Paradise*: Unpacking the Legacies of the Kansas and Oklahoma All-Black Towns." *American Studies* 46.1 (2006): 81–112. Print.

Jesser, Nancy. "Violence, Home, and Community in Toni Morrison's *Beloved*." *African American Review* 33.2 (1999): 325–45. Print.

Jimoh, A. Yemisi. *Spiritual, Blues, and Jazz People in African American Fiction*. Knoxville: U of Tennessee P, 2002.

Johnson, Barbara, "'Aesthetic' and 'Rapport' in Toni Morrison's *Sula*." *Textual Practice* 7.2 (1993): 165–72. Print.

Johnson, Charles. *Being and Race: Black Writing since 1970*. Bloomington: Indiana U P, 1988. Print.

Johnson, Diane. "The Oppressor in the Next Room." *New York Review of Books* (November 10, 1977). Print.

Jones, Bessie, and Audrey Vinson. *The World of Toni Morrison*. Dubuque, IA: Kendall/Hunt, 1985. Print.

Jones, Gayl. *Liberating Voices: Oral Traditions in African American Literature*. Cambridge, MA: Harvard U P, 1991. Print.

Jones, Tayari. "*Home* by Toni Morrison: Review." *San Francisco Gate* (May 6, 2012). Print.

Jordan, Elaine. "'Not My People': Toni Morrison and Identity." *Black Women's Writing*. Ed. Gina Wisker. London: Macmillan 1993: 111–26. Print.

Joyce, Joyce Ann. "Structural and Thematic Unity in Toni Morrison's *Song of Solomon*." *CEA Critic* 49 (Winter/Summer 1986–1987): 185–98. Print.

Juncker, Clara. "Unnatural Lives: Toni Morrison's Historical Universe." *Xavier Review* 32.1&2 (2012): 57–74. Print.

June, Pamela B. *The Fragmented Female Body and Identity*. New York: Peter Lang, 2010. Print.

Junker, Carstan. *Frames of Friction: Black Genealogies, White Hegemony, and the Essay as Critical Intervention*. Frankfurt: Campus Verlag, 2010.

Kachka, Boris. "Toni Morrison's History Lesson." *New York Magazine* (September 1–8, 2008): 90–1. Print.

Kakutani, Michiko. "Books of the Times: *Love* by Toni Morrison. Family Secrets, Feuding Women." *New York Times* (October 31, 2003). Print.

———. "Soldier Is Defeated by War Abroad, Then Welcomed Back by Racism." *New York Times* (May 7, 2012). Print.

———. "Worthy Women, Unredeemable Men." *New York Times* (January 6, 1998): 8. Print.

Kang, Nancy. "To Love and Be Loved: Considering Black Masculinity and the Misandric Impulse in Toni Morrison's *Beloved*." *Callaloo* 26.3 (2003): 836–54. Print.

Kastor, Elizabeth. "'Beloved' and the Protest: Why Black Writers Decried Book Award 'Oversight.'" *The Washington Post* (January 21, 1988). Final ed.: B1. Print.

Keenan, Sally. "'Four Hundred Years of Silence': Myth, History, and Motherhood in Toni Morrison's *Beloved*." *Recasting the World: Writing after Colonialism*. Ed. Jonathan White. Baltimore, MD: Johns Hopkins U P, 1993: 45–81. Print.

Khayati, Abdellatif. "Representation, Race, and the 'Language' of the Ineffable in Toni Morrison's Narrative." *African American Review* 33.2 (Summer 1999). 313–24. Print.

King, Debra Walker. *Deep Talk, Reading African-American Literary Names*. Charlottesville: U P of Virginia, 1998. Print.

King, Lovalerie. *Race, Theft, and Ethics: Property Matters in African American Literature*. Baton Rouge: Louisiana State U P, 2007.

——— and Lynn Orilla Scott, eds. *James Baldwin and Toni Morrison: Comparative Critical and Theoretical Essays*. New York: Palgrave, 2006. Print.

Klotman, Phyllis Rauch. *Another Man Gone: The Black Runner in Contemporary Afro-American Fiction*. Port Washington, NY: Kennikat, 1977. Print.

Konen, Anne. "Toni Morrison's *Beloved* and the Ghost of Slavery." *Beloved, She's Mine*." Ed. Genevieve Fabre and Claudine Raynaud. Paris: CETLNA, 1993: 53–67. Print.

Koolish, Lynda. "'To Be Loved and Cry Shame': A Psychological Reading of Toni Morrison's *Beloved*." *MELUS* 26.4 (2001): 169–95. Print.

Krumholz, Linda. "Blackness and Art in Toni Morrison's *Tar Baby*." *Contemporary Literature* 49.2 (2008): 263–92. Print.

———. "The Ghosts of Slavery: Historical Recovery in Toni Morrison's *Beloved*." *African American Review* 26.3 (Autumn 1992): 395–408. Print.

———. "Reading and Insight in Toni Morrison's *Paradise*." *African American Review* 36.1 (2002): 21–34. Print.

Kubitschek, Missy Dehn. *Toni Morrison: A Critical Companion*. Westport, CT: Greenwood, 1998. Print.

LaCapra, Dominick. *Writing History, Writing Trauma*. Baltimore, MD: Johns Hopkins U P, 2001. Print.

Lawrence, David. "Fleshly Ghosts and Ghostly Flesh: the Word and the Body in *Beloved*." *Studies in American Fiction* 19.2 (1991): 189–201. Print.

Lawson, Erica. "Black Women's Mothering in a Historical and Contemporary Perspective: Understanding the Past, Forging the Future." *Mother Outlaws: Theories and Practices of Empowered Mothering*. Ed. Andrea O'Reilly. Toronto: Women's P, 2004: 193–201. Print.

Lee, Catherine Carr. "The South in Toni Morrison's *Song of Solomon*: Initiation, Healing, and Home." *Studies in Literary Imagination* 31.2 (1998): 109–23. Print.

Lee, Dorothy H. "The Quest for Self: Triumph and Failure in the Works of Toni Morrison." *Black Women Writers (1950–1980)*. Ed. Mari Evans. Garden City, NY: Doubleday, 1984: 346–60. Print.

Lee, Sue-Im. *A Body of Individuals: The Paradox of Community in Contemporary Fiction*. Columbus: Ohio State U P, 2009. Print.

Leonard, John. "Travels with Toni." *The Nation* (January 17, 1994): 62. Print.

Lepow, Lauren. "Paradise Lost and Found: Dualism and Edenic Myth in Toni Morrison's *Tar Baby*." *Contemporary Literature* 28.3 (1987): 363–77. Print.

Le Seur, Geta. "Moving beyond the Boundaries of Self, Community, and the Other in Toni Morrison's *Sula* and *Paradise*." *CLA Journal* 46.1 (2002): 1–20. Print.

Levy, Andrew. "Telling *Beloved*." *Texas Studies in Literature and Languages* 331.1 (1991): 115–23. Print.

Li, Stephanie. *Toni Morrison A Biography*. Santa Barbara, CA: Greenwood Biographies, 2010. Print.

Lillvis, K. "Becoming Self and Mother: Posthuman Liminality in Toni Morrison's *Beloved*." *Critique* 54.4 (October 2013): 452–64. Print.

Liscio, Lorraine. "*Beloved*'s Narrative: Writing Mother's Milk." *Tulsa Studies in Women's Literature* 11.1 (1992): 31–46. Print.

Loichot, Valerie. *Orphan Narratives*. Charlottesville: U of Virginia P, 2007.

Lubiano, Wahneema. "The Postmodernist Rag: Political Identity and the Vernacular in *Song of Solomon*." *New Essays on Song of Solomon*. Ed. Valerie Smith. New York: Cambridge U P, 1995: 93–116. Print.

Luszczynska, Ana M. *The Ethics of Community: Nancy, Derrida, Morrison and Menendez*. New York: Continuum, 2012. Print.

Lydon, Susan. "What's an Intelligent Woman To Do?" *Village Voice* (July 1–7, 1981): 41. Print.

MacKinnon, Catherine A. *Toward a Feminist Theory of the State*. Cambridge, MA: Harvard U P, 1989. Print.

Macpherson, Heidi Stettedahl. *Courting Failure: Women and the Law in Twentieth Century Literature*. Akron, OH: U of Akron P, 2007. Print.

Madsen, Deborah L. *Allegory in America: From Puritanism to Postmodernism*. Basingstoke: Macmillan, 1996. Print.

Makward, Edris and Leslie Lacy, eds. *Contemporary African Literature*. New York: Random, 1972. (Morrison served as Project Editor.) Print.

Malmgren, Carl. D. "Mixed Genres and the Logic of Slavery in Toni Morrison's *Beloved.*" *Critique* 36.2 (1995): 96–106. Print.

Mandel, Naomi. "'I Made the Ink': Identity, Complicity, 60 Million and More." *Modern Fiction Studies* 48.3 (2002): 581–612. Print.

Marks, Kathleen. *Toni Morrison's "Beloved" and the Apotropaic Imagination.* Columbia: U of Missouri P, 2002. Print.

Marshall, Brenda. "The Gospel According to Pilate." *American Literature* 57 (1985): 486–9. Print.

Mathieson, Barbara Offutt. "Memory and Mother Love in Toni Morrison's *Beloved.*" *American Imago: Studies in Psychoanalysis and Culture* 47.1 (1990): 1–21. Print.

Matus, Jill. *Toni Morrison.* Manchester: Manchester U P, 1998. Print.

Mayberry, Susan Neal. *Can't I Love What I Criticize? The Masculine and Morrison.* Athens: U of Georgia P, 2007. Print.

——. "Visions and Revisions of American Masculinity in *A Mercy.*" *Toni Morrison: Paradise, Love, A Mercy.* Ed. Lucille P. Fultz. New York: Continuum Bloomsbury, 2013: 166–84. Print.

Mbalia, Dorothea Drummond. *Toni Morrison's Developing Class Consciousness,* rev. ed. Selinsgrove, PA: Susquehanna U P, 1991, 2004. Print.

McAlpin, Heller. "'Home': Toni Morrison's Taut, Triumphant New Novel." *NPR* (May 15, 2012). Audio, Print.

McCuskey, Brian. "Not at Home: Servants, Scholars, and the Uncanny." *PMLA* 121.2 (2006): 421–36. Print.

McDowell, Deborah E. "Harlem Nocturne." *Women's Review of Books* 9.9 (1992): 1–5. Print.

McDowell, Linda. *Gender, Identity and Place: Understanding Feminist Geographies.* Minneapolis: U of Minnesota P, 1999. Print.

McHaney, Pearl Amelia. "Southern Women Writers and Their Influence." *Cambridge Companion to the Literature of the American South.* Ed. Sharon Monteith. Cambridge: Cambridge U P, 2013: 132–4. Print.

McKee, Patricia. "Geographies of *Paradise.*" *New Centennial Review* 3.1 (2003): 197–223. Print.

Medora, Dana. "Justice and Citizenship in Toni Morrison's *Song of Solomon.*" *Canadian Review of American Studies* 32.1 (2002): 1–13. Print.

Mellard, James M. "'Families Make the Best Enemies': Paradox of Narcissistic Identification in Toni Morrison's *Love.*" *African American Review* 43.4 (Winter 2009): 699–712. Print.

Menand, Louis. "The War Between Men and Women." *New Yorker* (January 12, 1998): 78–82. Print.

Metress, Christopher. "Dreaming Emmett." *The Toni Morrison Encyclopedia.* Ed. Elizabeth Ann Beaulieu. Westport, CT: Greenwood, 2003: 105–7. Print.

Michael, Magali Cornier. *New Visions of Community in Contemporary American Fiction: Tan, Kingsolver, Castillo, Morrison.* Iowa City: U of Iowa P, 2006. Print.

Middleton, Joyce Irene. "Imagining Paradise." *Word-Work: The Newsletter of the Toni Morrison Society* 23.3 (Autumn 1991): 27–42. Print.

Mihan, Anne. *Undoing Difference*. Heidelberg: Universitätverlag Winter, 2012. Print.

Miller, Alice. *Breaking Down the Wall of Silence: The Liberating Experience of Facing Painful Truth*. Trans. Simon Worrell. New York: Dutton, 1991. Print.

Miller Budick, Emily. "Absence, Loss, and the Space of History in Toni Morrison's *Beloved*." *Arizona Quarterly* 48.2 (1992): 117–38. Print.

Mishkin, Tracy. "Theorizing Literary Influence and African-American Writers." *Literary Influence and African-American Writers*. Ed. Tracy Mishkin. New York: Garland, 1996: 3–20. Print.

Mix, Debbie. "Toni Morrison: A Selected Bibliography." *Modern Fiction Studies* 39:3&4 (1994): 795–817. Print.

Mobley, Marilyn Sanders. "Call and Response: Voice, Community, and Dialogic Structures in Toni Morrison's *Song of Solomon*." *New Essays on Song of Solomon*. Ed. Valerie Smith. Cambridge: Cambridge U P, 1995: 41–68. Print.

Moglen, Helen. "Redeeming History: Toni Morrison's *Beloved*." *Cultural Critique* 24 (1993): 17–40. Print.

Mohanty, Satya. "The Epistemic Status of Cultural Identity: On *Beloved* and the Postcolonial Condition." *Cultural Critique* 24 (1993): 41–80. Print.

Monteith, Sharon. *Advancing Sisterhood? Interracial Friendships in Contemporary Southern Fiction*. Athens: U of Georgia P, 2000. Print.

Montgomery, Maxine, ed. *Contested Boundaries: New Critical Essays on the Fiction of Toni Morrison*. Newcastle upon Tyne: Cambridge Scholars, 2013. Print.

Moore, Geneva Cobb. "A Demonic Parody: Toni Morrison's *A Mercy*." *Southern Literary Journal* 44 (2011): 1–18. Print.

Moreland, Richard C. *Learning from Difference: Teaching Morrison, Twain, Ellison, and Eliot*. Columbus: Ohio State U P, 1999. Print.

Morgenstern, Naomi. "Mother's Milk and Sister's Blood: Trauma and the Neo-Slave Narrative." *differences: A Journal of Feminist Cultural Studies* 8.2 (1996): 101–26. Print.

Mori, Aoi. *Toni Morrison and Womanist Discourse*. New York: Peter Lang, 1999. Print.

Mueller, Stefanie. *The Presence of the Past in the Novels of Toni Morrison*. Heidelberg: Winter, 2013. Print.

Murray, Rolland. "The Long Strut: *Song of Solomon* and the Emancipatory Limits of the Black Patriarchy." *Callaloo* 22.1 (1999): 121–33. Print.

Nicol, Kathryn. "Visible Differences: Viewing Racial Identity in Toni Morrison's *Paradise* and "Recitatif." *Literature and Racial Ambiguity*. Ed. Teresa Hubel and Neil Brooks. New York: Rodolpi, 2002: 209–31. Print.

Nnaemeka, Obioma. *Sisterhood: Feminists and Power from Africa to the Diaspora*. Trenton, NJ: Africa World P, 1989. Print.

Novak, Phillip. "'Circles and Circles of Sorrow': In the Wake of Morrison's *Sula*." *PMLA* 114.2 (1999): 184–93. Print.

Nowlin, Michael. "Toni Morrison's *Jazz* and the Racial Dreams of the American Writer." *American Literature* 71 (1999): 151–74. Print.

Ochoa, Peggy. "Morrison's *Beloved:* Allegorically Othering 'White' Christianity." *MELUS* 24.2 (1999): 107–23. Print.

O'Reilly, Andrea. "In Search of My Mother's Garden, I Found My Own: Mother-Love, Healing, and Identity in Toni Morrison's *Jazz.*" *African American Review* 30 (Fall 1996): 367–79. Print.

———. *Toni Morrison and Motherhood: A Politics of the Heart.* New York: State U of New York P, 2004. Print.

Otten, Terry. *The Crime of Innocence in Toni Morrison's Fiction.* Columbia: U of Missouri P, 1989. Print.

———. "Horrific Love in Toni Morrison's Fiction." *Modern Fiction Studies* 39 (1993): April 1995): 651–7. Print.

———. "'To Be One or to Have One': 'Motherlove' in the Fiction of Toni Morrison." *Contested Boundaries: New Critical Essays on the Fiction of Toni Morrison.* Ed. Maxine Montgomery. Newcastle upon Tyne: Cambridge Scholars, 2013: 82–95. Print.

Owens, Louis. "As if an Indian Were Really an Indian: Native American Voices and Postcolonial Theory." *Native American Representations: First Encounters, Distorted Images and Literary Appropriations.* Ed. Gretchen Bataille. Lincoln: U of Nebraska P, 2001: 11–25. Print.

Page, Philip. *Dangerous Freedom: Fusion and Fragmentation in Toni Morrison's Novels.* Jackson: U P of Mississippi, 1995. Print.

———. "Furrowing All the Brows: Interpretation and the Transcendent in Toni Morrison's *Paradise.*" *African American Review* 35 (Winter 2001): 639–51. Print.

Paquet, Sandra Pouchet. "The Ancestor as Foundation in *Their Eyes Were Watching God* and *Tar Baby.*" *Callaloo* 13.3 (1990): 499–515. Print.

Paquet-Deyris, Anne-Marie. "Toni Morrison's *Jazz* and the City." *African American Review* 35.2 (2001): 219–31. Print.

Parker, Emma. "'Apple Pie' Ideology and the Politics of Appetite in the Novels of Toni Morrison." *Contemporary Literature* 39.4 (1998): 614–43. Print.

———. "A New Hystery: History and Hysteria in Toni Morrison's *Beloved.*" *Twentieth Century Literature* 47.1 (2001): 1–19. Print.

Parrish, Timothy. "Introduction." *The Cambridge Companion to American Novelists.* Ed. Timothy Parrish. New York: Cambridge U P, 2013: xvii–xxxii. Print.

Patell, Cyrus R. K. *Negative Liberties: Morrison, Pynchon, and the Problem of Liberal Ideology.* Durham, NC: Duke U P, 2001. Print.

Peach, Linden. *Toni Morrison.* New York: St. Martin's, 2000. Print.

———. "Toni Morrison." *American Fiction after 1945.* Ed. John N. Duvall. Cambridge: Cambridge U P, 2012: 233–43. Print.

Peterson, Christopher. "Beloved's Claim." *Modern Fiction Studies* 52.3 (2006): 548–69. Print.

Peterson, Nancy J. *Against Amnesia: Women Writers and the Crises of Historical Memory.* Philadelphia: U of Pennsylvania P, 2001. Print.

Phelan, James. "Sethe's Choice: *Beloved* and the Ethics of Reading." *Ethics, Literature, and Theory: An Introductory Reader.* Ed. Stephen K. George. Lanham, MD: Rowman and Littlefield, 2005: 299–314. Print.

Podnicks, Elizabeth and Andrea O'Reilly, eds. *Textual Mothers/Maternal Texts: Motherhood in Contemporary Women's Literatures*. Waterloo, ON: Wilfrid Laurier U P, 2010. Print.

Portales, Marco. "Toni Morrison's *The Bluest Eye*: Shirley Temple and Cholly." *Centennial Review* 30 (1986): 496–506. Print.

Price, Reynolds. "Review of *Song of Solomon*." *New York Times Book Review* (September 11, 1977). Print.

Pullin, Faith. "Landscapes of Reality: The Fiction of Contemporary Afro-American Women." *Black Fiction: New Studies in the Afro-American Novel Since 1945*. Ed. A. Robert Lee. London: Vision, 1980: 173–203. Print.

Rabinowitz, Paula. "Naming, Magic and Documentary: The Subversion of the Narrative in *Song of Solomon, Ceremony*, and *China Men*." *Feminist Re-Visions: What Has Been and Might Be*. Ed. Vivian Patraka and Louise Tilly. Ann Arbor: U of Michigan P, 1983: 26–42. Print.

Rainwater, Catherine. "Worthy Messengers: Narrative Voices in Toni Morrison's Novels." *Texas Studies in Literature and Language* 33.1 (1991): 96–113. Print.

Ramadanovic, Petar. *Forgetting Futures: On Memory, Trauma, and Identity*. Lanham, MD: Lexington, 2001. Print.

Rampersad, Arnold. *Ralph Ellison: A Biography*. New York: Knopf, 2007. Print.

Raynaud, Claudine. "The Poetics of Abjection in *Beloved*." *Black Imagination and the Middle Passage*. Ed. Maria Diedrich, Henry Louis Gates, Jr., and Carl Petersen. New York: Oxford U P, 1999: 70–85. Print.

Reames, Kelly. *Toni Morrison's Paradise*. New York: Continuum, 2001. Print.

Reames, Kelly Lynch. *Women and Race in Contemporary U.S. Writing, From Faulkner to Morrison*. New York: Palgrave, 2007. Print.

Reed, Andrew. "'As if word magic had anything to do with the courage it took to be a man': Black Masculinity in Toni Morrison's *Paradise*." *African American Review* 39.4 (2005): 527–40. Print.

Reed, Harry. "Toni Morrison: *Song of Solomon* and Black Cultural Nationalism." *Centennial Review* 32.1 (Winter 1988): 50–64. Print.

Reyes, Angelita. "Ancient Properties in the New World: The Paradox of the 'Other' in Toni Morrison's *Tar Baby*." *Black Scholar* 17 (March–April 1986): 19–25. Print.

Rice, Alan J. *Radical Narratives of the Black Atlantic*. New York: Continuum, 2003. Print.

Rice, Herbert William. *Toni Morrison and the American Tradition: A Rhetorical Reading*. New York: Peter Lang, 1996. Print.

Richards, Phillip M. "*Sula* and the Discourse of the Folk in African American Literature." *Cultural Studies: Toni Morrison and the Curriculum*. Ed. Warren Crichlaw and Cameron McCarthy. London: Routledge, 1995. 270–92. Print.

Rieger, Christopher and Robert W. Hamblin, eds. *Faulkner and Morrison*. Cape Girardeau: The Center for Faulkner Studies, Southeast Missouri State U P, 2013. Print.

Rigney, Barbara Hill. *Lilith's Daughters, Women and Religion in Contemporary Fiction*. Madison: U of Wisconsin P, 1982. Print.

——. "'A Story to Pass On': Ghosts and the Significance of History in Toni Morrison's *Beloved.*" *Haunting the House of Fiction: Feminist Perspectives on Ghost Stories by American Women.* Ed. Lynette Carpenter and Wendy K. Kolmar. Knoxville: U of Tennessee P, 1991: 229–35. Print.

——. *The Voices of Toni Morrison.* Columbus: Ohio State U P, 1991. Print.

Rimmon-Kenan, Shlomith. "Narration, Doubt, Retrieval: Toni Morrison's *Beloved.*" *Narrative* 4 (1996): 109–23. Print.

Roberson, Gloria Grant. *The World of Toni Morrison.* Westport, CT: Greenwood, 2003. Print.

Roberts. John W. *From Trickster to Badman, The Black Folk Hero in Slavery and Freedom.* Philadelphia: U of Pennsylvania P, 1989. Print.

Rodrigues, Eusebio L. "Experiencing *Jazz.*" *Modern Fiction Studies* 39 (Fall/ Winter 1993): 748–52. Print.

Rody, Caroline. *The Daughter's Return: African-American and Caribbean Women's Fictions of History.* New York: Oxford U P, 2001. Print.

——. "Toni Morrison's *Beloved*: History, 'Rememory,' and a 'Clamor for a Kiss.'" *American Literary History* 7.1 (1995): 92–119. Print.

Rokotnitz, Naomi. "Constructing Cognitive Scaffolding through Embodied Receptiveness: Toni Morrison's *The Bluest Eye.*" *Style* 41.4 (2007): 385–408. Print.

Romero, Channette. "Creating the Beloved Community: Religion, Race and Nation in Toni Morrison's *Paradise.*" *African American Review* 39 (2005): 415–30. Print.

Rosen, Lois C. "Motherhood." *Toni Morrison Encyclopedia.* Ed. Elizabeth Ann Beaulieu. Westport, CT: Greenwood, 2003: 218–25. Print.

Rosenblatt, Paul C. and Beverly R. Wallace. *African American Grief.* New York: Routledge, 2005. Print.

Roynon, Tessa. *The Cambridge Introduction to Toni Morrison.* New York: Cambridge U P, 2013. Print.

Rubenstein, Roberta. *Home Matters: Longing and Belonging, Nostalgia and Mourning in Women's Fiction.* New York: Palgrave, 2001. Print.

Ruddick, Sara. *Maternal Thinking: Toward a Politics of Peace.* New York: Ballantine, 1989. Print.

Rushdy, Ashraf H. A. "Daughters Signifyin(g) History: The Example of Toni Morrison's *Beloved.*" *American Literature* 64 (1992): 567–97. Print.

____. "'Rememory': Primal Scenes and Constructions in Toni Morrison's Novels." *Contemporary Literature* 31.3 (1990): 300–23. Print.

Samuels, Wilfred D. and Clenora Hudson-Weems. *Toni Morrison.* Boston: Twayne, 1990. Print.

Sanna, Ellyn. "Biography of Toni Morrison." *Toni Morrison.* Ed. Harold Bloom. Philadelphia: Chelsea, 2002: 3–37.

Schapiro, Barbara. "The Bonds of Love and the Boundaries of Self in Toni Morrison's *Beloved.*" *Contemporary Literature* 32.2 (1991): 194–210. Print.

Scheiber, Andrew. "Blues Narratology and the African American Novel." *New Essays on the African American Novel.* Ed. Lovalerie King and Linda F. Seltzer. New York: Palgrave, 2008: 33–49. Print.

Schmudde, Carol E. "The Haunting of 124." *African American Review* 26.3 (1992): 409–16. Print.

Schreiber, Evelyn Jaffe. *Race, Trauma, and Home in the Novels of Toni Morrison.* Baton Rouge: Louisiana State U P, 2010. Print.

Schur, Richard L. "Locating *Paradise* in the Post-Civil Rights Era: Toni Morrison and Critical Race Theory." *Contemporary Literature* 45.2 (2004): 276–99. Print.

Scruggs, Charles. *Sweet Home: Invisible Cities in the Afro-American Novel.* Baltimore, MD: Johns Hopkins U P, 1993. Print.

Segal, Lynne. *Slow-Motion: Changing Masculinities.* London: Virago, 1997. Print.

Seward, Adrienne Lanier and Justine Tally, eds. *Toni Morrison: Memory and Meaning.* Jackson: U P of Mississippi, 2014. Print.

Sharpe, Christina. *Monstrous Intimacies: Making Post-Slavery Subjects.* Durham, NC: Duke U P, 2010. Print.

Shea, Lisa. "Georgia on Her Mind." *Elle* (2012): 236. Print.

Sherman, Sarah Way. "Religion, The Body, and Consumer Culture in Toni Morrison's *The Bluest Eye.*" *Religion in America.* Ed. Hans Krabbendam and Derek Rubin. Amsterdam: U V University P, 2004: 143–56. Print.

Showalter, Elaine. *A Jury of Her Peers: American Women Writers from Anne Bradstreet to Annie Proulx.* New York: Knopf, 2009. Print.

Sielke, Sabine. *Reading Rape.* Princeton, NJ: Princeton U P, 2002. Print.

Simpson, Ritashona. *Black Looks and Black Acts: The Language of Tony Morrison in* The Bluest Eye *and* Beloved. New York: Peter Lang, 2007. Print.

Skerrett, Joseph T., Jr. "Recitation to the Griot: Storytelling and Learning in Toni Morrison's *Song of Solomon.*" *Conjuring: Black Women, Fiction, and Literary Tradition.* Ed. Marjorie Pryse and Hortense J. Spillers. Bloomington: Indiana U P, 1985: 192–202. Print.

Sklar, Howard. "'What the Hell Happened to Maggie?': Stereotype, Sympathy, and Disability in Toni Morrison's 'Recitatif.'" *Journal of Literary and Cultural Disability Studies* 5.2 (2011): 137–54. Print.

Slattery, Patrick. *The Wounded Body: Remembering the Markings of Flesh.* Albany: State U of New York P, 2000. Print.

Smith, David Lionet. "What Is Black Culture?" *The House that Race Built.* Ed. Wahneema Lubiano. New York: Pantheon, 1997: 178–94. Print.

Smith, Denitia. "Toni Morrison's Mix of Tragedy, Domesticity and Folklore." *New York Times* (January 8, 1998): E1, E3. Print.

Smith, Valerie. *Self-Discovery and Authority in Afro-American Narrative.* Cambridge, MA: Harvard U P, 1987. Print.

___. *Toni Morrison: Writing the Moral Imagination.* Malden, MA: Wiley-Blackwell, 2012. Print.

Spallino, Chiara. "*Song of Solomon*: An Adventure in Structure." *Callaloo* 8 (Fall 1985): 510–24. Print.

Spargo, Clifford R. "Trauma and the Specters of Enslavement in Morrison's *Beloved.*" *Mosaic* 35 (March 2002): 113–31. Print.

Spaulding, A. Timothy. *Re-forming the Past: History, The Fantastic, and the Postmodern Slave Narrative.* Columbus: Ohio State U P, 2005. Print.

Spillers, Hortense J. "A Hateful Passion, A Lost Love." *Feminist Issues in Literary Scholarship*. Ed. Shari Benstock. Bloomington: Indiana U P, 1987: 181–207. Print.

——. "Mama's Baby, Papa's Maybe: An American Grammar Book." *African American Literary Theory: A Reader*. Ed. Winston Napier. New York: New York U P, 2000: 257–79. Print.

Stanley, Sondra Kumamoto. "Maggie in Toni Morrison's 'Recitatif.'" *MELUS* 36.2 (2011): 71–88. Print.

Steiner, Wendy. "The Clearest Eye: *Playing in the Dark*." *New York Times Book Review* (April 5, 1992): 17. Print.

Stepto, Robert B. *From Behind the Veil: A Study of Afro-American Narrative*. Urbana: U of Illinois P, 1979. Print.

Story, Ralph. "An Excursion into the Black World: The 'Seven Days' in Toni Morrison's *Song of Solomon*." *Black American Literature Forum* (Spring 1989): 149–58. Print.

Sudarkasa, Niara. *The Strength of Our Mothers: African and African American Women and Families*. Trenton, NJ: Africa World P, 1996. Print.

Sweeney, Megan. "'Something Rogue': Commensurability, Commodification, Crime, and Justice in Toni Morrison's Later Fiction." *Modern Fiction Studies* 52.2 (2006): 440–69. Print.

Tal, Kali. *Worlds of Hurt: Reading the Literatures of Trauma*. Cambridge: Cambridge UP, 1996. Print.

Tally, Justine. *Paradise Reconsidered: Toni Morrison's (Hi)stories and Truths*. Berlin: LIT Verlag 1999. Print.

——. *The Story of Jazz: Toni Morrison's Dialogic Imagination*. Hamburg: LIT, 2001. Print.

——, ed. *The Cambridge Companion to Toni Morrison*. Cambridge: Cambridge U P, 2007. Print.

——. *Toni Morrison's* Beloved: *Origins*. New York: Routledge, 2009. Print.

Taylor-Guthrie, Danille, ed. *Conversations with Toni Morrison*. Jackson: U P of Mississippi, 1994. Print.

Terry, Jennifer. "A New World Religion? Creolisation and Condomble in Toni Morrison's *Paradise*." *Complexions of Race: The African Atlantic*. Ed. Fritz Gysin and Cynthia S. Hamilton. Munster: Lit Verlag, 2005: 61–82. Print.

Thompson, Lisa. *Beyond the Black Lady: Sexuality and the New African American Middle Class*. Urbana: U of Illinois P, 2009. Print.

Thurman, Judith. "A House Divided." *New Yorker* (November 2, 1987): 175–80. Print.

Treherne, Matthew. "Figuring In, Figuring Out: Narration and Negotiation in Toni Morrison's *Jazz*." *Narrative* 11.2 (May 2003): 199–212. Print.

Troupe, Quincy and Rainer Schulte, eds. *Giant Talk: An Anthology of Third World Writings*. New York: Random, 1975. (Morrison served as project editor). Print.

Turner, Darwin T. "Theme, Characterization, and Style in the Works of Toni Morrison." *Black Women Writers (1950–1980)*. Ed. Mari Evans. Garden City, NY: Doubleday, 1984: 361–9. Print.

Updike, John. "Dreamy Wilderness." *New Yorker* (November 3, 2008): 112–13. Print.

Van Sertina, Ivan. *They Came Before Columbus*. New York: Random, 1976. Print.

Vickroy, Laurie. "The Politics of Abuse: The Traumatized Child in Toni Morrison and Marguerite Duras." *Mosaic: A Journal for the Interdisciplinary Study of Literature* 29.2 (1996): 91–109. Print.

——. *Trauma and Survival in Contemporary Fiction*. Charlottesville: U of Virginia P, 2002. Print.

Vrettos, Athena. "Curative Domains: Women, Healing and History in Black Women's Narratives." *Women's Studies* (October 1989): 455–74. Print.

Wade-Gayles, Gloria. "The Truths of Our Mothers' Lives: Mother–Daughter Relationships in Black Women's Fiction." *Sage* 1 (Fall 1984): 8–12. Print.

Waegner, Cathy Covell. "Ruthless Epic Footsteps: Shoes, Migrants, and the Settlement of the Americas in Toni Morrison's *A Mercy*." *Post-National Enquiries: Essays on Ethnic and Racial Border Crossings*. Ed. Jopi Nyman. Newcastle upon Tyne: Cambridge Scholars P, 2009: 91–112. Print.

Wagner-Martin, Linda. "'Closer to the Edge': Toni Morrison's *Song of Solomon*." *Teaching American Ethnic Literatures: Nineteen Essays*. Ed. John Maitino and David Peck. Albuquerque: U of New Mexico P, 1996: 147–57. Print.

——. *A History of American Literature from 1950 to the Present*. Malden, MA: Wiley-Blackwell, 2013. Print.

___. "Still Telling Women's Lives." *Writing Lives: American Biography and Autobiography*. Ed. Hans Bak and Hans Krabbendam. Amsterdam: VU U P, 1998: 283–99. Print.

——. "Teaching *The Bluest Eye*." *ADE Bulletin* (MLA), No. 83 (Spring 1986): 28–31. Print.

——. *Telling Women's Lives, The New Biography*. New Brunswick, NJ: Rutgers U P, 1994. Print.

——. *Toni Morrison and the Maternal: From The Bluest Eye to Home*. New York: Peter Lang, 2014. Print.

——. "Toni Morrison's Mastery." *Narrative Technique in the Writing of Contemporary American Women*. Ed. Catherine Rainwater and William J. Scheick. Lexington: U P of Kentucky, 1985: 191–205. Bibliography, Curtis Martin, 205–7. Print.

Walker, Alice. *In Search of Our Mothers' Gardens*. San Diego: Harcourt Brace Jovanovich, 1983. Print.

Walker, Melissa. *Down from the Mountaintop: Black Women's Novels in the Wake of the Civil Rights Movement, 1966–1989*. New Haven: Yale U P, 1991. Print.

Wall, Cheryl A. "Toni Morrison: Editor and Teacher." *The Cambridge Companion to Toni Morrison*. Ed. Justine Tally. Cambridge: Cambridge U P, 2007: 139–50. Print.

——. *Worrying the Line: Black Women Writers, Lineage, and Literary Tradition*. Chapel Hill: U of North Carolina P, 2005. Print.

Wallace, Kathleen R. and Karla Armbruster. "The Novels of Toni Morrison: Wild Wilderness Where There Was None." *Beyond Nature Writing: Expanding the Boundaries of Ecocriticism.* Ed. Kathleen R. Wallace and Karla Armbruster. Charlottesville: U of Virginia P, 1997: 211–30. Print.

Wallace, Maurice. "Print, Prosthesis, Impersonation: Toni Morrison's *Jazz* and the Limits of American Literary History." *American Literary History* 20.4 (Winter 2008): 794–806. Print.

Wallace, Michelle. *Black Macho and the Myth of the Superwoman.* London: John Calder, 1978. Print.

Wanzo, Rebecca. *The Suffering Will Not Be Televised: African American Women and Sentimental Political Storytelling.* Albany: State U of New York P, 2009. Print.

Wardi, Anissa Janine. "A Laying On of Hands: Toni Morrison and the Materiality of Love." *MELUS* 30.3 (2005): 201–18. Print.

——. *Water and African American Memory.* Gainesville: U of Florida P, 2011. Print.

Warner, Anne Bradford. "New Myths and Ancient Properties: The Fiction of Toni Morrison." *Hollins Critic* (June 1988): 1–11. Print.

Warrren, Kenneth W. *What Was African American Literature?* Cambridge, MA: Harvard U P, 2011. Print.

Washington, Teresa N. *Our Mothers, Our Powers, Our Texts: Manifestations of Aje in Africana Literature.* Bloomington: Indiana U P, 2005. Print.

Wegs, Joyce. "Toni Morrison's *Song of Solomon*: A Blues Song." *Essays in Literature* 9 (1982): 211–23. Print.

Weinstein, Arnold. *Nobody's Home: Speech, Self, and Place in American Fiction from Hawthorne to De Lillo.* New York: Oxford U P, 1993. Print.

Wen-Ching, Ho. "'I'll Tell' – The Function and Meaning of L in Toni Morrison's *Love.*" *EurAmerica* 36.4 (2006): 651–75. Print.

Wendt, Lana. "Toni Morrison Uncensored." Videorecording. Princeton, NJ: Films for the Humanities and Sciences, 1998. Visual.

Werner, Craig Hansen. *Playing the Changes: From Afro-Modernism to the Jazz Impulse.* Urbana: U of Illinois P, 1994. Print.

Wester, Maisha L. *African American Gothic, Screams from Shadowed Places.* New York: Palgrave, 2012. Print.

Widdowson, Peter. "The American Dream Refashioned: History, Politics and Gender in Toni Morrison's *Paradise.*" *Journal of American Studies* 35.2 (2001): 313–35. Print.

Wilentz, Gay. "An African-Based Reading of *Sula.*" *Approaches to Teaching the Novels of Toni Morrison.* Ed. Nellie McKay and Kathryn Earle. New York: MLA, 1997: 127– 34. Print.

——. "Civilizations Underneath: African Heritage as Cultural Discourse in Toni Morrison's *Song of Solomon.*" *Toni Morrison's Fiction, Contemporary Criticism.* Ed. David L. Middleton. New York: Garland, 2000: 109–33. Print.

——. *Healing Narratives, Women Writers Curing Cultural Dis-Ease.* New Brunswick, NJ: Rutgers U P, 2000. Print.

Williams, Dana A. "Dancing Minds and Plays in the Dark: Intersections of Fiction and Critical Texts in Gayl Jones's *Corregidora*, Toni Cade Bambara's *The Salt Eaters*, and Toni Morrison's *Paradise.*" *New Essays in the African*

American Novel. Ed. Lovalerie King and Linda F. Seltzer. New York: Palgrave, 2008: 93–106. Print.

——. *In the Light of Likeness – Transformed: The Literary Art of Leon Forrest.* Columbus: Ohio State U P, 2005. Print.

Williams, Lisa. *The Artist as Outsider in the Novels of Toni Morrison and Virginia Woolf.* Westport, CT: Greenwood, 2000. Print.

Williams-Forson, Psyche. *Building Houses out of Chicken Legs: Black Women, Food, and Power.* Chapel Hill: U of North Carolina P, 2006. Print.

Williamson, Jennifer. *Twentieth-Century Sentimentalism: Narrative Appropriation in American Literature.* New Brunswick, NJ: Rutgers U P, 2013. Print.

Willis, Susan. "Eruptions of Funk: Historicizing Toni Morrison." *Black American Literature Forum* 16.1 (1982): 34–42. Print.

——. *Specifying: Black Women Writing the American Experience.* Madison: U of Wisconsin P, 1986. Print.

Wisker, Gina. "Remembering and Disremembering *Beloved:* Lacunae and Hauntings." *Reassessing the Twentieth-Century Canon.* Ed. Nicola Allen and David Simmons. Palgrave Macmillan, 2014: 266–80. Print.

——. *Toni Morrison: A Beginner's Guide.* London: Hodder, 2002. Print.

Wolfe, Joanna. "'Ten Minutes for Seven Letters': Song as Key to Narrative Revision in Toni Morrison's *Beloved.*" *Narrative* 12.3 (2004): 263–80. Print.

Wolff, Cynthia Griffin. "'Margaret Garner': A Cincinnati Story." *Massachusetts Review* 32 (1991): 417–40. Print.

Wood, Michael. "Sensations of Loss." *Aesthetics of Toni Morrison.* Ed. Marc C. Conner. Jackson: U P of Mississippi, 2000: 113–24. Print.

Woodward, Kathleen. "Traumatic Shame: Toni Morrison, Televisual Culture, and the Cultural Politics of the Emotions." *Cultural Critique* 46 (2000). 210–40. Print.

Woolf, Virginia. *Mrs. Dalloway.* London: Chatto, 1925. Print.

Worden, Daniel. *Masculine Style: The American West and Literary Modernism.* New York: Palgrave, 2011.

Wyatt, Jean. "Giving Body to the Word: The Maternal Symbolic in Toni Morrison's *Beloved.*" *PMLA* 108 (1993): 474–88. Print.

——. "*Love's* Time and the Reader: Ethical Effects of Nachtraglichkeit in Toni Morrison's *Love.*" *Narrative* 16.2 (May 2008): 193–221. Print.

___. *Risking Difference: Identification, Race, and Community in Contemporary Fiction and Feminism.* Albany: State U of New York P, 2004. Print.

Yaeger, Patricia. *Dirt and Desire: Reconstructing Southern Women's Writing, 1930–1990.* Chicago: U of Chicago P, 2000. Print.

Yalom, Marilyn. *Maternity, Mortality, and the Literature of Madness.* University Park: Pennsylvania State U P, 1985. Print.

Yardley, Jonathan. "Toni Morrison and the Prize Fight." *The Washington Post* (January 25, 1988). Final ed.: C2. Print.

Yohe, Kristine. "Enslaved Women's Resistance and Survival Strategies in Frances Ellen Watkins Harper's "The Slave Mother: A Tale of Ohio" and Toni Morrison's *Beloved* and *Margaret Garner.*" *Gendered Resistance: Women, Slavery, and the Legacy of Margaret Garner.* Ed. Mary E. Frederickson and Delores M. Walters. Urbana: U of Illinois P, 2013: 99–114. Print.

Young, John K. *Black Writers, White Publishers: Marketplace Politics in Twentieth-Century African American Literature.* Jackson: U P of Mississippi, 2006. Print.

Yukins, Elizabeth. "Bastard Daughters and the Possession of History in *Corregidora* and *Paradise.*" *Signs* 28.1 (2002): 221–47. Print.

Zauditu-Selassie, Kokahvah. *African Spiritual Traditions in the Novels of Toni Morrison.* Gainesville: U P of Florida, 2009. Print.

Online Sources

The Toni Morrison Society online news and bibliography: www.tonimorrisonsociety.org

Index

CPSIA information can be obtained
at www.ICGtesting.com
Printed in the USA
LVOW01*2314050216
473954LV00008B/321/P

9 781137 446695